STARS SCREAMING

STARS SCREAMING

JOHN KAYE

Atlantic Monthly Press
New York

Published simultaneously in Canada
Printed in the United States of America

FIRST EDITION

Library of Congress Cataloging-in-Publication Data
Kaye, John.
     Stars screaming / John Kaye. — 1st ed.
          p.   cm.
     ISBN 0–87113–691–0
     I. Title.
     PS3561.A8857S73   1997
     813'.54—dc21   97–9368

DESIGN BY LAURA HAMMOND HOUGH

The Atlantic Monthly Press
841 Broadway
New York, NY 10003

10 9 8 7 6 5 4 3 2 1

For my son, Jesse
and for H., who tried so hard

★

STARS SCREAMING

★

PART ONE

THE CAST

Welcome to Hollywood

"Pretty legs," a sailor on leave says to his buddy, while they watch Grace Elliot stroll by the racks in front of Nate's News. "Reminds me of this gal I knew back in Davenport. Julie Lagerson. Looked as cool as a cucumber, but if you pushed the right button she got hotter than a five-alarm fire."

Overhearing their conversation, Nathan Burk says, "She's wearing a ring, boys, so I wouldn't get any ideas."

"Yeah?" the sailor says innocently. "Ideas about what?"

Then his buddy says, "Her husband's probably overseas. How do you know she ain't lookin' for it like all the rest?"

"That's right," the sailor says, and Grace Elliot spins around slowly and fixes the two of them with a hard stare.

"Looking for what?" she asks them.

Before they can respond, a peach-colored Packard con-vertible pulls around the corner and parks in front of the newsstand. Behind the wheel is a handsome young man with deep dark eyes and long, black, slick hair.

"Be right there, Mr. Fonda," Nathan Burk shouts, and he races over a copy of the *Omaha World-Herald*. After the driver pays for the newspaper and the enormous automobile speeds away, Grace Elliot asks, "Was that Henry Fonda?"

"Yes, it was. He comes by every day."

"I can't believe it," she says with a sigh. "I saw him in *The Grapes of Wrath* right before I left home."

"Me too," the sailor says.

"So did I," says his buddy, excited that they all have something in common. "I saw it with my dad the day before I enlisted. We're farmers just like the Joads."

"He should get an Oscar for that one," says a mournful-looking old woman with bloodshot eyes who is standing nearby. She's wearing hospital slippers and a ratty gray coat that's stained with food. "If he don't, they should investigate the whole deal."

"I agree," Grace says, nodding.

"Me too," says the sailor.

"So do—"

"Nobody asked you two," the old woman snaps, and she sends a gob of spit next to their feet. "Now get the hell away from this gal before I kick you both in the family jewels." The old woman feints with her foot and the two sailors jump backward. "A woman alone on this boulevard is like raw meat hanging from a tree in the jungle."

"They're just lonely," Grace Elliot says, and she pulls the latest issue of *Modern Screen* off the rack in front of her. On the cover is a picture of Lauren Bacall and Humphrey Bogart dining at Romanoff's. "I can handle guys like that."

"Yeah? Didn't look like it to me," the old woman says, while she watches Grace Elliot flip through the magazine. "You thinkin' of becoming an actress?"

"Maybe. If I'm lucky."

"You got any talent?"

"I hope so," she says, exchanging the copy of *Modern Screen* for a copy of *Photoplay*. "I won a beauty contest back home."

"Big deal," the old woman says, and Grace Elliot hears her fart. "Every two-bit twat in Hollywood is Miss This or Queen of That."

Moving away, Grace Elliot says, "I've got a contract, too."

"For what?" The old woman hoots. "A hundred and fifty a week to be atmosphere until you can cozy up to some fat-cat producer. Then what? You give him a little action, and he lets you say a line or two in a scene that ends up in the shitter. Listen to me, honey," the old woman growls, as she follows Grace up the block. "Do yourself a favor and go back home."

Grace Elliot shakes her head.

"I've been there and back, sweetheart! Listen to me! All they want is a couple of squirts between your legs, that's all! Take my advice and pack your bags and get back on whatever train—"

"No!" Grace Elliot suddenly screams into the old woman's face. "I'm never going home! Ever!"

A nerve pulsates in the old woman's forehead as she slowly backs up the street. When she reaches the corner, she lifts one of her feeble hands and points to the sky. "Let us pray to God for this woman," she says after a long silence, and then, looking around furtively to make sure no one is watching, she turns and disappears into a crowd of tourists crossing Hollywood Boulevard.

★

One

Burk and

Sandra

June 1969

Ray Burk, hungover, nervous, and clearly disappointed with his life, was parked on Larchmont Avenue, just south of Melrose, killing time before his Monday meeting with Dicky Solomon, the producer of *Magnetic North,* a futuristic cop show and the highest rated new series on CBS. Paramount Pictures was located one block east on Gower, and from where he was sitting Burk could see a billboard showing Ryan O'Neal and Ali McGraw locked in an amorous embrace.

He thought, Give me a break, the same words he'd said out loud earlier that morning, after Sandra had quoted the latest item of gossip she'd culled from Joyce Haber's column in the *Los Angeles Times.*

"He was spotted in Chez Jay over the weekend," she told Burk while they were sitting in their tiny breakfast nook. "Joyce says his marriage is in real trouble."

"Sandra—" Burk said; then, hearing the anger in his voice, he stopped and picked up the sports section.

"What is it, babe?"

Burk shook his head.

"Tell me."

"Give me a break, Sandra. Okay?"

Sandra stared at Burk as she crunched her toast. When she reached for her coffee, her robe fell open and her right breast swung free, exposing the nipple, "Tell me what's wrong, Ray."

Burk shook his head. From the living room he could hear Louie singing along with the puppets on *Sesame Street*. He knew without looking that his son was sitting cross-legged in front of the television, surrounded by his Legos and his army men, with a bowl of soggy Shredded Wheat balanced in his lap.

"Ray?"

"Nothing, I told you." I'm just confused, he wanted to say. Then he said it. "I'm just confused."

Sandra sat quiet for a while, trying not to show how worried she felt inside. Then she reached across the table and combed her fingers through his hair. "You hate your job," she said. "Don't you, Ray?"

"It's bullshit. Being a censor is bullshit. It's not who I am."

"I know."

Burk stood up and crossed to the sink. After he washed his cup, he turned and glanced at the clock above the stove. "It's almost nine," he said. "I gotta go. I have a meeting."

Sandra watched him walk into the dining room and take his wallet and keys off the table, then got up and followed him to the front door. When he turned to bend down to kiss her, she put her arms around his waist and pulled him close. "Things will get better," she whispered. "I know they will."

"Okay."

"I believe in you, Ray."

"I know."

Burk kissed her tenderly on the forehead and stepped back from their embrace. He was moving forward when he heard her say, "Didn't you forget something, Ray?"

He turned and saw Sandra leaning against the doorframe. "Your son," she said. "You forgot to say good-bye to your son." Burk took a step toward her but she waved him away. "Go. You're late."

"Give him a kiss for me," Burk said.

"Better yet, I'll give him two and a hug to boot."

Burk got into his car and switched on the ignition. Before he backed out of the driveway, he looked up and saw Sandra still standing in the doorway, staring at him with a desperate sparkle in her eyes. Feeling his heart tremble, Burk lifted up his hand and waved goodbye. Sandra, her face still scared, waved back, then she turned away from the street and walked into their house.

"I'm not changing a thing. Right, Gillian?" Dicky Solomon said, winking at his leggy British secretary as she ushered Burk into his office. "Not a fucking word."

Opening his script, Burk said, "My first note is on page ten."

"Shove your notes, Burk. I got a twenty-one rating and a thirty-five share of the audience. I got a hit show without your notes."

"On page ten," Burk continued affably, ignoring the circles of perspiration that were forming underneath his arms, "we'd like you to lose the line 'Screw you, pal.'"

"Screw *you,* pal," Dicky said, but Burk saw him delete the line in his script. "What else?"

"On page twenty-four," Burk continued, "we—"

"We? What's this *we* bullshit?" Dicky shouted. "You *personally* want to lose this stabbing on page twenty-four. Right, Burk?"

"Right," Burk admitted, playing along. He noticed Dicky smile.

"Then for you it's out," Dicky declared loudly, gazing at Burk with satisfaction as he flipped on his stereo and lit up a joint.

And for the next thirty minutes, while Dicky got loaded and they listened to side one of "Tommy," Burk patiently argued his way through the rest of the script. By the time Gillian popped her head in the door to announce that Sandra was on the phone, Burk had convinced Dicky to make nearly all the changes that Charly Orth, his boss and Director of Program Practices for the network, had mandated that morning.

Burk said, "Tell her I'll call her when I get back to my office."

"No. Take it," Dicky said, getting up quickly and moving around the desk. "I gotta go down and check on the sets. We're through here, right?"

"I guess so."

On his way out the door, Dicky said, "This is a nowhere gig for you, Burk, but you do a good job. I'll see you next week."

Burk waited until Dicky closed the door before he picked up the phone.

"Ray?" He heard Sandra's whisper when he lifted up the receiver. "Are you on?"

"Yeah. I'm right here. You okay?"

"Uh-huh. I just got back from doing the laundry. While I was folding your jeans I started to miss you, so I thought I'd give you a call."

"How did you find me?"

"How do you think? I called your office and Lorraine gave me the number. You mad?" Burk remained silent. "Ray? Did you hear me? I said I missed you."

"Yeah, I know. And there are lots of times I miss you, Sandra. But—"

"But what?"

"Just leave a message next time, okay? I'll call you right back."

"That sometimes takes hours. By that time I don't miss you so much," Sandra said, and one of Dicky's phone lines began to ring. It rang three times before Gillian picked it up. "Is Dicky there with you?" Sandra asked.

"No. We're finished."

"What about us, Ray? Are we finished too?"

"Come on, Sandra."

"Are we?"

Burk let out a long sigh. "No. We're going to be fine," he said, but moments later, when he hung up the phone, he could still hear the terror in her voice.

A month earlier, on a foggy and rainy Saturday morning in May, Burk and Sandra and Louie went for a drive up the coast to Santa Barbara. On their way back to LA the rain ended, and the sky was more blue than gray when Dicky Solomon's red Corvette drew alongside Burk at a stoplight in Brentwood. Beside Dicky, holding a blond cocker spaniel puppy, was a boy around Louie's age.

"That's him," Burk said to Sandra, pointing with his chin.

"Who?"

"Dicky Solomon. The producer I told you about."

"That fat bald guy. You're kidding me."

"Don't stare," Burk said quickly.

When the light changed to green, Louie said, "That boy's got a puppy."

"Follow him," Sandra said to Burk.

"What for?"

"I'm curious."

"Daddy?"

"What?"

"Can I get a puppy someday?"

"We'll see."

"Say yes, Daddy."

"We'll see," Burk said again, and he pulled into the right lane.

Dicky Solomon drove west on Sunset, his Corvette moving easily through the curves. At Allenford he downshifted into second and turned right. When he reached San Vicente, he stopped at Playtown, a toy store on 26th Street that had just opened that weekend.

"Why are we stopping?" Louie asked Burk, while they idled in a red zone around the corner. "Are you getting me a toy?"

"No, honey," Sandra said, "but if you're good maybe we'll let you stay up and watch 'The Wild Wild West.'"

Dicky left Playtown and made a stop at the Liquor Locker on Montana before he drove up to his hillside home in Mandeville Canyon.

"Eighteen fifty-seven," Sandra said to herself, as she opened her purse and took out a pencil.

Burk said, "Why are you writing down his address?"

"I don't know," Sandra said, shrugging. "Maybe we'll send him a Christmas card."

"Why would we do that? We're not friends of his."

"You're work friends."

"No we're not."

"You said he likes you," Sandra said, turning toward him. "Maybe he can help you get a better job."

Burk shook his head, keeping his own eyes averted. "Forget it, Sandra. Dicky Solomon could care less about my life."

After Burk made a U-turn and they were coasting slowly down the canyon road, Louie said, "Maybe someday I'll get a puppy dog."

Sandra said, "Maybe," and she pushed a button on the radio, changing the frequency from AM to FM. "Just Like a Woman" was playing on KPPC, and Sandra sang the words along with Dylan while she closed her eyes and eased down in her seat. When the song ended, she turned and smiled at her son. "Maybe you will, sweetheart."

★

Santa Anita was closed on Mondays, so after she washed the breakfast dishes and dropped Louie off at nursery school, Sandra spent the rest of the morning working on the five-thousand-piece jigsaw puzzle that was spread over the dining room table. The title of the puzzle was "Storm," and depicted on the cover of the box was an ink-black sky split by a thin bolt of lightning. Swelling underneath the heavy clouds were huge waves just a shade lighter than the sky.

"Just sky and water?" Burk had said the night before when he saw the picture on the box. "That's it? Nothing else?"

"Lightning," Sandra added.

"That's gonna take you forever."

"That's the point," Sandra said, dumping the pieces on the table. "It's supposed to take forever."

By noon Sandra had finished three beers and a small section of the sky when her concentration was interrupted by the telephone. I'm not in the mood to talk to anyone, she decided, and she put her hands over her ears. But the phone continued to ring patiently until she finally raced into her bedroom and screamed, "Okay, I hear you, I hear you, goddammit!" After waiting for two more rings to steady herself and catch her breath, she lifted up the receiver and let five full seconds pass without speaking. Then, almost in a whisper, she said, "Hello?"

"Mrs. Burk," a woman responded immediately, "this is Mrs. Pincus, Louie's teacher at the Goodtime Nursery School."

"Yes."

"Louie's been acting a little odd lately, and I thought we should talk about it."

Sandra lit a cigarette and sat down on the edge of the unmade bed. She took a deep drag, and gray smoke curled into the sunlight that poured through the open window and stroked her face. "What does he do?" she asked.

"It's what he doesn't do," the woman said. Her voice was cold, remote. "In class he refuses to speak or answer questions, and during playtime, instead of interacting with the other boys and girls, he spends the entire hour walking backwards around the edge of the yard."

"Is he bothering anyone?"

"No. But that isn't the point."

"What is the point?"

"He's not making friends," the woman said in a softer, more concerned voice. "I think it would be easier for him if he did. I think he would be happier."

Sandra stretched out on the bed and blew a smoke ring toward the ceiling. "It's just a stage," she said. "I'll discuss it with my husband."

"I tried to call him earlier today."

"You called him first? Don't you call the child's mother first?" Sandra said, sitting up. "Isn't that the way it generally works?"

"Yes, generally. But I've had trouble reaching you in the past. Last Friday, for example—"

"I was at Santa Anita last Friday, like I am every afternoon during the week. Except Mondays. I'm an expert handicapper," Sandra bragged; then she glanced at her wristwatch, as if she had an appointment to keep. "Can I speak to Louie, please?"

"He's taking his nap. If you like I can wake him."

"No. Don't."

Sandra heard a door slam in the house next door, and the sound startled her.

"Mrs. Burk?"

She didn't answer. Her body was rigid, her mouth dropped open in fear.

"Mrs. Burk? Are you there?"

"Yes."

"I think we should discuss this in person."

"No."

"But—"

"Stop it!" Sandra said, springing up from the bed. Her eyes were wide and her heart was beating in her throat. "There is nothing wrong with my son!"

Sandra was in the kitchen heating up take-out pizza when Burk came home from work that evening. On the dining room table, next to the small section of clouds she had pieced together that morning, was a note that said, *I'm pregnant.*

Burk looked at her inquiringly. "True?"

"Yes."

"Wow."

"Is that a happy wow or a sad wow?"

"I'm not sure."

"I want this baby, Ray."

"Okay. But—"

"I really do!"

That night, while he and Sandra lay side by side in the darkness with their bare shoulders touching, Burk replayed the conversation he'd had with Louie right before he put his son to bed.

"Mom's sad," he told Burk.

"She is? How do you know?"

"Because this afternoon, while we were driving home from nursery school, I looked over and saw a tear fall off her chin."

"Did you ask her what was wrong?"

"No."

"Then maybe she wasn't sad, because sometimes people cry when they're happy."

"No."

"Some people do."

"Tears are what happens when the glass breaks behind your eyes. If you swallow them you can die."

"Did your mom tell you that?"

"No. The bird did."

"What bird?"

"The big black bird."

"Where is that bird, Louie?"

"You can't see him."

"Why?"

"Because he's inside my head, behind my eyes . . . behind the glass."

"Is he always there?"

"No. Just sometimes. He'll come tonight if Mom forgets to tuck me in and kiss me good night."

* * *

Much later that night, his body fatigued but his mind too restless to let him sleep, Burk switched on the radio. From 3 to 4 A.M. each morning on KMPC, late-nite talk show host Ray Moore invited his listeners to call in and "share a moment from your childhood, a story or anecdote that is either happy or sad. It doesn't matter which, because we're here to listen and open our hearts, not to judge."

The first caller, a woman from Monrovia, spoke about a crush she had had on a boy in the fourth grade. "Donnie Randolph was his name. I sat right behind him at Warner Avenue Elementary," she told Radio Ray. "No one ever called him Donald or Don. It was always Donnie. He was smart—but he was a cutup too, always turning in his seat to make faces at his friends or toss notes down the aisle. But he never looked at or spoke to me. Not once during the whole semester, even when I gave him a card on Valentine's Day. Do you know how that made me feel?" the woman asked Radio Ray, her voice close to tears. "It made me feel like the ugliest little girl in the whole world."

"Maybe he was just shy," Radio Ray said. "What else do you remember?"

"All those weeks sittin' there in class, hopin' he would smile at me or say hello or even tease me. And I remember how my fingers ached to reach out and straighten his shirt collar so I could touch his hair. Sometimes I would bend my head forward and dare myself to kiss him on the neck—but of course I never did."

Radio Ray said, "I suppose you were in love with him."

"Yes, I suppose I was."

"What do you think he's doing now?"

"Your guess is as good as mine. Selling insurance. I don't know," she said and paused. "Maybe he's dead."

"Maybe he is, but maybe he's listening right now. I know this is a long shot," Radio Ray said, "but if you're out there listening, Donnie Randolph—"

"My name's Margerie Willis," the woman said, her voice brightening. "Warner Avenue Elementary, class of 'forty-seven. I hope he remembers me."

"I hope so too."

A few minutes later a woman with a southern accent told Radio Ray that she once knew a boy named Donnie in Gulfport, Mississippi, the town where she was raised. "But we used to call him Wonderhead, 'cause his bucket was shaped like a loaf of bread. Get it? Wonderhead, Wonder bread."

Laughing, Radio Ray said, "Was his last name Randolph?"

"His name was Donnie. That and his big-ass head is all I can remember."

After a station break and a commercial for a weight reduction powder imported from Canada, Radio Ray took a call from a man who said he was using the pay phone outside the Vogue Theatre on Hollywood Boulevard.

"My name is John Beal," he told Radio Ray, "and I'm from Omaha, Nebraska. You familiar with Omaha, Ray?"

"As a matter of fact I am, John Beal. I worked at KKOW back in the summer of 'fifty-two."

"I was nineteen years old that summer," John Beal said.

Out loud, Burk said, "Gene was twelve and I just turned ten."

"I stayed at the Hotel Sherwood," said Radio Ray, "right up the street from the Greyhound station."

"I rode the dog a few times," John Beal said.

"It's a good way to travel across America. Cheap, too."

"Ray, did you ever eat at Chloe's?"

"Many times."

"I used to bake their pies," John Beal said proudly.

"I didn't have much of a sweet tooth, John. But I sure remember that meat loaf."

"Shoulda tried the pies. Then we would have something to talk about," John Beal said, and the line went dead.

Burk put his hand on the receiver and left it there for several seconds before he dialed.

"Last call," Radio Ray said with a regretful sigh. "You're on the air."

"When I was ten years old I didn't make Little League," Burk said, hearing the bed groan slightly as he stood up and moved the phone into the bathroom. "Neither did my older brother, Gene. The coach told my dad I took my eye off the ball and my arm was too weak. He said Gene was too slow. But Ricky Furlong made it," he said, and his voice began to quaver. "He lived across the street, and we all tried out together. And when we drove home that day, he was in front with my dad . . . and me and Gene were in back. I didn't feel that was right. I felt we should've been up there with him, no matter how bad we did."

"What about your mom?"

"She was gone. She left my dad when I was eight. She wasn't around for anything."

"That's tough," Radio Ray said. "I'm sorry."

Burk grimaced. "Yeah," he said, his voice sounding hurt, "so am I."

After Burk came back to bed, Sandra tried to maneuver herself into his arms, but his shoulders tensed and he rolled out of her embrace.

"What's wrong?" she asked him.

"I'm not in the mood."

"Well, I am."

"I'm sorry."

Sandra let her hand slip between her thighs. Burk said, "Don't, please."

"Why not?"

"Let's talk."

"No. I don't want to talk," she said, and Burk could feel the bed move.

"Stop it," Burk hissed.

"Then fuck me!"

"No," Burk said loudly. Then, in the dark, he saw his son move slowly into the bedroom. "Louie? What's wrong?"

"I'm scared."

"There's nothing to be scared of," Sandra said, sitting up. "Go back to sleep."

"I heard noises."

"You were just imagining."

"No."

Burk said, "He was hearing us. We were loud. Weren't you, honey?"

Louie shook his head. "Outside," he said, pointing. "I heard noises outside."

Burk heard Sandra sigh as he slid out of bed. Just below the window, in the moonlit yard next door, water spurted from the nozzle of a long yellow hose lying unwound in a flower bed. Several yards away, in the center of the backyard, an empty swing squeaked as it moved back and forth on the rusty chains.

Louie said, "It was the man next door. That's who I heard. That's who woke me up. Right, Daddy?"

Burk squeezed Louie's hand. "Right," he said. "He was watering his lawn."

Louie glanced over his shoulder. "Mommy?"

"What?"

"It was the man next door."

"I heard."

"I'm not scared anymore."

"Good."

"I'm going back to sleep."

After Louie shuffled out of the bedroom, Burk remained by the window looking into the night, listening to the water running from the hose and the squeak of the swing set and the sound of the bedsprings, as his wife's breathing grew faster and faster, and the distance between them grew wider and wider.

★

Two
Burk and
Bonnie:
Dream
Lovers

December 5, 1969

Six months later Burk was drinking at Ernie's Stardust Lounge toward the end of the day when he learned that his wife had miscarried after the running of the fifth race at Hollywood Park. During this same telephone conversation he also discovered that he had been fired from his job.

"Sandra's at Brotman Hospital," his secretary, Lorraine, told him.

"Is she all right?"

"Physically, she's fine. You can pick her up after six." Another phone rang in the background and Lorraine put him on hold. When she came back on the line, she said, "Charly feels you should take a few days off."

Burk felt his chest suddenly tighten with anxiety. "What else did he say?"

"He asked me where you've been lately."

"What did you tell him?"

"I told him I didn't know."

Burk was silent a moment. "Lorraine?"

"Yes, Mr. Burk."

"Am I going to be fired?"

"I don't know."

"But maybe I am?"

"Mr. Burk—"

"C'mon, be straight with me."

"Mr. Burk," Lorraine said, keeping her voice steady, "I think you should be worrying about your wife right now."

"I *am* worried about my wife. I'm always worried about her. But I'm worried about my job, too."

There was silence on the other end of the line. Burk knew he was gone. There was nothing more to say, so he hung up the phone and walked back to the bar.

"My wife just lost our kid," Burk told Miles, the bartender.

"He'll turn up. How old is he?"

"Twenty-two weeks."

"Twenty-two weeks? You mean—"

"He's dead. She had a miscarriage at the track."

"Jesus, you better get your ass out there."

"Yeah, I know. As soon as I finish this beer," Burk said, and as Miles gave him a quizzical look. "If that's okay with you."

Miles shrugged. If thirty years behind the bar had taught him anything, it was when to back off if he sensed that a conversation with a customer was beginning to sound peculiar. Burk usually acted like a normal guy, but then so did James Earl Ray, a regular for a while at the Stardust Lounge. Except to order a drink ("Another tall screw, bub"), Ray never uttered a word to anyone, and the only time he left his stool was to play "Tennessee Waltz" on the jukebox. But one day he didn't show up, and the next time Miles saw him, James Earl Ray's ice-cold eyes were staring down from the television screen above the bar. "Can you believe it?" someone said at the time. "All those hours he was sittin' here, that crazy cracker was workin' out how he was gonna bag that jig."

Burk punched P-5 on the jukebox and checked his watch. It was nearly five o'clock. He knew he better get moving if he was going to have enough time to pick up his son, Louie, at nursery school and drop him off at his dad's house for the night before driving out to the hospital.

. . . Dream lover where are you
With a love that's oh so true
With a hand that I can hold
And a love that's oh so bold . . .

The panic that he'd been holding down swelled and washed over Burk like a black wave as he whispered the lyrics to the song playing on the jukebox, and for a brief but frightening moment it seemed that he had made a terrible mistake with his life. "Can this be really happening?" he said softly to himself as Bobby Darin's velvety voice followed him out of the Stardust Lounge into the fading afternoon sunlight on Hollywood Boulevard.

★

The first time Burk heard "Dream Lover" was in 1959, ten years earlier, on a moonlit night in Palm Springs during spring break.

He and his best friend, Timmy Miller, had driven down to the desert right after school was out on Friday, and by the time they reached the outskirts of town—where traffic was backed up bumper-to-bumper with carloads of teenagers from all over Southern California—they knew where all the parties were that evening. The motel mentioned most often was the Regency Arms.

"A bunch of sluts from Santa Ana stay there," a fat kid with greasy sideburns told them as he pulled alongside Timmy's '55 Chevy on Palm Canyon Drive. "Last year this chick took on everyone in town. She called herself Daisy Crazyfuck. I'm horny as hell, so I'm counting on her showing up this year."

But Burk never made it to the Regency Arms, or to any of the other motels that weekend.

"It was one of those lucky deals that just happened," Burk told Sandra a few weeks before they were married. They were lying in bed, trading puffs off the same cigarette. "Timmy was up in our room, taking a nap, and I was out by the pool, catching the last rays of the day. I didn't even notice her when she put her towel down next to me."

"Yeah, right."

"It's the truth. Really."

"What was her name?"

"Laurel."

Sandra laughed.

"What's so funny?" Burk asked her.

"Think about it, Ray," Sandra said, sending a loop of smoke toward the ceiling. "The first time you get laid and her name is Laurel, as in victory. What did she look like? Wait! Don't tell me! She had a face full of freckles, really pretty turquoise eyes, and a body that was close to perfect. Right? And you were sealed together forever the moment she asked you to spread Coppertone on her shoulders."

"She made it all seem so easy."

"Easier than me?" Sandra said, moving her hips closer to his. "I slept with you on the first date. Remember?"

"This was different."

"How?"

"Sandra," Burk said, as she rested her fingertips on his thigh, "I was in high school."

That Friday night Burk and Laurel drove deep into the desert, into a narrow canyon, stopping finally to watch a sky filled with purples and reds. When the stars came out they opened a quart of rum and drank it straight from the bottle, passing it back and forth while they cautiously exchanged bits and pieces of their lives. Eventually they ran out of things to say, and there was a pocket of silence after a song ended on the radio.

"Laurel," Burk said shyly.

"Uh-huh."

"Do you think it would be all right if—"

Before Burk could get the rest of the words out of his mouth, Laurel leaned across the seat and kissed him softly on the lips. "You're a sweet boy," she said, and she put his hand between her cheerleader legs. "I'm really glad I met you."

Later, while they were making love in the backseat of Timmy's car, the deejay on the local station announced that the request line was open. A gentle breeze stirred the desert air, and a girl's sleepy voice came over the radio. "This is Daisy," she said, "and I want you to play 'Dream Lover' by Bobby Darin."

"Who do you want me to send it out to?" the deejay asked her. There was a long silence. Then Daisy said, "To . . . everyone."

"Is that really a true story?" Sandra said to Burk as she pulled him close.

"On my life."

"What else do you remember?"

"How deep the silence was in the desert after the song ended, how dead still it seemed. I remember the sounds of our breathing, and when I came I remember hearing the metal couplings of a windmill squealing on a nearby mesa."

"Did you love her, Ray?"

"Yes, I think so. I mean I told her things that I never told anyone, except you."

"Like what?"

"Like the time I plagiarized a term paper for my American History class."

"What did she say?"

"She just laughed. She said she cheats on tests all the time. And then I told her about my dad, how he was screwing this woman on our block. I told her both those things."

"Your two biggest secrets."

"Then, they were."

"Do you still love her, Ray?"

"No."

"Are you sure?"

"Yes."

"Do you still love me?"

"Are you kidding?" he said, searching for her nipple with his mouth. "Yes, I still love you."

★

It was nearly six o'clock, and Louie was still sitting on the front steps of the Goodtime Nursery School. He had his Dodger cap pulled low over his eyes, and his Fred Flintstone lunch pail was balanced on his knees. The rest of the kids had already gone home, but Louie wasn't frightened. No matter how late it got, someone always came to pick him up. But he wished they would come pretty soon, because today was not such a good day at the Goodtime Nursery School; all morning long, while he was supposed to be painting or learning to read or playing outside, that big black ugly bird kept popping up on the TV screen inside his head. The bird just sat there behind his eyes, squawking, making Louie squawk too, until his teacher finally told him to leave the classroom.

But that afternoon after the big black bird flew away, the number 232 came up on the screen, and for the rest of the day that was all Louie would say, repeating the number 232 over and over, driving all the kids crazy, until Mrs. Pincus, his teacher, called his mom. She wasn't home, and his dad wasn't at his office, so all his teacher could do was make Louie sit on the porch by himself.

"Daddy!" Louie shouted when he finally saw Burk's car pull up to the curb. "You're here. You're finally here."

"Yeah," Burk said, as his son tore across the grass and hurled himself into his arms, "I'm finally here."

"I'm very concerned," Nathan Burk said, as he stood in his kitchen, watching his son chop vegetables for Louie's salad. "I think there's something mentally wrong with her."

"Dad, don't worry about it," Burk said. "She's been acting a little strange lately, but—"

"Ray, last week she attacked a woman at the supermarket because she took her parking place. You don't do something like that if you're sane. No wonder she lost the baby."

Burk started to speak but stopped when Louie walked into the kitchen, holding a large stuffed frog. "I'm hungry, Grandpa," he said.

"Just hold your horses, little man."

"He can't," Burk said, "because he's already holding a frog." Louie laughed, and Burk lifted him into the air. "So how do you want your hamburger, Louie?"

"Rare."

Burk reversed the Dodger cap on Louie's head and kissed him on the nose. "Just like Daddy. Right, Louie Louie?"

"Right."

"It's Screwy Louie these days," Nathan Burk said.

Burk glanced at his father. "What's that supposed to mean?"

Nathan Burk turned away from his son's gaze. "That's what the kids call him at nursery school."

"Who told you that?"

"He did," he said, looking over his shoulder at Louie.

"That's not true," Burk said. "They don't call you that, do they?"

"Sometimes they do, Daddy," Louie said.

"Why?"

Louie lifted up the frog to hide his face. "They just do," he said.

Burk's father brought the salad over to the table in the dinette. "Here," he said to Louie. "Eat."

Louie slowly lowered his frog. But when he picked up his fork, there were tears brimming in his eyes. "When is Mom coming home?" he asked Burk in a worried voice.

Shortly before Burk left for the hospital to pick up his wife, he slipped into the basement of his father's house. Behind the water heater, protected by a tarpaulin, were two medium-sized cardboard boxes that belonged to his older brother, Gene. Inside each box were over a hundred vintage rock-and-roll records, all of them in mint condition.

Burk was searching for "Cool Daddy" by the Thrills, a regional R & B hit from 1956 on the Proud Dog label. This particular 45 would not be considered valuable were it not for the B side, "Daddy's Big Dick," a studio-party outtake that was unintentionally recorded and mistakenly distributed in parts of west Texas and New Mexico. Seventeen copies were sold before the master was destroyed and the record pulled off the racks.

King Kong, a drug dealer Gene busted during the Watts riots, had a copy in his safe along with four kilos of heroin. "That spade skated a year in the joint when I saw that maroon-and-gold label," Gene told Burk when he brought the record by his house. "I even let him keep the smack."

Before dealing in rare rock-and-roll records and, later, in autographs and other memorabilia, Burk's brother had been a cop for seven years, joining the force right after he flunked out of college in 1960. A tenacious investigator and absolutely fearless, Gene had risen quickly through the ranks and twice was nominated for Policeman of the Year, the last time in 1966, the year before he resigned.

"Law enforcement is not for me anymore," he told Burk the day after he came back from the Monterey Pop Festival. "I'm gonna hang it up."

And that was that. The next day Gene turned in his badge.

Burk wondered what Gene would do if he found out someone stole one of his prized records. He had killed two men in the line of duty, but Burk doubted that Gene would shoot his own brother. "Screw it. I could use the money, but it's not worth the risk," he heard his voice say out loud, and he decided to put the record back.

"Daddy!" Louie shouted from upstairs. "Where are you?"

Burk snapped off the light. In the dark! he wanted to scream.

Doctors and nurses wearing sea-green surgical masks hurried past Burk as he stepped off the elevator on the second floor of Brotman Hospital. As he had been directed, he turned left at the nurses' station and nearly collided with two orderlies who were backing a stretcher out of the radiology lab. On the stretcher was a boy around Louie's age, with a shaved head and a long thin tube inserted into his throat. Using some fancy footwork, Burk was able to maneuver around the little guy, who stared up at him with pale, pain-ridden eyes that looked ready to cry. When he arrived at room 207—Sandra's room—the door was partly open, and the overpowering odor of bourbon wafted into the hallway.

"Come on in," Sandra said, without looking up from her *Racing Form*. Her plastic ID bracelet was still fastened to her wrist, but she was sitting, fully clothed, in a chair by the bed. "I only have one more race to scope out and we can split."

"No rush," Burk said. "Take your time."

Sandra scribbled some numbers on a note pad.

Burk stared at his wife. She was missing a sock, and her maternity dress was ripped underneath the arm. "I think Louie's having some problems at school," he said.

"That Screwy Louie business."

"How long has that been going on?"

"Awhile."

"He's upset by it."

"Kids can be jerks at that age," Sandra said, still not looking up. "I wouldn't worry about it."

"My dad is the one who's worried," Burk said, and he drifted over to the window facing the parking lot. Down below he saw a young black girl on metal crutches flanked by her parents. Her pelvis was curved by some terrible disease, and she slowly and painfully dragged herself toward the hospital entrance. "And he's worried about you, too. He thinks you should see a psychiatrist."

For a while they were silent. When Burk turned around, he noticed the empty pint of Wild Turkey that was sitting on the dinner tray. "Do you think I'm crazy?" Sandra finally said.

"I don't know. Maybe talking to someone isn't such a bad idea."

"I talk to people every day. I talk to you. I talk to Louie. I talk to the guys at the track. I—"

"Sandra?"

"Huh."

"Look at me."

"What?" she said, and she raised her eyes for the first time. "What do you want, Ray?" He pointed at the empty bottle of Wild Turkey. "Hernando brought that," she said.

"Who's Hernando?"

"Just a friend. A jockey I know. He cashed my ticket for me in the fifth."

"You had the exacta?"

"I had it up the ying-yang, Ray," she said, and she folded up her *Racing Form*. But her hands were trembling when she stuck it inside her purse. "Well, aren't you going to ask me?"

"Ask what? How much you won?"

"No. About the baby. It was a boy," she said, as she stood up. "A baby boy."

Burk's body faltered a moment. He closed his eyes and tried to get his mind cleared. Then he took a deep, quieting breath, letting it out slowly as he followed her out of the room. While they were walking toward the elevators, Sandra let her head rest against his shoulder. "So how was your day?" she asked him.

"Not so good."

"What happened?"

"Well . . . I got fired."

"That's awfully strange." Sandra lit up a Marlboro while she studied Burk's reflection in the windshield. They were on the Hollywood Freeway, traveling north toward the San Fernando Valley, toward their home. "You're telling me the truth? You haven't been to work in the last six weeks?"

"I check in."

"Then you leave. And you start . . . driving?"

Burk nodded. "So where do you go?" she asked.

"Hollywood. East of Vine. I have this special route I take." Burk started to draw a map in the air. "Sunset east to Gower, north to Franklin, east again to Western, south to Hollywood Boulevard, east to Normandie, et cetera, et cetera."

"Around and around you go."

"More or less."

"Without stopping."

"I stop for gas," Burk said. He flipped on his turn blinker and edged into the right lane. "And sometimes I stop at this bar for a few drinks. But mostly I just drive. I have to."

Sandra said nothing for several seconds. Then: "You have to."

"Yes," Burk said, and he struggled against the urge to be up there right now, on the boulevard, cruising slowly in the right lane, contemplating the bewildered and humorless men and women as they moved in and out of the bars and the cafeterias and their thinly furnished rooms: Hollywood's lowlife, the dispossessed and the checkmated, surrender splashed on their faces like birthmarks.

"No wonder you got fired, Ray."

"I shouldn't be a censor. You know that."

"What should you be?"

Burk pulled off the freeway. "I don't know. Something else. Something creative."

Before Burk took the job at the network, he was working as a research assistant for Hornaday Productions, a documentary film company that specialized in making educational and industrial films for large multinational corporations. It was a highly respected outfit, destined to move into commercial television and feature films, and everyone told Burk he was crazy to quit, even though the network was doubling his salary.

"A fucking censor?" Gene said, stunned, unable to look him in the eye. "That's the stupidest thing I've ever heard."

But Joe King, the network honcho who recruited Burk, convinced him "it would be for six months max, a corporate pit stop before they move you over to the creative side, into program development, where a high-octane guy like you can really take off."

That was eighteen months ago.

An ambulance, siren screaming, shot past Burk's car as he crossed the intersection of Gower and Fountain. "Hobart," Burk said, pointing to a side street. "Three blocks up is Harold Way. That's where Gail Russell lived right before she died."

"Who's Gail Russell?"

"This actress. She was in *Wake of the Red Witch* with John Wayne. She went to Santa Monica High."

"How do you know about this stuff?"

"I pick it up."

"Where?"

"Around."

At Sunset and Western they passed a group of venereal men with irrelevent lives who were idling in front of a no-name bar with the windows blacked out. Guarding the darkened doorway was an oversized man sitting in a wheelchair, wearing a porkpie hat and fingerless gloves. A dog-eared Bible was open in his lap and he was drinking bourbon from a large paper cup.

Sandra said, "What's that place?"

"It's called the Bat Cave."

"What goes on in there?"

"Gail Russell was married to Guy Madison back in the fifties. In 1961 they found her dead in her apartment, surrounded by bottles and vials of pills."

"Ray, what goes on in the Bat Cave?"

"You really want to know?"

"Yes."

"Girls dance naked."

"And?"

"And sometimes a guy will give them some money, and the girl will give him a pencil flashlight to look up inside her."

Sandra leaned back against the door. She looked perplexed. "What are they looking for?"

"I don't know," Burk said. "The end of the Vietnam War, maybe."

Sandra smiled but her lips remained closed. "You really are weird. You know that?"

"Yeah, I know. But you know who is *really* weird?"

"Who?"

"The guy who used to live here." Burk turned left on Normandie and parked in front of a four-story brick apartment. "Dr. Cyclops."

Sandra suddenly sat up. "Bullshit."

"Seventeen thirty-one Normandie. You can look it up."

"Swear to God?"

Burk nodded. Then he said, "Remember?"

On their very first date, when they were both students at the University of Wisconsin, Burk and Sandra drove three hundred miles in a snowstorm to see Bob Dylan perform at a club in Minneapolis. After the show, after singing "Don't Think Twice, It's All Right" about a million times in their crummy motel room, they made love for the first time. But years later, what they remembered most about that night was not the sex, which was clumsy at best, but how much they laughed when Albert Dekker, the actor who played Dr. Cyclops on the late late movie, shrunk his helpless victims down to the size of tiny dolls.

After the movie ended and the night started to fade into daylight, Sandra reached under the covers and said, "Well, I'm sure glad he didn't shrink this." She was still laughing when Burk came inside her, and afterward, when the blue sky shone through the flimsy curtains and he apologized for being too fast, she held his shoulders tight and whispered, "No, sweetheart, you were just fine."

When their son was conceived later that winter, Burk and Sandra shared an apartment above the Three Bells, a biker bar in Madison. For that entire semester, for hours at a time, two songs were played over and over on the jukebox: "Louie Louie" by the Kingsmen and "Wooly Bully" by Sam the Sham and the Pharaohs.

"I can't decide," Sandra said as they listened to the music pound below them.

"I think we should go with just plain Louie," Burk said.

"You sure? What about Louie with Louie as his middle name?"

"If you really want to," Burk said, realizing with a pang of doubt that the decision was now final.

★

When Burk woke up in the middle of the night there was an unfamiliar odor in the bedroom. "Sandra," he called out in a low voice. He could hear her breathing, but the space next to him was empty. "Sandra," he said again, louder.

"Here."

"Where?" Burk sat up and tried to adjust his eyes to the darkness. "Where are you?"

"Turn on the light."

Burk recognized the iron smell of blood a split second before he saw her standing naked in the corner of the room. She was holding a straight razor by her side, and blood was flowing freely from a large X she had carved in her stomach. "I had a baby ghost in my tummy," she said in a small voice, "and I had to let it out."

The punch that knocked Sandra unconscious also broke her jaw.

"It was the only thing I could do," Burk tried to explain to the paramedics after they loaded her in the ambulance. "I thought she was going to kill herself."

"If you say so," one of the paramedics said.

"You don't believe me?"

"We'll believe anything," said the other paramedic. "Isn't that right, Terry?"

"Whatever."

Burk called his brother from the hospital.

"Sounds like she's pretty fucked up," Gene said.

"Her jaw's gonna heal okay, but she'll have scars on her stomach."

"No big deal."

"I'm not crazy about scars, Gene."

"What difference does that make? You guys are through." Burk didn't say anything. "Right?"

"I guess."

"You guess. Come on, Ray, your wife is mentally ill."

"She's my best friend, Gene."

"Yeah, I know. But she belongs in a nut ward." Burk didn't disagree, but he suddenly felt terribly alone. "Ray?"

"I'm here. I'm thinking."

"Don't. You'll get a headache."

"I'm pretty fucked up behind all this."

"You'll pull it together. You have to. You got a kid."

Several seconds passed in silence. Burk spoke first. "I got fired today."

"That had to happen."

"Yeah, I know. It was the wrong job."

"I told you that. Go home and get some rest," Gene said. "Okay?"

"Okay."

"We'll talk tomorrow."

"I'll be out."

"Where?"

"I don't know . . . driving."

Burk hung up the phone and drove back to his house. Before he went to sleep, he walked into Louie's bedroom and turned off the light. After he closed the door, a car moved slowly down Valley View Lane, and twin beams of light pierced the darkness inside his son's room— and the bars on a baby's crib were shadowed on the wall.

The next day, the day after the Rolling Stones came to California, Burk met Bonnie Simpson.

★

Burk was parked on the corner of Beverly and Rampart with the hood up and the motor running. He gunned the engine. The rpms started to build up, and he heard the same thin whine that had worried him a few minutes earlier, right after he pulled away from Ernie's Stardust Lounge. It definitely wasn't the transmission or a valve—he knew that—and the temperature gauge was normal, which ruled out the radiator and the water pump. It's either a wheel bearing or a worn-out belt, Burk decided, as he switched off the ignition and got out of the car.

"It's the torque converter or the power steering." Burk was looking under the hood when he heard her voice. "That's my guess, anyway."

"I think it's a belt," Burk said.

"It's not a belt sound," she said.

Burk turned around: She had a wide face, suntanned and freckled, and when she smiled—as she did when Burk looked her way— thin lines were splintered in the delicate skin next to her eyes.

"That's a whine, like a kid crying. A belt sound is more like a singing noise."

"Then it's the torque converter?"

"Maybe," she said, reaching into her purse for an apple. "But I'd lean toward the power steering. You want an apple?"

"No, thanks."

"You sure? I got tons."

"I just ate."

Inside her purse, along with several red and green apples, was a map to the movie stars' homes.

"Apples are a wonderful source of energy," she said. "Low on calories, easy to digest." Burk started to lower the hood. "Wait," she said. "Let me check something first."

Before Burk could stop her, she ducked underneath his arm and unscrewed the top of the power-steering unit. "I *knew* it," she said triumphantly.

"Knew what?"

"You're almost out of fluid. Check it out."

Burk leaned forward. He could smell lilac perfume on her neck, and when he dropped his eyes he could see the tops of her breasts through the neck of her blouse. "What does it mean?" he said.

"Could have a leak. Only one way to find out."

"How?"

"How?" she repeated, rolling her eyes. "By looking under the car, dummy." She took a large bite out of her apple, and with her mouth full she said, "If nothing's dripping, that means you're probably okay. Just gotta add some fluid."

Burk dropped into a crouch. The ground underneath the engine was dry.

"Well?" she said, and Burk saw his car sag as she hopped up on the fender.

"I don't see anything," he said.

"Good."

Burk stood up. She took another bite of her apple and pointed to the movie-star map that was unfolded on her lap.

"Where's Tigertail Road?"

"In Brentwood."

"Is that far?"

"Ten miles."

"That's where Henry Fonda lives," she said, with a mysterious smile. "I just loved him in *Mister Roberts*."

"Yeah, he was pretty good in that," Burk said, although he preferred Fonda's performances in his earlier films, especially Westerns like *The Ox Bow Incident* and *My Darling Clementine*. "You like the movies?"

She nodded; then she crossed her legs and her loafer dropped off her foot and fell into the gutter. "Would you mind getting that for me?" she said.

Burk reached down for the shoe, and she stretched out her leg. Underneath her plaid pleated skirt he could see her bare thighs and, farther up, shaded, a triangle of black hair. "My name's Bonnie Simpson," she said.

Burk gripped her calf for support. "Ray Burk," he said, and he slipped on her shoe.

Burk bought a can of power-steering fluid at the Chevron on Melrose and Wilcox. On their walk back, Bonnie told him he reminded her of someone she knew in Detroit, an engineer friend of her first husband. "Rick Hardesty," she said. "Same build, and you wear your hair the same way. Over to the side." And a few minutes later, while they were approaching Burk's car, she told him why she got divorced. "It's the same old story," she said. "He stopped loving me and he stopped touching me, and after awhile the parts of my body became as obsolete as the fins he designed on the 'sixty-five Bonneville. But, hey, that's all in the past." Bonnie took Burk's hand, but when he gazed at her she turned her head away slightly, her eyes solemn and her lips pursed in concentration. After a few steps she let his fingers slip away. "The past doesn't mean anything now. Isn't that right, Ray?"

Burk shrugged. "I guess."

They walked the next block without speaking, and when the silence became awkward, Burk said with grave seriousness, "You don't remind me of anyone I've ever met."

Bonnie stopped and turned to look at him, studying his face with a faint grin. "Really?"

"You don't," Burk said. "Really. It's the truth."

As Burk drove west, toward the ocean, he tried to explain to Bonnie what it was like to grow up in LA during the fifties, how it was no big deal to put five hundred miles on your car every weekend when you were sixteen or seventeen years old, especially in the summertime.

He said, "You could knock off half of that just by tooling up and down the Sunset Strip or Hollywood Boulevard on Friday and Saturday nights. A side trip out to San Bernardino or Riverside for the drag races or a quick shot down to the Pike, this sleazy amusement park in Long Beach, and you could clock another couple of hundred miles on your speedometer, easy. And sometimes, if the waves were right, me and Timmy Miller used to get up before dawn on Sunday mornings and surf down the coast, beginning near the county line and following the swell south until we finally ended up just below San Diego." *Just below* meaning just below the border at the Blue Fox Saloon in Tijuana, where a pretty Mexican whore would give Burk and Timmy simultaneous hand jobs while they threw down shots of tequila and watched a large dog and a naked woman pretend they were falling in love.

After they passed Beverly Hills and UCLA, Burk took a right on Bundy, and they began to climb into the hills above Sunset. Outside, the light was failing, and the overcast sky was beginning to darken. "Not much time left to see houses," Burk said.

"That's okay," Bonnie said. "Just as long as I get to see where Henry Fonda lives. If we're lucky we'll see him in person, because sometimes he stands outside and washes his car in his driveway."

Burk laughed. "Who told you that?"

"This lady I knew back in Detroit. Her cousin took one of those Hollywood Fantasy Tours, and the driver mentioned it."

"That," Burk said, "is one of the most ridiculous things I ever heard."

"It's true, really." Bonnie gave Burk a smile out of the side of her mouth. Then she unhooked her safety belt and said, "You'll see."

Burk turned left on Carmelita, and the narrow road grew steeper. Bonnie turned in her seat, letting the hem of her skirt rise over her knees. "Are we getting close?"

"I think so," Burk said, and he felt the front of his jeans begin to bulge. "I haven't been around here since high school, when me and my buddies used to drink beer up on Mulholland Drive."

"Mulholland Drive. That's a lovers' lane, isn't it?"

"Used to be."

"Did you ever bring girls up there when you were in high school?" There was an awkward pause, and Burk had to fight down the impulse to reach out and touch her pale, smooth thighs. "Well," Bonnie said with a playful smile, "did you?"

"Sometimes."

"Back in Michigan everyone used to go out to this golf course near the lake. My best friend's sister—this girl named Jane

McDowell—had sex for the first time on the fourteenth green. Talk about freezin' your buns off. Of course the word got out, and for the rest of the semester all she heard was 'McDowell is the easiest par three in the county.' Hey, listen!" Bonnie's head was cocked toward the engine. "Do you hear it?"

"Hear what?"

"The whine," she said. "It's gone."

Burk grinned. "You're right."

"Stick with me, Ray, and you'll go places," Bonnie said, making a fist and chucking him under the chin. Then she winked and said, "Pull over."

"Pull over?"

"Uh-huh."

"Why?"

Bonnie reached out and turned the key, killing the engine. "Because we're taking a break," she said, and she started to unbutton her blouse. "Okay?" Burk sat, saying nothing, surprised by her frankness. "Okay?" she said again.

"It's not even dark."

"It will be."

"But—"

"Shhh." She was on her knees now, leaning forward, kissing his forehead, his eyes, and the corners of his mouth. "Everything's going to be fine. I promise. Just relax."

Burk was still breathing hard, so he didn't hear the first drops of rain when they started to patter on the roof of his car. Later, when his voice came back, he said, "I guess we can forget about visiting Mister Roberts tonight." Bonnie smiled and leaned back in the seat. She had the window down partway, and droplets of water sparkled in her hair like silver beads.

"Yeah," she said, her smile now becoming secretive. "Only some kind of fool would be washing his car on a night like this."

The rain had stopped, and flower children in their bright gypsy garb crowded the crosswalk as Burk pulled up to a stoplight on Sunset and Larrabee. Across the street was the Whiskey A Go-Go, where the Flying Burrito Brothers were third-billed to Elvin Bishop and the

British rock group Traffic. A truck was parked outside the front entrance, and two sweat-streaked roadies were unloading an amplifier the size of an icebox.

On the corner, a pale thin girl dressed like a zen archer was hawking an underground newspaper. "Death all day in the USA," she said over and over, in a singsong voice, as she pointed to the bold red-lettered headline that screamed ALTAMONT.

When the light turned green, Bonnie said, "I was in LA once before. Twenty years ago. I was thirteen, and I came out here to visit my mother. She died while I was here."

"How?" Burk asked her.

Bonnie frowned and looked out the window. "She burned to death in a fire."

"When she was twenty-four she entered this statewide beauty contest and she won. And guess what: A talent scout saw her and offered her a chance to take a screen test in Hollywood. All expenses paid. Just like you read about. But it really did happen to her."

Burk and Bonnie were parked in front of the Argyle Manor, a two-story mustard-colored apartment house on the northwest corner of Argyle and Franklin. While Bonnie was speaking, Burk could see a yellow-haired woman in a bathrobe standing by a window on the second floor. She was nursing a baby as she talked on the phone. When the woman hung up, Bonnie said, "No one knew she had a six-year-old daughter. I was like this big secret."

"Where was your dad?"

"Overseas. In the war. I ended up staying with my grandparents."

Burk didn't say anything. Somewhere in the neighborhood a dog began to bark, and his hand involuntarily closed into a fist.

"What's wrong, Ray?"

Burk shook his head. "Nothing. I was just thinking about my kid's dog. I bought him this beagle puppy last week," he said, staring off, "and Monday it disappeared. It jumped out of my wife's car while she was driving Louie home from nursery school." Burk turned and looked at Bonnie. "Out the window. It jumped out the window, into the traffic on the freeway. Louie screamed at her to stop, but she had the radio turned up so loud she didn't hear him until it was too late. I told him the dog would find its way home, but he didn't believe me."

"Of course he didn't."

"I don't think he'll ever forgive me."

Bonnie hunched forward a little, and Burk felt her hand gently touch his leg. "You feel trapped, don't you, Ray?"

Burk waited a moment, then he nodded his head. "Yeah, I do."

"I know what that feels like," Bonnie said. "I was trapped too. Trapped and scared and alone. But I'm not alone now," she said into his eyes. "I'm with you."

"Make yourself at home. There's some paper cups under the sink," Bonnie said, and she walked into the bathroom and closed the door.

Burk looked around. Except for a couch that folded into a bed, her apartment was totally bare. No furniture. No dishes. No pictures on the walls. No books or magazines. Not even a radio. She could have moved in that very day—and it occurred to Burk that maybe she had.

After he found the cups and poured himself a drink, Burk leaned against the breakfast bar and listened to the conversation coming from the apartment next door. "I didn't come all the way out here from Tulsa to sing backup for no one," a girl snarled. "Sheryl, honey," a man casually replied, "you'll fuck the dude if that's what it takes to make the rent." "*That* I might do," the girl said, and Burk heard a shrill laugh followed by the sharp sound of a hand striking flesh.

"Hi." Bonnie was standing in the kitchen doorway with her skirt off and her blouse unbuttoned to her waist. "So," she said, reaching for the paper cup that Burk was holding, "do you want to hear the rest of the story?"

★

In the spring of 1942, Bonnie's mother, Grace Simpson, took the Union Pacific railroad from Buchanan, Michigan, to Hollywood, California. And by the end of that same year, while her husband—a marine corporal—was crossing the Pacific on a troop carrier, she was acting in her first movie.

"My father never knew she was in a beauty contest or that she went to Hollywood or any of those things," Bonnie said. She and Burk were sitting cross-legged on the bed, in their underwear. "My mom said he would've jumped ship if he knew she left me back home."

Burk took a sip of scotch. "Yeah, that's a pretty strange thing to do," he said.

"Strange. I call it brave."

"I don't know."

"I do," Bonnie said. "Sometimes you gotta take some risks with your life. Like we're doing now, Ray. Right?" Bonnie reached behind her back and unhooked her bra. Then she looked at him with unmistakable affection and said, "Let's get under the covers."

After they made love for the second time that night, Bonnie told Burk that her father was killed on the island of Corregidor shortly before her mother's first movie was released in 1943. The day after the funeral, Grace Simpson took the Union Pacific back to Hollywood, where she made nine more movies, most of them B Westerns.

"They were just bit parts," Bonnie said, as she slipped out of bed and stood naked by the window. "She never had more than a few lines. But for some reason she started to get this following among soldiers and sailors who were returning home from the war. She even started to get fan mail. And do you want to know what's really strange? All of them said the same thing, that Mom reminded them of . . . of the girl they left behind."

Quietly, Burk crossed the room and joined Bonnie by the window. "I came out to visit her in 1949," Bonnie said, taking his hand, and she looked up at him with a small sad smile. "We were going to take a vacation together, but Max Rheingold wanted her to be in *The Crooked Man,* this gangster picture he was producing. He tried to fuck my mom," she said matter-of-factly. "He tried to fuck her in his office when he interviewed her for the part. I was right there, sitting in a chair outside the door. I heard her scream and I ran inside and made him stop."

"How?"

Bonnie hesitated before she answered. "I got between them," she said. She pointed toward the hills. "Look, you can see the *H.*"

"The what?"

"The *H* in the Hollywood sign. See?" Bonnie took a step backward, and Burk's erection nudged her hip.

"I see it," Burk said. "I see it every day."

Bonnie's hand dropped down between his legs, and she began to stroke him gently with the tips of her fingers. "Do you believe me?" she whispered.

"What?"

"That stuff about my mom and Rheingold."

"If you said it happened, then I guess it happened."

"It happened," Bonnie said positively, "just exactly like I told you."

Burk laced his fingers around her waist and pulled her close. "Then tell me the rest," he said.

"When I'm damn good and ready," she said, and held his eyes for a long time. Then she smiled and led him back to the bed.

"Even though it was the biggest role she had ever been offered, Mom was so frightened of Rheingold she almost turned it down. Finally, a week before shooting started, Lindy Dolittle, the director and an old friend, convinced her to change her mind."

Bonnie shifted her body on the bed so she could look straight into Burk's eyes.

"The script called for the final shoot-out to take place at a remote mountain cabin, and we ended up going up to Big Bear Lake on location. There was all sorts of rough-and-tumble action that week, so Mom was doubled a lot, which was fine with me because that meant we could spend more time together. Some mornings we went hiking way up in the mountains, far away from the cast and crew. In the afternoon, if it was warm enough, we would sunbathe naked by a narrow stream that was hidden in a grove of pines. We never really talked about much, or if we did I don't remember. Still, I don't think I have ever felt as calm as I did then, lying next to her, staring up through the tree branches at the clouds floating across the sky.

"But one afternoon she woke up from a nap and told me about this dream she had. She said she was on the Union Pacific and she was coming out to Hollywood for the first time. It was night. They were passing through the Rockies. 'I began to hear this sound,' she said, 'like a child sobbing. At first I thought it was the wind whistling outside or the steam from the engine. But when we passed over the Colorado River into Arizona, these sounds I heard, these sounds of mourning, got louder and louder, and by the time we entered the California desert I began to hear this terrible pounding inside my skull. Finally the conductor came into the car, and I asked him what this awful noise was. He said it was the stars. They were grieving, he said. But when he got close to me I saw that he wasn't the conductor at all. He was wearing the uniform of a marine corporal.' He told my mom that the stars were crying for her, but if she turned around, he told her, by the time she passed back through the Red River Valley she wouldn't hear the crying anymore. But she said she couldn't turn back because she was going out to Hollywood. 'Then you'll have to get used to the sound,' he told her, and he wished her good luck. As soon as he left the car my mom saw a light glowing in the distance, a light that grew brighter and brighter until she recognized it as the headlight of a locomotive heading in the opposite direction. But when she looked outside she saw no other tracks, just sagebrush and sand. Still, the train kept coming, phantomlike. Then with a flash it silently passed by, disappearing into the night, leaving behind the tumbleweeds blowing across the desert and the stars screaming in her ears. And then she woke up."

After Bonnie finished speaking, Burk stared at her for what seemed like thirty seconds. The silence was broken by a telephone that started to ring in the apartment next door. It rang six times before it stopped.

"Pretty late to call someone," Burk said.

"Maybe someone's trying to call you at your house, Ray."

"Maybe."

The phone rang again, but this time just once.

"Ray?"

"Yeah?"

"I made up that story."

Burk's head was resting on Bonnie's stomach. He kept quiet for a while, letting her words echo in the darkness, before he said, "Everything?"

"Just the dream part. That was mine. Not my mom's."

"But everything else—"

"Was true. Okay?"

"Okay," Burk said, and he slid his tongue along the thick scar that bisected her lower abdomen. "Finish your story."

"On the final day of shooting, Rheingold arrived on location in a long white limousine. I was sitting under a tree, holding a stray cat, when he called Dolittle over to discuss the final scene, a complicated sequence that would require split-second timing if they went for one take. 'Don't blow it,' I heard Rheingold say to Dolittle. 'Get it the first time.' And then he glanced at me and said, 'I want it to look real, so don't double the girl.' Dolittle told him there was no point in taking chances on the last day, that he could get everything he needed in close-ups, but Rheingold just shook his head and said, 'Do it my way.'"

An alarm clock went off somewhere in the apartment building, and Burk started to hear a morning deejay begin to yak over the radio.

He closed his eyes, trying hard to concentrate on Bonnie's story, even though he knew she was going to tell him something that he didn't want to hear.

"In the script Mom was playing Elizabeth Springer, a young housewife who gets kidnapped during a small-town bank robbery. After the police show up and surround the cabin where the robbers are hiding, they were supposed to lob a tear-gas canister through a window to flush them out. The special-effects guy had rigged up this harmless smoke bomb, which was Mom's cue to come running out-side—followed, of course, by the bad guys. And that's the way it was rehearsed all afternoon.

"But later that evening, when they did it for real, when the smoke bomb went off, the cabin roof exploded into the air and the sky turned as red as blood. Mom was not the first one out, but the last. I heard her screams before I saw the flames shooting up from her hair like ruby flares. The stuntmen all rushed forward, but when they ripped off her burning dress, charred strips of skin fell to the ground like pieces of dead bark . . . and she lay there burning to death right in front of my eyes."

A week later, on the Sunday after her mother's funeral, a man named Jack Rose drove Bonnie downtown to Union Station. Once more she had a ticket on the Union Pacific, but this time she was not riding home to Michigan. She was on her way to another city in the Midwest, Omaha, a city in Nebraska where her child would be born, in room 706 in the Hotel Sherwood.

"I had a boy," she told Burk, "and I named him Bobby."

Burk did not remember falling asleep, but when he opened his eyes there was a patch of cheerful midmorning sunlight where Bonnie's tangled hair should have been. After a few moments—enough time to find his Marlboros and notice that her clothes were gone—he realized he was alone.

It was impossible for Burk to believe that Bonnie had suddenly disappeared forever, that he would never again touch her skin or feel her tongue fill his mouth. From the very first moment he saw her on the street, he felt connected to her in a way he didn't understand. There was something in her wholesome but troubled features—the way she looked so deeply into his face, the chaos and pain buried behind her frantic eyes—that overpowered his mind and made his heart do a mad little dance.

"She probably went out for some groceries," Burk decided, saying the words out loud to the four bare walls, but he was already feeling that awful ache of loneliness as he lit up the first of the ten cigarettes he would chain-smoke during the next two hours.

Later that afternoon, when he stepped outside the Argyle Manor, Burk was approached by two determined-looking men with thick chests and dark, quick eyes.

"Freeze," one of the men said, cutting Burk off as he started toward his car. "Police. Put your hands in the air."

★

In local news, an unidentified armed woman was shot and critically wounded this afternoon in Brentwood, outside the luxurious home of movie producer Max Rheingold. Although details at this time are sketchy, apparently the woman was riding a Starline Fantasy Tours bus when she suddenly pulled a .22–caliber pistol and ordered the driver to stop. She tried to force her way onto Mr. Rheingold's property, which is located across the street from the estate owned by actor Henry Fonda.

Burk was listening to KNX All News 1070 as he drove west on the Ventura Freeway. He was on his way home after the police had questioned him for three hours.

"Tell them everything you know about this broad," Gene had told Burk when he finally got through to him at the station. "These guys are good guys; I used to work with them. Tell them the truth and they'll cut you loose."

"I told them everything," Burk said.

"They don't believe you, Ray."

"Then that's too bad."

Burk heard his brother take a deep breath on the other end of the phone. "Ray?" he said in a calm voice.

"Yeah?"

"They know you. Okay? They work undercover east of Vine and they see you around. Other people see you too. And they tell the cops."

"They see me driving. That's all I do."

"Day after day? Hour after hour? What the fuck's going on with you?"

"Nothing."

"Nothing?"

"I just drive, Gene."

"Is that it, Ray? You just drive. Is that why your ol' lady is in the hospital with a broken jaw, your ass is in jail, and Louie cries himself to sleep—"

"Bye, Gene." Burk hung up the phone, and he told the police everything they wanted to know about Bonnie Simpson. He told them how they first met, and he described the sweet smell of her perfume and the slope of her shoulders as she leaned under the hood of his car. He even told them how her bones and muscles felt underneath his hands when her long, smooth legs were wrapped around his waist. He told them she was raped as a child, about the scar on her lower abdomen and the possibility of a child somewhere. He told them about her dream. About the stars and the sounds they made.

Burk told them everything. But he didn't tell them that he loved her.

Louie's Big Wheel was sitting in front of the garage as Burk pulled into his driveway. When he switched off the ignition he heard the phone ringing inside his house, but he waited outside, breathing in the crisp cool air, until it stopped.

Before he went to sleep, he turned on the radio. On KMPC, Radio Ray Moore was speaking to a man with an angry voice.

"I struck my boy today," the caller told Radio Ray. "Not with my fist. I slapped him. But I slapped him hard enough to flame up his cheek."

"Why did you do that?"

"I caught him in the garage. He had the top off the paint thinner and his nose stuck inside the can. Those fumes can turn your brain goofy. I told him that before, but he don't listen to me."

"How old is he?"

"Twelve."

"Pretty young for that kind of stuff."

"Too young. That's why I had to draw the line. The next time I catch him in there he's gonna get a real beating."

"I'd think twice about that."

"I didn't call you for advice, Radio Ray."

"Why *did* you call me?"

"I wanted to get it off my chest."

"What are you hiding in the garage?"

"What do you mean?"

"I don't know. You sound like there's something in there you don't want him to see."

"What're you talkin' about? All I got in there is my camping gear, a lawn mower, and my tools."

"You got a tackle box?"

"Hell, yes. Of course I got a tackle box."

"The tray on top, that's where you keep all your lures and flies. Right? And maybe some hooks. What do you have underneath?"

"Nothin'."

"Nothing? Really?"

"I got some leader and a deck of playing cards."

"That's it?"

"And some insect repellent."

"What else?"

"Nothin'."

"You got something else down below, don't you? Something you're ashamed of. What is it, dope? Dirty pictures? Condoms? What do you have in there?"

"Nothin'! I got nothin'! Stop pushing me!"

There was a long pause. Radio Ray waited but the caller didn't speak.

"Apologize to your boy," Radio Ray said, breaking the silence. "Go in now and tell him you're sorry."

"He's asleep."

"Wake him up. Tell him you love him. Do the right thing."

"I don't know."

"Do it."

"But—"

"Do it. *Now.*"

The next morning, when Burk saw the picture in the *Los Angeles Times,* he knew right away that something was wrong. Two paramedics were loading Bonnie's body into the rear of the ambulance, but in the right-hand corner of the picture, in the gutter, Burk saw something that looked like a shoe. "Move aside," Burk said out loud to the cop in the picture, who was blocking his view. "Move aside or pick up her shoe. That's her loafer, you dumb shit! Pick it up! *Pick up her fucking shoe!*"

Gene called later that afternoon. He said, "I just spoke to my guys down at headquarters. It's all bullshit. They checked with the Screen Actors Guild, and they have no record of an actress with the name Grace Simpson. Ellen, Faith, Heather, Helen, yes. No Grace. No one close to that. Zip."

"Maybe she changed her last name. Actors do that all the time."

"Ray, listen to me. This chick—"

"Forget it, Gene. I'm not interested."

"What do you mean?"

"I don't want to hear it."

"You don't want to hear the truth? What're you, fuckin' crazy?"

No one spoke for at least a minute. Finally, Burk said, "P-Five."

"What?" Gene said.

"'Dream Lover.' P-Five on the jukebox at Ernie's Stardust Lounge. That's where it all started."

"I'm not following you, Ray."

"'Dream Lover,' Gene."

"I know the tune. Bobby Darin. B side—"

"P-Five. Palm Springs. The desert. Darin. A lavender sky. Laurel. The chick in the trophy case. It's all right there."

"Where?"

"Behind my eyes, Gene. The movie. I just have to splice it together, and you'll see how all this is connected. All of it. The whine in my power steering, Dr. Cyclops, James Earl Ray, Rheingold, Ricky Furlong—"

"Ricky Furlong?"

"And Clay Tomlinson too. I can't leave them out, Gene. Clay and Ricky changed our lives. I'll put them right next to those guys muff-diving at the Bat Cave. What do you think?"

"I don't know, man."

"You don't know, Gene? You're my brother. *How the fuck could you not know?*"

★

Three
Gene and
Clay:
Throwing
Down

From shortly before Christmas in 1941 until he suffered a mild heart attack in the spring of 1972, Burk's father Nate owned and operated Hollywood's busiest newsstand. Located eight blocks west of Vine, on the corner of Las Palmas and Hollywood Boulevard, the racks at Nate's News stretched south for nearly an entire city block.

Nathan Burk sold all the major dailies and newspapers of record, both foreign and domestic, but it was really his wide selection of oddball magazines (some stashed under the counter) that kept the sidewalk on Las Palmas crowded with customers twenty-four hours a day, seven days a week. Along with the familiar newsweeklies like *Time* and *Life,* Nate's was the only newsstand in the city to stock such maverick journals as *Naked Church Choirs, Amputee Love,* and *Coffin & Tombstone,* the monthly trade magazine for the mortuary industry.

But unlike other news dealers, Burk's father rarely returned his unsold magazines. Instead, every Saturday morning Burk and his older brother, Gene, would box the leftovers and hand-dolly them over to Yesterday's Pages, the used book and magazine store that their father owned on the corner of Cherokee and Selma. Yesterday's Pages was managed by Nathan Burk's cousin Aaron Levine, an ex-prizefighter and occasional movie extra who grew up next door to gangster Buggsy Siegel on the Lower East Side of Manhattan.

Aaron was also an alcoholic, the kind of blackout drinker who would disappear for days or sometimes even weeks at a time, ending up hospitalized or incarcerated in cities as far away as Galveston, Texas, or Tacoma, Washington, with absolutely no memory of how he got there. After these binges, Nathan Burk would always pay for Aaron's transportation back to Los Angeles, sometimes even hopping on a plane himself to serve as his personal escort. But whenever he demanded that his cousin stop drinking, threatening to fire him if he didn't comply, Aaron would just shake his head and stubbornly say the same thing: "I'm just a punch-drunk drunk and that's all I plan to be, so if you don't like me the way I am, Nate, you can just tell me to get lost."

But that was something Nathan Burk could never do.

★

"Because he's your cousin, Dad. Right?"

"No, Ray. Not because he's my cousin," Nathan Burk told his younger son on a muggy Saturday afternoon during the summer of 1949.

They were sitting at a window table in Mike Lyman's Vine Street Delicatessen, eating corned beef and chopped liver sandwiches. A block away was the Hollywood Pantages Theatre, where Burk had spent the morning watching cartoons and a Western serial starring Hopalong Cassidy and Buster Crabbe.

"Because he saved my life."

"He saved your life?" Burk's eyes opened wide and his lips were poised over the straw inside his bottle of Brown's Cream Soda. "Really?" Burk's father nodded. "How?"

Nathan Burk took a bite out of his sandwich and followed that with a fork piled high with cole slaw. "There was this big dumb Irish kid in our neighborhood," he said, speaking around the food in his mouth. "Jack Moriarty was his name. He was a bully, the kind of bully who used to beat up on kids for no reason. He just liked to hurt you. If you fought back he hurt you worse. Of course, he would never mess with me if I was with Aaron. But if he caught me alone on the street, he would either pinch my nipples or knuckle-punch me in the small of the back. I hated that boy," Burk's father said sharply. "I used to pray every night that he would die."

Nathan Burk paused for a moment and let his eyes travel around the restaurant. His narrow lips were working silently, and Burk could see a tiny speck of mustard in the corner of his mouth.

"One Saturday morning," he went on, pushing aside his plate and shifting his attention back to his son, "I was sitting in the subway station waiting for the train up to the Polo Grounds. I was on my way to see the Dodgers play the Giants. When I heard the subway I stood up, and that's when Moriarty grabbed me from behind in a bear hug. 'Look what I got,' he yelled. 'I got Big Nose Burk, the Jewish Jerk.' Then he began to laugh like a madman while he carried me over to the tracks. I screamed for help, but everyone ignored us or figured we were just a couple of kids horsing around. I'm absolutely certain he would've thrown me in front of the train if Aaron hadn't shown up right at that very moment. A split-second later, and I would've been dead."

Burk's father stopped speaking and glanced at his reflection in the delicatessen window. Outside, a gray-bearded man dressed in a hooded black robe walked up the sidewalk, carrying a white owl in a cage. Across Vine Street, movie producer Max Rheingold was standing in front of the Brown Derby smoking a long black cigar. With him was a woman wearing skin-tight red toreador pants and six-inch red spiked heels. A large red leather purse hung from her shoulder, and when she stepped to the curb and ducked inside the waiting limousine, Nathan Burk realized it was the aging ingenue who regularly came by his newsstand each week to pick up her hometown newspaper, the *Buchanan* (Michigan) *Bugle*. Her name was Grace Elliot, and he first saw her one evening in the spring of 1942.

She was remarkably fresh and innocent looking then, her face round and glass-smooth, and her long, very auburn hair was tied behind her head in a ponytail. But now her once-clear face had a rough and unfinished look, and there was purplish eye shadow on her eye-lids and carmine lipstick slashed across her shapely mouth.

"What happened, Dad?"

Burk's father turned away from the window and stared at his son, puzzled. "Where?"

"At the subway station. What happened at the subway station with the bully?"

"Oh, there," Burk's father said, closing his eyes, straining to bring that part of the past back into focus. "Well," he said, "Aaron was going to the ball game that day too. And he brought along his favorite bat, figuring that afterwards, if he was lucky, he would get one of the Giants to sign it. But when he got to the subway station and he saw what was going on, he—"

"Aaron let that kid have it," Burk said, sitting up straight. "He smashed him with his bat. Right?"

"That's right," Burk's father said. "But once Moriarty let me go, Aaron dropped his bat and used his fists to sock him in the jaw. He went down real hard, but he got back up with a big smile plastered on his face. He said, 'Try to hit me again, sheeny,' but when Aaron cocked his right hand, Moriarty laughed and said, 'Screw you, Jew,' and he turned around and jumped in front of the train."

Burk was silent. He looked stunned. Finally, he said, "You mean he committed suicide?"

"Yes, he did," Burk's father said, and he signaled the waitress for the bill. "And that, my son, is the end of the story."

★

Ten years later, on the Saturday afternoon that Burk's older brother Gene was scheduled to fight Clay Tomlinson in the parking lot at Will Rogers State Beach, Timmy Miller's aquamarine '55 Chevy turned the corner on Las Palmas and idled in front of Ruffino's, the take-out pizza joint that sat directly across the street from Nate's News. "Maybe Baby" was playing on KRLA, and nestled underneath Timmy's arm was a sharp-featured girl wearing dark sunglasses, and very tight white shorts.

"This is PK," Timmy said to Burk, as he climbed into the rear seat.
Burk nodded. "Nice to meet you."

"Same here," PK said, without turning her head.

PK's name was really Patty Kendall, and later that day Burk
would learn that her father, Kenny Kendall, was an out-of-work
actor and that she'd recently moved to the west side from Canoga
Park, a suburb on the northern edge of the San Fernando Valley.
Timmy had picked her up that morning, hitchhiking into Hollywood.

"That's where I work," PK said to Timmy, as they cruised past
the Grauman's Chinese Theatre. "I got the job because my mom
knows the manager. She's a waitress at the Cinegrill," she said, pointing across the street at the Hollywood Roosevelt Hotel. "Before that
she was a cigarette girl at Ciro's."

Burk leaned forward and rested his arms on the front seat. "My
parents used to celebrate their wedding anniversary at Ciro's."

"No kidding," PK said. "Maybe my mom sold them cigarettes."

"Maybe."

"I bet they noticed her for sure. She's got really long dyed blond
hair and boobs out to here. Some people think she looks like Mamie
Van Doren, except she's older. My mom, that is."

Timmy said, "PK was in Goody-Goody last week when Tomlinson
knifed that guy from Westchester."

Burk felt his heart begin to thump. He glanced nervously at PK.
"You were there?"

PK nodded, her back to him. Then she lifted up her sunglasses
and swiveled around in her seat: Freckles were sprinkled across her
forehead, and up close her blue eyes were as soft as faded denim.
"You're scared. Aren't you, Ray?"

"Yeah. I am."

"I would be too."

Burk felt slightly embarrassed. They pulled up to a light, and
he shifted his eyes away from PK's face. "I just can't fuckin' believe
he's back in LA. What's it been, Tim? Five years?"

"At least."

"Nobody thinks Gene will show. But they're wrong."

There was a long pause. Timmy lit up a Marlboro and took a
drag, waiting for the traffic to move before he glanced into the rearview mirror. "Don't worry, Ray. Gene's gonna kick his ass."

★

Gene Burk turned thirteen on August 27, 1953. Summer ended two weeks later, and he rode his new sky-blue Schwinn two-wheeler across the schoolyard at Ralph Waldo Emerson Junior High School. A muscular boy that Gene didn't recognize was standing alone near the bike rack. His hair was the color of brick, and he was wearing a dirty white T-shirt and jeans that were ripped in both knees.

"Hi," Gene said, after he parked his bike. "My name is Gene Burk."

"Who cares what your name is?" the boy sneered, and he walked away without shaking Gene's hand.

By the first recess it was common knowledge that the new boy, Clay Tomlinson, had moved to Los Angeles after both his parents and his older sister were killed in a car wreck on the Indiana turnpike.

"It happened over the Fourth of July," Suzy Farrel whispered to Gene during homeroom. "They were coming back from the state fair in Indianapolis."

"Who told you that?"

"Lisa Sutter. She overheard Miss Gardner telling Mr. Fields in the library. They said it was a miracle he survived."

Before the day was half over, more rumors about Clay's background were passed along between classes and during lunch hour in the cafeteria: he had an older brother who died in Korea (true); the uncle he was living with, Luke Tomlinson, was a professional golfer (false: he managed a driving range in Panorama City); his sister was a dead ringer for Joanne Dru and she was planning to become an actress before her life ended tragically at the age of nineteen (half true: Shirley Tomlinson was blond and almost unbearably beautiful, but at the time of the accident she was engaged to her high school sweetheart and studying to be a veterinarian at Indiana University in Bloomington); and so on.

"Tomlinson always seemed a lot older than thirteen," Timmy said to PK as he drove west on San Vicente Boulevard. At Ocean Avenue he turned right and they followed a long line of cars down Channel Road to the Pacific Coast Highway. "For one thing he had a beard, plus he smoked like a fiend and he already knew how to drive. I remember one Saturday we saw him cruising through Westwood in his uncle's raggedy old pickup. He was sittin' real low in the seat like a pachuco, and he was wearing biker shades like the ones Brando wore in *The Wild One*." Timmy laughed and caught Burk's eye in the rearview. "You remember that, Ray?"

Burk nodded, he seemed disoriented for a moment as his memory jumped backward, past that day to another day, to a cool clear autumn afternoon in 1953. He remembered walking into a room he shared with his brother and finding him facedown on his bed, crying.

"Some new kid at school smacked him around," Burk's father told him over dinner. "He busted up his lip and gave him a shiner."

"Why?" Burk asked.

"I don't know. He wouldn't tell me."

★

"There wasn't any reason," Gene told Burk later in the darkness of their bedroom. "I was just going over my math homework with Carla Powers and he walked up and slugged me in the face."

"What'd you do?"

"I tried to grab his arms but he punched me again."

"Did you fight back?"

"I couldn't."

"Why?"

"I was afraid he'd hurt me."

"He did hurt you, Gene. Look at your face."

The next day, Friday, between fourth and fifth periods, Clay Tomlinson pulled Gene behind the metal shop and doubled him over with a right hand under his heart. Gene instantly lost his breath, and tears oozed out of his eyes as he desperately tried to gulp air. A crowd quickly gathered and someone shouted "Fight him, Gene!" but, later, all Gene could remember was that split second of pain after the bell rang and Tomlinson's final blow glanced off his cheekbone, sending him to his knees.

Silence weighted the air that afternoon while Burk and his older brother rode their bikes home from school. Finally, at a stoplight,

Burk pointed to the discolored lump that was growing next to Gene's ear. "Are you gonna let him beat you up every day, Gene?"

"Eventually he'll lay off."

"How do you know?"

"He will. As soon as he sees I won't fight back he'll lose interest."

They sat for a while without speaking. Several cars and a bus passed by, the gray exhaust curling in front of their faces. Suddenly Burk stood up on his pedals and peeled off to his right. Over his shoulder he yelled, "I don't want a coward for an older brother, Gene. That's not fair."

It rained in Los Angeles the following Monday, so Burk's father took the day off to watch the Brooklyn Dodgers play the New York Yankees in the fifth game of the World Series. With the score tied three all and Duke Snider at the plate in the sixth inning, the phone rang. When he picked up the receiver, a voice he didn't recognize said, "Is this Gene Burk's father?"

"Yes it is."

"This is Mr. Lockridge, the principal at Emerson Junior High School. Your son has been injured."

Nathan Burk's mind went blank for a moment. "What happened?"

"We're not sure. Either he fell or he was pushed out of the boys' rest room on the second floor of the classroom building. The ambulance has just arrived." Through the other end of the receiver, Burk's father could hear the radio account of the World Series playing in Lockridge's office. Snider took a called third strike and Lockridge said, "Fortunately, a hedge broke his fall. Right now it looks like a broken collarbone and some cuts and bruises. They'll be taking him to St. Johns Hospital in Santa Monica. Do you need the address?"

"No. I know where it is. I'll be right there."

Nathan Burk hung up the phone and gazed at the TV: Jackie Robinson was trying to score from first on a Gil Hodges single. "He's rounding third," the announcer cheered, "and he's heading for the plate. Here comes the throw from Mantle and—"

"Safe," Nathan Burk whispered, his fists clenched, barely able to breathe. "Let my boy be safe."

Because there were no eyewitnesses and Gene refused to cooperate with the investigation by the police, Tomlinson could not be linked

directly to the "accident." Nevertheless, Mr. Lockridge suggested to
Tomlinson's Uncle Luke that, "given the circumstances, it might be
better for everyone if you withdrew Clay from Emerson and sent him
to one of the other junior high schools in the district. That way he'll
get a fresh start."

"I can't handle the boy," Luke Tomlinson said, and he decided
instead to ship his nephew back to Indiana. And for the next two years
Clay was in and out of trouble, spending a six-month stretch at Clinton,
a boys' reformatory in Terre Haute that was later to claim Charles
Manson as one of its alumni.

★

"After Gene had his cast removed, he took the trolley into Hollywood
and told my dad he wanted to learn how to fight. That was on a
Monday," Burk told PK after they passed the Santa Monica Pier. They
were in a snarl of traffic, and he had to raise his voice over the crash
of the waves and the radios playing in the cars around them. "That
afternoon there was a speed bag and a heavy bag installed in the back
room of Yesterday's Pages. The next day he went into training with
my cousin Aaron."

Timmy said, "I used to go up there with Ray and watch, and at
first it was pretty hilarious to see this tubby kid and this old drunk
rope-skipping down Hollywood Boulevard and shadowboxing in the
store windows."

"Gene was overweight but he wasn't clumsy," Burk assured PK,
"and he picked up stuff quick, too, because Aaron was a helluva
teacher when he wasn't up the street at Ernie's getting bombed on
gin." Burk glanced toward the ocean; then his head went back and
he began to laugh. "You should've been there when he taught Gene
how to throw a left hook."

"We just got through seeing *River of No Return* at the El Rey,"
Timmy said, and he was laughing now as his mind went back to that
Sunday. "We were walking down the block, and all of a sudden we
heard Aaron shouting, 'Rotate your hips! Rotate your hips! Leverage!
Leverage!' I said to Ray, 'Is he teaching Gene to fight or fuck?' We
didn't know what the hell was going on. Then we walked into the back

room of Yesterday's Pages and saw that Aaron had all these pictures of fighters pasted on the walls, pictures of these famous left-hook artists from the past that he tore out of back issues of *Ring* magazine. Guys like Stanley Ketchel and Benny Leonard and Ike Williams. And there was Aaron with his shirt off, skinny as a string bean, his pants slippin' down over his butt, firing left hooks at the heavy bag. And each time he would throw a punch he would shout, 'Rotate your hips!' *Bam! Bam! Bam!* I couldn't believe it and neither could Ray, because Aaron hit that sucker so hard it felt like the store was shaking."

Burk said, "Aaron trained my brother for a couple of months, but he knew, like I knew, that sooner or later Gene would have to find out if he could execute—you know, take care of himself against someone punching back, not a bag. So one day he took me and Gene and Tim downtown to the Main Street Gym.

"There was this colored guy, Lee Calhoun, who was working out for the Golden Gloves or something, and Aaron knew his trainer, and he asked him if he'd let his fighter spar a few rounds with Gene. It wasn't supposed to be a real fight—I mean, Gene was only thirteen and this guy already had a bunch of amateur fights—but as soon as the bell rang Calhoun ran across the ring and began pounding the shit out of Gene. By the end of the round he could barely keep his hands up, and blood and tears were running down his face.

"Aaron knew he'd made a mistake, that he'd overmatched Gene, but when he told him between rounds that he was gonna call it off, Gene said, 'No. Don't stop it! Let me finish! If I quit now, I'll always quit.' So Aaron let him fight, and during the next two rounds he took a terrible beating. But he didn't go down, and by the end of the third round everyone in the whole fucking gym was on their feet cheering for Gene." Burk paused, and PK twisted around in her seat to look at him. "You couldn't believe how proud I was, PK."

PK nodded her head, her eyes fixed on his. "He's your big brother, Ray. You *should* be proud of him."

★

When word went out on Friday night that Gene Burk and Clay Tomlinson had agreed to fight the following afternoon, the news trav-

eled by phone through the Southland's teen grapevine in less than
an hour. And by 9 A.M. the next morning, upwards of five hundred
kids—all of them vibrating with excitement—began to arrive at Will
Rogers State Beach, driving in from cities as far east as Riverside
and as far north as Bakersfield.

Former child actors Dean Stockwell and Bobby Driscoll rolled
up together in a shiny new Corvette, and Brandon de Wilde, the kid
from the movie *Shane,* was spotted drinking straight vodka from a
silver flask, surrounded by a pack of slender surfers with dark sun-
tans and bleached-white hair. By noon the parking lot was filled and
several legendary street fighters from years past were making their
presence known, swaggering through the milling crowd, knocking
people aside: bad asses like Jack Boise, Eddie Del Campo, and the
notorious Dockweiler twins, two giant mulattos with sweat glistening on their bulging muscles and their crudely shaved heads. Even
Carl Linger rode up from Long Beach, along with ten members of
the Hell's Angels chapter he joined after he was paroled from San
Quentin.

Clay Tomlinson was off to the side, leaning against the fender
of his '53 Olds Starfire, dragging on a Pall Mall, his lean and long
muscled arm around "nympho" Nancy Leeds, a skinny cocktease from
Tarzana, who was shaking her hips and grinding her pelvis to the
rock-and-roll music blasting over the car radio. Idling nearby, watching her with an air of contempt, were a knot of Mexicans from Boyle
Heights, part of the White Fence, LA's oldest and largest street gang.

When Gene came through the crowd, followed by Burk and
Timmy and Patty Kendall, a girl shouted, "Here he comes! Here
comes Gene Burk!" and suddenly all the voices and laughter and
conversations ceased, leaving only a murmuring silence and the
scuff of feet as a narrow lane was formed that opened into the center of the parking lot.

Taking his time, but moving confidently and with no anger showing in his face, Gene walked right up to Tomlinson and said, "I'm
ready when you are, Clay."

Tomlinson said, "You mean you're ready to die," and Gene
grinned.

"I don't think so," he said, and a space around them cleared fast.

Laughing to himself, Tomlinson pinched off the burning end of
his cigarette and lunged for Gene, grabbing him around the neck and

wrestling him to the ground. Gene was caught off guard, and, before he could react, Tomlinson was already pounding his head on the concrete. Burk quickly pushed his way to the front of the adrenalized mob and screamed, "Don't quit, Gene!" and with a sudden burst of strength Gene was able to separate himself and scramble back to his feet.

The next time Tomlinson came at him, Gene feinted to his right and jabbed him in the face. Tomlinson took a step backward and started to spit blood. Gene double-jabbed him again; then he threw a right cross that split open his eyebrow. Tomlinson howled in pain and the crowd behind Burk surged forward, knocking him to the ground. For the next thirty seconds, while a wave of bodies swept over him and a jet streaked by overhead, the air was filled with cheers and screams and the sound of thudding fists.

As soon as he pulled himself to his feet, he saw Gene and Tomlinson trading punches, with Gene getting the best of it, his right hand clubbing the side of Tomlinson's head. Very soon more fights began to break out. Everywhere you looked, blood was flying and kids were punching and kicking each other and rolling around on the parking lot or down on the warm yellow sand.

By the time the police arrived, Gene had Tomlinson backed up against Timmy's car, and he was hitting him with punch after punch—not roundhouse punches, either, but neat sharp rights and lefts to the head, the kind of punches he learned in the back of *Yesterday's Pages*. Both of Clay's eyes were closed, his lip was all busted up and lopsided, and blood poured out of his nose, soaking the hairs on his chest.

Finally, when the cops pulled him away, Gene turned and looked over his shoulder at his younger brother. Smiling through a mouth filled with blood and broken teeth, he said, "Nobody's ever gonna call me a coward again, Ray. Fucking nobody."

The police ran a check on Clay's car, found out it was stolen, and loaded him into the back of a black-and-white. Burk and Tim and PK drove Gene over to the emergency room at St. John's, where it took a doctor and two nurses a good hour to stitch up his face.

On his way home that night, Gene stopped at Billy's Bop City, a record store on Lincoln Boulevard. He bought an album by The Meadowlarks and a single by Fats Domino. When he finally fell asleep, leaving the ecstasy and terror of that long day behind, "I Want to Walk

You Home" was spinning on the phonograph, playing over and over and over until Burk woke up and finally switched it off. The next morning, after he got up and flipped over the record, Gene realized that his father was standing awkwardly in the doorway of his room. His expression was blank, concealing his worry.

Gene laughed through his swollen lips. "I guess I look pretty bad."

Nathan Burk nodded his head slowly. "Yeah. You do," he said, but when he tried to laugh along with his son, the sound was blocked by a swelling in his throat.

Gene stepped forward and put his arms around his father's shoulders. "It's okay, Dad. It's over," he said. "I won."

"I know you did," Nathan Burk said, and Gene could feel his pounding heart. "This morning I was scared. Now I'm just . . . proud."

Four

Max

and

Jack

December 6, 1969

When dawn broke on the day that Burk kissed Bonnie Simpson for the last time, a red-lead band of sky flared above the eastern horizon. With the first thin light came the Santa Ana winds, and by 5 A.M. that morning the sky framed outside Max Rheingold's bedroom window was streaked with indigo and silver clouds, trailing silky threads the color of sunburned flesh.

Rheingold had already been up several times during the night, roused first by distant sirens and the yowling of neighborhood dogs, later by the warm winds whirling through the canyon. Finally, he was jolted awake for good by a sharp, stabbing pain deep inside his rectum.

"Jesus Christ," he said under his breath, and he reflexively reached for the bottle of Demerol he kept in the top drawer of his nightstand. He chased down three pills with a gulp of leftover wine and closed his eyes, counting backward from one hundred while he listened to the bedroom shutters vibrate and the branches of the avocado and lemon trees scrape against the side of his house.

Gradually the painful pounding behind his testicles began to subside, and Max reached between his legs, continuing to count down slowly through the teens until his right leg started to twitch. At thirteen he lost his breath. When he silently shaped the number seven with his lips—which just happened to be the precise age of the little girl with the Shirley Temple curls he was sodomizing in his sexual fantasy—a small puddle of semen suddenly flooded his navel.

After he ejaculated, Max nearly fell back to sleep until a garbage truck backfired loudly as it labored up Tigertail Road. The truck's radio was tuned to KGFJ, and the driver, a black man with a deep bass voice, was singing along with "Everyday People," the current hit by Sly and the Family Stone.

Max reached for the telephone and dialed time. "Six-fifteen and thirty seconds," announced the recorded voice and Max yawned, relaxed in the knowledge that he still had two full hours before his meeting with Jack Rose. But as his lungs filled with air, Max noticed a seed of discomfort begin to grow in the region of his sphincter. "Not again," he whispered, and then, as the pain expanded and a mist of tears covered his eyes, he screamed, "What the fuck is going on?"

"Not to worry," Artie Schlumberger had told Max earlier in the week, after he slipped his finger out of Max's anus and stripped off the latex surgical glove. "I don't feel any lumps or masses and, as far as I can tell, the bleeding is from one of your hemorrhoids."

"What's that mean, 'as far as I can tell'?"

"It means I'm a urologist, Max," Artie said carefully, "not a proctologist."

"But everything seems okay?"

"Yeah," Artie said, and he hesitated for a moment, debating whether to send Max up to see Herman Frick, the rectal guy on the seventh floor. "Of course you're a little enlarged up there, but that's standard for a guy your age."

Max grunted. "Don't give me 'your age' bullshit. I probably get laid more than you do, putz."

Artie grinned good-naturedly, forgetting about Herman Frick as he now remembered how much he despised Max Rheingold.

"So what about something for the pain?" Max said as he hitched up his pants and tightened his belt.

"Aspirin should be all you need, Max."

"But just in case."

Artie took a seat behind his desk and swiveled his chair so he could gaze out the open window behind him. The northern sky, a bright ceramic blue when he awoke that morning, was now smeared with a rust-colored haze. "I don't think it's a good idea," he finally said.

"I'm not interested in what you think. It's not your asshole."

"That's true, Max." Artie spun round and opened the top drawer of his desk. He took out a prescription pad and held it up. "But it's my medical license."

"Be serious, kid."

"I am serious. This is it," Artie said while he scribbled a prescription and passed it across the desk. "No more scams."

"What scams? What're you talking about?" Max said, grinning innocently as he pocketed the prescription. "I would never ask you to write a bogus script for me, Artie. Ever."

Bogus script. The irony in that statement was not lost on Artie as he watched Max Rheingold light up a long cigar and waddle slowly out of his office. Because twenty years earlier, during the Red Scare, when the House Un-American Activities Committee came to Hollywood to root out Communists and Communist sympathizers in the motion picture industry, Artie's father, Samuel Schlumberger—a highly sought-after scriptwriter who fought against Franco in the Spanish Civil War and was an earnest supporter of all good liberal causes—was suddenly denied employment.

But Schlumberger (like many Hollywood writers who were blacklisted in the fifties) continued to turn out movie scripts for a small group of independent producers. Sometimes he wrote under a pseudonym, but more often than not a friendly but politically untainted writer would allow his name to be used on Schlumberger's work. For a small fee, of course.

One of Samuel Schlumberger's scripts, falsely credited to Amos Solomon, was a low-budget noirish tale of revenge that Max Rheingold produced for Keystone Pictures in 1948. Starring Kenny Kendall and

Ellen Hamel, *Careless Love* did unexpectedly well at the box office, especially in the South and Midwest, and Max (in a gesture that was uncharacteristically generous) rewarded Schlumberger with a small share of the movie's profits.

The day he received his bonus check for ten thousand dollars, Samuel Schlumberger placed the money into a trust account for his eight-year-old son, Artie.

"For his education," Samuel Schlumberger told his family.

"What about me?" Artie's older sister, Maria, asked.

"With your looks, who needs money?"

"But Dad," she protested, "that's not fair."

Her father laughed. "Who said life is fair?"

Samuel Schlumberger died suddenly of a brain aneurysm on September 9, 1963, and that Sunday a small funeral was held at the Hillside Memorial Cemetery, the favored final resting place for Hollywood's well-known Jews.

Artie flew in from Baltimore, where he was attending medical school at Johns Hopkins University. He took a taxi from the airport to the cemetery, making one quick stop at the Paradise Lounge, a strip joint on Century Boulevard just west of the airport. With his cab double-parked by the curb, he sat on a ripped vinyl bar stool, surrounded by pimps and prostitutes, watching an impassive, unsmiling Oriental woman dance topless to the jukebox. After three watered-down drinks, he walked outside and bought a pint of scotch to go at the cut-rate liquor store on the corner.

He drank openly throughout the Kaddish, but he never shed a tear. "I was crying inside," he explained to his sister afterward, while she drove him back to the airport. "Is there anything wrong with that?"

Over Christmas vacation Artie flew back to Los Angeles. Maria picked him up at the airport, and once again they drove over to Hillside, where they said a silent prayer over Samuel Schlumberger's grave. While they were walking back to the car, Artie told his sister that he felt guilty about the money he'd received from their father. "You were right. It wasn't fair. You should've got something too," Artie said.

"But I did get something," Maria said, and she opened her wallet and displayed a photograph of a dust-colored pony standing inside a small corral. "I got Emma," she said, pointing to the picture.

"Dad got you a pony?"

"No. Max Rheingold did," she said, flipping to a picture of herself sitting on the same pony. She was wearing white tennis shorts, sneakers, and a blue T-shirt that was pulled tight across her scrawny chest. Standing next to her, frowning, was a little girl with amber-colored hair and apple-green eyes.

Artie said, "How come I never knew?"

"Because Dad told me never to tell anyone. Not even Mom. He swore me to secrecy."

"Who's the girl with you?"

"Her name was Bonnie. She was with Rheingold when the chauffeur picked me up from school. Her mother was an actress," Maria said, her face growing serious. "That day, while we were out riding, we got caught in a thunderstorm. We got drenched and the chauffeur took us back to Rheingold's house so we could take a hot bath and get some clean clothes.

"While we were sitting in the tub, Max walked into the bathroom with this weird smile on his face. When he unzipped his pants and started to masturbate, Bonnie leaned over and whispered, 'Don't cry,' and when I tried to climb out of the tub she held my wrist tight. 'Stop it,' she said. 'Just let him do it till he's done.' After thirty seconds or so he came, and a big glob of semen jumped out of his penis and landed on my knee. Bonnie put a hand over my mouth so I wouldn't scream, keeping it there until he finally left the bathroom.

"As soon as I got home that afternoon I told Dad what happened, but he didn't say a word until it was time to go to sleep. Then, while he was tucking me in, he said, 'I don't think it would be such a good idea to go riding anymore.' I said, 'Neither do I,' and he turned off my light and kissed me good night.

"Before I closed my eyes I could hear Mom and Dad listening to the *Lucky Strike Hit Parade* on the radio downstairs in the living room. I fell asleep right after they played the number-one song for the week. It was sung by Patti Page."

Artie said, "Let me guess. 'The Doggy in the Window'?"

"No."

"'Changing Partners'?"

"No."

"'Mockin' Bird Hill'?"

"Nope."

"What?"

"'Tennessee Waltz.'"

★

Max's meeting with Jack Rose did not go well.

"I don't need a partner," Jack said, after Max casually suggested they produce a picture together. "I'm doin' fine."

"Things could change, Jack."

"Then I'll adjust."

Several heads turned as Glenn Ford entered the Polo Lounge. As he passed by their table he nodded to Jack, and Max said, "He still looks good."

"Good enough to eat," said their waitress, a middle-aged woman with a long jaw and slightly crossed eyes. After she took their order, Max said, "Remember that sneak we went to back in 'forty-two? That Rosalind Russell picture—"

"*My Sister Eileen.*"

"That's the one. He was there that night."

"Who?"

"Ford. He sat right in front of us. You were with that Mexican broad you used to represent. Lucy Something."

Jack shook his head. "You lost me, pal."

"Come on, Jack. You guys were an item." Max snapped his fingers. "Lucy Alvarado, that was her name. I used her in *Bleeding Kansas,* the gangster flick I shot up in Lone Pine."

Bleeding Kansas made a modest profit and Max used Lucy in two more films, both quickie Westerns; then she caught Harry Cohn's eye at the Trocadero one evening and he put her under contract at Columbia Pictures. But three months later he changed his mind and decided to put the studio's effort behind his other Latin discovery, Margarita Cansino, better known as Rita Hayworth.

"She's a great fuck," Harry Cohn told Jack Rose on the day he dropped Lucy's option, "but she can't sing and dance like my other spick."

Max saw Lucy next at Eartha Kitt's opening at Ciro's, and from time to time he would run into her at the Florentine Gardens or the

Colony Club, always drunk and dressed to kill with a different man on her arm, usually some garishly dressed musician that she would introduce as "my new lover boy."

He last heard from her on Halloween night in 1950, when she left a message with his answering service. "Pray for me, Max," she said, in words so slurred that she could hardly be understood by the operator. "Pray for Lucy Alvarado."

The next morning she was found dead on the floor of her apartment. The coroner's report said she'd overdosed on morphine.

"I need a picture," Max said to Jack while they were waiting for their cars. The wind had increased along with the temperature, and dead autumn leaves danced and cartwheeled down the long sloping driveway in front of the hotel. "You listening to me, Jack?"

"Be realistic, Max."

"I am being realistic. Why do you think we're having breakfast? Because we're friends, Jack. For almost thirty years! And friends help each other out."

Jack's face remained impassive as he watched his sleek brown Jag pull to the curb.

"I need a picture," Max said again, his voice becoming higher as he geared up his nerve. "Let's do something together. We'll make a fortune." Jack started to step away but Max delayed him with a hand on his sleeve. "Jack, you gotta help me."

"I'm already rich," Jack reminded Max, and gently pulled his arm away. "I don't need a partner. I'm sorry."

"That's right. Just brush me off," Max said loudly as Jack tipped the parking valet and slid behind the wheel of his Jag. "You don't need me. You don't need anyone. But don't forget about *her*," he called out, his voice sounding vengeful. "Don't forget about Lucy Alvarado."

Instead of heading directly home, Max drove west on Sunset until he reached the Pacific Coast Highway. At Topanga Canyon Road he stopped at a small grocery for a six-pack of Hires Root Beer and a package of chocolate Malomar cookies. He continued driving north with the windows down, becoming more and more comforted by the sound of the ocean and the Mozart symphony playing on KFAC. Near Point Dume his eyes became heavy, and a mile or so later he pulled into a deserted parking lot adjacent to Zuma Beach. He took off his tie, loosened his belt, stretched out on the seat, and began to hum, almost inaudibly, the theme from the movie *High Noon*.

Thirty minutes later an ancient Studebaker turned into the parking lot with gas-blue smoke spewing from the exhaust. The driver jumped out, wearing a full Santa Claus suit, complete with white beard and wig. With him was a carload of unruly, hungry-looking children, who pummeled each other as they raced down to the sand. Lagging behind, tugging a Dalmatian puppy on a rope leash, was a girl of about ten with fuzzy blond hair and red welts on her ankles.

"Violet," she screamed, and a stiff ocean breeze lifted her sun dress over her hips, "you better be good, or I'm gonna hurt you bad."

Max chuckled; then he saw the little girl staring at him through the windshield.

"Who are you?" the little girl asked, yanking the leash so hard that the puppy yelped as she flipped over on her back.

"My name is Max."

"What are you doing here?"

"I'm resting," Max said, reaching for his cock and feeling it grow. "Come over here."

"Why?"

"I want to show you something."

"Come on, Julie," a little boy shouted, the wind carrying his voice up from the shoreline. "Come on!"

"I gotta go," the little girl said. "I gotta go find my dad."

As the little girl skipped away, a large wave crashed on the beach and a single cloud slid by the sun, darkening the ocean.

An hour later a Starline Fantasy Tour bus turned right off Sunset and moved slowly up Tigertail Road. Bonnie Simpson was sitting in the seat directly behind the driver, whistling tunelessly while she rolled up her movie star map and gently slapped her thigh. When the driver said, "Now we are approaching a house that is owned by Henry Fonda," Bonnie removed a .22 caliber pistol from her purse. Then, with an expression of gravity on her face, she pointed the pistol at the driver's head and said, "Please pull over."

★

Five

Bonnie:

With Cameo

Appearances

by Ricky Furlong

and Clay Tomlinson

Bonnie Simpson left Omaha in 1950, shortly after her son was born, and for the next three years she cropped her hair short like a boy and traveled aimlessly around the Midwest, spending most of her time in a series of detention centers and juvenile jails. Around the time of the grain harvest in the summer of 1953, she was caught hopping a freight in western Kansas and sent to live with a foster family on a farm outside of Topeka.

There everything she did was wrong, and she was beaten and repeatedly raped by her foster father and his teenage son. She finally escaped on Christmas Day, in the middle of a brutally cold winter, but shortly afterward she was taken into custody in Joplin, Missouri, where she was found living in an abandoned soap factory. She became a ward of the state and was transferred to the Mapleton School for Girls in Bascom, a town located high up in the Ozark Mountains.

Bonnie was released from Mapleton on May 18, 1954, her eighteenth birthday, the same day that a boy named Clay picked her up hitchhiking near Davenport, Iowa, in the heat of the afternoon. He was driving a faded blue 1950 Pontiac that he'd stolen the day before from a parking lot in Terre Haute, Indiana.

They drove west for the next six hours without exchanging a word, stopping only to gas up or take a leak. Near Omaha, Nebraska, Clay lowered the radio and coasted to a stop on the shoulder of the highway. "We're broke and nearly out of gas," he said, his slit eyes staring ahead. "I gotta do a crime."

"I'm not gonna help you," Bonnie said.

"That's okay," he replied, adjusting the rearview mirror as he accelerated back into traffic. "I didn't ask."

When Clay pulled in front of the Orpheum Theatre in downtown Omaha, there was a long line of young people waiting to see *A Star Is Born,* starring Judy Garland and James Mason.

Bonnie said, "I met Judy Garland once. I went to a party at Bing Crosby's house, and she was there."

"Sure thing."

"I did. I even went to the horse races with her and Van Johnson and Janet Gaynor. Audie Murphy was there too."

"And I'm Ted Williams."

"Don't believe me."

"I don't."

Bonnie opened the door and stepped inside the shade from the marquee. "I'll be sitting in the sixth row," she said over her shoulder as she walked toward the box office. "On the aisle."

Two hours later, during the second feature, Clay fell into the seat next to Bonnie. After a few long breaths, he said, "I got seventy dollars."

"I don't want any."

"It's for gas, stupid."

"You're a criminal."

"So what?"

"And you're gonna get caught, too, if you keep it up. How old are you?"

"None of your business."

"You're way younger than me. I know that. You could change, but you probably won't."

"You don't know nothing about me," Clay sneered, squeezing her arm so hard that tears came to her eyes. "Not a goddamn thing."

An elderly man holding a flashlight appeared in the aisle next to them. He shined the yellow beam into Clay's face. "Everything okay here?"

Clay raised his hands to block the light. "Yeah. Everything's fine."

"He ain't bothering you, is he?" the old man asked Bonnie.

Bonnie shook her head.

"You sure?"

"Yes."

As soon as the usher disappeared up the aisle, Clay unbuckled his jeans and stuck Bonnie's hand inside his underwear. "Jack me off," he said, his mouth close to her ear. "Okay?"

Bonnie felt him thicken inside her fingers. When she squeezed him, he made a sharp moan that drew a look from the couple seated across the aisle. "That was quick," she said, half smiling as she slid down in her seat. "I hope it felt good."

Clay didn't reply.

As she continued to stroke him, Bonnie opened her shirt and uncovered her breasts. "Here," she said, and she pulled his face to her chest. "Kiss me."

When she felt Clay's mouth close on her nipple, Bonnie took in a breath and her lips shaped the words *I love you.* But she didn't mean them and she never let them out of her throat.

After the movie ended, Clay decided to steal another car. "The Pontiac's too hot," he told Bonnie as they walked south on Douglas. "Anyway, I think the alternator is ready to go." He stopped in front of Chloe's Diner on North Dodge. "I'll meet you here in awhile. Okay?"

Bonnie thought for a moment, not quite meeting his eyes. Then she glanced across the street and her face seemed to sag. A black woman in a white maid's uniform came out of the Hotel Sherwood with a four-year-old boy. They were holding hands.

Clay said, "What's wrong?"

Bonnie looked dazedly at the two figures moving away from her, still holding hands, and when they disappeared around the corner she turned and stared at Clay, her flat voice hiding the deep ache inside her chest. "Nothing. Nothing's wrong."

An hour later, while Clay Tomlinson was coasting slowly out of the Sears parking lot in a shiny silver 1953 Chevy, Bonnie Simpson was riding in a Greyhound bus moving south on U.S. 75.

"A girl said to give you this," the waitress at Chloe's told Clay when he entered the nearly empty restaurant. She handed him a folded napkin. Inside was a Topps baseball card with Ted Williams's picture on the front. "She also said to be careful."

Clay felt his mouth go dry. "Just 'Be careful'? That's all she said?"

The waitress nodded. "Yes," she said, "that's all."

Around midnight that evening, Bonnie's bus stopped for gas and oil at a small service station in Morgan City, Louisiana. Outside, giant mosquitoes swarmed around the headlights, and above their high whine Bonnie heard a gentle blues playing on the jukebox in the diner next door. The song was "Please Hurry Home" by B. B. King.

★

December 3, 1969

Indian summer followed Bonnie across the Great Plains as she rode another Greyhound bus west from Detroit in 1969. Along the way she was struck by the number of young people they passed traveling on foot. The men had hair down to their shoulders, and they were dressed mostly in blue jeans and boots and Mexican shirts. Many had guitars slung over their backs. Flutes and tambourines were in evidence, too, along with dogs and young children, some carried papoose-style by strong-boned girls with daisies strung through their long blond hair.

For a while Bonnie found it odd that these dusty vagabonds rarely beckoned to the passing traffic with their thumbs. But it became clear to her after several miles that this was unnecessary, because the similarly dressed travelers who picked them up in their junky cars and vans already knew their destination.

"They're all goin' to San Francisco," said Bonnie's seatmate, a man somewhere over the age of seventy, with a shock of white hair and bright baby-blue eyes. "They're having this big musical deal with the Rolling Rocks or something. I saw it on the news. . . . Hey, check that out," he said, turning in his seat as they passed a Day-Glo school bus that was parked on the shoulder of the highway with cottony black smoke billowing from the engine. A bundle of men were gathered around the open hood while the women—some of them topless—sunbathed on the roof. "Now that's what I call sightseein'."

Bonnie laughed a little while the bandaged fingers of her right hand fidgeted nervously with the broken zipper on the red imitation-leather purse that was resting on her lap. Inside—along with her wallet and her bus ticket to Los Angeles—were four apples (two red and two green), a leftover turkey sandwich wrapped in tinfoil stained with blood, a bleacher ticket stub from a Boston Red Sox–Detroit Tigers game she attended with her therapist back in the summer of 1968, three black-and-white photographs (including one of her mother in Hollywood, circa 1942, standing in front of the entrance to Paramount Pictures), four hundred and forty dollars in twenty-dollar bills, rolled tight and secured by a thick black rubber band, and a .22 caliber pistol.

"Where you goin'?" Bonnie's husband, Freddie Bousquet, had asked her on Sunday night, when he saw her folding her clothes into the cheap canvas suitcase that was now resting in the luggage rack above her head.

Bonnie told him LA.

"You leaving me?"

"I guess."

"I could stop you," he said, following her into the kitchen. "You know that, don'tcha?"

Bonnie's hand reached for a knife. Trying to remain calm, she spread some mustard on two pieces of rye bread, before she sliced a tomato and carved the leftover Thanksgiving turkey. "But that means you'd have to kill me."

Freddie laughed, but he stopped laughing quickly when he saw the thread of blood spilling into the sandwich from a deep gash in Bonnie's thumb. "Jesus," he said. "You fuckin' sliced the shit out of yourself."

"It's just a nick," Bonnie said lightly, and she used the back of her hand to wipe the perspiration off her forehead, leaving behind a jagged red streak above her eyebrows.

"You're gonna need stitches in that. I'm serious. We're goin' to the hospital," he said, but when he reached for her wrist, Bonnie jerked her hand away, and several drops of blood splattered on his face and the white-tiled floor.

Freddie struck her face with the back of his hand, drawing more blood out of one nostril, but Bonnie remained silent, standing motionless, staring at him blankly until the wall phone rang and he roughly pushed her aside and nearly knocked over a chair in his hurry to grab the receiver.

A woman said, "Is Bonnie Simpson there?"

"Yeah, she's here."

"May I talk to her, please?"

"For you, cunt," Freddie said loudly, and Bonnie, shaking inside and trying to control herself, turned her back on him and ran cold water from the sink over her hand. "I said it's for you," he yelled once more, jabbing her in the back with the mouthpiece several times before he flung the receiver on the counter next to the toaster and stalked out of the kitchen.

Bonnie wrapped her thumb in a paper towel and lit a cigarette, waiting until Freddie was out of earshot before she picked up the phone. Then, softly, she said, "I told him."

The woman on the other end sighed deeply. "That's good," she said.

Bonnie took a step backward so she could see through the hallway into her bedroom. Freddie was rooting through her suitcase with both hands. When he looked up and saw her staring at him, the muscles went tight in his face.

"Bonnie, are you still on the line?"

"Uh-huh."

"You remember what I told you way back when?"

"Yes," Bonnie said, watching transfixed as Freddie opened his fly and sent a stream of urine onto her freshly laundered clothes. "I remember."

★

"You're not crazy," Bonnie's therapist, Rosellen Clark, told her when she first came to see her at the Wayne State Mental Health Clinic in downtown Detroit.

"I'm not?"

"Nope."

"Then what am I?"

"You're just . . . depressed."

Bonnie remained silent for a moment. "I'm just depressed, that's it?"

"That's it."

"But—"

"You're sad. You cry. Your husband beats you. That does not make you crazy," Rosellen explained. "In fact, you're normal compared to some of the folks I see every day. For instance, earlier this morning, this white fellow walked in here and claimed he was turning into a piece of cheese. Called himself Monterey Jack and took a seat on the floor right over there in the corner next to those bookshelves. Said he had to stay in a cool dark place or else he'd get all moldy and his skin would turn as green as grass. He said it with a straight face, too."

Bonnie didn't laugh or even smile as she gazed past Rosellen's shoulder with her head inclined to the side, listening, it seemed, to the small fan purring in the corner of the room. Presently, a fly buzzed through an open window and circled Rosellen's large Afro twice before it landed on her framed MSW certificate that hung on the wall behind her head.

"I have to go," Bonnie said, sliding back her chair and standing up.

"What's your hurry?"

Bonnie pointed to the clock on Rosellen's desk. "I've been here an hour."

"At least."

"Then my time is up, isn't it?"

Rosellen shook her head no. "We got lots of time, sugar. Relax."

"I'll come back next Wednesday," Bonnie said, and she took a step backward and reached for the doorknob. "We can talk more then."

Rosellen checked her calendar and frowned. "I'm taking next Wednesday off," she said. "I've got tickets to see the Red Sox play the Tigers. But I'm free the Wednesday after that."

Bonnie shrugged.

"Wait! I've got a better idea. Why don't you come with me?"

"To a baseball game? Are you kidding?" Bonnie asked. Her tone was suspicious. "Can you do that?"

Rosellen smiled at her. "You can do anything you want if you're tryin' to help someone. At least that's the way I see it."

Bonnie stood, thinking, her hand still on the doorknob. The door clicked open and she said, "I don't know. Maybe."

"No maybes. Gotta put it on my schedule right now. Yes or no."

"Okay," Bonnie said, and for the first time that day she smiled. "Sure. Why not?"

The following Wednesday, at noon sharp, Bonnie Simpson met Rosellen Clark at the will-call window in the parking lot in front of Tiger Stadium. The temperature was already in the 90s and climbing, and by the time they reached their seats in the upper deck in left field, Rosellen's tawny face shone with sweat and Bonnie's white cotton blouse was clinging to her back.

After Denny McLain struck out the side in the first inning and the cheering around them stopped, Bonnie told Rosellen how she celebrated her thirteenth birthday on June 6, 1949, the day after she arrived in Los Angeles for the first time, from Buchanan, Michigan.

"I went to Chasen's, this fancy restaurant. I was with my mom," she said wistfully, closing her eyes for a moment as she stepped back slowly through her past. "I had a steak and a Caesar salad and a piece of chocolate cake for dessert. I think it was the best dinner I ever had. That summer I saw the ocean for the first time, and I took my one and only tennis lesson, and I got a crush on a man named Terry Tibbles. Terry's middle name was Nicholas. So naturally everyone called him TNT, a nickname that just fit perfect with the job he had on the movie set in the mountains where we stayed for a while; he made things explode.

"'I can make the stars cry,' he told my mom one night outside our cabin by the lake. The porch light was off, but the brightness from the moon threw their shadows against my wall. Soon their faces came together and I heard their lips touch, and right then I knew what I wanted most was to have a man hold me in his arms at night. Someone to hold me tight."

In the bottom of the seventh inning a bizarre incident took place down on the field. The bases were loaded with two out and Tiger manager Sparky Anderson sent up a pinch hitter for the weak-hitting right fielder, Earl Fulton. His name was Ricky Furlong, and he struck out on three blistering fastballs to end the rally and the inning.

But instead of turning and walking back to the dugout, Furlong remained at the plate with the bat cocked uselessly behind his ear, staring out at the now-vacant infield. Time was called and both managers and all four umpires convened at home plate. Several minutes went by as they stood in a close circle around Ricky, scrutinizing him dumbly as they tried to talk him off the field. Eventually they gave up and Sparky motioned to his dugout, and two of Ricky's teammates came out and lifted him up by his elbows, transporting him back to the clubhouse like a cracked marble statue.

"There's something seriously wrong with that boy," Rosellen told Bonnie after the game, while they were walking through the parking lot in the shimmering heat. "He's going to need help. Lots of help."

★

December 6, 1969

The overcast morning light was an hour away, and a mild Santa Ana condition was blowing in vagrant breezes from the northeast when Bonnie Simpson's bus pulled into Los Angeles on Thursday, one day behind schedule. After she bought a cup of coffee and a postcard at the Greyhound station on Vine Street, she strolled up to Sunset Boulevard and sat patiently on a bus bench while the night sky faded into a mixed hue of silver and gray clouds.

The traffic was sparse, but cars with single men driving would beep their horns lightly as they passed by her corner. They must think I'm a prostitute, Bonnie said to herself, as she watched a blue Cadillac circle the block twice before pulling to the curb in front of her. "Need a ride?" the driver, a fat man, asked her, but Bonnie turned her face away and directed her gaze in the opposite direction. "You sure?" he said. "I can make it worth your while."

Bonnie remained silent and the fat man called her an ugly name under his breath. The stoplight blinked to green, and Bonnie heard the car window close up electronically as the Cadillac rolled slowly through the intersection.

When the light turned red again, a city bus stopped to discharge a potbellied man in his early thirties, with a big, doughy face and dirty red shoulder-length hair. He proceeded to the corner, where he unfolded a canvas chair and propped up a sign by the lamppost that read MAPS TO THE MOVIE STARS' HOMES. He took a seat and glanced at Bonnie, and when he smiled she noticed that a large chunk of his lower jaw was missing.

Bonnie smiled back and said, "Good morning."

The man inhaled. "Yes, it is," he said, the side of his face collapsing as the air pushed the words out of his mouth. "It's a wonderful morning."

After she rented her apartment in the Argyle Manor, Bonnie took a shower and walked the three short blocks down to Hollywood Boulevard. She bought a street map and a copy of *Photoplay* at Nate's News on Las Palmas; then she crossed the street and continued west until she reached the Grauman's Chinese Theatre.

The last time Bonnie was in Los Angeles, in 1949, she and her mother spent the better part of a Sunday afternoon wandering through the forecourt of Grauman's, examining the celebrity footprints and handprints that were embedded in the concrete. Bonnie remembered seeing a pretty young woman sitting in a wheelchair in front of the box office, weeping like a child. Suddenly, the woman threw herself on the ground and began clawing at the cement, screaming, "He loves *me*, only *me*! I was the only one he loved!"

Bonnie's mother said, "Don't stare," and she pulled her away from the circle of tourists who instantly gathered around the woman. Crossing the street, Bonnie overheard a man say, "Her name was Marla Casey. She played a dance hall girl in *Stampede*. She was having an affair with Rod Cameron. When he broke it off she threw herself off the roof of her apartment building."

The warm wind swayed the tops of the palm trees on Melrose Avenue as Bonnie stood in front of the main entrance to Paramount Studios. From her pocketbook she took out the photo of her mother posed against the high walls.

"That's my mom," Bonnie said to the guard standing in the kiosk by the front gate. "She used to work here."

The guard glanced at the photo while he waved through a black Cadillac convertible with a sleek-looking blonde behind the wheel.

Bonnie said, "That was—"

"Faye Dunaway," interrupted a young man standing on the sidewalk a few paces away. He wore faded Levi's, a blue T-shirt, and a Detroit Tigers baseball cap with the bill turned up. "I got her yesterday on her lunch break," he said, holding up a leather autograph book with a floral cover. "Today I got my eyes peeled for Marlon Brando. Wouldn't that be something if I got *his* autograph, Gill?"

The guard exchanged a look with Bonnie. Then he winked at her. "Yes, that's right, Ricky," he said, talking through his smile. "It sure would."

To Bonnie the young man said, "Last week Peter Fonda almost ran me down with his motorcycle. That's why Gill makes me stand over here, out of the way. I got his father's autograph here, too," he said, and he held up a page with a signature scrawled in green ink. "*I* didn't get him, my dad did. His name was Benny Furlong. He worked on a lot of his pictures. *Grapes of Wrath, The Long Night, Fort Apache,* lots of 'em. Was your mom an actress?" he said, looking over her shoulder at the photograph she was holding. Bonnie nodded. "What was her name? Maybe I have her autograph."

"No," Bonnie said. "You never heard of her."

"My dad's got tons of people in here you never heard of: Carla Baxter, Kenny Kendall, Lucy Alvarado. Nobody's ever heard of them," he said, and he pushed his face close to hers. "Come on, tell me."

Bonnie shook her head. "I gotta go," she said, backing up.

"Where?"

"I got things to do," she said. "And don't try to follow me."

"Follow you? You're no one. Why would I follow you?"

"Just don't."

When she returned to her apartment, Bonnie moved the armchair over to the window and sat staring down at the street until the twilight shadows fell across her patient face, darkening the room.

"I'm here," she said out loud, right before she dozed off. "I'm finally here."

It was after midnight when she awoke and heard the radio playing in the apartment beneath her. Radio Ray Moore was saying, "Let's spend an hour talking about our fears, the things that make our hearts pound in the middle of the night. You're on the air."

A woman called in, a high school teacher, and said she was afraid of the noise in the cafeteria at her school. She said, "When I'm in charge during lunch, and I hear loud talking and the plates and trays banging, it puts the fear of God in me."

"What are you afraid of?" Radio Ray asked her.

"I'm afraid something's going to happen."

"What?"

"Something. I don't know. Don't badger me, Ray, I just get afraid."

"I'm afraid of dyin'," a man named Leon said to Radio Ray. "That's what I fear the most. That don't make me special, does it, Ray?"

"No. Of course not. It's something we all have to face sooner or later. How old are you, Leon?"

"Twenty-seven."

"You're a young man."

The caller said, "What frightens *you*, Radio Ray?"

"Bowling alleys and flamingo tattoos."

"That's pretty weird."

"And dominoes remind me of tombstones."

In the apartment below, Bonnie heard a woman say, "Will you turn that off, please?"

"I'll turn it down," a man said.

"No!" the woman shouted. "Turn it off."

"I'm afraid of fire," the next caller said, a boy, and Bonnie sat up with her eyes open wide. "I'm afraid of the flames and the smoke. I'm afraid of getting burned. I'm afraid, but I set them anyway."

Radio Ray said, "You set fires?"

"Yes."

"You need help."

"I know."

"Tell someone. Your mom or someone at school. A teacher. They'll get you help."

"Miss Morris knows who I am."

"Who?"

"Miss Morris. She called earlier. I recognized her voice. She knows about me. I want to burn down the school."

"People would die."

"I know."

"You need to talk to someone."

"I'm talking to you, Ray," the boy said, and a moment later someone downstairs switched off the radio.

Six

Becoming a Writer and Losing a Wife

December 13, 1969

One week after Bonnie's death and Sandra's miscarriage, Burk was sitting in the living room of his house on Valley View Lane, surrounded by open boxes and wrapping paper and the wooden tracks for the Hot Wheels set he was trying to assemble for his five-year-old son. When the phone rang in the kitchen, Louie dropped the metal race car he was building and shouted, "Mommy!" and for a split second Burk, too, thought it was Sandra, but then he remembered that his wife was unable to speak over the phone, that her jaw was still wired shut.

"Happy Hanukah, Ray." It was Timmy Miller, calling from Berkeley, where he'd been living since 1963, the year he graduated from Cal and opened a used book store on Telegraph Avenue. Burk and Timmy had spoken often on the phone, but the last time they saw each other was in June, when Timmy flew down for their tenth high school reunion, an event that Burk chose not to attend.

"I was thinking about you, Tim."

"Yeah?"

"No shit."

"Daddy."

Burk put his hand over the mouthpiece. "I'll be off in a couple of minutes, Louie."

"Is that Mom?"

"No. It's Uncle Tim. Mommy's still in the hospital. She can't talk on the phone yet, remember?"

"Oh, yeah, that's right. But when her face stops hurting, she can. Right?"

"Right."

"You didn't mean to hurt her, did you?"

"No. I was trying to save her life."

"Ray?"

"Sorry, Tim."

"You want to call back?"

"No, that's okay. Louie?"

"Yeah?"

"Why don't you watch *Gumby*. When I'm through on the phone, I'll finish putting together the Hot Wheels."

"Okay."

"Tim?"

"Yeah?"

"I was thinking about PK. We had some cool times, didn't we?"

"Sure did."

Louie turned away from the TV and stared at Burk. "Are you talking about Mom?"

"No."

"Who are you talking about?"

"This girl I knew in high school. She and I and Uncle Tim were friends. We took a trip once."

"Is she gonna live with us now?"

"Don't be silly."

"Good."

"Tim?"

"What?"

"I think I have a great idea for a movie."

* * *

"Now what? The Wedge? Dana Point? San Diego?" Timmy asks Burk. They are sitting at a corner table in the Blue Pelican, a dilapidated diner that is built on weather-worn pilings overlooking the ocean near Capistrano Beach. On the jukebox the Shirelles are singing "I Met Him on a Sunday," and outside the sun has fallen behind the thick dark clouds massed on the horizon, casting an eerie purplish light over the solitary surfer still riding the waves. "Or we could go to TJ, then drive down to Baja and surf Rosarita on Sunday."

"Whatever you want," says Burk, shrugging, his attention shifting to the sway of PK's hips as she walks out of the ladies' room and crosses back to their table.

"Or we could zoom."

"Zoom?" Burk glances at Timmy, who is now grinning slyly. "What's that?"

"This thing we do."

"Who?"

"Me and PK. It's kinda hard to describe. She'll tell you," Timmy says as PK sits down in the chair next to him and plucks a Pall Mall out of the pack lying in the center of the table.

"Tell him what?" she says, lighting up.

"About zooming."

PK takes a long drag and exhales slowly, looking away as she lets the smoke come out a little at a time. "I met him on a Sunday and my heart stood still," she sings, her voice off key as she tries to imitate the Shirelles' lead singer.

Timmy says, "Come on, PK, show him."

PK glances at Burk. Then, yawning, she says, "I don't know."

"You have to. He's my best friend."

PK, after a short silence, reaches into her purse and removes a harmless-looking nasal inhaler, a two-inch plastic cylinder with one end rounded off to fit snugly into a nostril. In 1959, this particular inhaler—brand name Rexall Nasalex—had been banned by the FDA and pulled off the shelves of every drugstore and supermarket in the state. But it took several weeks for the directive to reach some of the more remote communities in Northern California, and there were still isolated pharmacies in Humboldt and Trinity counties where the Rexall Nasalex had not been replaced by Rexall Mist, a four-hour spray containing the benign active ingredient oleic acid, rather than the pure Benzedrine that PK's father discovered one evening on a *Bonanza* location, when he and a couple of his actor buddies cracked open the Nasalex and squeezed the speed-saturated cotton filter into their coffee.

"So whattaya think?" Timmy says, catching Burk's eye as he and PK roll the Nasalex back and forth across the Formica table. "You want to try it?"

The plastic cylinder stops in front of Burk. He picks it up and closes his hand around it. "What happens to you?"

Timmy and PK look at each other. "Everything." PK laughs. "Everything that you ever wanted to happen."

At 9 A.M. the next morning, Burk drove his dented Chevy down to the neighborhood Thrifty Drugs. He bought ten 8-by-14-inch yellow legal tablets, an electric pencil sharpener, and four boxes (of one dozen) No. 2 Ticonderoga pencils. When he arrived home he made a second pot of coffee, drank a cup while he reread the sports section, and then walked into his den and wrote *Fade In* on the top left-hand corner of a blank yellow legal page.

Six weeks later, Burk completed the first draft of *Zoomin'*, a lightly fictionalized account of the drug and sex-soaked odyssey that he and Timmy and Patty Kendall took ten years earlier, in the winter of 1959.

"I bet it's terrific," Sandra said. "When can I read it?"

"I don't know. I think I'll wait till I hear from some agents."

"If you don't want to show it to me, that's okay too."

"No," Burk said, "I do. I just want to wait."

That night Burk and Sandra made love for the first time since she'd been released from the hospital. It was quick and tense, and the warm excitement he used to feel when she kissed and fondled him was gone. After she came in a series of quiet spasms, there was a sad silence in their bedroom, a silence that was more intense, it seemed to Burk, than if he were truly alone.

Finally Sandra said, "That wasn't one of our best, was it? I bet right now you wish I'd disappear off the face of the earth."

"That's not what I'm feeling."

"What are you feeling, Ray?"

"Scared."

"Of what? Of being stuck with me for the rest of your life?"

"Sandra—"

"Stuck with a wife who has a miscarriage at the races and tries to stab herself to death. A normal wife doesn't do that. And a normal mother misses her son when she's away."

"You love Louie, you know you do."

"I don't feel like I belong here anymore, Ray. I feel like I belong somewhere else."

"Where?"

"*I don't know,*" Sandra cried out suddenly. "*I just don't know.*"

The following day Burk mailed his script to five agents. Of the five, two—Ben Marino from Creative Management Associates and Ronny Gold at William Morris—he knew from CBS. Both were second-tier variety agents, assigned to hand-hold the singers and comics who appeared on the *Red Skelton Show* and the *Smothers Brothers Comedy Hour,* two of the shows that Burk covered when he was a censor.

Burk called them personally, and each promised to pass *Zoomin'* along to their literary departments as soon as it arrived at their offices. As it turned out, they were the first two agencies to reject his screenplay.

"A few interesting scenes but, on the whole, this story is unbelievable," wrote a junior agent at the Morris office. The following day the script came back from CMA with the word NO stamped across the title page in huge red letters.

By the end of the second week the rest of his scripts had been returned in the mail. Ziegler-Ross and the Sunset Plaza Group dismissed his efforts in identical language: *Sorry, this is not the kind of material we're looking for.* The only encouragement came from Irving Kaplan of Premiere Artists. He wrote:

> *I enjoyed reading* Zoomin' *very much. For a first draft this is extremely well conceived. Good luck. Irv.*

On Friday afternoon, Burk drove down to the post office and mailed off ten more copies of his screenplay. When he returned home, Sandra was sitting at the dining room table in the muted light, still in her bathrobe. By her elbow was a vodka Collins, and his script was open in front of her. She said, "I'm on page eighty-three. I think it's really good."

The tension in Burk's face slowly disappeared, replaced by an expression of surprise. "You're kidding?"

"No, Ray, I'm not."

"It works?"

"So far it does."

"It's not getting slow or anything?"

"Ray?"

"Yeah?"

There was a pause. Then, looking up, Sandra said, "Did this stuff really happen?"

"Some of it did."

"The motel is real?"

"Yeah."

"And this girl PK, she fucked all those marines. That's true?"

"We were high, Sandra."

"Yeah, I guess. What about the boy who dies when Timmy takes him surfing in the middle of the night?"

"That's made up. No one dies."

"Did *you* fuck her too?"

"Who?"

"The girl, PK."

"Finish the script."

"I mean in real life. Did you fuck her, Ray?"

"Does it matter?"

"Just tell me."

Burk nodded just perceptibly. "Yes," he said. "I fucked her."

Ten days later, Burk received a call from Maria Selene, an agent at Rheinis and Robins, a small but prestigious literary agency in West Hollywood. "I read *Zoomin'* over the weekend. I found it quite interesting," she told Burk, in a voice that was cool but not unfriendly. "You may have some talent, Mr. Burk. I think we should set up a time to talk. How does three-thirty on Wednesday sound?"

"Three-thirty? That's fine."

"Do you know where we are?"

"I think so," Burk said, scanning the submission list that he kept taped on the wall above his desk. Checking the address, he said, "You're at 9255 Sunset, right?"

"The penthouse suite. I'll see you Wednesday."

After he put down the phone, Burk felt light-headed. A warmth spread throughout the center of his chest, and the phrase *you may have some talent* kept repeating itself inside his head as he wandered from room to room in a semidaze. On his third pass through the kitchen he saw Sandra pull her car into the driveway. Next to her on the seat was a basket of laundry. Before she turned off the engine she bent forward and her head fell out of sight, searching, Burk was certain, for the pint of Smirnoff that she kept under the seat.

Moments later, when he met her on the front porch, she slid past him quickly and silently, making no sign with her eyes that she even recognized him. In the bedroom where he followed her, he said, "What's wrong? What's going on?"

Saying nothing, Sandra put the laundry on the bed. Then, as if in a trance, she unzipped her skirt and walked into the bathroom. Turning away from the open door, Burk said, "I have some good news. I just got off the phone with an agent."

There was no reply. When he heard the toilet flush he turned around. Sandra was standing in front of the mirror, staring at her reflection while she squeezed skin cream from a tube into the palm of her hand.

Burk said, "Did you hear what I said?"

Sandra nodded, almost smiling now as she pulled up her blouse and rubbed the viscous white liquid into the thick scars that cross-hatched her stomach.

"She thinks I have talent. I'm going to meet with her on Wednesday."

Sandra's fingers slowly crept inside her underpants, and her knees buckled slightly as she started to stroke herself.

"You're not gonna say anything. You're just gonna stand there, staring at me while you jerk off. Is that what you're gonna do?"

Sandra hunched her shoulders and a few ragged locks of hair fell over half her face. Then, closing her terrified eyes, she whispered, "Leave me alone, Ray. Just leave me alone."

★

"Small and dark, with big ears. That's how I imagined you." Those were Maria Selene's first words after Burk walked into her office. "I guess I was wrong."

Maria held out her hand and Burk sized her up. She was pretty but older than he'd imagined, at least forty-five, with salt-and-pepper bangs and a big sexy mouth.

"Producers hate tall writers. They're harder to intimidate. You sit here," she said, pointing at a low gray couch against the far wall; then she followed him across the room and sat in an armchair facing him. On a glass table between them were a bowl of mixed nuts and a pile of movie scripts. Burk's draft of *Zoomin'* sat on top of the stack with an official Rheinis and Robins label attached to the cover.

Maria pointed at the script. "Don't get your hopes up. I can't sell it. It's way too bizarre."

"Most of it's true," Burk said. "It really happened."

"So did the plague. *Zoomin'* goes in the drawer," Maria said sternly. She reached for a handful of nuts and popped several into her mouth. "However, we would be extremely interested to know what you're planning to write next. Any ideas?"

"Nothing full blown, just a character I'm interested in."

"Yeah? Tell me about him."

"His name is Smart Art. He's a street mime in San Francisco. But what he likes to do best is work plastic."

Maria leaned forward a little. "'Work plastic'? What does that mean?"

"It means he's the world's greatest credit card counterfeiter," Burk said, forgetting to add that this character was based on a true story he'd read in *Crimestoppers,* the monthly magazine for the National Association of Police Chiefs, that he'd picked up earlier in the week at his father's newsstand.

Maria was silent for a few seconds. "A street mime who counterfeits credit cards," she said, beginning to nod her head enthusiastically. "That's a character we haven't seen before. Do you have a title?"

"*Mr. Plastic Fantastic.*"

"Nice."

Burk shrugged. "Now all I need is a story to go with it."

Maria grinned. "You know what nine out of ten screenwriters have engraved on their tombstones: *finally, a plot.*"

Burk finished the first draft of *Mr. Plastic Fantastic* in eight weeks. "It's not perfect. The third act still needs to be fine-tuned," he told Maria Selene over the phone. "But overall I think it works."

Withholding her excitement, Maria said casually, "If you can get a copy to me today, there's a chance I could get to it over the weekend." Burk said he would send it over by messenger, and they made an appointment to meet the following Wednesday. "That'll give the boys a chance to read it too. It sounds like a winner," Maria said, and when Burk hung up the phone in his den he could hear Louie furiously pedaling his Big Wheel up and down the driveway next to their house. A moment later when he pulled aside the curtain and the sweet, smiling face of his son passed by the window in the waning light, Burk felt something deep and warm stir inside him, a feeling he could only describe as a father's love.

It was nearly eight o'clock when Sandra arrived home from Hollywood Park. "I got stuck in traffic," she said to Burk, as she nonchalantly opened her purse and dumped a thick wad of cash on the dining room table. "I know I shouldn't have stayed for the ninth, but I had a hunch on the exacta."

Burk heard the refrigerator open and close, and when Sandra entered the living room she was holding a bottle of ginger ale. She took a seat on the opposite end of the couch and put her feet up on the cushion, giving Burk a brief look before she began to browse through the latest issue of *Rolling Stone.*

Sandra had been on the wagon for over a month, and her dirt-dark eyes—without the glaze of alcohol—sparkled in their deep sockets. Her body, too, seemed more alive. Gone was the fat around her hips, and her legs, long and lean, fit snugly inside her faded blue bell-bottom jeans. For the first time in weeks Burk felt himself become sexually aroused, but when he reached out to caress her ankle, Sandra drew back her foot and swatted his hand away with the magazine.

"Where's Louie?" she asked, without looking up.

"Sleeping."

"Already?"

"He was tired."

"It's not even nine. He never goes to sleep before nine. I didn't even get a chance to say good night."

"You weren't here."

"I know that, but still . . ." she said, her voice dying away as she stood up and walked into their bedroom.

After she did her nightly exercises and took a long hot shower, Sandra reentered the dining room and started to add up the cash that was now stacked in neat piles on the table. "One hundred and sixty-five and change. I already counted it," Burk said from the couch. "That's almost two grand in six weeks."

"Really?"

"Really."

Sandra took a seat at the table and began filling out a bank deposit slip. "I guess I'm on a hot streak," she said.

"You've won thirty-four days in a row. That's not a hot streak, that's amazing."

"I've got a system, Ray. I told you that," she said irritably, then she pulled a copy of the *Daily Racing Form* out of her purse. "See?" Inked in the margin next to each horse's past performance were odd symbols and complicated algebraic calculations. "Here," she said, pointing. "This is how I do it: Speed divided by claiming price times a factor of two, plus or minus weight allowances and track variants, equals this number. Each horse gets a number," she said, and she snapped a rubber band around the money and dropped it into her purse. "The higher the number, the better the horse. It's that simple."

At first Burk thought she was joking, expecting her at any moment to break out laughing. But when he tried to encourage her with a smile she said, "What's so funny?"

"Nothing. I was just—"

"Don't you get it?"

Burk stared at Sandra, wondering if she was going insane, a thought that had crossed his mind more than once over the last six months. "Yeah, sure," he said finally, nodding. "I get it."

On Tuesday, the next racing day, Burk decided (somewhat guiltily) to follow Sandra when she left for Hollywood Park. Sitting upright and holding the steering wheel in both hands, she drove south on the San Diego freeway, passing La Tijera, the exit nearest to the track. At Century Boulevard she got off and made a quick right. She drove two blocks and pulled into the parking lot behind the Paradise Lounge.

"It was one of those sleazy cinder-block dives near the airport," Burk told Gene, when he called him later that night. "It reminded me of the Bat Cave."

Gene said, "I think I know what you're gonna tell me, Ray."

"I'm gonna tell you that I don't think Sandra has a system for picking horses, okay? That's one thing I'm gonna tell you. And I'm gonna tell you I understand now why she bought the new Creedence album last week. You know why? Because up there on stage, shaking her tits to 'Green River,' is Sandra Burk, my wife. And you know something else, Gene? Even with all those scars she looked good. Trim, tan, sexy, with a big smile on her face. You hear me? A *big* smile. Then you know what she did? She dropped her bikini bottom and walked to the edge of the stage and hit 'em with the pay dirt, stuck her cooze right in their faces. Can you believe it, Gene? Can you fucking believe it?"

After a short silence, Gene said, "What did you do?"

"Nothing. I just walked out."

"Did she see you?"

"I don't know and I don't care. If she did, she didn't say anything when she got home. Just dropped the cash on the table like she always does, like she made another score at the track."

"She's doin' it for you, so you can finish your script."

"She looked really happy up there, Gene."

"Don't overthink it. At least she's not drinking."

"She's developed a following, too. Clyde, the owner, said there's a whole shitload of men who get off on women with scars."

"Ray, I gotta go."

"What am I gonna do?" Burk said. His voice was desolate.

"Forget about her, Ray. Just take care of Louie and keep writing. Okay?"

"Okay."

"'Bye."

★

"You first," said Rick Rheinis, glancing at Maria Selene, who was sitting next to Burk on the red leather couch in Sid Robins's office. "Can you hear us okay?" Rheinis said, leaning forward in Sid's chair to adjust the volume on the speakerphone.

"Loud and clear," said Sid's voice, patched in from New York, where the night before he'd attended the Broadway opening of *Big Fellas,* a new play by Joshua Flood, a Rheinis and Robins client.

"I had a problem with the piece," Maria said.

"We all did," echoed Rheinis. "But that's not to say there weren't things we liked. Right, Sidney? . . . Sidney? . . . Sidney, you there?"

"What?"

"I said—"

"One sec, Rick, I got a room service guy in here with my lunch."

Burk nervously fumbled for a cigarette, dropping it on the carpet before he could put it in his mouth. When he picked it up he glanced at Maria. She started to speak but was interrupted by Sid's voice.

"Okay," he said, "I'm back."

Rheinis said, "We were talking about Ray's script."

"Refresh my memory."

"*Mr. Plastic Fantastic.*"

"Oh, yes, of course, some wonderful stuff. Ray?"

"Yes, sir."

"You are an extremely talented guy."

Burk smiled. "I'm glad you liked it. I wasn't sure if—"

"Whoa, wait! I said you were talented, not that I liked it." Burk flushed. He glanced at Maria, trying unsuccessfully to catch her eye. "To be candid, I couldn't make it past page forty-eight. It was too . . . busy." Maria and Rheinis stared at the speakerphone, nodding. "I recommend we don't send it out."

Careful not to look at Burk, Rheinis jingled the change in his pocket for a few seconds. "I've got a meeting at Fox at noon," he said, checking his watch as he stood up. "I'll call you this afternoon, Sidney. Say hello to Joshua."

After Rheinis left the office, Maria said, "Without the solid development of a single story you've got nothing, Ray."

Burk felt his face burning. "I thought I had a story."

Maria said, "So did we. But it got lost in the side issues and subplots."

"Maybe Smart Art—"

Maria shook her head. "Smart Art worked fine, Ray. So did Lily and Rockabye Ralph. So did the car chase through Chinatown and the shoot-out on the Golden Gate Bridge."

"But it lacked flow, coherence. I didn't hear that tom-tom beating underneath the words. I didn't know who to root for," Sid's voice said. "And without a rooting interest there's no climax potential. No climax potential means . . . no climax . . . and soft box office."

For several seconds, the only sound in Sid's office was the hiss of long distance. "It was just a first draft," Burk finally said, feeling shamed and outraged at the same time. "I could do a rewrite."

"That's up to you," said Sid's voice. "But it might not be worth the effort." Then, changing the subject, he said, "Maria, I spoke with Jack Rose. I think he's ready to commit on the Berliner project."

While Sid and Maria openly discussed agency business over the speakerphone, Burk idly flipped through a copy of *Daily Variety*. He let fifteen minutes pass—by then the color had left his cheeks and he'd almost retrieved his pride—before he stood up and walked out of the office.

"Basically they agreed with you," Burk told Sandra when he came home that afternoon. They were sitting in armchairs on opposite sides of the living room. Outside the wind swirled and a light rain was falling. "They said it was garbage."

"That's not what I said. I said it was too complicated."

"Too complicated?"

"Right."

"Fuck complicated."

"You asked me and—"

"I worked hard on that script!"

"I know you did. I *saw* you," she said loudly. "I was here, Ray."

"No you weren't. While I was writing and taking care of Louie, you were down on Century Boulevard, dancing naked for a bunch of fucking perverts."

Burk stood up.

"Ray, wait—"

"Fuck you, Sandra."

Sandra stared at Burk, and for the first time in their marriage she saw real hatred in his eyes. After a long silence, he walked past her into the dining room. "I'm going to pick up Louie," he said, in a voice that was unforgiving, and he could not see the sadness erupt in her face as he picked up his car keys and walked outside.

Sandra's car was gone from the driveway when Burk came back from the Goodtime Nursery School. "Mommy's left. She's not coming home," Burk heard his voice say, knowing this even before he saw that her suitcase was missing, along with her shopping bag filled with old racing forms.

Louie suddenly looked frightened. "For how long?"

"For just a little while," Sandra told Louie later that evening. She was calling him from a motel in Riverside. "I'll be back before you know it."

"It's raining. It's not safe to drive in the rain."

"It's just drizzling."

"But the roads are slippery."

"I'll be careful. I promise."

Louie turned his head as Burk walked into the living room. His arms were folded tight across his chest. "Daddy's gonna miss you."

"I'll miss Daddy."

"Will you call us?"

"Every night."

"You promise?"

"Swear to God."

"I bet she comes back tomorrow," Louie said to his father, looking around expectantly after he hung up the phone. "She'll be sitting right here on the couch when I come home from school. Right, Daddy?"

"Maybe."

"I bet."

Louie kept his eyes closed on the ride home from nursery school the following afternoon. "She's probably stuck in traffic," he said when he saw the empty driveway on Valley View Lane. "She'll be home in a little while." And before he went to bed, in a voice that Burk could barely hear, Louie said, "Wake me when she calls. Okay?"

Burk said, "For sure," but Sandra didn't call that evening like she'd promised, or the next. Two weeks went by and Louie stopped looking for her car when he came back from school, and by week three he didn't dash to the phone each time it rang.

Still, every night he got down on his knees by the side of his bed and asked God to bring his mother home safely, and then he would get underneath the covers and lie motionless, moving his lips silently as he replayed their last conversation, wondering why she would lie to him like that.

Once she did come home, in a dream, and Louie threw off his blankets and shouted, "She's here, she's here!" repeating these words over and over as he ran through the darkened house. When Burk finally found him, he was standing on the front lawn with tears rolling down his face, staring into the outer dark. "She's here . . . I know it," he said in a tiny voice. "I saw her."

Burk felt a terrible sadness sweep through his chest as he reached for his son's hand. "No, Louie, you were just dreaming," he said, and he led him back to bed.

★

Louie's nursery school day ended at three o'clock, the same time Burk finished writing, and most afternoons on their way home they would stop at a small park on Balboa Avenue near Encino. There Louie would ride his Big Wheel or play on the monkey bars while Burk sat at a picnic table and edited the script pages he'd rewritten that morning.

One day a young woman took a seat on the bench across from Burk. "You write?" she said, and Burk nodded. "So do I," she said, and from her purse she removed a professionally typed screenplay with the Columbia Pictures logo on the cover.

Her name was Loretta Egan. She was in her early thirties, pretty but thin, with bold eyes and dark, curly hair. Her script, *Cold as Ice,* a sexy thriller starring Clint Eastwood, was set to begin filming in the fall. "It's my fourth original but my first sale. I can't believe it's really gonna happen," she told Burk. "What about you, any credits?"

"No. Not really. Actually I just started writing six months ago."

"You have an agent?"

"Maria Selene. She's with Rheinis and Robins."

"They're good. You must know what you're doing."

Burk shrugged. "I thought I did," he said, then he told her about *Mr. Plastic Fantastic,* the negative response he'd received.

"What's it about?" she said.

Burk started to explain the plot. Halfway through, Loretta said, "Stop. I can't follow it."

"I guess it *is* pretty complicated," Burk laughed, not altogether surprised by her bluntness. "When I'm done with this draft it will be a lot clearer. Maybe you could look it over before I turn it in. I mean, if you're not too busy."

Before Loretta could reply, Louie rolled up on his Big Wheel. Following him on a tricycle was a little girl with pale yellow hair that hung in front of her shoulders.

"This is Emily," Louie said. "She's five too. Say hello to my dad, Emily."

Emily said hello; then she pointed behind her to a bench by the swings. "That's my mom with the pink sweater. She's crying. Yesterday was her birthday."

Louie said, "Emily's dad left her like Mom did. Tell my dad how long he's been gone."

"No."

"Please?"

"No."

"Pretty please."

"All right," she said, and her lips began to shake. "He's been gone a million trillion billion years."

Burk said, "That's a long time."

That night while Burk lay awake listening to Radio Ray Moore, Louie tiptoed into his room and slipped into bed next to him. In a few minutes he was asleep, so he didn't hear the call Radio Ray took right before he signed off for the news. The caller, a woman, would not reveal her name, but she told Radio Ray that she was a regular listener. "I've never called in before," she said, "but my husband did once."

Radio Ray kept her on the line when he went into a station break, and during the network news that followed she told Radio Ray that she was staying at the Silverado Motel in Las Cruces, New Mexico.

Off the air, she said, "I'm lying here in bed on my back, and across from me, on the wall above the TV, is a painting of a little girl seated at a small wooden table with her ankles crossed and her hands folded neatly in her lap. Through the window in the picture a horse can be seen grazing in a field filled with yellow daisies. And beyond the horse, on the horizon, is a single gray cloud.

"Right now I can't see the picture because it's pitch dark, but once in awhile a car will pass by and the headlights will flash across the wall of my room—and for an instant I might see the little girl or the horse or the cloud that is getting ready to rain."

The caller stopped speaking and began to hum a melody that sounded familiar to Radio Ray Moore. A moment later, he heard someone pounding on her door. The caller continued to hum, louder, and the man in the background yelled, "Open the fucking door, Sandra, you goddamn cunt!"

The ON THE AIR light blinked on inside Radio Ray's booth, flashing red like blood spurting from a vein. At that moment Louie rolled over and whispered something in his sleep. To Burk, who was half awake, it sounded like "Come home," but he wasn't sure. It may have been only a long deep sigh.

On the morning of August 15, 1970, Burk accepted a collect call from his wife. She explained that she was in jail in Victorville, a city in the high desert one hundred and fifty miles northwest of Los Angeles. She said she'd shot a man named Shay Carson, a cowboy from Bozeman, Montana, and the nation's finest calf roper, and that she'd been charged with murder.

That was the bad news.

The good news came later that afternoon when Maria Selene phoned Burk, informing him that Jerome Sanford, the head of production at Paramount Pictures, had finally read his script, *Zoomin'*. She'd sent it over as a writing sample, and he liked it enough to pass it along to Jon Warren, a protégé of John Houston and the hottest young director in Hollywood. Warren told Sanford that he wanted it to be his next project.

All this came out of the blue, because Burk had not spoken to Maria in four months, since he'd turned in his third rewrite of *Mr. Plastic Fantastic*. By this time all the money he'd borrowed from his father had run out, and whatever writing career he thought he had was over. In fact, he'd just taken a job that day selling men's shoes at a department store in Westwood. He was walking out the door when Maria called.

"That's amazing," Burk said, after Maria told him the news.

"There's only one problem," she said, making it sound minor. "He wants to set the story in 1969. Can you make that work?"

"I don't know."

"If you can't, there's no movie. Warren's the key. Think it over and I'll set up a meeting."

★

Jon Warren lived on Alta Way, a narrow private road that cork-screwed into the hills off Benedict Canyon. The house, shaped like an L, sat high on a cliff and was surrounded by evergreens and a ten-foot-high white sandstone wall that was made even whiter by the bright sunlight.

"William Morris sends me ten scripts a week. They're all dogshit. But I read yours in one sitting," Jon Warren told Burk. They were sitting under an umbrella on the pool terrace. Not too far away a slim and supple blonde lay topless on an air mattress floating in the water. "It moved like a fucking gun. Only one problem: your story. It's dated," Warren said, and he stood up. He was wearing a clean white T-shirt, khaki shorts, and beaded Mexican moccasins that he kicked off his feet when he stepped up on the diving board. "The fifties are fucking square compared to the social revolution that's going on today. You dig what I'm saying?" Warren stripped off his T-shirt. His body was lean and muscular, and the diving board creaked and bent under his weight when he walked out to the end and flexed his knees. "Think about it, man. The Beatles, the Dead, Hendrix, Warhol, Leary, Antonioni. These cats are fucking explorers that are sailing into the unknown. We're all zooming today."

"What I wrote about really happened," Burk said. "Most of it, anyway."

"Desire and denial! That's what drives a story," Warren said, springing high in the air, and the loud snap of the diving board echoed across the canyon. "Goals," he said, landing hard. "Immediate or long-range, but your characters must be moving in a particular direction." Warren looked down at the beautiful blonde floating beneath him. Her eyes were closed and she was very lightly massaging her nipples with the tips of her fingers. "What I liked about your script was the originality," Warren said, shooting Burk a smile before he unzipped his khaki shorts and threw them by the side of the pool.

Burk looked away, embarrassed, directing his gaze toward a slender palm tree in the center of the lawn. Nonetheless he found himself becoming aroused as Warren bounced lightly on the board with his erect penis straining toward the ice-blue sky.

"I liked the energy, the craziness, the unpredictability. But you were way too close to your material, too close to shape it dramatically, too close to free that part of your unconscious that pulls the reader along on a journey they never want to end. A story has to get me here," Warren said, pointing to his erection. "Yours didn't." Warren grabbed his cock and jerked it fast several times. "You dig what I'm saying?"

Before Burk could reply Warren was already in the air, his body arched gracefully, his stiff cock causing a large ripple as he knifed through the surface of the water. When he reappeared in the shallow end, Burk said, "I have an idea."

"Of course you have an idea. You're a fucking writer," Warren said, a bemused smile on his face as he watched the blonde strip off her bikini bottom and paddle toward him on the raft. "And a damn good one, I might add."

FROM: Jerome Sanford
TO: Robert Evans
DATE: October 26, 1970
Received the first draft of *Pledging My Love,* an original screenplay by Raymond Burk that Jon Warren is committed to direct. I finished it last night and thought it was wonderful. The plot (which I don't want to ruin for those who have yet to read it) concerns the surprise arrival of two former high school classmates at their ten-year reunion.

(1) Ricky Horton—a once-gifted athlete who suffered a mental breakdown on the field during his first major league game.

(2) Barbara St. Claire (Sinclair in high school, with the emphasis on the "sin")—a B-movie actress whose career was derailed when a scandal sheet revealed that she'd appeared in a stag film while she was a senior in high school.

What brings these two together is their obsessive need to find Eric Baldwin, another classmate of theirs who has dropped out of sight. Their search takes them on a journey through the bloody heart of Los Angeles, beginning on the night of the reunion and ending on the morning of the Manson killings, when the painful event from the past that unites this threesome is finally revealed.

I found this to be an incredibly compelling script, with relationships and situations that are unique and speak to today's marketplace. That Jon Warren wants to direct makes this project that much more exciting. I am recommending that we move forward quickly to get this in production.

Below are just a few of the casting ideas I jotted down this morning:

Ricky	Barbara	Eric
Bob Redford	Jane Fonda	Jack Nicholson
Warren Beatty	Diane Keaton	Bruce Dern
Jon Voight	Sally Kellerman	Al Pacino
Jeff Bridges	Ellen Burstyn	Dennis Hopper
James Caan	Tuesday Weld	
Peter Fonda		

From *Daily Variety,* November 9, 1970:

"Pledging . . ." Pledged to Paramount
Pledging My Love, *an original screenplay by Raymond Burk, has been purchased by Paramount Pictures. Described by VP Jerome Sanford as a "mythic psychological thriller,"* Pledging *will be produced and directed by Jon Warren beginning in the spring of 1971. Jack Rose will executive produce.*

On the same day that Paramount announced the sale of his screenplay, Burk recognized Loretta Egan's blue Volvo parked on

Balboa Avenue next to the park. She was sitting, reading a magazine, on a blanket spread out on the grass near a large brick barbecue.

Louie jumped out of the car and ran across the grass field, leaving Burk behind to carry the Big Wheel over to the picnic benches,
where he remained seated for a full five minutes before Loretta looked
up from her magazine. He waved hello, but she didn't wave back or
speak, merely stared at him as if she were trying to place his face.

"Ray Burk," he finally said.

"Yes, I remember," she said, then looked back at her magazine.
"Columbia canceled my movie. Eastwood pulled out. He's gonna make
Dirty Harry over at Warner's with Don Siegel."

Burk lit a cigarette and waited a respectful few seconds before
he spoke. "That's really a bummer. I'm sorry."

"I found out on Friday. They were already building sets. I was
that close, Ray. That fucking close."

Burk nodded sympathetically, while he puffed on his cigarette
without inhaling. Nearby, another woman in a white bikini was
lying on the grass with her face up to the sun. A pair of dark glasses
and an open magazine rested on her lap.

Turning back to Loretta, Burk said, "Maybe if I made you dinner it would cheer you up."

Loretta laughed, but her face was filled with sadness. "Maybe,"
she said, "but I seriously doubt it."

Burk shrugged and dropped his cigarette on the grass, stepping
on it. "I think it's worth a try."

Loretta followed Burk back to his house. After they shared a beer and
listened to side one of *Blue*, the latest album by Joni Mitchell. Loretta
agreed to stay with Louie while Burk went out for groceries. He
bought a bottle of Chianti, a three-pound chateaubriand, two heads
of romaine lettuce, and all the ingredients to make a Caesar salad
from scratch. By the time he got home, it was dark and he found
Loretta and Louie sprawled on the living room rug, playing Monopoly.

"I used to play games with my mom," Louie told Loretta, while
Burk was standing outside on the patio, lighting the barbecue. "But
we could never finish, because she would always drink too much and
forget what she was doing."

Loretta rolled the dice and landed on Pennsylvania Avenue, a
property owned by Louie that was already decorated with four bright-

red houses. "You owe me four hundred dollars," Louie said, holding his hand out, palm up.

Loretta slowly counted out three gold hundreds and two blue fifties. "Here you go, Mr. Moneybags. Spend it wisely," she said. She caught Burk smiling at her through the sliding glass doors. "And save some for your dad."

"My dad doesn't need any money. He's gonna be rich."

"Oh? He is?"

Louie nodded his head; then he rolled the dice and advanced to a railroad that he already owned. "They're going to make his movie," he said, as he pushed the dice across the board. "Your turn."

Loretta heard a cabinet in the kitchen open and close. A moment later Burk came into the living room holding the bottle of red wine and two long-stemmed glasses.

"How come you didn't tell me?" Loretta said, glancing at Burk after she passed GO and collected two hundred dollars from the bank.

"Tell you what?"

"About your movie. Louie said you got a green light."

Burk stood quietly for a moment. Then he said, "It was in today's *Variety*. I thought you saw it."

"I don't read the trades," Loretta said, accepting the glass of wine Burk was holding out. "They depress me and make me jealous."

"Are you jealous of me?"

Loretta paused to take a sip of wine and a drag off the cigarette burning in the ashtray by her elbow. "Of course I am," she said mildly, "but I'll get over it."

On Louie's next roll he was told to pick a card that sent him directly to jail. "Goody! I get to go to jail," he said, giggling happily. "Now I can visit with my mom."

Burk was still standing above them, and Loretta looked up and whispered, "He misses her terribly."

"Yeah, I know he does," Burk said, his voice choking up. He turned back toward the kitchen. "I'm gonna go put on the steak."

After they were done eating, Burk cleared the table and washed the dishes while Loretta and Louie continued their game. In less than an hour Loretta was bankrupt.

"That was fun," Louie said, giving Loretta a hug. "You're a good loser. A lot better than my dad."

"Oh, yeah? What's he do?"

"He says bad words."

"Really?"

"Sometimes. Not all the time."

"Does he ever let you win?"

"Never," Burk said from the kitchen. Then he told Louie to put on his pajamas and get ready for bed.

When Burk reappeared in the living room after reading Louie to sleep, all the lights were off and Loretta was lying on the couch with one hand propped behind her head and the other lightly stroking her thigh. After he switched on the stereo and adjusted the volume, Burk took a hit off the joint that she was now holding in the air above her head.

"You know what I want?" she said, shifting her body so Burk could stretch out next to her.

"No, what?"

"I want to screw your ears off," she said, laughing, and she rolled on top of Burk and covered his face and neck with tiny kisses. "I want to celebrate your victory today, Mr. Hollywood."

Burk remained silent and lay very still, his eyes straying around the room.

"Well? You're not going to say anything?"

"I'm worried about Louie," Burk said. "So I don't think you should spend the night."

Loretta, laughing without showing surprise, sat up quickly and pulled her sweater over her head, revealing small but perfectly formed breasts. "I don't want to spend the night," she said, in a voice that made it clear she was telling the truth. "I just want a good fuck. Do you think you can handle that, Ray?"

There was a long silence before he said, in a tone that was quiet and controlled, not wholly committed yet to the erection that tightened his pants, "Yes, I think I can handle that."

★

On January 12, 1971, Sandra Burk pleaded no contest to voluntary manslaughter in Victorville Superior Court. She was given a two-year sentence to be served at the California Women's Prison in Frontera, a small rural community located twenty-five miles east of Los Angeles.

"She'll be up there with the Manson chicks," Gene told Burk when they spoke that evening.

"Wonderful."

"Relax. She'll be on the street in less than a year. When are you gonna see her?"

"She doesn't want any visitors."

"What about Louie? Does he know where she is?"

"I'm gonna tell him tonight."

"Poor kid. How's he doin' otherwise?"

"Great."

"Leaving LA was the right move, Ray."

"I know. Berkeley's cool. Timmy's bookstore is doin' great, too. He's thinking of adding an art theater next door."

"Say hello."

"I will."

"When are you coming down?"

"We start shooting in May."

"I'll see you then."

"For sure."

"Ray?"

"Yeah."

"No more driving."

★

PART TWO

FIVE DAYS

IN THE

BREAKDOWN

LANE,

THREE

WITHOUT

WEATHER

Welcome to
Hollywood II

When the Young Man from Omaha steps out of the Hotel
Sherwood on 16th and Dodge, he feels the scorching summer
wind shift suddenly from east to west. A gust of fiery air
burns his eyes and billows his shirt, and, overhead, a row of
dirty gray clouds swells and rolls across the sky, dragged by
the wind.

The Young Man turns south on Dodge, and through the
city's skyline he sees more clouds begin to gather and thicken
and darken the horizon. Later on, that afternoon, the sun will
disappear and the sky over the high plains will be as black as
tar, and before the day is over the Young Man will hear the
deafening sounds of thunder and lightning battling in the
heavens, while hailstones the size of fifty-cent pieces hammer
down on the roof of his bus.

This is the fourth time the Young Man has set out on
this journey, and he feels his heart tick fast when he sees the

familiar logo of the greyhound dog extended over the sidewalk at the end of the block.

"I am leaving everything behind," the Young Man tells
Daniel Schimmel, his uncle and the owner of the Hotel
Sherwood, right before he departs for Los Angeles. "Tomorrow when my bus crosses the Rockies, a new life will erase my
old life and I will be ready to make my mother's final wish
real."

After his nephew left the hotel, Daniel Schimmel sat silently for several moments, frowning as his eyes roved uneasily around his office.
On the wall beside the window was a poster from the old Omaha
Orpheum Theatre. The poster, faded yellow and curling at the edges,
announced the opening of a vaudeville show on August 27, 1928—
the very last to play the Orpheum, as it turned out.

Headlining the revue was songstress Lenora St. Folette, and
preceding her were Elmer Freedom and His Performing Dachshund,
Celia and Her Doves, acrobats the Campos Brothers, and Sad Sack
the Clown; listed at the very bottom of the poster in the smallest type
was the comedy team of Schimmel and Rheingold.

Following his lunch in the downstairs dining room, Daniel
Schimmel came back to his office and dialed Max Rheingold's number in Los Angeles. As he waited for Max to pick up, he sat back in
his chair and lit a cigarette, reflecting on their shared past while
he watched an occasional bird curve through the air outside his window. After the tenth ring he put the handset back in the cradle. Out
loud, in a voice without emotion, he said, "I tried to warn you, Max.
Que sera sera."

Seven

Monday:
Ricky Meets
Bobby and
Burk Is
Barred from
the Set

Principal photography on *Pledging My Love* commenced at 8 A.M., Monday, May 17, 1971. Earlier that same morning, while Burk was sipping coffee and skimming the *Daily Variety* in his room at the Beverly Hills Hotel, Ricky Furlong was curled up on his daybed in the St. Francis Arms, staring numbly out his grime-coated window on the fourth floor.

Located three doors east of Western Avenue on Hollywood Boulevard, the St. Francis Arms was once a convenient oasis for many distinguished East Coast writers and actors who came to Hollywood for brief assignments at one of the many studios within walking distance. John Garfield came and went over the years, and so did John O'Hara and F. Scott Fitzgerald, before they gravitated west to the Garden of Allah apartments on the Sunset Strip. But that was back in the thirties and forties. Since then the St. Francis had deteriorated along with the neighborhood, and today the guests were a miserable collection of bums and barflies—grief-struck men and women with watery eyes and oily faces that were permanently flushed.

When the sky was light, Ricky left the hotel and walked down to Tiny Naylor's, the twenty-four-hour diner on the northeast corner of La Brea and Sunset. And he—like Burk—was reading a copy of the *Daily Variety,* but Friday's edition, which included a chart listing all the movies currently in production at each studio, along with the cast and other so-called "above the line" or creative personnel.

"Elliott Gould's starring in something at Universal," Ricky told Rose, his waitress, when she brought his coffee and a menu. "He sure got big all of a sudden. When I first got his autograph at the *Funny Girl* premiere, he was just some guy married to Barbra Streisand."

Rose smiled. She was an ordinary-looking woman in her early thirties with a melancholy face and short dark hair that fit her head like a black beanie. Ricky sat in her section because he liked her not-too-bright smile, and the way she inflected the end of her sentences reminded him of Danny Lomax, a shortstop from Charlotte that he was secretly in love with in 1961, when he hit .351 and was voted Rookie of the Year in the Carolina League.

Rose said, "I hear Goldie Hawn's doing a picture with Warren Beatty down the street at Columbia."

"I already got her at the sneak of *Cactus Flower.*"

"She was good in that."

"I didn't see it," Ricky said. He picked up the menu and ran his finger down the breakfast entrees. "I think I'll have the hamburger patty and eggs, with the patty rare and the eggs up."

"Tomatoes or potatoes?"

"Tomatoes."

Rose plucked the menu out of Ricky's hands and stuck it under her arm; she wrote up the order and clipped the check on the metal cylinder that spun in front of the kitchen slot. A fat black cook working over the big iron range stared at the check, then through the slot at Rose. "You know who was in here this morning?"

"Who?"

"Guess."

"Paul Newman."

"Guess again."

When Rose hesitated, the cook said, "Marlon-fucking-Brando, that's who."

Ricky stared at the cook. He was smiling a wide smile and blisters of sweat popped off his forehead and his cheeks. Rose lit a cigarette, leaving it burning in an ashtray while she moved down the counter, wiping away the crumbs and the coffee stains. "You're teasing," she said.

"Booth three," the cook said, pointing with his right hand and using his left to crack two eggs in a frying pan that sizzled with grease. "Over there by the window. Ask Randi."

"Ask me what?" said a bony-tough waitress who was totaling up a bill by the register.

"About Brando."

"I waited on him. What's the big deal?" Randi asked, speaking rather loudly as she looked in Ricky's direction.

Ricky dropped his eyes into his lap and watched his agitated fingers refold his napkin. He knew Randi disliked him: A few weeks earlier, while he was leaving the restaurant—before the glass door had even closed behind him—he'd heard her say, "How can you stand waiting on that creep, Rose?"

"I don't think he's a creep," Rose had said, springing quickly to Ricky's defense.

"Yeah? So what do *you* call a guy who wears a baseball cap indoors and spends all day collecting autographs from movie stars? He's a fucking creep if I ever saw one."

After finishing his breakfast, Ricky left Tiny Naylor's and walked north toward the intersection of Highland and Sunset. Once he reached the corner, he stood rigid and confused for several seconds, before he turned east, staying on the south side of the boulevard, where the stars of Gloria Grahame and Fred Astaire and several other of his favorite actors were enshrined on Hollywood's Walk of Fame. At Las Palmas, he stopped at Nate's News and paged quickly through the latest issues of *Photoplay* and *Modern Screen.* As a general rule browsers were discouraged at Nate's, but Phil Lasky, the grim-looking manager who roamed up and down the racks, honking "Pay or move on," never hassled Ricky, knowing he would always purchase something, even if it was only a package of Necco wafers or Beeman's spearmint gum.

Ricky continued east on Hollywood Boulevard. Near Seward a tall man in a wrinkled gray suit fell into step beside him. His gray hair and mustache were neatly trimmed, and he carried with him a battered black medical bag and a blue umbrella. As they passed the lurid display of lingerie in the windows of Frederick's of Hollywood, he introduced himself to Ricky as Dr. Breeze. "What do you make of those crotchless panties? Doesn't leave very much to the imagination, does it?" he said, tapping the tip of his umbrella sharply against the window glass. "Pretty soon they'll be showin' live sex in there. After that, all bets are off. Right?"

Ricky nodded but remained silent, keeping his eyes on the sidewalk and the stars passing underneath his feet.

When they paused for a red light at Cahuenga, Ricky felt the doctor's fingers tighten on his sleeve. "How's your health?" the doctor asked, his voice suddenly intense, his eyes large and soulless. "Tell me how you're feeling."

The light changed and Ricky pulled his arm away as he stepped off the curb. "I'm feeling fine," he said.

"I can give you a checkup."

"No, thanks."

The doctor dug through his medical bag until he found a badly wrinkled diploma. "Here. I'm Maxwell Breeze," he said triumphantly, trotting now to keep up. "See, I'm a board-certified dermatologist from the University of South Florida. I have many offices in Los Angeles, the nearest of which is four blocks away, behind the All American Burger on Bronson."

Once they passed the Taft building, Ricky heard the doctor begin to wheeze. "Slow down," he called out, his breath strained. "I can't keep up."

Ricky looked over his shoulder with an apologetic expression. "I'm sorry," he said. "I can't. I've got things I have to do."

Ricky crossed the boulevard at Wilcox and sidestepped a bedraggled group of hippies bunched in front of Do-Rite Donuts, hawking blotter acid and Malaysian hash. In the next block he encountered a girl no older than thirteen with a dazed, drugged smile on her sunpeeled face. She was wearing thigh-high red boots, silver hot pants, and a see-through blouse with a large battery-operated crucifix attached to her chest that blinked on and off. A few feet away a bigbellied man wearing just a soiled T-shirt was evacuating his bowels in the doorway of Kurtz's electronics. "Don't you dare look at me!" he screamed, as Ricky hurried past.

Then, just before he reached Vine, Ricky noticed a young man kneeling in the center of the sidewalk. He was thin and small-boned, and his round face was already damp with sweat as he furiously polished one of the coral terrazzo stars on the Walk of Fame.

Ricky paused and the young man looked up, probing him with his eyes as he continued to rub the chamois cloth across the nameless star in front of him. His ill-barbered hair was cut close to his skull, and next to him on the sidewalk was a can of Brasso, a root beer in a paper cup, and an open package of Hydrox cookies.

As he stared at Ricky, the young man's eyes seemed to change from green to a deeper green—the eyes of an ageless child, Ricky thought, recalling a line from a poem he'd once read. "Will you be my friend?" the young man asked, looking in his lap and then back at Ricky's face.

Not understanding why, exactly, but feeling united with this boy in some strange way, Ricky said, "Sure, I'll be your friend."

Late that same morning, when Bobby Sherwood moved into Ricky's room at the St. Francis Arms, he would say, "I knew it would happen like this. It always does when I dream it will."

★

Burk swiveled his chair and looked out the window of his office. The sky was a ceiling of deep blue, except for a few bruised clouds that were scattered over the Hollywood Hills. Directly below him a thin dark-complected man in his thirties was standing in the pale sunlight outside Stage Three, smoking a cigarette and reading the *Hollywood Reporter*. A gray Borsalino was tilted rakishly on his head and a shoulder holster was visible underneath his topcoat. Above the stage door, the red light was pulsating, indicating they were filming inside.

Laughter came from down the hallway and Burk spun around and sat back in the chair, staring at the blank walls and empty bookcases. After several seconds he picked up his phone and dialed Loretta.

"Guess what?" he said, trying to sound upbeat when she picked up. "I've got my own parking place. I don't have to park in back with the rest of the peons."

Loretta yawned. "That's nice, Ray."

"Al Pacino drove on the lot in front of me."

"Ray?"

"Yeah."

"I thought you started shooting at eight."

"We did."

"So how come you're not on the set?"

Burk glanced at the memo he found on his desk when he arrived, then he said, glumly, "Warren wants to work with the actors alone for the first week. He said having the writer around right at the start might make them less spontaneous."

"When did he tell you this?"

"He didn't. He wrote me a memo."

"What are you supposed to do?"

"I don't know. I feel like shit."

"I can imagine."

Outside, the light above the stage door blinked off. The actor wearing the Borsalino put out his smoke with his shoe, but when he reached for the door handle Robert Evans suddenly exploded by him, into the sunlight, followed by an overweight man wearing a beard and thick horn-rimmed glasses.

"Check this out," Burk said. "I can see Evans and Coppola arguing in front of the *Godfather* stage. I hear they're way over budget."

"Brando's supposed to be wonderful," Loretta said, and there was a long pause that Burk did not try to fill. "Look, Ray, I'll be in my office around eleven. Call me if you want to talk."

Burk sucked in his breath. "It's fuckin' bullshit," he said, his voice soft but now filled with rage. "I wrote the script. I should be there, hangin' out. That's the whole reason I'm down here. Jesus. . . ."

Burk's voice trailed off. Loretta said after a short silence, "I gotta go. Call me later."

When the line clicked, Burk hung up hard and got to his feet, waiting a few moments before he called Maria Selene. Nora, her secretary, said she was on a long distance call. "That's okay. I'll wait," Burk said, glancing over the interoffice mail that was placed on his desk earlier that morning, along with the memo from Warren.

According to the daily call sheet, the cast and crew would be at Griffith Park all day, shooting scenes four through nine in the newly revised script—scenes that focused on the relationship between Barbara Sinclair and Ricky Horton on the morning after their high school reunion. The night shots would be completed later that month, and the reunion itself—the movie's opening scene—was slated for the second week. Tuesday the location would move to the Raincheck Room, a downscale bar on Santa Monica Boulevard where Tom Crumpler, the actor playing Eric Baldwin, was scheduled to step in front of the camera for the first time.

Burk had seen Crumpler earlier that morning, checking into the hotel. Slouched by his side, trying to look both interesting and bored, was a waifish blonde dressed in black velvet hip huggers and a Garbo-esque hat. According to Eddie Bascom, the head bellman and the hotel's coke dealer, she was the current girl of the moment on the New York scene and "very proper pussy."

"I already heard," Maria told Burk when she came on the line. "Warren called Sanford last night, and Sanford got me at home this morning."

"What did you say?"

"Honestly?"

"Honestly."

"I said that keeping you away from the set was stupid, that Warren was acting out of fear and ego. I told him I thought your presence would be a major asset to the film."

"If he starts improvising," Burk said, "he's gonna ruin the script."

"I know. Sanford agrees, but he wants to see the dailies before he steps in."

"That's bullshit," Burk said, his voice going up. "I should be on the set right now."

"Don't yell at me, Ray. Okay? I'm on your side. You can call and complain, but you can't yell at me."

Burk felt a drumroll of fear inside his chest. "I don't know what I'm supposed to do."

"Take a drive. Go to the beach. You're getting paid, what else do you want?"

Burk said nothing as he held the phone tight against his ear. A hummingbird zoomed by the open window and a gust of warm air blew inside, sending the call sheet off the desk on a short flight to the floor behind his chair. When he bent to pick up the paper he glanced outside: Two men with blond beards and worn Levi's were unloading scenery from a truck parked by the stage. A secretary in red heels and a tight white miniskirt walked by, and one of the men reached out playfully to pinch her on the ass. She slapped his hand away without missing a step, saying, "You can look but you can't touch," and continued up the street, turning around in a circle once so they could see her dazzling smile.

The men laughed at the same time, and Burk heard the line go dead in his ear.

As Burk left the building, he passed by a suite of offices on the first floor with DICKY SOLOMON PRODUCTIONS lettered on the door. These offices were empty now—Dicky and his staff were in Hawaii shooting *Curved Balls,* a sitcom pilot for CBS that was based on the exploits of two retired baseball players who open up a private detective agency in Honolulu—but Burk smiled to himself, wondering what Dicky would think when he pulled into the Paramount lot the following week and observed Burk's name on the parking space next to his.

Burk and Dicky had spoken only once since Burk was fired from the network—in January, when Sandra was convicted and sent to prison. Dicky said he'd followed her case in the *LA Times,* where it was on the front page of the Metro section for three straight days. "What a crazy broad. With the right plot there could be a TV movie in there someplace," he told Burk. "Or a small feature. Great role for Ann Margret or Tuesday Weld." Burk said he didn't think he'd feel comfortable participating in something like that. "I don't want you involved," Dicky had said, his voice extremely cold. "I just wanted to check out your vibe."

"I hope you drop the idea," Burk had said disapprovingly, and he assumed Dicky had, because he never heard from him again, and when a list of his future projects was recently summarized in the trades, Sandra's story was not mentioned.

After he bought a pint of Cuervo Gold and a package of beef jerky at White Horse Liquors on Western Avenue, Burk drove his rented red Mustang convertible north into Griffith Park. A sign with the Paramount logo pointed toward a parking lot adjacent to the carousel. A fat teamster sat in a folding chair by the entrance.

"Name?" he asked, looking up from the crossword puzzle in his lap. He wore blue aviator sunglasses and a black satin jacket with *Larry* stitched in red across the breast.

"Burk. Ray."

The teamster picked up a clipboard and used a nicotine-stained finger to run down a list of names. "I don't see Burk," he said. "What do you do?"

"I'm the writer."

"You're not on the list."

"So you're telling me I can't park here," Burk said, louder than he intended.

The teamster shrugged. "I don't make the rules," he said, evading Burk's eyes as he rocked slightly in his chair, "so don't get in my face."

"I'm not in your face. I'm just asking you a simple fucking question."

The teamster shook his head in mild surprise and reached into his jacket for his walkie-talkie. "Chuck, Larry up in the lot," he said, glancing at Burk as he spoke into the mike. "Got a problem."

A voice crackled through the static. "What's the deal?"

"Fella here says he's the writer. I don't have him on the list. You better send up Myers."

"Will do."

Glancing off to his left, Burk could see the grips pulling cable and setting up lights near the carousel. Along with Hillary Yawky and Ben O'Reilly, the actors portraying Barbara Sinclair and Ricky Horton, the scene required twenty hippies—"atmosphere," as the call sheet referred to them—but the extras he saw lounging around the set looked bogus: too many beads, bells, and Mexican serapes; costumed freaks in polka-dot bell-bottoms and fake fur vests, not the street kids he described in the script with "sickly white skin and burnt-looking eyes, shining with hate."

Burk picked out Jon Warren amid the crew members. He was standing next to Chickie Green, the cinematographer, both of them supervising the placement of the camera. "Prick," Burk said, under his breath, and took a long slug of tequila. When he lowered the bottle, he saw a man with a beard and long blond hair jogging across the parking lot. In his hand was a walkie-talkie with the antenna pulled out all the way.

"You really the writer?" the man asked Burk, looking at him admiringly while he caught his breath. Burk nodded and the man smiled. "Fuckin' great script."

Burk absorbed this compliment for a few moments before he said, "Thanks."

"Thank *you*," the man said, crouching down to extend his hand through the window. That's when Burk noticed the coiled snake tattooed on his neck. "Snake Myers. First AD."

"Ray Burk."

Snake spit on the ground between his feet. "I do not know why they always have to fuck with the writer. I mean, if it wasn't for you, none of us would be working." Snake's indignation and his smile made Burk's anger begin to dissipate. "But you can rest easy, Ray, your stuff is playing excellent. Everything we got this morning was outasight."

"What about the first scene between Barbara and Ricky?"

"What about it?"

"Did it work?"

"*Work?*" Snake rolled his eyes and looked at Burk, incredulous. "It fucking cooked. And they did it *line* for *line*. Ben wanted to improv part of the ending, but Warren said, and I quote, 'When you're ready to say what's on the page, I'll turn on the camera.'"

"Warren said that? Really?"

"I shit you not."

"Was Ben good?"

"Intense, man. He was *intense*," Snake said, and he pointed to the tequila in Burk's lap. "You mind if I have a taste?" Burk passed the bottle through the open window and Snake tipped it up to his mouth for two long swallows. "Let me tell you something," he said, closing one eye and peering down at the set. "I know everyone thought Warren was crazy to cast unknowns in those parts. At least Crumpler's done a soap. But the chick, that took some cojones, man. The word in the street was that Fonda was considered."

"Dunaway too. Paramount almost canceled the picture when Warren changed his mind."

Snake squeezed Burk's shoulder, uncapped the tequila, and swallowed again. "Fucker knows what he's doing. I don't know where he found those people, but they're good. I mean they're fuckin' *real*."

"Unlike those hippies down there."

"Tell me about it. Fuckin' casting blew it," Snake said, getting to his feet. He shaded his eyes, looking off to the west where the sun was burning through a cloud shaped like a gray heart. "But don't worry, I got my people down on the boulevard bringing in a new batch." Snake flashed Burk a wink. "And remember, everyone down there on this picture believes in your script." Snake handed back the bottle and rapped the hood twice with his knuckle. "Picture time," he said. "I gotta get back to work."

Burk shifted his car into reverse and made a U-turn in front of a studio van that was pulling into the parking lot. Inside were the new extras: unpleasant-looking men and women with pallid faces that were gouged with failure and disillusionment. A woman with a yellow bruise on her cheek caught Burk's eye. When he smiled, the boy in the seat behind her—he was ten at the most—leaned out the window and spit on Burk's windshield. Burk gave him the finger and the kid gave it back with both hands, spitting and cursing, until someone shouted, "Cool it, Alan," and pulled him back inside by his hair.

Burk continued driving through the park until he found an open but nearly empty parking lot on Los Feliz Boulevard, next to the riding stables. Using a narrow footpath that circled around the tennis courts and the children's zoo, he was able to approach the movie's location undetected through a dense wood. A dove called softly while he rested for a moment in the shelter of a mammoth oak tree; then, lighting a cigarette, he crouched down to watch the activity below him through the haze and rising heat.

Jon Warren was sitting in his canvas chair, talking to the wardrobe designer, an uptight-looking woman wearing purple pedal pushers and purple-tinted granny glasses. After a few moments he dismissed her with a wave, got up, and moved over to where Chickie Green was watching the grips build the camera platform. They were joined by Snake Myers, who tapped his watch and pointed at the clouds rolling in from the west. Warren nodded his head. Then he took Myers by the elbow and walked him over to a trailer that was used as a dressing room and toilet. There was a short conversation that ended when Myers slipped what looked like a vial of cocaine into Warren's hand and strolled off wearing a crooked grin.

Burk heard a sound behind him and turned and saw a boy standing motionless a short distance away: the same boy with the fever-red eyes who spit on his windshield earlier that morning. A woman, emaciated and as white as salt, appeared from behind a large gray rock and stood there next to the boy in a rectangle of sunlight, twisting her hands nervously.

Burk was suddenly aware that he recognized this odd pair. Two years ago, when he drove endlessly through the streets of East Hollywood, he used to see them several times a week, noticing them because the mother—that's who he assumed she was—always seemed to be in such a tremendous hurry, speed-walking up the sidewalk with the boy pulled along in her wake, running every few steps to keep up.

The first time he saw them he thought the boy was late for school, but then he began seeing them not only in the morning but at odd hours in the middle of the day, moving at the same frantic pace, their heads bobbing crazily as they deftly quick-stepped through the traffic on some unknown mission.

One time they nearly collided with Burk while he stood outside Ernie's Stardust Lounge, lighting a cigarette with his back against the wind. When they passed by, he saw the woman's mouth moving silently, her expression both a grimace and a grin. The boy's face had an odd air of mischief, and there was an Archie comic book rolled up in his rear pocket. Who were they? Burk wondered at the time. And why were they always in such a rush? If they were really mother and son, where was the father, and why wasn't the boy in school?

Burk stood up. "Who are you?" he asked the woman, keeping his voice low and one eye on the boy.

The woman didn't answer, just stared at him with a madwoman's eyes, swallowing and working her jaw. Finally the boy said arrogantly, "Who the hell are *you*?"

"I asked you first."

The boy grinned slightly and made a weird gesture with his right hand, like he was getting ready to salute. "They said they'd pay us," the woman said in a lifeless voice, "but Alan don't want to do that."

"Do what?"

"They want him to be someone else's child."

"I want to be with my mom," the boy said, seizing her hand.

"They don't want me in the movie," the woman said. "They say I don't look right."

Burk's facial expression tightened slightly. He felt annoyingly vulnerable. After several seconds he turned away and looked down at the set. The catering truck had arrived and two long tables were being filled with huge platters of food. Nearby, a couple of extras in costume were throwing a Frisbee across the grass behind an empty bandstand. "I've seen you before," Burk said, bringing his eyes back to the woman. "Both of you. I've seen you walking through Hollywood."

The woman took a step forward, still holding the boy's hand. "We've seen you, too."

"What're you doin' up here?" the boy said quickly, staring at Burk with a strange combination of boldness and fear.

"I'm hiding."

"From who?"

"From—"

"Everyone," the woman said, her face taking on an almost life-like color. "He's hiding from everyone. Just like us."

"Where are you calling from now, Ray?"

"Ernie's. This bar on Hollywood Boulevard."

"Are you drunk?"

"I've had a few."

"You sound drunk," Maria said. Burk dropped a quarter into the jukebox and punched P-5. When Maria spoke again, her voice was stern but careful. "Ray, listen to me. It wasn't such a good idea to show up at the location."

"I wrote the movie, Maria."

"And everyone knows that, especially Warren, but he's calling the shots. So just let him do his job. Okay?"

"What about dailies?"

"What about them?"

"Do I get to see them?"

"I don't know. I'll talk to Sanford. Again, it's up to Warren. If he doesn't want you in the screening room, then it's tough shit. I've got to take another call," Maria said suddenly. "I'll get back to you as soon as I hear anything."

When Burk came back to his bar stool, there was a fresh shot of Cuervo Gold waiting for him. Miles told him it was on the house. Burk thanked him silently with a nod and a woman down the bar said, "How's your kid?" Burk turned and looked at her: one eye was closed and she was squinting over the top of her cigarette. "He don't remember me," the woman said to Miles, exhaling a great cloud of smoke.

"It's been a long time, hon. Almost two years."

"My hair used to be blond and wavier. I used to wear it like Esther Williams. This is not my real hair," she said to Burk.

Miles said, somberly, "Alice's been sick."

"I'm sorry," Burk said.

"Down below. In the hot spot. But I'm fighting it," she said, her lips twisting into a painful grin. She was silent once more, then: "So, back to your son. Louie, right?" Burk nodded, wondering, How does she know this? "What is he now, six?"

"He'll be seven in June."

"I'm sixty-two and a half," she said, chuckling softly, and Miles was smiling now too. "You still don't remember me, do you?" Burk shook his head. "Alice. Alice McNair. I worked at Columbia, in wardrobe."

"Okay," Burk said, nodding, his memory finally becoming unsnagged. "Sure."

"We used to talk about the old days. I worked with Rita Hayworth on *Cover Girl.*"

"Now I remember."

"Before chemo I was like this," Alice said, making a large circle with her arms.

Miles said, "Alice was at the track the day your wife had the miscarriage."

"That's right. I was there," she said with certainty. "I was standing right alongside her in the grandstand. Of course I didn't know you guys were married until later that evening. When Miles told me the story I put two and two together." Alice leaned forward and looked Burk in the face. "Boy, she could sure play the horses."

Burk stopped a smile and made a thoughtful face. "You know," he said, "I don't remember talking about Sandra and Louie in here."

"Talked about them all the time," a man behind him said in a sardonic voice. Burk looked over his shoulder: A stringy white-haired man sat alone at a table against the far wall. He wore a dirty tweed hat, and his hands and arms trembled with Parkinson's disease. "Of course, you were so liquored up you don't remember."

"That's Martin Epstein," Miles said. "He used to sit here." Miles slapped the bar with his palm. "Right under the TV."

"Until my arms started flappin' and knockin' over glasses and ashtrays. Now he's got me down here in the flats where it's safe."

"Martin owned the magic shop over on Wilcox," Alice said. "Martin's Magic Kingdom. When we lived on Yucca I used to bring my boy by almost every day after school. He made me buy loads and loads of those little red and blue metal soldiers."

"The Civil War guys. I had a set of those," Burk said. "I saved them and gave them to Louie."

Miles caught Burk's eye. "Alice's son died in Vietnam," he whispered, shielding his mouth with his hand. "Paratrooper."

Martin Epstein raised the cane that was resting in his lap and pointed the rubber tip at Burk. "I knew him since he was a kid. Him and his brother. Came in on Saturdays. Am I right?" Burk didn't remember but nodded anyway. "I knew your father, too," Martin Epstein said. "So did all the big-shot actors—Fonda, Mitchum, the whole bunch. They all got their hometown rags from your dad. 'I'll meet you down at Nate's'—how many times did I hear that? Or 'Goin' down to Nate's; I'll be back in ten.'

"I remember when he first came to town with your mom. Had the little stand over on Gower and Fountain. Carried the trades and the *Racing Form* and the local dailies. That was it. Then—bingo— couple of years later he's over on Las Palmas with racks runnin' from here to Tijuana. If I remember correctly, it was Frank Havana who set him up there."

"My dad worked his ass off," Burk said. "Nobody set him up anywhere."

Martin Epstein made a guilty face. "Havana and your dad were friends," he said, bowing his head. "I know that for sure. Seen them every week sittin' ringside at the Hollywood Legion Stadium." Martin Epstein's hand jerked in front of his face, pretending to part a curtain that shielded his eyes. "Can see it now, like it was yesterday. Max Baer is fightin' some colored stiff, and sittin' on the aisle in the sixth row is Frank Havana. Beside him is your dad and his cousin Aaron Levine. On the other side, Max Rheingold."

"Max Rheingold?" Burk said the name as if he were hearing it for the first time. Then he laughed nervously, gazing into his glass for several seconds before he finished his drink.

No one spoke for a while, and the only sound was the whir of the ceiling fan and the clink of beer glasses as Miles stacked them behind the bar. "I'd like to hear a song," Alice said at last.

Burk took out a coin and turned it over in his hand several times, examining it closely. "I'll play P-Five," he said. "That's 'Dream Lover.'"

"You just played that," Miles said.

"That's okay. I like that song," Alice said.

"No. I'll play something else," Burk said.

"Play something by Gogi Grant," Martin Epstein piped up. "'The Wayward Wind' is one of my favorites."

"That fella's changed," Miles said, speaking in a low voice as he watched Burk feed quarters into the jukebox. "The first day he came in here, he was wearing a coat and tie. Hardly said a word. When he did open up, he talked about his wife, how much he loved her, but that sometimes she acted so queerly he didn't think he knew her at all."

"You can't ever know a woman," Martin Epstein said. "Even without her clothes on, she's one of God's great mysteries."

Miles glanced at Martin Epstein and they stared at each other until Alice said, "That day at the track I noticed her right away. She had one of those faces that was beautiful and miserable at the same time. She had four winners and the Daily Double."

Miles absorbed this information with a nod as he poured himself a slug of gin and knocked it down neat. Burk came back to the bar and Alice smiled at him, but he turned away from her watery eyes. A moment later the front door opened and a black sailor peeked inside and scanned the bar.

"Can I help you?" Miles asked him.

"I'm lookin' for my partner. He ain't here," the black sailor said, his face looking embarrassed as he stepped back outside.

As the blade of sunlight vanished from the floor, Burk let his mind carry him back to that exhilarating afternoon when he met Bonnie Simpson for the first time. Behind his squinted eyes he saw her walking next to him, her hands buried deep in the pockets of her unbuttoned coat, her laughing face raised to the sky.

Miles reached out and patted Burk's shoulder. "What's goin' on?" he said. "You look a little lost."

Burk nodded and swallowed hard. Bonnie's sunlit face was gone, but he could still hear her laughter in the back of his head. "I feel lost," Burk said, surprised by the pain gathering in his stomach. Then he stood up and dropped a five-dollar tip on the bar. On his way out he said, "I'm not sure I'm ever coming back to this place."

* * *

That night around 2 A.M. Radio Ray received a call from a man named Clark. He said he was a graduate of Princeton University.

"I graduated with a degree in Library Science," he said. "Right now I'm working at a local university, which I will not name. I'm having a difficult time at my job. Why? Because I'm in love with a colleague. Her name is Diana."

"Diana. That's a pretty name. Does she—?"

"Please let me finish."

"Sorry, I didn't mean to interrupt."

"I know what you're going to ask me," Clark said in a high voice. "No. She does not know I love her. We have never spoken."

"But you did say you were colleagues?"

"She works in Periodicals. I'm in the History section."

"Maybe you should introduce yourself."

"No. No matter what I said it would be wrong."

"How do you know?"

"I know."

"Then by not speaking to her—"

"Not speaking to her is ecstasy!"

There was a long pause. Then Radio Ray spoke firmly. "You said at the beginning of this call that you were having a difficult time. Maybe you would like to explain what—"

Clark cut in. His voice trembled. "I want to follow her home at night. In the morning I want to watch her run. Later, I want to surprise her in her house—"

"Wait a sec—"

"Naked, sweating, her eyes filled with raw fear."

"Clark—"

A pitiful moan, then softly: "I need to be inside her secret heart."

★

Eight

Tuesday:

Burk Goes

Back to

the Set

AND

Bobby

Remembers

Omaha

May 18, 1971

Burk woke up on his back with a hard-on tenting the sheet above his waist. While he amused himself with his right hand, his empty mind was filling slowly with erotic images left over from his last dream. In one he saw himself standing naked against a stark white wall. Kneeling in front of him with their eyes half closed were two women, a brunette and a redhead, both with hair reaching to the middle of their backs. They were fondling him—the redhead stroking his balls, the brunette licking his cock. In the background other unseen women were speaking softly, murmuring encouragement.

Burk climaxed violently, his face grimmacing with each convulsion. When he finally opened his eyes he saw drops of semen sliding through the hairs on his chest, glistening like the trail of a snail. In the corner of his vision he also noticed the message light blinking on the phone beside his bed.

After he lit a cigarette and ordered coffee from room service, he dialed the hotel operator. "You have a message from Boyd Talbott," she told him. "He said you could reach him on the set."

"Is that it?"

"Loretta Egan also called."

"When?"

"Nine-thirty."

Burk checked the alarm clock on his nightstand. It was ten-fifteen. Although he was a heavy sleeper, he rarely slept through a ringing phone. "Did you put her through?"

"No. You instructed us to hold all calls."

"That's strange," Burk said. "I don't remember doing that."

The *LA Times* arrived with the coffee and Burk drank three cups, two quickly, but savoring the third while he browsed through the sports page. Soon his serenity was interrupted by a commotion in the room next door, followed by Tom Crumpler's angry voice: "Get the fuck out of here, you stuck-up cunt! Now! And don't fucking come back!" A door slammed, and Burk swung his legs out of bed. It was not a good sign when a featured actor in your first film was either drunk or going through cocaine withdrawal at ten in the morning, two hours before he was due on the set.

The phone rang and Burk dropped the newspaper on the rug before he put the receiver to his ear. Loretta said, "I think we should give this a rest for a while." Her voice vibrated, slightly out of control. Before Burk could speak, the hotel operator broke in, saying, "I've got an emergency call from Boyd Talbott."

Loretta cleared the line and the phone clicked twice before Talbott spoke. "Ray, you on?"

"Yeah, I'm here."

"You're tough to reach." Talbott's voice was cold and deliberate, with a trace of the British accent he'd picked up while he attended the London Film School between his junior and senior years at Yale. When he graduated, Paramount hired him as an intern, assigning him to *Pledging My Love* as Warren's assistant. "Jon would like to know if you could knock off a short scene at the bar, before Crumpler arrives."

Burk waited for Talbott to go on. When he didn't, Burk said, "What kind of a scene?"

"Just something brief, to give us the flavor of the place."

"I thought I did that with the dart game."

"Perhaps, but—"

"And later when the waitress gets pissed off at the stuntman who—"

"What Jon thought would be interesting," Talbott said, cutting in cautiously, "would be a scene between a couple of out-of-work actors. They're both drunk, complaining about all the stuff they've had repossessed over the last few months. One guy has lost his car, a convertible he bought when he was a regular on a series; the other actor—he's younger, just married—has had his living room set pulled out. Maybe the bartender chimes in about his Master Charge, how he went five hundred over the limit and the marshal showed up on his doorstep to reclaim it in front of his kid. A quick two-pager."

"You're sure we need it?"

"Absolutely. See what you can work up," Talbott said. "When you're done, bring it by the set."

★

Later that same morning (while Burk labored over a scene that would never be filmed), Bobby Sherwood sat listlessly by the window in the room he shared with Ricky Furlong, watching the traffic pass by in front of the St. Francis Arms. Up the street a bus pulled to the curb in front of Ernie's Stardust Lounge, discharging a blind black man wearing a lemon-colored suit and a panama hat.

A large-boned and clumsy-looking nurse stepped off next and began walking up Hollywood Boulevard. She was in her sixties and her gray hair was pulled into a bun, except for one loose strand that fell across her face. The way her shoulders rolled when she walked reminded Bobby of Mrs. Hooten, a guest from California who stayed regularly at the Hotel Sherwood during the month of August.

> "I don't have any relatives in Omaha," she tells Bobby one morning when they ride down in the elevator together. She is wearing plaid Bermuda shorts and a wide-rimmed straw hat. "They're all dead, or they moved away like I did. But I like to come back every year, especially during the harvest season when the memories of my childhood are the fondest."

Mrs. Hooten never speaks of these memories to Bobby,
but late one evening when the dining room and the
Cornhusker Lounge are closed, he sees his uncle chatting
with her in a quiet corner of the lobby. They are seated on a
small banquette, so engrossed in their conversation they don't
hear Bobby crawl slowly across the worn carpet to a hiding
spot behind a large potted plant. "I was there that night. I
was at the Orpheum," she tells Bobby's uncle. "My dad took
us, my big brother and me. I was nineteen and Dave was
twenty-two."

"David became a doctor, didn't he?"

"Yes, he did. A radiologist. We were both home from
college that summer. He was a senior at Nebraska and I was a
sophomore at Creighton, majoring in journalism. We finished
bringing in the wheat on Friday, and seeing the vaudeville
show that night was Daddy's treat. I had never seen a live
stage show before, and in the back of my mind was the possibility that I might write about it for my journalism class."

"A review?" Daniel Schimmel says, smiling.

"Possibly."

"Did you?"

Mrs. Hooten pauses before she replies. "No, I didn't."

"Why?"

"It was too painful. Why they hated you so much I never
understood."

Here Daniel Schimmel loses his smile. "We weren't
funny."

"You were awful. True. This is very true."

"Max was drunk. You remember that, of course?"

"Max? You mean—"

"My partner, Max Rheingold. The fatty with the stove-
pipe hat and the oversized shoes. You must remember him
vomiting onstage."

"Yes, of course. We thought it had to be part of the act.
And such profanity," she says with disgust. "They beat him,
didn't they?"

"They beat us both. And not just the people who were in
the audience."

"The police?" Daniel Schimmel nods. "Mr. Rheingold
exposed himself," Mrs. Hooten whispers, "didn't he?"

"Yes, he did."

"We couldn't believe our eyes."

"It was the last vaudeville show in Omaha, ever."

"I remember a clown called Sad Sack and a gentleman with a dog act."

"Elmer Freedom. He beat me bloody with his fists. His dog took several chunks out of Max's legs."

"Elmer Freedom. What a wonderful name. My lover Miriam will laugh so when she hears it. There was also a lady with birds."

"Celia and her doves, but she never got to go on. We were the last act."

"Yes. But I remember seeing her afterward, outside the theater, running down the street toward the bus station with a cage in each hand. What a queer sight."

"Max was on the same bus, on his way west with three dollars in his pocket. Me? I spent two days in the hospital, then two more days here recuperating, before I went downstairs to work in the kitchen."

"You told no more jokes?"

Daniel Schimmel shakes his head. "None."

"They threw tomatoes at you."

"And two days later I was peeling them into boiling water for the vegetable soup."

"A comedian in the kitchen."

"I was a fraud, but Max was a bigger fraud."

"His johnson was formidable, as I recall."

"His johnson?"

"You've never heard that term? His dingus, how about that?"

Daniel Schimmel laughs. "That I understand."

"It was formidable," she repeats.

"What did your father say?"

"He said, 'Sometimes it never pays to leave the farm.'"

This time they both laugh.

"What happened to that man?" Mrs. Hooten asks Daniel Schimmel, her face becoming serious.

"What happened to Max Rheingold?" Daniel Schimmel leaves the question in the air, while he removes his glasses and gazes off into the blur of the lobby. When he turns back toward her, he says, "That's a long story."

"I bet it is," Mrs. Hooten says, and smiles. "Why don't you begin and I will let you know if I become bored."

★

Burk circled the block twice before he found a metered parking space in front of the Mayfair Market. Directly across the street was the Raincheck Room, where crew members were milling about or drinking coffee in small huddles, obviously on a break. An overweight cop loaned to the production for the day was waving cars around the cables and lights that blocked off the lane by the curb.

Burk used his Levi's to dry his palms before he got out of his car. When he looked up he saw Talbott appear in the open doorway of the Raincheck Room. He was wearing a blue button-down shirt, knife-creased chinos, and shiny cordovan loafers without socks. The script he was holding against his chest was protected by an expensive leather binder.

The light flashed to green, and a white Cadillac glided to a stop in front of the bar. The woman driving had jet-black hair and a sharp profile. Jon Warren was sitting in the passenger seat. He was wearing dark shades and a straw cowboy hat, which he tilted back on his head when the woman leaned to kiss him on the lips. There was some good-natured whistling and scattered applause from the crew, and when Warren opened the door and stepped into the sunlight he bowed deeply, removing his hat in a sweeping gesture. Then he threaded his way through the cables and lights, nodding to Talbott in a perfunctory way before he disappeared inside the bar.

Snake Myers loped out of the Mayfair Market and caught up to Burk in the middle of the crosswalk. "What's shakin', my man?" he said, clapping Burk on the shoulder. "Snake Myers, remember?"

Burk nodded. "Yeah, sure."

"So, what's up?"

"Not much."

"Just in the neighborhood?"

"Not really," Burk said. He held up his script. "I'm dropping off some revisions."

"New pages. That's cool," Myers said, and a goofy smile worked its way across his face. "Give 'em to me and I'll make sure they get to Warren."

"Talbott wants to see them first."

"Talbott's a punk," Myers said, looking around impatiently once they reached the other side of the street. "Fuck him."

"He works for Warren, so—"

"He's a studio snitch. He works for himself." Myers turned away, and Burk saw a pint of Old Grand Dad in the pocket of his jeans. "See you around."

Burk was moving toward Talbott when Warren stepped outside the Raincheck with his arm around Chickie Green. They went off to one side and spoke in hushed voices, deciding which lens to use for the next shot. When there was a lull in the conversation, Burk said to Warren, "I've got the scene worked out."

Warren glanced at Burk, holding his eyes for the briefest of moments, and then looked past him, distracted. "Let's go with a twenty-five millimeter," he said to Chickie, putting a viewfinder up to his left eye. "We'll start on the billboard and pan down to the street; then we'll pick up Crumpler and follow him into the bar."

"You want me to light the phone booth?"

"Yeah. But keep everything flat."

When Warren lowered the viewfinder, Burk held out his type-written pages. "Here they are," he said.

Warren looked over at Talbott, who was now standing just behind his right shoulder.

"The business in the bar," Talbott said finally. "Before we see Crumpler."

"Oh, yeah," Warren said, nodding. "I thought we could put some topspin on the opening."

"I nailed it," Burk said. Talbott reached out, but Burk ignored him. "I want Jon to read it first."

"Don't need to. I've decided to improv it," Warren said, and gazed off down the street. "I'm gonna use some old character actors, guys you would recognize but who don't work much. I'm just gonna let them riff about the biz, keep it real, let the cameras roll, and see what we get." Warren turned his head and looked at Burk with a smile that was both meek and superior. "I think it's gonna be cool."

Burk said, "I spent all morning on this. You should've let me know before I did the work."

"I just came up with it," Warren said, beginning to ease away. "I'm sorry, man."

After Warren disappeared into the bar, Talbott blinked his eyes and tried to look contrite. He said, "If it's any consolation, he's been shooting your pages word for word. This is the first thing he's changed."

Burk remained silent, fighting back his anger as he watched a long black limousine double-park in front of the Raincheck. Before the driver could open his door, Tom Crumpler stumbled out of the backseat with an idiot smile plastered on his face.

Someone said, "That dude is righteously fucked up," and an electrician with a weight lifter's body took Crumpler by the arm and led him inside the bar.

Burk turned and started back up Santa Monica Boulevard. He passed Snake Myers, who was leaning against a camera truck speaking softly into a walkie-talkie. Burk heard Warren's voice over the light interference. He said, "Make sure Burk is off the dailies list, and under no circumstances do I want him on the set while we're shooting."

Burk ducked inside the Billiard Den and called Loretta from the pay phone by the men's room. She was currently officed at Universal, polishing an original screenplay, *Scorched,* the story of a sexually precocious teenager living in Las Vegas with her showgirl mom and a retarded brother. Hal Ashby was supervising the rewrites but had not yet committed to direct.

"What did you mean this morning?" Burk asked Loretta when she picked up.

"Just what I said: that we should take a break, not see each other for a few weeks."

"Are you seeing anyone else?"

"I can see anyone I want, Ray."

"That's not what I asked."

A dull-looking kid with half-shut eyes came out of the men's room and leaned against the wall across from Burk. He was wearing baggy sweatpants and broken leather sandals that were patched together with duct tape. "You gonna be long?" he asked Burk, smiling in an unfriendly manner.

"Awhile."

"How long's awhile?"

Before Burk could reply, Loretta said, "Who're you talking to, Ray?"

"Some hippie kid waiting to use the phone. I'm at the Billiard Den."

"That's across from the Raincheck. I thought you weren't supposed to go by the set."

"Warren wanted me to revise a scene. I just dropped it off."

The kid against the wall said, "I gotta call home to Rockford, Illinois, and I gotta do it soon so my folks can wire me the cash."

"I'm bringing Louie down this weekend," Burk said to Loretta, keeping one eye on the kid. "Sandra wants to see him on Sunday."

"When did you find this out?"

"I got a letter from her last week."

"How come you never mentioned it?"

"I don't know," Burk said. He sounded evasive. "I've got a lot of things on my mind."

"Yeah, right," Loretta muttered, clearly annoyed.

"It's been almost two years since he's seen her. That's a long time."

Loretta started to speak, then stopped. The kid against the wall took out a dime and held it up to Burk's face. "I gotta make a call," he said. "It's important."

Burk was going to tell the kid to fuck off but there was something crazy in his ratlike eyes, a look that made him seem ready to explode.

"I gotta get back to work," Loretta finally said. "Let's talk in a couple of days."

Burk ate a taco and a big, sloppy burrito at a fast-food stand on Robertson. Loitering at a table nearby were a group of derelict teenagers who looked deeply stoned on acid. A girl wearing a purple velvet Salvation Army dress glanced at Burk and smiled. Pinned over her right breast was a button that said *If it moves, fondle it.*

The boy next to her stood up suddenly to order a strawberry shake. He wore a belt of bells and a blue shirt with the signs of the zodiac all over the front and sleeves. At the counter he did a weird little dance, tossing his head about and flailing his arms awkwardly. Suddenly he stopped and turned around, his eyes taking on a weird glow as he unsuccessfully tried to stare Burk down.

By now it was nearly four o'clock, closing in on the cocktail hour, and Burk decided he needed a drink fast. But instead of driving back to his hotel, he took Robertson north to Sunset, made a quick left, and pulled into the parking lot next to the Cock and Bull. A few spaces away, he noticed a high-breasted blonde get out of a white Corvair. She was wearing a red silk blouse and white Levi's that were so tight that Burk could see a crease between her legs. He followed her inside and watched her walk past the bar, joining actor Mike Connors in a back booth.

At the far end of the bar Aldo Ray was playing liar's dice with a pudgy man dressed in a dark suit that fit him too snugly through the chest. When Burk took a seat nearby, he overheard Aldo Ray say, "Fucker's got a hit series, and all of a sudden he's got more gash than Errol Flynn."

The pudgy man nodded, meeting Burk's eyes for a brief moment before he said, "I worked with him on *The Baron of Arizona*. We were both kids."

"Vincent Price and Ellen Drew. Who directed that?"

"Forgot. Budd Boetticher, I think. No, wait. . . ."

Burk said, "Sam Fuller."

"That's right," the pudgy man said, and Aldo Ray shot Burk a look.

"McQueen was in here yesterday," said the bartender. He was a swarthy man with shrewed eyes that were sunk deep into his face. "He was with Lee Marvin and what'sisname, his other motorcycle buddy."

"Keenan Wynn," the pudgy man said. "Talk about a guy who can put away the booze."

Aldo Ray lit a cigarette and took a quick drag. "Christ," he muttered, "I'd drink too if my old lady ran off with a fag."

Mike Connors stood up. On his way to the cigarette machine he waved to Aldo Ray and his pudgy friend. "Mike's a good guy," Aldo Ray said.

"Yeah?" The pudgy man sounded unconvinced. "If he's such a good guy, how come you're not doing a guest shot on *Mannix?*"

"Aldo don't work the small screen," said the bartender, after he poured himself a shot of Johnnie Walker Red.

"That's right. I'm a movie star," Aldo Ray said, and everyone at the bar grinned, especially those who were familiar with the notorious stag reel that he did back in the early fifties with stripper Candy Barr.

The stacked blonde sitting alone in the back booth was now staring at Aldo Ray. Her lips parted in a small, canny smile that hardened her eyes. The bartender leaned across the bar. He said, "Her name's Cherry, which obviously she isn't."

Aldo Ray nodded and ran his fingers through his short blond hair. "So much pussy, so little time," he said, his gravelly voice sounding detached while his small blue eyes caromed off the bartender and landed on Burk's face. "You an actor?"

"No," Burk said. "I'm a writer."

"That's good. Too many fuckin' actors in this town."

"And not enough good writers," the pudgy man said. "How'd you know about Fuller? You're too young to remember that flick."

"My dad knew him. He used to come by his newsstand."

"Which one is that?"

"Nate's News on Las Palmas."

"So you're Nate's kid? No kidding." Aldo Ray said, smiling for the first time. "I liked Nate. Good man. He had the only place in town that carried my hometown paper. The *Crockett Courier*. Crockett, California. Good town. Clean. Good people. The opposite of this shithole."

The door to the restaurant opened and Robert Culp walked inside with a stunning dark-haired woman hanging on his arm. She was wearing blood-red lipstick, and a red velvet jumpsuit that was at least a size too small.

Burk and the pudgy man both turned and watched the hostess seat them in a booth across from Mike Connors.

"You working on anything?" Aldo Ray asked Burk.

Burk nodded. "A movie I wrote is in production at Paramount."

Aldo Ray arched an eyebrow. "As we speak?"

"It started shooting on Monday."

"What's it called?"

"*Pledging My Love.*"

The pudgy man glanced at Burk, his face showing more interest. "The Jon Warren picture. I was supposed to read for something next week. Some kid's stepfather, I think. You wrote it, huh?" Burk smiled. "Congratulations. Maybe you could put in a good word."

"Give the kid a break," Aldo Ray said.

"I just saw you in a *Wild, Wild West*," Burk said to the pudgy man.

"Two weeks ago. I played a Russian strongman in a traveling circus."

From down the bar, Burk heard a short, humorless laugh. When he turned he saw a man hunched over his drink, one eye closed, the deep lines in his face visible in the unsteady light. "I haven't worked in a year," he said. "Twelve goddamn months since I've had a fuckin' part, and these no-talent cocksuckers waltz in here like they own the world."

The bartender took a step in the man's direction and said, "Easy, Kenny. Settle down."

"Settle down, my ass!" the man said. "Don't tell me to settle down or I'll wipe up the floor with your skinny ass." The man lit a cigarette and flipped the match into the ashtray. "What the fuck you lookin' at?" he said to Burk. "Huh?"

"Nothing," Burk said and glanced at Aldo Ray, who just shrugged.

The man dragged on his cigarette and angrily shook around the ice in his glass. Picking up the phone, the bartender said, "I'll call you a cab, Kenny."

"Okay, Petey-sweetie," the man said with an exaggerated lisp. "You call me a cab and I'll call you a train."

"Guy was a hell of an actor," Aldo Ray said, dipping his shoulder toward Burk as he lowered his voice. "You recognize him?"

"Kenny Kendall," Burk said, trying to keep his lips from moving too obviously. "I knew his daughter back in the fifties."

"PK," the pudgy man said, nodding. "She hangs out at the Melody Room. Nick Adams used to fuck her. Hell, everyone used to fuck her."

Kenny Kendall made a gun with his thumb and forefinger and pointed it at the pudgy man. "Bang, you're dead!" he said, and pulled the imaginary trigger. "Bang! Bang! Bang! You're all fuckin' dead."

After Kenny Kendall's cab arrived and Pete the bartender and a busboy helped him outside, Burk used the pay phone to call in for his messages. "Maria Selene, that's all," the hotel operator said. Burk tried her office, but Nora told him she'd left for the day.

On his way back to the bar, Burk saw Mike Connors sitting alone in his booth. On television his face had a strength that was missing in person. He winked at Burk, smiled, and quickly averted his eyes.

The blonde with the ample chest was now standing next to Aldo Ray, hugging his arm. "I told Mike I recognized you," she was saying, "but I wasn't sure, so I thought I'd come up close for a better look."

The pudgy man elbowed Burk lightly in the ribs. "They were neighbors in the same apartment building when Aldo first came to town."

"The Argyle Manor," said the blonde. "That's when you were dating Wanda and I was going with Rory Calhoun. Aldo fixed my fridge one afternoon," she said, grinning slyly as she peeked over her shoulder at Mike Connors. "One thing led to another. Right, Aldo?"

Aldo Ray nodded as he stubbed out his cigarette. He pointed at Burk. "This is Ray Burk. He's a writer."

"He's too cute to be a writer," the blonde said, squeezing Aldo Ray's arm; then she tossed her hair behind her shoulder and Burk noticed a large irregular mole beneath her left ear.

"I knew someone who lived at the Argyle Manor," Burk said. "She was from Michigan. I met her a couple of years ago."

"This was back in the early fifties," the blonde said.

"She was here then too," Burk said. "In 1949."

The blonde reached across the bar and placed her hand over Burk's wrist. "Was she your girlfriend, Ray Burk?"

"Who?"

"The girl from Michigan."

"No," Burk said, wincing when he felt her nails bite into his skin. "Just someone I knew."

Mike Connors called out the blonde's name. It sounded to Burk like Arlene. She released Burk's hand and said, "I gotta go"; then she slipped a business card into Aldo Ray's pocket. "That's my service," she said, moving away. "Call me."

Aldo Ray looked at the bartender. "I thought you said her name was Cherry."

The bartender shrugged. "That's what she called herself last week," he said. "Maybe she's got two names. Maybe that's her nickname. What do I know? I just mix drinks at this joint."

"Don't get hot," the pudgy man said.

"Her name was Bonnie Simpson," Burk said, and Aldo Ray turned and gazed at him with a confused expression.

The pudgy man said, "He's talking about someone else, Aldo."

"The day I met her it was hot and muggy. She was wearing a camel's hair blazer and lilac perfume. On her feet were brown penny loafers with soles that were worn thin. I think about her constantly."

"The writer's telling us a story," the pudgy man said.

"No. This really happened," Burk said slowly, as if he was having an inner dialogue with himself. "This is someone real. There was a picture of her in the paper."

Aldo Ray and the pudgy man exchanged a silent glance. The bartender untied his apron, and a new man came on duty. He was older, in his mid-sixties, with serious eyes and thinning gray hair.

"Bonnie Simpson." Aldo Ray said her name and shook his head from side to side.

"I think about her constantly," Burk said once more. "She had all these delicate lines in her face, and when I first saw her I could feel my body needing her hands, my skin needing to feel her touch."

Aldo Ray said, "That name mean anything to you, Mel?"

The bartender said, "What's that?"

"Bonnie Simpson."

The bartender slowly turned back the cuffs of his shirt and checked his watch against the clock on the counter behind him. "No," he said. "No. I can't say it does."

Burk said, "Her mother was an actress. Her name was Grace."

"I had an agent named Grace," said the pudgy man. "Grace Foster. Worked for Harry Gold."

The bartender poured himself an inch of scotch and chewed his lips while he tugged his shirt away from his belt. "Grace Simpson. No. Don't ring a bell."

"Elliot. Grace Elliot," Burk said, his eyes fixed on Aldo Ray's face in the mirror behind the bar. "She was from Buchanan, Michigan. She liked to wear the color yellow, and butterscotch was her favorite flavor. Elliot was her maiden name."

The pudgy man said, "We get the picture, but what's the point?" And from somewhere in the shadows behind him, Burk heard Robert Culp say, "We leave now we can be in Vegas in six hours. Tell me yes and I'll get us a suite at the Sands."

"She's dead," Burk said, standing up to pay his tab. "She died in a fire. She burned to death."

★

It was close to 10 P.M. when Burk arrived back at the Beverly Hills Hotel. There were four pink phone message slips waiting for him at the front desk, and he sorted through them quickly as he crossed the lobby, pausing briefly when he noticed Warren Beatty leave the Polo Lounge arm in arm with his latest girlfriend, the beautiful British actress Julie Christie. They were Hollywood's newest golden couple and Burk slowed his step to bask in their starlight, letting Beatty pass by so close their shoulders nearly touched.

Just before he stepped inside the elevator Burk caught a glimpse of Eddie Bascom. Now dressed in street clothes—a pink rayon shirt and flared cranberry slacks—Eddie was walking down the stairs from the mezzanine with his bellman uniform slung over his shoulder on a wooden hanger. With him was Gus Tolos, the bartender from three to midnight in the Polo Lounge and, according to many sportswriters, the best schoolboy athlete in the history of Los Angeles.

As the elevator closed and ascended to the third floor, Burk recalled the afternoon he first heard the name Gus Tolos. It was in the spring of 1958. Gus was only a sophomore, but he led Hollywood High School to the city basketball championship, scoring forty-six points in the title game.

"The next morning the *LA Times* called me the Golden Greek," Gus told Burk late one afternoon after most of the lunch crowd had emptied out of the Polo Lounge. "But to the chicks down at State Beach that summer I was Gus God. Now look what I'm doin'." He glanced down the bar. "You wanna know what happened?"

"What?"

"I became a drunk. A falling-down, tongue-chewing drunk. For ten years I lived on skid row. But not anymore," he said. "I beat it. In July I'll be sober one year."

Burk said, "That's terrific. Congratulations."

Gus shook his head. "No. Don't congratulate me. I had nothin' to do with it. God just showed me the light, and I've been walkin' toward it ever since."

In the short silence that followed, Burk's mind was tugged back to the winter of 1969, when Sandra attended her one and only Alcoholics Anonymous meeting.

Burk dropped her off at a clubhouse on Ohio Street, just east of Sepulveda, but when he came back an hour later she had disappeared. Around midnight he found her outside the King's Head, a rowdy Scottish pub on Broadway and Third, in Santa Monica. Her hands were cuffed behind her back and two cops were loading her into the back of a patrol car.

"She threw a beer stein at the bartender," said one of the cops when Burk identified himself as Sandra's husband. "He told her she was too drunk to play darts and she freaked out. Almost tore the guy's head off."

"Shit like this happen often?" the other cop asked Burk.

Burk laughed softly at this question but did not reply. Then he glanced at Sandra, and with a casual shrug he said, "Sometimes it does."

Burk dialed room service and ordered up a Caesar salad and a Bloody Mary; then he flicked on the TV and called Loretta three times in the space of an hour, hanging up at once each time her service picked up. Around midnight he dialed the Carousel Escort Service and requested that a light-skinned black woman be sent up to his room.

"Tall or short? Any preference?" he was asked by a woman with a deep, resonant voice.

"Over five feet."

"Esmeralda is available. She's from the island of Jamaica."

"Is she pretty?"

"As a sunset over Montego Bay."

"I'll be waiting."

"Room number, please?"

"Three-one-seven."

"It's now twelve-oh-six. She will be at your door in twenty minutes."

Under the shirts in his dresser, Burk found a green-tinted vial that was half filled with cocaine. He dumped the contents on the glass covering his bedstand and chopped out several thick lines, using the laminated edge of his Writer's Guild card. He tooted three right away, planning to save the rest for Esmeralda, but five minutes later, when Loretta called, he said, "One sec," put the receiver underneath the pillow, and inhaled the rest.

"Do you have company?" she asked Burk when he came back on the line.

"What do you mean?"

"Like, is there someone in your room, Ray? If there is, just tell me and I'll hang up."

"There is no one here, Loretta."

"We're not exclusive, Ray. You can fuck anyone you want, not that you need my permission. I assume you haven't been faithful,"

Loretta said, trying to sound indifferent, and Burk took a breath to avoid a quick response. "I know I said we should take a break, but now I wonder what difference it would make. We're not in love. Why keep up the charade?"

"We don't have to," Burk said, the cocaine giving his voice a confident edge; but in another part of his mind he could hear the hollowness of his words, and he knew he would be sorry for them later on, around 4 A.M., after he'd fucked Esmeralda and she'd left with his three hundred dollars, when his heart was throbbing with fear and he was pacing back and forth across the room, pulling at his dick, talking to himself, making up movie ideas and wise and funny things to say to Loretta when he called her back to apologize early the next morning.

Into this uneasy silence Loretta said, "We can still be friends."

There was another long pause, and this time the silence was so deep that Burk thought Loretta had disconnected. When, finally, he heard her breathing into the phone, he said, "Fuck friends. I don't want you as a friend. I want . . ."

"What do you want, Ray? Tell me."

Burk shook his head. The coke was wearing off fast. He began to feel panicky, out of control. "I want—" he started, then stopped.

"What? Jesus, Ray. *What?*"

★

Nine

Wednesday: The Weather Changes AND Burk Drives Back to the Argyle Manor

May 19, 1971

When he awoke on Wednesday morning, Burk was puzzled to see a dead gray sky hanging over the city like a soiled sheet. And, except for a brief period in the late afternoon on Thursday, when a thin blue stripe appeared on the rim of the horizon, the sky would remain utterly unwelcome and empty of light for the next three days, clearing finally on Saturday morning, just an hour before Louie's plane arrived at the airport.

As soon as he ordered a pot of coffee from room service, Burk sat up carefully and leaned back against the pillow propped up behind him, listening alternately to the pounding inside his head and the phone ringing in the room next door. He closed his eyes, keeping them closed until the ringing stopped, the angry sound replaced by running water and Tom Crumpler's high off-key voice singing Dylan's "Don't Think Twice."

Involuntarily, Burk found his mouth being shaped into a smile. He was thinking back to that weekend in 1964 when he and Sandra saw Dylan in Minneapolis. On the drive up she took Burk by surprise, saying, "I'm your girlfriend now. Okay? Is that what you want?" Burk said yes, and later that night, before they made love for the first time, while he held her in his arms, he said, "I never in a million years thought I could be with someone as pretty as you."

And Burk remembered Sandra rising up on her elbow and staring down at his face. "You're a cool guy," she said, the light from the television flickering over her breasts. "You know that, Ray? You really are."

Burk recalled how frightened he was of the new feelings of tenderness that surged inside him.

"What's wrong?" Sandra asked him, when she felt his body stiffen and his face turn inward.

"Nothing," Burk said. "I'm just crazy about you and . . ."

"And . . . what?"

"And I'm scared."

"Of what?"

Burk said nothing for a few moments. Then his words came out in a rush: "Scared you'll leave me. Scared you'll never love me as much as I love you."

The humidity had increased, dampening Burk's neck and back as he drove past the Paramount lot and turned left on Bronson. He continued north to Sunset and turned right. At Western Avenue he turned left again, and two long blocks later he pulled up to a stoplight on Hollywood Boulevard. Next to him was a 1960 Buick Riviera driven by a thin black man with a hawk face and iron-gray hair and sideburns. A hand-lettered sign on the driver's side door said I LOVE A WHITE WOMAN.

It was four in the afternoon and Burk had been driving since noon, circling the same twenty blocks, using the wipers intermittently to sweep away the mist that settled on the glass. He stopped only once, around two-thirty, to purchase some gas and make a collect phone call.

"I'm driving again," he'd told Timmy Miller. He was calling him from the Chevron station on Beverly and Normandie, one block from where he'd first encountered Bonnie Simpson two years earlier. "And I'm really freaked."

"I know. I can hear it in your voice."

"Yeah? You can?"

"You sound weird, Ray."

"I feel weird," Burk said, staring across the street at the Hollywood Hacienda Motel. The only car in the parking lot was a mud-splattered white '66 Chrysler with Oklahoma plates. "Like I could do something out of control."

"Maybe you should come back up."

"I can't. I'm going out to see Sandra on Sunday. That's why I called. I want you to put Louie on a plane Saturday morning." There was a pause, and Burk caught himself staring at a woman standing in the motel parking lot. She had thick legs and a hard-looking face. A lean, muscular man stood in the doorway of one of the rooms, speaking to the woman with his arms folded over his naked chest.

Finally Timmy said, "You think that's a good idea?"

"What?"

"Louie comin' down."

"He wants to see his mom. It's been a long time," Burk said. "I gotta go. Leave a message with the flight number at the hotel. Tell Louie I love him."

Burk dropped the phone into the cradle, but he remained in the booth with his hand on the receiver while the fat woman crossed the street. As she angled toward him he could see the flesh jiggle on her thighs and the smirking grin on her doughy face. "Ten bucks for a blow job. Fucking Okie can suck his own dick," she sneered under her breath, her bleary eyes raking Burk up and down as she lurched up the sidewalk.

The stoplight turned green on Hollywood Boulevard and Burk drove north to Yucca and turned left. At the corner of Argyle and Franklin he found a parking space behind a U-Haul that was filled with furniture.

An old man in a wrinkled black suit was maneuvering a shopping cart up the sidewalk, groaning with each step. On his head was an oversized fedora that nearly covered his ears. As he shuffled by the Mustang, he gave Burk a false smile and Burk smiled back, noticing for the first time the small wooden sign that was stuck in the ice plant in front of the Argyle Manor. It said APARTMENTS FOR RENT— 1 AND 2 BEDROOMS.

Burk lit a cigarette and looked off, down the street. He wondered what the chances were that Bonnie's old apartment was available. He thought, if it was, it might be a neat place to hide out, to be alone with his thoughts; not a place to eat or sleep, he'd still use the hotel for that, but a place where he could read or maybe try to begin a new project, a secret place.

The more he thought about this idea the more he could feel something move inside him, a building need to be inside that room, to have his name taped over the mail slot downstairs.

The gray light outside was growing dimmer and Burk started to feel drowsy. In his half-sleep a memory returned, bringing with it a feeling of helplessness.

> Bonnie is standing at the door of her apartment on the morning she left, her face tilted to one side. Outside, the sun is climbing ominously over the neighboring rooftops. "Don't worry, Ray," she says, in a voice that is strong and confident. "I'm not going far. I'll be back. I promise."

The building's owner was a tall, very lean woman in her seventies. Her large eyes were dark and beautiful, and she was wearing a long black evening dress that grazed the top of her black suede pumps. She said her name was Lillian Ohrtman.

"I'm staying here temporarily, until I find a new manager," she told Burk outside the half-open door to her apartment. "Norman Swain, my former manager, died last Saturday of cirrhosis of the liver and other complications due to alcoholism. What kind of work do you do, Mr. . . . ?"

"Burk. I'm a writer."

"How delightful. Books? Plays? Films?"

"Films."

"My second husband was a film writer. Perhaps you may have heard of him. His name was Lionel Lewis."

"Wasn't he blacklisted?"

"Yes, he was," she said, ignoring the phone that started to ring in her living room. "Are you interested in renting an apartment, Mr. Burk?"

Burk felt his body tense. "Is nine available?"

The phone rang for a third time before a man picked up and said hello. Lillian Ohrtman said, "Have you lived here before?"

Burk shook his head, but his eyes moved up to the second floor. "No. But someone I knew once did."

A young man with wet lips and dark floppy bangs came to the door. He was dressed in a black tuxedo with a maroon cummerbund. "That was Drew," he said in a cold voice. "I told him we would pick him up in twenty minutes."

"This is my son, Mark," Lillian Ohrtman said to Burk, but neither man stuck out his hand. "We're on our way to the Hollywood Bowl. André Previn is conducting a program of Broadway show tunes. But first we're going to have a picnic on the grass with Mark's friend Drew."

"He's my lover, not my friend," Mark said with exaggerated dignity. "Why do you refer to him as my friend? You know I hate that."

"Well, then, he's *my* friend," she said with a little laugh, but still keeping her eyes on Burk. "Last week Drew and Mark and I saw Harry Belafonte at the Greek Theatre. We had a lovely time. The night was so clear we could count all the stars in the sky. I despise weather like this," she said, frowning. "Don't you, Mr. Burk?"

"It's okay once in awhile. For a change."

Mark rolled his eyes. "Oh, Mother, will you stop? He doesn't want to talk about the stupid weather. He wants to rent an apartment." He turned and walked back inside, leaving Burk and Lillian Ohrtman alone on the front steps.

In the window of the apartment next door Burk could see a woman dressed in a white bathrobe. Pink rollers were in her hair, and the stub end of an unfiltered cigarette dangled from her lower lip as she pushed a vacuum across the rug. When she caught Burk staring at her, she stopped and looked back at him with her hands on her hips.

Burk dropped his eyes and Lillian Ohrtman said, "Once, in the summer of 1931, when I was living in Venice, there were forty-two straight days of overcast skies. Roger Armstrong, my first husband and Mark's father, ran a ride at the pier. Of course, the attendance was way down and we almost starved. I was studying painting at UCLA, but I had to quit and become a saleslady at the May Company. I was terrible at selling, and ultimately I was fired. Things became so desperate that I entered one of those dance marathons. A movie was finally made about those contests."

"*They Shoot Horses, Don't They?*"

"Yes. That's it. A wonderful film," Lillian Ohrtman said, the color rising in her cheeks. "The Fonda girl was superb and so was Gig

Young. What a ladies' man he was! For a short time he went out with an actress friend of mine. Her name was Lucille Vickers. Metro had her under contract until she was blinded by a klieg light during *Apache Warpath,* her first film. A terrible accident."

Mark reappeared on the front steps. He was holding a full-length mink coat and a small black purse. After he slipped the coat over his mother's shoulders, she said, "Number nine is vacant. If you would like to rent it, it will be two hundred and fifty dollars per month, plus a fifty-dollar security deposit."

Once more, Burk glanced at the apartment next door. The woman in the white bathrobe was gone, but a small lapdog was standing on the back of the couch with his paws moving up and down on the window, scratching the glass. "Can I write you a check?" Burk asked.

"Can't this wait until morning?" Mark said, his breath smelling of rum as he swung his face toward Burk. "I told Drew to be waiting in front of his apartment. He'll be freezing cold."

Lillian Ohrtman opened her purse and took out a ring of keys. She slipped off one key and took hold of Burk's arm and moved him toward the sidewalk. "We're going to hear songs from *Showboat,*" she said, pressing the key into his palm. "And *Oklahoma* and *Porgy and Bess.* We're going to have a glorious evening." Lillian Ohrtman turned and smiled at her son. "Well, my boy, are you coming or not?"

"Are we bringing him too?"

"No, of course not," she said, and to Burk she said, "Spend the night if you like. The apartment is clean, and there are fresh linens in the closet."

They shook hands and Burk said, "I'll give you a check tomorrow. Is that all right?"

"It certainly is."

Bonnie's apartment was just as small and dingy as Burk remembered. The only changes were in the kitchen, where a new refrigerator hummed softly and the faded yellow walls were now covered with wallpaper that was vertically patterned with pink and yellow roses. Next to the sink was a jar of instant coffee and a painted ceramic cup with ducks parading around the circumference.

As he waited for the water to boil, Burk stripped off his clothes and began to masturbate standing up in the center of the living room. Exciting himself was difficult in this joyless atmosphere, and as he rocked back and forth, jerking himself violently, his elbow caught the lamp next to the window, toppling it to the floor. The bulb shattered, sending shards of glass across the room, and seconds later, when he came, a cat began to meow on the landing outside his door.

Burk used the soles of his feet to rub his semen into the rug; then he carefully swept up the glass with a whisk broom he found underneath the sink. For the next few minutes he lingered in the kitchen over his coffee, listening to a radio that was playing in a distant apartment. The song, "Back in My Arms Again" by the Supremes, was one of those tunes Burk and Sandra had heard over and over on their trip across the country in 1964.

Burk shook his head to erase Sandra's face from his mind. Then he looked back into the living room and saw his bunched-up clothes sitting in a pile. Marlboro cigarettes from a pack in his shirt had spilled on the floor, and the blue-striped tip of one sneaker was peeking out from underneath the couch.

Two years earlier, on the day they met, Bonnie was standing where he was now, leaning back against the kitchen counter with her blouse open, grinning slyly, a breast balanced in each hand while Burk sucked on the hardening nipples.

"Tell me about my tits," she asked him.

"They're great."

"Great? That's very descriptive. Are you sure you're a writer?"

"They're full and soft and—"

"Bigger than you expected."

"As a matter of fact, they are."

"Everyone tells me that."

"Everyone."

"Guys."

"Guys you've fucked."

Bonnie looked down and smiled. "If they saw my tits, yes, I probably let them fuck me. Are you jealous?" By now Burk was on his knees. Bonnie's skirt and panties were down and his tongue was between her legs. "Wait," Bonnie said, her body sinking slowly to the floor. "You don't have to answer that right this second."

In her bedroom later, Burk told Bonnie the truth when she'd asked him if he'd ever cheated on his wife. "Well, you have now," she said, and laughed loudly. "Freddie cheated on me all the time. But cheating is the wrong word, because he didn't hide it. More than once

I came home and caught him giving it to some tramp he'd picked up. In our bed, no less."

Burk said, "I'm surprised you didn't kill him."

"If I'd loved him I might have."

Daylight had vanished by the time Burk finished putting on his clothes. For several minutes he sat tense and alert on the couch, chain smoking Marlboros in the dark, listening to the clanging of pots and pans in the apartment below. From the same apartment he heard a woman sobbing loudly, a desperate sound that was followed by the howl of a dog.

Burk put out his cigarette and moved to the window. Outside, the leaves were darker than the sky, and down below, on Argyle, a boy of ten or eleven was bouncing a tennis ball underneath a street-lamp. His light-colored hair and his faded, ill-fitting clothes reminded Burk of Ricky Furlong and those late summer nights when they played ball in the street in front of their houses.

"How come Gene never plays ball with us anymore?" Ricky asked Burk one evening.

"He's older. He's got other things to do."

"Is he mad 'cause I'm better than he is?"

"You're not that much better."

"Yes, I am."

"No, you're not."

But it was true: Ricky was the best. At twelve he could already throw a fastball so hard that Burk would feel the sting in his palm all through the following day.

In time the boy on the street was approached by a large, ungainly woman wearing a gray sweater and shapeless gray trousers. She carried two shopping bags under her arms and looked out of breath. They stood close for awhile, chatting, the boy staring down at his feet. Then the woman abruptly turned and looked up at Burk with a scolding smile.

Burk took a step backward and the phone rang, taking him by surprise. In the shock of the moment he picked up the handset. "Hello?"

"Steve?" A man's voice, thick and tentative.

"I'm sorry," Burk said, "Steve doesn't live here."

"Where is he?"

"I don't know."

Burk heard a disappointed sound. "Is this Duke?"

"No."

"I need to get a message to Steve. Or Duke. Either one. It's important."

Burk said, "I can't help you."

"Listen, schmuck," the man said, his voice flaring with anger, "don't fuck with me."

Burk counted to five, silently; then he said, "Steve moved."

"Okay, I get it," the man rasped. "He moved in with Duke, right? And that broad from Tulsa. What's her name? Wanda or Ruby or something. Not Tulsa, Lubbock. Piece of truck-stop trash from the Panhandle. Fingering her was like putting your hand in a horse's mouth. Goddamn Lake Erie between her legs."

"I gotta get off," Burk said, and he heard the man moan softly. "If I see Steve, who should I say called?"

"Tony," the man said in a half whisper. "Tell him Tony. He can find me at the Spotlight Bar, on the corner of Selma and Cahuenga. Tell him to bring Wanda and her wet pussy."

Burk hung up the phone, took a deep breath, and let it out slowly. Sweat trickled down his ribs, and his insides were wrenched into a knot. He quickly lit another cigarette and kept the match burning while he checked his watch: 9:26. On what day? Tuesday? Wednesday? Thursday? Wednesday, that's right. Louie arrives on Saturday. And Sunday night they will be on a plane back to Berkeley together. Home. Fuck this place. I'm gone.

The phone rang again and Burk seized the receiver, saying, "Listen to me, Tony! Okay? I just rented this apartment and the phone was left on by mistake. I don't know Steve or Duke or this slut from Lubbock. I don't know you or anyone else from the neighborhood. I drive, Tony. That's what I do. And I rarely talk to people. Are you listening to me, Tony? Huh?"

There was a long, intense silence on the other end of the line. Then, in a concerned voice, Lillian Ohrtman said, "Are you all right, Mr. Burk?"

"Mrs. Ohrtman?"

"Yes, it's me," she said, her voice rising over the applause building in the background. "I'm at the Bowl, in the manager's office. I was worried. I'd forgotten that the electricity was off. I didn't want you sitting in the dark. Is that what you've been doing?"

"Part of the time, yes."

"There are some candles in the cupboard over the sink. On the left."

"I was just on my way out," Burk said.

"Oh, you're not," Lillian Ohrtman said, sounding disappointed as the orchestra began to play "Everything's Coming Up Roses," Ethel Merman's show-stopping number from the Broadway show *Gypsy*. "Are you all right?" she asked once more.

Burk stood up. The phone cord was wrapped around his foot, and he kicked it away. "I don't know," he said weakly. For an instant, in the air around his face, he could smell the unmistakable odor of Bonnie's perfume and the minty taste of her breath.

"If it gets too chilly, there's an extra blanket in the closet next to the bathroom."

"I can't spend the night."

"Where would you go?"

"I have a place."

There was a brief silence, then Lillian Ohrtman said, "Mary Martin performed tonight, as a surprise guest. She sang, 'I Won't Ever Grow Up' from *Peter Pan*. I thought Mark and Drew were going to die."

Burk said, "Someone named Tony called for a Steve somebody."

"Pay no attention."

"But—"

"Steve Caudabeck did not pay his rent," Lillian Ohrtman said in a clipped voice. "That's why he was evicted, plain and simple. If Norman Swain was not so ill he would've been gone weeks ago. I'm sorry, Mr. Burk, but I have no sympathy for deadbeats."

"I'll pay my rent," Burk said defensively.

"Of course you will," she assured him. "You're a fine young man. Writers are wonderful tenants."

"But I won't be here all the time."

"That's up to you. Now I must get back to my seat," she said, in a more genial tone. "Mark will be concerned. I just wanted to make sure you were all right."

"I'm fine."

Not long after Lillian Ohrtman clicked off, Burk heard a car door slam, followed closely by the sound of footsteps moving swiftly up the stairway to the second floor. A woman's shadow passed by the curtains and Burk whispered Bonnie's name, forgetting for the briefest of moments that she was no longer alive.

Three police cars were parked in front of the Beverly Hills Hotel when Burk drove up at 2 A.M. "Crumpler was arrested. He beat the shit out of the room service waiter," Eddie Bascom told Burk as they rode up together on the elevator. Eddie's eyes blinked rapidly as he spoke, and he nervously began to clench and unclench his fist.

"Was he hurt bad?"

"The homo? Crumpler fractured his cheekbone," Eddie said, looking pleased. "The story's all over town. It made the eleven o'clock news but they botched it. It's gonna be the lead in Joyce Haber's column on Friday. She'll get it right," he said, winking, an admission that his job at the hotel included selling gossip as well as cocaine. The elevator opened and Burk stepped into the hallway. "Ciao, baby."

Burk examined the phone message slips he was holding. Maria Selene had called three times, at 4:35 P.M. and twice between eleven and eleven-thirty, when, Burk guessed, she'd heard about Crumpler's arrest. There was also a message from Timmy, with Louie's flight information, and one from Gene. None from Loretta.

As he approached Crumpler's room, Burk heard a voice say, "We can't do anything about the assault. That's a done deal. The fag's already filed charges. The rest of the stuff can be finessed."

Crumpler's door was cracked a few inches, and Burk could see Jerome Sanford leaning against the fireplace. His beefy face sagged with fatigue, but even at this late hour he was dressed immaculately, in a style that some young executives at Paramount had begun to imitate: gray flannel slacks and a dark blue blazer worn over a light or dark blue polo shirt left unbuttoned at the throat. The edge of the bed hid the lower part of his legs, but Burk assumed that his sockless feet were snug inside his brown suede moccasins.

Burk had met Sanford only once, for drinks at Musso & Frank a few days after Paramount purchased his screenplay. That evening Sanford wore khakis and a light pink button-down shirt with the cuffs folded above his elbows. He ordered back-to-back extra-dry martinis, straight up, and with a low, intense voice he confided to Burk that he'd recently separated from his second wife, Ruthie Galan, a young actress who was a regular on *Eden Valley,* a nighttime soap that was NBC's answer to *Peyton Place.*

"Tight pussy but a room temperature IQ," he had said, winning from Burk a slightly embarrassed laugh. "Right now I'm staying with my first wife, or more correctly in her guest cottage, where my daughter generally stays when she isn't spreading her legs for whatever rock-and-roll band she's chasing around the country." Sanford mumbled something inaudible and shook his head. "I'm not usually this crude," he said apologetically. "I'm sorry."

Burk said, "She's a teenager. She's rebelling. It's a phase."

"No," Sanford said, stabbing an anchovy in his Caesar salad. "No. I wish that were true. She's a slut."

They each had three more martinis before Maria arrived, as planned, for dessert. By then the discussion had switched back to Burk's script, which Sanford drunkenly described as a "goddamn brilliant piece of work."

A man with his back to Burk was sitting on Crumpler's unmade bed. He and Sanford were listening to another man, who was standing behind the door, out of Burk's vision. He said, "Look, the last thing we want to do is make it hard for the studio. As far as we're concerned it was a simple assault. Crumpler thought the kid was making a pass and he belted him."

Sanford said, "So what you're saying is we can work together on the drugs business."

"Absolutely," said the man behind the door, keeping his eyes on Sanford as he moved into the center of the room. He was short and blond, around forty, and his shirt and coat were pulled tight against his broad chest. His Scandinavian face was both serious and serene. "We don't make promises we can't keep."

"Give me a figure," the man on the bed said, as he produced a large vial of cocaine and flipped it into the air. His partner reached out and let the bottle fall into the palm of his hand. "Say, five big ones."

"Sounds good to me."

"Two and a half each. That work for you, Jerome?"

Sanford nodded his head, his face showing no expression as he reached for his wallet. "Yes," he said. "I think that works fine."

* * *

At some point before he went to sleep, Burk switched on the radio. The news ended, and Ray Moore took a call from John Beal. He told Radio Ray he was working the graveyard shift at the Norm's on Vermont and Sunset. "I'm bussin' tables and washin' dishes, but I plan to be workin' on the grill by Christmas. They seen my résumé," he said. "Two years at Chloe's in Omaha. Three at Shoney's in Stillwater. Another eighteen months at the Stuckey's on the Ohio Turnpike. I can cook some food, Ray. You can count on that."

Radio Ray said, "I bet you make a dandy club sandwich."

"If the turkey's fresh I do."

"At home I use fresh tomatoes from my garden."

"Only way, Radio Ray."

"You miss Omaha, John Beal?"

"I miss the sky."

Burk tuned out the next caller, a cabbie named Fred who told a series of idiotic jokes involving women and fish. The caller after him, a man with a voice full of pain, spoke only three words, "Love the doomed."

Following a Chevy commercial, a woman who chose to remain anonymous called in to complain about her husband. "I got varicose veins and he says my legs are unsightly. What can I do? He knew I wasn't Betty Grable when he married me, for cryin' out loud. I mean, come on, he ain't no Cesar Romero himself. He's only five foot four," she said, keeping her voice low. "Just a little bitty man with a potbelly and a wrinkled butt. Sometimes it's hard for me to keep a straight face while he's undressin'. But, hell, I love him, so I try to make the best of it."

Burk listened to Radio Ray take two more calls, the last from a man named Ted who said he'd been drinking nonstop for three days. "Seventy-two hours straight. I need help," he said, pleading. "If I don't stop I'll crumble up and die."

Radio Ray said, "The best I can do is give you the number of Alcoholics Anonymous."

"Oh, really," Ted said dubiously. "Is that the *best* you can do? I need compassion, someone to care about me."

"I care about you, Ted."

"No, you don't. If you did, you'd offer to come over and be with me, to put a damp washcloth on my forehead and tell me everything's going to be all right."

"You sure you've been drinking?" Radio Ray said.

"Why would I lie?"

"You don't sound drunk."

"Did I say I was drunk? *No,* stupid. I said I've been drinking. Four quarts of Scotch and a case of beer in three days. I've been coughing up blood for a week."

Radio Ray said, "I think Alcoholics Anonymous is the place for you, Ted."

Ted suddenly lost his temper. "I am not an alcoholic! Don't call me that name! Forget about me! Butt out! I don't need your help. My neighbor will help me," he assured Radio Ray. "Mrs. Otis. Mrs. Candace Otis will care for me."

"That's great, Ted," said Radio Ray, surprised by the sarcasm he heard in his voice. "Let us know how things work out."

"We'll drink rye whiskey and watch the fish swim in the fish tank. When it gets light outside, she'll make flapjacks, and I'll run back to my place for the pure maple syrup my son sent me from Massachusetts last Christmas. Yessir, we'll have a fine old time. After breakfast we'll drink some more and I'll end up napping on her couch. If I'm lucky I'll wake up."

"I'd think about AA."

"You think about it, Ray. I'm gonna get drunk."

★

May 20, 1971

Burk switched off the car radio and turned north on Kenmore. At Clinton he slowly pulled around a mangy dog that was lying in the center of the street. One paw dangled helplessly in the air, and blood was caked around a wound in his neck. A boy of six or seven sat dry-eyed on the curb. His elbows rested on his knees and his face was supported by the heels of his hands.

Burk lowered his window. "Is that your dog?" he asked, and the boy looked up at him. Lank dirty-blond hair fell over his ears and dull glassy eyes peered out of a face that was the color of the street. "Is it?" The boy nodded. "Don't you think you should move him?" The boy shook his head. "Why?"

"My mom said not to touch him," the boy said and looked away.

"Yeah, that's probably a good idea," Burk agreed. He told the boy that he had a son his age.

"Does he have a dog?"

"He had one, but he got lost."

"My dog's dead," the boy said, pointing to the dog in the street.

A thin haggard-looking woman with dyed red hair came around the side of a narrow apartment building. Following her was an elderly black man carrying a shovel and a green garbage bag.

"Lester's gonna take care of Fellow," the woman said to the boy.

The black man nodded. "Gonna dig him a nice grave. Yes I am."

"Fellow? Was that your dog's name?" Burk asked the boy.

The boy remained silent for a few moments, licking his lips. "No. His name was Goodfellow," he said, giving this information in a toneless, almost dead voice. "We called him Fellow for short."

The black man moved into the street and poked the dead animal with his shovel. "Yep, he's gone," he said.

"Who're you?" the woman said to Burk. "How come you're double-parked here talkin' to my son?"

"I saw the dog in the street and stopped. I thought I could help," Burk said.

"I told you not to talk to strangers," the woman said to the boy, kicking him lightly in the hip with the toe of her sandal. "You don't know who this person is."

The boy stood up and dusted off his pants. Ketchup and mustard stains covered the front of his T-shirt, and his filthy socks were bunched around his ankles. "I'm going inside to watch *Speed Racer*," he said.

The woman took a step forward and measured Burk with her eyes. "You mind your own business," she said, looking down at him. "You understand? Now get outa here."

Burk continued driving: Hobart, Van Ness, Mariposa, Vermont, back up to Hollywood Boulevard and moving west; he turned left on Cummings and double-parked in front of a nondescript apartment built around a courtyard that was filled with cast-off furniture and other debris. A woman dressed in a nightgown and slippers was standing on her doorstep, brushing her hair.

In the late 1940s, Hollywood tough guys Tom Neal and Steve Cochran shared a flat at this address. Tim Holt lived next door until *The Treasure of the Sierra Madre* was released in 1948. All three, Miles had told Burk, were regulars at Ernie's Stardust Lounge.

Bronson. El Centro. Gower. Ivar. Argyle. Vine. Crossing Sunset and Vine always gave Burk a rush of energy. The Greyhound station stood one block south, and he parked in front to watch the new arrivals, mostly young people in their teens, runaways, their faces not quite so fresh and hopeful as they were in '67, during the Summer of Love, when they came to San Francisco and Hollywood in droves from cities all over the U.S. By 1969 that twinkle in their eyes was fading. By 1971 it was gone. Their faces were hard now, unyielding, their shoulders slumped from the bedrolls on their backs.

Lexington. De Longpre. Leland Way. Back down to Sunset and east again. At Serrano, Burk stopped at the Von's market for a tin of sardines. In the checkout line he stood behind a dark-skinned woman carrying a straw purse. She said her name was Nadia, that she was newly divorced. Burk took her back to the Argyle Manor. On the way up the stairs she tripped, skinning her knee.

They ate sardines on Triscuits and drank dark beer from Mexico. "You have sad eyes," she told Burk when she was straddling him.

"I *am* sad."

"I can make you happy."

Burk said they had to leave soon. When she asked him why, he said, "I have to drive."

In the deepest part of himself, where his own private wisdom burned the brightest, Burk recognized that his compulsive need to drive (and whatever he was searching for in the hot stillness of the street) was entwined somehow with the impossible feeling of loss he woke to each day. And he knew also that all the women he had loved the most had turned away from him and deepened that awful emptiness.

Except for Bonnie Simpson.

Yes, Bonnie had left him in the sleepy comfort of her room in the Argyle Manor back in December of 1969, but she had meant to return; Burk knew that for certain and was bleakly reassured by the knowledge. Still, two years later, the mysterious and sacred joy that he felt during the brief time they spent together was unexplainable to him, one more piece of the strange puzzle that had become his life.

But as he drove through East Hollywood and scanned the faces on the street, a thought came forth that quickened his heartbeat and rocked his mind: Maybe he had been looking for Bonnie all along— and miraculously he had found her. Maybe out of some strange shapeless chain of events that was his life and hers—and the lives of all the desperate and brokenhearted people that the sun outlined each day outside his windshield, their spirits crushed, their footsteps following their narrow shadows—they were destined to have one moment, one single day, where he got to see her laughter light up her eyes and feel the strange magic in her body when they came together in the afternoon light.

For the next few blocks Burk felt a surge of happiness as he recalled Bonnie's smiling face, and he felt himself smiling, too, as he searched out his eyes in the rearview mirror. In time, Bonnie's face disappeared and another face came alive in his mind, surprising him as it broke through the layers of time: the gentle, painfully serious face of Laurel Adams.

★

With Laurel in the desert that first time in 1959, when her clothes came off and he was moving inside her in the backseat of Timmy Miller's car, Burk felt it was all right to say that he loved her. And Laurel said she felt the same way. "But I can't say the words. Not yet," she told Burk. "But I will."

Incredibly, Burk never spoke to Laurel again once they left Palm Springs at the end of spring break. Whenever he called her house, her mother said she was either in the shower or over at a friend's. Once her younger sister picked up and claimed Laurel was at the library, studying for a test.

"What time will she be home?" Burk asked her.

"I don't know," her sister said, in an oddly detached voice that almost seemed rehearsed. "But I'll tell her you called."

For three weeks Burk waited for Laurel to return his call, but she never did. On the night of his seventeenth birthday he got drunk and foolishly dialed her number from a pay phone outside Stan's Drive-In in Hollywood. It was after midnight and her father was audibly enraged when he found out who was on the line. He told Burk that Laurel was going steady with another boy and not to call their house anymore.

"No. That's bullshit. You're wrong," Burk said, shouting over the traffic that swished by on the street. "She loves me."

Later that week Burk received a postcard from Laurel. On the front was a picture of the motel where they met. On the back she wrote:

I have a boyfriend, Ray. I lied to you. I'm sorry.
Please don't hate me. And don't call me anymore.
Thanks,
Laurel

The following Monday, Burk cut all his classes and took the Santa Ana Freeway south to Orange County. Laurel lived a few miles from Disneyland, in the city of Buena Park, and by eleven o'clock that morning Burk was parked in the students' lot behind her high school. He sat listening to rock and roll on KRLA until the lunch buzzer sounded. Then, after a quick walk around the block to calm his nerves, he entered the campus through an open gate and boldly followed a stream of students into the cafeteria.

He recognized Laurel's flirtatious laugh before he saw her at a table sitting next to a boy dressed sharply in pressed Levi's and a blue button-down shirt. In a moment they were joined by a pack of happy-sounding kids—jocks and student government types—the same elite social crowd that ran Burk's high school and every other high school in Southern California.

Burk went through the food line and found a seat at a table that was not quite in Laurel's line of sight. As he secretly watched her and her boyfriend holding hands and cracking jokes, he felt his face burn and twitch and his mouth curl into an angry grimace. For half a minute he cursed her under his breath, ignoring a fat sulky girl who took a seat across from him, blocking his view. When he stood up to leave, Laurel turned her head and Burk was certain that she saw him drop his serving tray in the rack by the door and walk outside.

Burk wept all the way back to Los Angeles, and it was close to four when he pulled off the freeway on Vine and circled the quiet streets of East Hollywood for two hours, letting the monotony of the moving cars and his unconnected impressions calm his throbbing mind. When he got home that evening and his father asked him why he wasn't in school—the vice principal had called the newsstand twice that day—Burk told him the truth.

"I'm sorry," Nathan Burk said, putting his arm around his son's shoulder. "It's a terrible thing to lose someone you love."

"Is this the way you felt when Mom left?"

"Yes."

"How long does it take to go away?"

"The pain? I don't know. But it will go away, Ray. Eventually."

★

Burk stopped at White Horse Liquors to buy a pint of scotch and some cashews and drove back to the Argyle Manor. He was standing in the kitchen, pouring his third drink, feeling oppressed and confused and wanting to weep, when he heard someone knocking lightly on the door. He went into the living room and pulled aside the curtain. Through the veiled light he saw Lillian Ohrtman staring at him. She wore a white linen dress and a matching pillbox hat.

"Today is my thirtieth wedding anniversary," she said to Burk, once he opened the door. "Lionel would still be here, too, if those cowardly bastards didn't drive him to an early grave. My second husband was a screenwriter like yourself. I told you that, didn't I?"

Burk nodded. They were both standing just inside the doorway to the apartment.

"He committed suicide. They found him slumped over his typewriter. He died in Mexico, in the Yucatan. He drank rat poison, mixing it with one-fifty-proof rum. The last words he typed were 'Nothing ever felt this good.'" Lillian Ohrtman took off her hat and walked around the room once before she sat primly on the couch. "Aren't you going to offer me a drink?"

The phone rang in the living room while Burk was in the kitchen.

"Yes?" Lillian Ohrtman said, picking up the receiver in the middle of the second ring. "Who? No, Steve Caudabeck is not here. Well, yes, I'm sorry also. No, this is not Rita Bledsoe and no, you cannot suck on my pussy." Lillian Ohrtman slammed down the phone and made a clucking sound with her tongue. "The nerve," she said, straightening her back.

Burk came back into the living room with two glasses of scotch. He sat down on the couch, and Lillian Ohrtman reached out and rested her hand on his thigh. They were both silent for a while, and then she leaned close and said, "I got married at the Methodist Church on Camden Drive in Beverly Hills. The reception was at the Ambassador Hotel in the Coconut Grove. All the major mucky-mucks were there: Zanuck, Cohn, Warner; Louella and Hedda, of course; and Gregory Peck and Henry Fonda. All of them. You could not believe what I looked like. I have pictures. They don't lie."

Lillian Ohrtman studied Burk's face as her arthritic fingers labored to unbutton his Levi's.

"I was ridiculously lovely. My body was perfection. All the men wanted to dance with me, and I remember the heat of their bodies as they drew me in close. In my ear they told lewd jokes, and when my back was turned away from Lionel I allowed their hands to rub my buttocks. I obliged them because they were drunk and overstimulated, like I am now." Lillian Ohrtman's head sagged into Burk's lap. "Later that night—my wedding night—in the penthouse suite, Lionel and I made great love. I remember when I did to him what I'm going to do to you now, he said, 'Good Lord, Lil, you're going to suck the paint right off the goddamn walls.'"

Shortly before he drove away that evening, Burk encountered Mark Ohrtman on the street outside the Argyle Manor. He wore a dark blue smoking jacket over white silk pajamas. "I saw your name in the *Daily Variety.* You have a movie in production called *Pledging My Love.* True?" Burk nodded his head. "And you're staying at the Beverly Hills Hotel," Mark Ohrtman said. He reached into his smoking jacket and produced a matchbook from the Polo Lounge. "Am I correct?"

"That's right," Burk said. "But I'm not comfortable there all the time."

"Of course you're not," Lillian Ohrtman said. She was standing outside her apartment, hugging her shoulders against the cool air. "It's a hotel. You're looking for a homier spot. Someplace real. Where you can make friends."

Lillian Ohrtman walked forward until she was standing next to her son. Upstairs, Burk heard a phone ring in his apartment. He took a step toward his car and Mark Ohrtman said, "Drew, my lover, does Rona Barrett's hair. She knows what happened the other night in the hotel. She has good sources. They say that actor beat up the waiter on purpose."

Moving away, Burk said, "As far as I know it was an accident."

"No," Mark said, blinking his heavy-lidded eyes, "that's not what Drew says."

"It has the makings of a wonderful scandal," Lillian Ohrtman said. Her lips were set in a bemused smile. "Actor punches room service waiter. I've had my share of waiters." She laughed. "Oh, yes, I have. Waiters, pool boys, beboppers, even writers. Yes, even writers."

Burk was now seated behind the wheel of his Mustang. On the opposite side of the street a young couple walked by wearing Levi's and light parkas. Their arms encircled each other's waists. "Look," the girl said, tilting her head as she pointed toward the sky. "Look at all the stars."

A window shade went up in a small stucco house squeezed between two apartment buildings. A woman said, "Keep it down out there. We're tryin' to watch TV."

"This is what Drew heard," Mark Ohrtman said. He was speaking to Burk, but only his shadow on the sidewalk was visible from inside the car. "He heard the actors in your film, the main actors—the three leads—were rehearsing a scene in the hotel room. A very intense scene, where real emotions had to be revealed. They'd been rehearsing all night, according to Drew's sources. They were rehearsing a scene that was written by you that takes place in a motel. Isn't that right?"

"I've always liked motels," Lillian Ohrtman said. "They made me feel so . . . so wanton."

In the rearview mirror, Burk saw Mark Ohrtman make a face.

"What?" Lillian Ohrtman said.

Before her son could respond, Burk started his engine. His headlights came on, but Mark Ohrtman's face darkened. "They attacked him for no reason," he said. "How *dare* they?"

"It wasn't their fault. They were rehearsing a scene," Burk said. "It was an accident."

"He was given a copy of the script," Mark Ohrtman said. "He was told to play the part of a young Marine lance corporal. You know who I'm talking about, don't you?"

Burk did not reply. His radio was on very low and he could hear someone speaking to Radio Ray. The voice sounded familiar.

"The room service waiter was flattered to be asked to rehearse. What a stroke of good fortune, he thought. I'm an actor. If I'm good, maybe they will help me get the part. It's possible."

"Anything's possible in Hollywood," Lillian Ohrtman said, with a pained smile.

"But something went wrong inside that hotel room. There was liquor and drugs, according to Drew's sources. Things became too intense, too sexually intense, perhaps. The boy was attacked, we know that. His jaw was broken and nine stitches were taken in his eyebrow. That we know for sure, Mr. Burk, Mr. Screenwriter."

Burk put the Mustang in gear and began coasting toward the end of the block. In the rearview he saw Mark and Lillian Ohrtman turn away from the street. They were clinging to each other.

A car came up the block, the glare of the headlights making Burk shield his eyes. He heard a dog in the neighborhood bark twice and Lillian Ohrtman's voice came out of the near dark. "Hush, dog," she said, and then her thin shadow vanished from the sidewalk.

★

"My mother got shot playing tennis in Miami Beach," Gene told Radio Ray as Burk crossed La Cienega and eased the Mustang over to the curb. It was close to 2 A.M., and a thick ghostlike fog had swallowed the rooftops and billboards on Sunset, bringing the visibility down to twenty yards. Parked in front of him was a white limousine with the hazard lights blinking. "She was playing on the clay courts next to the Roney Plaza. It was a Mafia hit, but the guy they were gunning for—Joe Pallazi—was playing mixed doubles on the next court over. Actually, that's a lie, Ray, but that's the story my dad told me when she left home. He heard it from a guy who hung around the newsstand, a bookie named Izzy Wachtel. That's how Izzy's wife died," Gene said. "What really happened was my mom was visiting her sister. She lived in New York, but each summer they met in a different city for a vacation away from their husbands. That year it was Miami, and my mom met this guy, Ted Sloss. He owned a restaurant in Biscayne Bay. But instead of just having an affair, she moved in with him. He ended up dumping her for a chick who groomed horses out at Hialeah. Six months later my mom came home. But to my dad she was dead. He told her, 'Esther, you're dead. You're gone.' She said, 'I still love you, Nate,' but he said, 'I'm sorry, you can't live here.' So she found a place on Ocean Park and Twenty-third, a few blocks away, and she started comin' by every day. I guess I was around ten when this happened, maybe nine. Am I boring you, Ray?"

"No, not at all," Radio Ray said, his voice perfectly honest. "You're not boring me at all."

"What about your listeners? I could be boring them. If you like, I'll give you another story. I've got millions. I'm a cop. I could spin cop stories till the cows come home. Actually I *used* to be a cop," Gene said, dropping his voice. "But in my head I still am."

"Thanks for calling."

"I'm not through talking."

"For tonight you are," Radio Ray told Gene and his audience. "I'll be right back."

Burk called Gene from the phone booth on the corner of Kings Road and Sunset. "I heard you," Burk said. "I was listening. That story you told was bullshit."

"Part of it was true. She went to Miami. She met a guy."

"She didn't come back."

"Sometimes she did."

"Twice a year. Once during the summer and once over Christmas. And the guy's name was Polse, not Sloss. Meyer Polse. And he was from DC. He owned a chain of furniture stores. Three in Baltimore, three in Roanoke, Virginia."

"You don't remember, Ray. You were too young."

"I remember everything."

"Late spring, 1949. She took us up to Lake Arrowhead. Do you remember that?"

"That was before she left, before she went to Miami."

"We were driving up the Angeles Crest Highway. When it got real steep and the elevation changed, I got this terrible pain in my ear. She said it would go away but it didn't. And she wouldn't stop. Remember? I was lying in the backseat, screaming, and you were reading comic books in front. Finally she pulled over in this small town just before Big Bear. She asked at a gas station for a doctor, and they sent us to this guy who lived above a laundry. The first thing I saw was a framed picture of a prizefighter he had on his wall, some skinny lightweight who trained up there, Young Teddy Berle, I think that was his name. Fought Ike Williams for the championship in 'forty-seven. Aaron knew who he was right away when I told him. There were other pictures too, of actresses and actors, people he prob-

ably treated while they were on location. None of them looked familiar. I mean, John Wayne wasn't up there, or Hoot Gibson, or Bob
Steele, or the Bowery Boys. But I was cryin' so hard by then all their
faces were blurred."

"Gene—"

"You were outside, in the car, oblivious. You didn't see the guy.
He had these yellow jagged teeth and his breath smelled like cigarettes and wine. I can smell it now as we talk. No office, either. Just
this crummy room, that's all. That's where she took me."

"You always had earaches, Gene. They went away."

"This one didn't. It felt like someone was running an ice pick
through my head. The doctor said I had a blister in my ear. He told
me he was gonna pop it. I was lying on the couch, on my side. Mom
was behind me someplace, but I couldn't see her face. When I wasn't
looking the doctor knelt down and stuck this long silver needle into
my ear."

"Jesus."

"No shit. I never felt a pain like that. Pus and blood just poured
out of my head. I'm not kidding you, *poured* out. This happened, Ray,
while you were outside reading Archie and Little Lulu and Batman."

"Gene, I just remembered something."

"The pictures on the wall. A lot of unknowns."

Burk said, "Grace Elliot died in Big Bear in 1949."

"There you go, Ray."

"What're you telling me, Gene?"

"We never got to go camping, did we? Remember? The forest
rangers stopped us because of a fire. A fire in the mountains, he said.
It was true. We could see the smoke and flames and hear sirens. Mom
got real upset. She said we came all the way from LA. The forest
ranger said he couldn't let us through. I was glad. I wanted to go home.
I was in so much pain."

"I don't remember this."

"You blocked it out, Ray. You blocked my pain. That's what
you do."

Gene waited for a response but Burk said nothing. Outside the
glass a chauffeur was bouncing nervously from foot to foot. Burk
cracked open the door and the chauffeur said, "My limo broke down,
mate. I hafta call these blokes a taxi before they get too excited."

"Who are they?"

"T. Rex," the chauffeur said, naming a newly popular English band that was headlining the Whiskey A Go-Go on Saturday night. Their hit—"Bang a Gong"—was a weirdly sinister piece of trash-glam disco that gave Burk bad vibes.

"I gotta get off," Burk told Gene. "Someone needs to use the phone."

"When we came down out of the mountains, around Redlands, my ear started to feel better. I remember the reception on the radio cleared up too. Mom found a baseball game—the LA Angels were playing the Hollywood Stars—and we kept it on all the way home."

"I gotta go," Burk said.

"The next day was a Sunday. She took us to the beach, and later we went to a movie at the Village Theatre in Westwood. Something with Burt Lancaster, about Indians. Afterward, she dropped us off and that was that. We didn't see her again until Christmas."

There was a manila envelope waiting for Burk at the front desk when he arrived back at the hotel. Inside was a memo from Boyd Talbott that he read through quickly as the elevator took him up to the third floor.

DATE: May 20, 1971
FROM: Boyd Talbott
TO: Ray Burk
RE: Upcoming scenes
Have tried to reach you by phone for three days. No luck.

1. Scene #88. Jon feels that Eric should drive a '57 Chevy instead of an Olds Starfire. More interesting to shoot. Does it matter to you?

2. In #46 (flashback) Eric and Barbara are parked on Mulholland. They pick up WSLX, Nashville, on the radio. Is that possible? Does it stretch our credibility? Perhaps they could pick up a station in a state closer to California. For example: KOMA—"where it's mighty pretty in Oklahoma City."

3. Jon thinks we should actually see the Marine drown in Act III (Scenes 142 and 143). We should not leave the audience confused. Ambiguity at this point would be counterproductive.

4. We may need a polish on Barbara's speech on 87–88 (#131). She sounds a little too poetic.

5. The scenes that follow (#131–135), at the Coral Reef Motel, when they view the stag film that Barbara made in 1959: Jon feels there should be less dialogue. Look it over. If you agree, see what you can trim. I could also see losing Ricky's speech where he's talking about playing ball in Tulsa.

And finally, regarding the recent incident at the hotel. We have been advised by the studio not to talk to the press. Everyone at Paramount is quite upset (naturally), and there has been some talk about suspending the production, though I think that is unlikely. Jerome Sanford has spoken to Maria and she will pass along what our position will be, if she hasn't already done so.

If you need to reach me over the weekend, here is my number at my home: 555–1161.

Ciao,

Jim

Burk was rereading the crisply typed memo as he stepped off the elevator. When he reached for his room key, Crumpler's door suddenly flew open, revealing a powerfully built middle-aged man wearing a trench coat with a sprig of mistletoe pinned high on the lapel.

"I thought you were the bellman," the man said to Burk. "I just called the front desk. I told him I wanted a new room. There's bloodstains all over the wall by the lamp. Looks like a goddamn torture chamber."

The man took a small bottle of pills out of his trench coat. He popped a capsule into his mouth and threw back his head and swallowed. "Percodan," he said, pounding his chest with his fist. "Twenty milligrams. Use it to calm me down when I fly."

Burk left the door slightly ajar as he walked inside his room. The phone was ringing. "You gonna answer that?" the man said. He was now standing just inside Burk's doorway, pointing at the white phone ringing urgently on the night table. "Or you gonna let it ring all night?"

The telephone rang one more short ring and stopped. The man's hand was resting on the doorknob. The belt on his trench coat had loosened, showing Burk his belly button and a triangle of pale heavy flesh. He said, "Drug sales are down all over. Especially in the Northwest, my number-one market. They fall again next quarter, I could be in big trouble. I could get fired."

Burk made a sympathetic sound as he sank down on his bed and began to slowly untie his shoes.

"I don't do well in LA. Never made my quota here. The fucking doctors are prima donnas. They buy all their shit from the young reps from Upjohn and Merck. They don't like me, for some reason." For a moment the man's face looked deeply perplexed. "Today was bad. I got treated like shit. But tomorrow I'm driving to San Diego. San Diego's always been a good town for me. I'll be okay. Don't worry. I'll be fine as soon as they move me out of this room."

Once more Burk's phone began to ring.

"I would answer that," the man said, demonstrating the action in the air. "If it was me I'd snatch it right up. How do you know it's not an emergency, an accident of some kind, a loved one injured?" Burk stood up and the man took a step backward, into the hallway. "How do you know that?"

"I don't," Burk said politely. He closed and locked his door before he took off his clothes and crawled into bed.

Sometime later, in the deepest part of the night, he woke up and heard someone laughing crazily outside his door. Then, suddenly, and apparently for no reason, the laughing stopped and there was a sharp cry of terror and anguish, followed by a long, pitiful moan.

Burk got out of bed quickly and stood paralyzed for a moment in the center of the room, listening to his heart pound and the odd whimpering sounds on the other side of the wall. Sweat broke out on his neck, and his hand began to tremble, but when he finally stepped through his growing fear and jerked open the door, the hallway outside his room was mysteriously empty.

Eleven

Friday: Burk Goes to Jail and Bobby Visits Max Rheingold's House

Los Angeles Times   *May 21*

JOYCE HABER

Assault and battery charges were dropped against Tom Crumpler, the young actor who was arrested Tuesday night at the Beverly Hills Hotel. According to my sources, Ted Davis, the hotel employee and the injured party in the late-night melee, has accepted a monetary settlement from the hotel and Crumpler himself. Studio publicist Leo Katz denied that Paramount was involved in the settlement in any way. "We didn't ante up a penny," he said, "and rumors that Davis will play a role in the film are totally false."

Jerome Sanford, studio VP, referred all calls to Jack Rose, executive producer of Pledging My Love. *Rose said, "It was an unfortunate incident. I've talked with Crumpler and he knows he made a mistake. He assures us there will be no more problems."*

My attempts to speak with Crumpler or his costars were unsuccessful. Speaking for Director Jon Warren, his assistant Boyd Talbott said, "Crumpler's performance in this film is extraordinary. That's all that's important from our standpoint." We'll see.

Burk was driving east on Franklin when he saw the red light strobing on the police car tailgating his bumper. A moment later the siren came on, and he moved into the curb lane and rolled to a stop in front of Immaculate Heart High School.

On the radio James Taylor was singing "Country Road" and Burk sat very still, waiting for the cop to appear. Not far away was a bus stop where a young girl was moving her lips while she read the current issue of *Scientific American*. Resting next to her on the bench was a blood-colored case for a trumpet or a clarinet.

The clock on the dash said it was four minutes after one. Burk had been driving for three hours but remembered nothing since he'd spoken to Loretta earlier that morning. He'd called when he awoke and she'd told him she was leaving town.

"Just for a few days," she'd said, in a strange, uninflected tone. "I'm going out to the desert to finish the script." She was traveling with a man, her new lover; he could read it in her voice. "I'll talk to you when I get back."

"Come on over to the hotel, Loretta."

"I have to pack."

"I need you this morning."

"You need to fuck me."

"Come on."

"No."

"Please . . . please. . . ."

"No."

When Burk hung up, he could hear a man laughing in the hallway outside his room. "Come on over," he said, cruelly mimicking Burk's voice. "I need you this morning. Come on . . . please."

The cop was wearing mirrored sunglasses and sharply tapered sideburns that were at least an inch longer than regulation. After Burk gave him his license, he turned away, saying, "Keep your hands on the steering wheel where I can see them."

Burk exhaled slowly while he watched the cop's long frame recede in the sideview mirror. A yellow jacket buzzed against the windshield, and to the east a hawk circled in the dark sky over Griffith Park.

The police radio popped and crackled and the girl on the bus bench put down her magazine and stared at Burk with a curious, almost cryptic expression on her face. For a moment Burk's eyes went out of focus and he thought of his son. He imagined Louie in a classroom flooded with sunshine, surrounded by boys and girls eager to be his friends. His smile never seemed brighter.

"Your license has expired," the cop said to Burk.

"What do you mean?"

"On April thirtieth, your birthday. I'm going to have to take you in," the cop said, taking a step backward and letting his hand rest on the top of his baton.

Burk didn't move. The girl on the bus bench said, "What're you gonna do, arrest him for having an expired license?"

The cop dropped his head so he could see over the top of his shades. "Yes," he said to the girl. "I am."

A motorcycle cop pulled around the corner and parked behind Burk. Another patrol car was speeding west on Franklin. A city bus crossed through the intersection and the girl on the bench stood up. "What a waste of taxpayer dollars," she said, in a snide voice. "No wonder my dad says all cops are jerks."

The bus was double-parked next to Burk's Mustang. The driver, a black woman with a dignified face, was smiling through the open door. "I seen him," she said to the cop, making a circle with her thumb and forefinger. "I seen him driving round and round."

While Burk was being questioned by detectives at the Hollywood police substation on Cole Street, Bobby Sherwood and Ricky Furlong were standing in front of Max Rheingold's house on Tigertail Road. On his lawn was a For Sale sign with a red SOLD sticker pasted diagonally across the front.

"Twenty-two twenty-four. That's where he lives," Bobby said, consulting a small spiral notebook he was holding.

"That's where he *used* to live," Ricky said. "Tomorrow I'll call the realtor. I'll find out where he moved."

"What if they won't tell you?"

"I'll find him, Bobby. Don't worry."

"But—"

Ricky put his hand over Bobby's mouth. "Relax, sweetheart. Just relax."

On their way back down to Sunset, they stopped in front of a hacienda-style mansion on Carolwood Drive. Parked in the driveway was a maroon Bentley convertible with its top down.

Ricky said, "Frank Sinatra lived here back in the 1950s, before he got divorced. I went to grammar school with his oldest daughter, Nancy."

"She's cute," Bobby said. "And she's got a cute voice, too."

"One Saturday she invited me to a birthday party at her house. A circus tent was set up in the backyard, and there were clowns, a magician, and a real cotton candy machine. There was a pony ride, too. And that day a boy named Alex Becker fell out of the saddle and cracked his skull open on a sprinkler head. He was rushed to the hospital and stitched up, but he never came back to the party. Later on I heard that Frank gave the Becker family a ton of money not to file a lawsuit."

Bobby turned and looked into Ricky's face. "You were popular in school, weren't you?"

"Sort of."

"I wasn't."

"That's okay," Ricky said, smiling at Bobby in a motherly way, "you're popular with me."

From the tennis court on the property next door they could hear the rhythmic *thwack* of the ball as it was stroked back and forth across the net. The court was built below the main house and was protected from the wind by a green tarp that was attached to a tall chain-link fence.

"I hated school. I was always picked on," Bobby said, as he cut through the thick larkspur that grew from the sidewalk up to the base of the fence. Through a tear in the canvas he saw a boy and a girl— both teenagers with blond wavy hair—facing each other on opposite sides of the court. The girl was lovely looking, with large freckles on her neck and arms and long narrow legs. Zinc oxide protected her nose from the sun, even though the sky was the color of wet clay. "You have no idea what it was like, Ricky."

"You're trespassing," Ricky said. "Come on back."

Bobby fastened his fingers on the fence, squeezing the cross-hatched squares until the blood drained out of his knuckles. "They chased me and bullied me," he said, beginning to hear a distant ringing inside his head, a tinkling sound, as if two champagne glasses were brought together in a toast by his ear. "They pushed me down in the schoolyard and kicked me in the side and in the back."

Ricky walked into the larkspur and stood behind Bobby. The girl on the other side of the fence was walking briskly around the perimeter of the court, gathering up the loose tennis balls, using her racket to spank them into the air.

Bobby made a disagreeable face as the ringing grew louder inside his head. But now the sound was different, like the screams of angry children. Bobby said, "They would chase me and I couldn't get away, because there was always a fence to stop me, a fence like this one. So I used to climb way up, above their hands, and I would hang there until a teacher on the yard duty would chase them off. Nobody came sometimes, and I would stay up there the whole recess, ducking away from their taunts and the rocks and sticks that were aimed at my head. They said I was mental. The girls even made up a song about me: 'The boy on the fence without any sense.'"

Bobby closed his eyes. His temples were pounding from the sharp pain that spiraled into his ear. On the court the game had stopped, and the young players were standing by an open gate, trading swallows from a bottle of soda.

Bobby said, "I have to find Max Rheingold."

"I know you do, Bobby."

"I have to find him soon."

Burk walked out of the Hollywood police station just after midnight. The air was damp and cold, the sky pitch black and starless. He'd been interrogated for more than four hours by two vice detectives and Gene's former partner, Eddie Cornell. "If you weren't his brother we would've locked you up," Cornell told Burk privately, before he was released.

"For what? I haven't done anything."

"You're pissin' people off. That's what you're doin'. Nobody likes to see someone driving around their neighborhood for hours on end. It makes them feel . . . paranoid."

"I like to drive."

"Then find someplace else," Cornell said. "Drive around Beverly Hills. Drive up to Mulholland, down to the ocean. Just stay the fuck west of La Brea."

"No," Burk said, and Cornell gave him a look of unguarded anger. "I belong here."

On his way out of the station, Burk picked up his wallet and his watch at the booking desk. "Almost forgot," the sergeant on duty said. He handed Burk a coffee-stained copy of *Pledging My Love.*

Burk said, "Where did this come from?"

"I guess they found it when they went through your car."

One of the vice cops who had interrogated Burk was pouring coffee into a paper cup. His hair was tied in a ponytail, and a large gold medallion hung around his neck. "Good read," he said, looking in Burk's direction but speaking to the booking sergeant. "He'll get my five bucks."

Burk walked up Cole to Cahuenga, then followed Cahuenga north to Hollywood Boulevard. The traffic was light, and what pedestrians he saw he heard first by their amplified footsteps. At Selma, a soldier wearing a green beret stood behind a bus bench at parade rest: a silent sentry with a face that could be made out of wax. A black dog with an open wound on its neck trotted along the gutter, pausing to look back once at the soldier before skittering into an alleyway filled with packing crates and a dumpster brimming with foul-smelling garbage.

Burk glanced into the alley and saw a black man lying on a mattress, jacking off, his lengthening penis lit up by the hellish glow of a red lantern. A woman who Burk could not see said, "Come on in and play with us, darling."

When he came to Hollywood Boulevard, Burk crossed to the north side of the street. A police car with its lights high-beamed followed him for a block, rolling slowly in the right lane. Near Cherokee he passed an empty news peddler's kiosk and thought quickly of his father, newly arrived in Los Angeles, standing inside a similar shed, shivering in the lonely lamplight.

From somewhere Burk heard the weak sound of a radio and Radio Ray's voice. He tilted his head back and raised his eyes. In an upper-story window was a woman with false-looking hair and a once-lovely face. She was leaning out, looking down, elbows propped on the wooden ledge. Another face was at her hip, staring with wide child's eyes. From inside the darkness of this room, an unknown voice on the radio said, "I've got the air conditioner on but I'm still sweating. I don't know what to do."

"Call a doctor," Radio Ray suggested, coolly.

"No. I can't."

"Why?"

"Because when the virus leaves my body, my soul will disappear too."

"I don't believe that," Radio Ray said.

"I can feel my spirit burning like a whip across my back. My fucking skin looks like the inside of a watermelon. But I know that this fever is God's judgment. His fingerprints are all over my body. I thought he would protect me, but I was wrong."

Burk followed the old trolley tracks down the boulevard until he reached Gower; then he turned south. After a block he arrived in front of KMPC and peered through the locked double glass door. A tall security guard in light khaki clothes was standing in front of the elevators. He was well over six feet, with blond hair and blond eyelashes. When he saw Burk, he came forward and unlocked the doors. "What can I do for you?" he asked.

"I want to speak with Ray Moore."

"He's on the air."

"I know that."

The guard's jawline seemed to tighten and he rocked back on his heels. "You want to speak to Ray Moore, you have to call him on the telephone. You want to see him in person, you make an appointment during regular business hours." He turned and pointed. Burk followed his finger to a large clock above the elevator. "See that red second hand? When it crosses the twelve, I don't want to see your face outside this glass."

"Do you think I'm crazy?" Burk asked him.

The security guard looked at Burk while he bolted the door. His lips twitched just before he spoke: "I don't know what you are."

Burk walked east on Sunset, pausing on a freeway overpass, fighting both vertigo and the urge to jump to his death.

He turned and looked to the north: A dome of fog sat over the black hillside like a gray helmet. He heard the sound of weeping. His head did a quick swivel and his eyes fell on a man slumped on a bus bench. A blanket covered his shoulders. The man looked Burk over for several seconds before he whispered, "Set me on fire." Burk's eyes shifted to the ground, where a red gas can rested between the man's feet. "Pour it on me and light me up," the man said.

A dog barked in the hills. Burk turned in a circle, to make sure he was alone in the street. Then he shook his head and continued walking, stepping around a pile of human stool that sat by the curb.

Just before he reached Western, Burk passed by the entrance to the Bat Cave. Through a slit in the curtain shielding the door, he saw a woman dancing buck naked on a U-shaped stage. She was thin, with spidery limbs and a pussy that was shaved bare. In her right hand she held a thick wedge of chocolate cake.

A man with mascaraed eyes put a five-dollar bill on the stage. The dancer smiled and settled into a crouch that put her private parts in front of his painted face. "Eat me up," she said, and shoved the cake deep into her thighs.

"Believe I will," said the man, leaning forward. "Yes, I believe I will."

Larry Havana rolled his wheelchair through the curtain. A long flashlight rested in his lap. He clicked it on, and a cloud of insects swirled around the beam shining in Burk's face. "Looks like you're freezing your ass off," Havana said, smiling. "Five dollars gets you in."

Burk backed away from the light. "I'm okay," he said.

Inside the bar the dancer was massaging the customer's neck while he tongued globs of cake out of her crotch. "Gonna have to charge you for peeking," Havana said to Burk. His smile was different now; he was mocking him. "No freebies in the pussy game. Nope. I cannot have any of that."

"My dad knew your father," Burk said.

"Yeah? My father knew lots of people."

"Nate's News. Nathan Burk. That's my dad," Burk said with some pride. "Your father put out dirty magazines that my dad sold underneath the counter."

A black bouncer came through the curtain carrying a bottle of bourbon and a plastic cup filled with ice. Eyeballing Burk, he said, "Everything cool out here, boss?"

Havana nodded. "Everything's fine, Clifford."

"Man be chowin' down in there."

"Five dollars a slice is as good as it gets."

"Best deal in town, boss."

The bouncer walked back inside the club and Burk said, "When you were a kid, my brother used to push you around Hollywood. His name was Gene. One summer your dad gave him a job selling movie star maps."

Havana regarded Burk for a moment while he used his hands to squeeze circulation into his thin, crippled legs. "Gene. Yeah. I know him. He became a cop. He got fired, right?"

"He quit."

"What's he doin' now?"

"He helps out my dad. And he's got a side business collecting old rock-and-roll records."

"I collect pussy," Havana said, and he barked out a laugh.

A Lincoln Mark VII with smoked windows rolled up in front of the Bat Cave. It sat idling for several seconds before the window on the passenger side came down, revealing an old man with a crumpled face and light blue eyes. "How late you open?" the old man asked.

"We never close," Havana replied.

A playful leer passed across the old man's face, and the big car slid forward, followed by vapors of gray smoke. One taillight was out; the other was reflected in the street, a scarlet eye socket staring up from a lost world.

Burk started walking away. Havana said, "Be seein' you, Burk."

"Maybe."

"Bring your brother by. I'd love to say hello. No peekin', though. You peek, you pay."

Burk turned north on Western, ducking into a cold wind. In the middle of the block, a barely pubescent blonde stepped out of a late model Buick. She was wearing a short white diaphanous dress that outlined the silhouette of her naked body. After the driver took off, burning rubber, the girl said, "What are you doin' up so late? You lookin' for a date?"

"No."

"Cruisin' for guys?"

"No."

"You sure?"

"I'm on my way back to my car. It's on Franklin."

"I'll walk with you."

"Why?"

" 'Cause I feel like it. Put your arm around me," the girl said, looking back over her shoulder as they started up the street. Burk pulled her close, and she moved his hand so it covered her breast. "Feels good, huh? I bet you got a rod," she said. She stopped and pressed her body closer. "Yeah, you do."

"I'm tired," Burk said, pulling away.

"Your dick ain't. I'll jack you off for three bucks."

"No."

"Blow job for seven-fifty."

"Look—" Burk said, then stopped. The car that dropped her off had circled the block and was now parked across the street. The engine was running and the radio was playing "The Great Pretender," an oldie by the Platters.

"Is that your pimp?" Burk asked the girl.

"Might be."

The girl stared at Burk until he met her eyes. She was breathing heavily, her expression both hungry and tender. Burk reached into his pocket and took out a wrinkled ten-dollar bill. He said, "I'll give you this if you leave me alone."

The girl shook her head. Now she looked amused. "We gotta do something."

"I don't want to do anything," Burk said, trying not to look or sound frightened.

A voice from the Buick said, "Dance with her." Burk looked at the girl, wondering if this were a joke or some kind of code. "Dance with her," the voice said again, and this time the girl stepped forward and slid her arms around Burk's waist.

The radio was turned up and Tony Williams's lead voice soared over the street:

Oh, yes, I'm the great pretender,
Pretending that you're still around. . . .

Burk put his hands on the girl's hips as she steered him into the middle of the street. He felt awkward, swaying flat-footed, her thighs pushed into his.

After one verse, the girl took Burk's hand and put it between her thighs. "Dancing makes me so hot," she said, raising her skirt. "Feel how wet I am." Burk tried to step away, but the girl pulled him back. "Don't," she warned him under her breath. "He'll get pissed."

"We have to get out of the street."

"We will when the record's over."

An empty bus slowly passed by, the headlights splashing their faces. Burk raised his hand; his fingers were coated with blood. He looked down: more blood ran down the girl's thighs, spotting the white line in the center of the street. "I'm flowing," she said, relieved. "That's good. That means I'm not pregnant."

The song on the radio ended and they broke apart. The driver, a black man, was outside his car, leaning against the fender. He was dressed in loose-fitting white duck trousers that reminded Burk of pants worn by workers in a hospital. Perhaps he was an orderly or a male nurse, making ends meet as a part-time pimp.

The black man said, "Thank the man for the dance."

The girl looked at Burk. A quick smile as she reached out and touched his arm. "Thanks."

"Ask him if he needs a ride some place."

"Do you need a lift?" Burk shook his head. "Are you sure?"

"Yes, I'm sure. I'll see you around," he said, and began walking north on Western. It began to drizzle, the long thin drops tickling his neck like a shower of pins. On the corner a bundle of newspapers sat underneath a streetlamp. Charles Manson was on the front page, wearing a fiend's face. Burk crouched in the darkness and wiped his bloody hand across Manson's coal-black eyes: two deliberate strokes that left an X as red as a curse.

An Interlude: Catching Up with Max

Max Rheingold's prostate surgery took place in the spring of 1971. He spent six days in St. John's Hospital in Santa Monica, where he received only two visitors, producer Jack Rose and actor Kenny Kendall.

On the Sunday before he was released, Jack Rose offered Max the use of his cabana at the Beverly Hills Hotel. "Sit around the pool. Read, swim, take it easy," Jack said. "Charge anything you want."

Because he was nearly broke and his house on Tigertail was on the brink of foreclosure, Max should have been enormously relieved by Jack's generosity. Deep inside he *was* grateful, but there was also another part of him that felt Jack owed him this favor, and more. "I've been a stand-up friend," Max told Kenny Kendall, when he came by a few minutes later, after visiting hours were over. "You know what I mean?"

"Fuckin'-A."

"I remember when he was a nobody agent with a one-room office on Gower. Jack Rose, bullshit. In the old days he was Jake Rosenkrantz.

Him and his brother Sheeny Saul grew up two blocks away from me on Mulberry Street. Both of them ran with Buggsy Siegel and Lou Dashowitz and the rest of the Jewish mob. Saul became a loan shark and a waterfront enforcer. Jake became Jack the Torch."

Kenny Kendall took a half pint of gin out of his pants. "Jack the Torch?"

"He was an arsonist for the mob. Back in the thirties he did two years in Sing Sing and another two in Dannemora."

"He did time? You're kidding me."

"That's a fact. And when he got out the second time, he told Siegel he was tired of playing with matches. He said he wanted to come to California. The next day Meyer Lansky met him at Grand Central Station. Meyer gave him an envelope with ten grand inside, and off he went."

Kendall was staring out the window. "Now look at him," he said. "That fucker's rich as shit. His cabana, big deal. He could rent you a whole fuckin' bungalow." Jack Rose's Jag was parked in a space by the main entrance. In the passenger seat was a voluptuous black woman wearing dark glasses in glittering gold frames and a bright green scarf. When Jack breezed outside, she took off her scarf and shook out her thick reddish hair. "Got himself some poontang, too."

"She's a dancer on *Rowan and Martin's Laugh-In*," Max said. He sat up with a groan and pushed aside the curtain. "He always liked that dark stuff."

"Back home we called that splittin' the black oak."

Max grunted a laugh, and a bell rang somewhere in the hospital. Seconds later a Chinese nurse walked swiftly into Max's room. "No good to drink in hospital," she said, frowning at Kendall while her fingers found the pulse in Max's wrist. "Set bad example. Against rules. Please put away."

"In the navy we used to call *that* 'slant-eye pie,'" Kendall said to Max, staring at the nurse without expression as he uncapped the bottle and raised it to his lips. "I got some of that myself."

The nurse checked Max's blood pressure and entered the results in the chart that hung by a chain from the end of the bed. She was almost out the door when she stopped and turned around slowly and gave Kendall an inquisitive look, as if she were trying to see into the darkness of his mind. Several seconds passed. Then, in a quiet but savage voice, she said, "You no good. You no good at all."

* * *

Beginning in June, when his strength and appetite began to return, Max started each morning with a brisk one-mile walk through Beverly Hills, followed by a plate of lox, bagels, and cream cheese at Nate and Al's delicatessen on North Beverly Drive. Most of the time Max invited himself to sit with Mort Finkel and Stan Lapidus, two sketch writers for Danny Kaye that he knew back in the forties, when he was a producer at Monogram and they were one of several teams hacking out comedies for Ma and Pa Kettle.

The week they were fired—the same week Stan's wife gave birth to their first child—Max hired them to polish a screwball Western he was developing for Chill Wills and Ken Maynard. He paid them generously and under the table, a favor that Mort and Stan had never forgotten, making them inclined to be unfailingly pleasant whenever Max decided to squeeze into their booth.

However, there were many people in this early morning crowd, including Max's urologist, Artie Schlumberger, who were familiar with the darker side of Max's past, and they would mutter disgustedly behind his back when he walked inside. Several were openly hostile.

One morning comedian Jack Carter told him he was a "total piece of garbage," and when Max stood up to challenge him, Buddy Hackett "accidentally" dumped a bowl of cream of wheat into his lap. This convulsed Phil Silvers and Milton Berle and the other comics at Buddy's table, and Flip Wilson nearly spit out his French toast when Rich Little slid out of the booth and began a walk up and down the aisle with his legs splayed apart and his hands flapping at his sides, imitating Max's distinctive waddle.

The abuse stopped one Sunday morning after Max pulled out a loaded .45 and stuck it underneath Shecky Greene's chin. "You've been insulting me for weeks," Max said, his hand shaking as he clicked off the safety. "One more time and I'm gonna blow your fuckin' head off."

Mildred, the silver-haired hostess, dialed the police, and Max was arrested ten minutes later, at the corner of Rodeo Drive and Little Santa Monica, calmly waiting for the light to change while he scratched his nuts and munched on a bagel slathered with lox and cream cheese. A week later the case was dropped when Shecky Greene refused to press charges. "Max is connected. Sinatra let

Shecky know it was a bad idea," Danny Kaye was overheard telling George Burns at the Hillcrest Country Club, and everyone nearby nodded knowingly.

Because he was forbidden to patronize Nate and Al's for one year, Max now ate his breakfast alone at the counter in the coffee shop downstairs in the hotel. The rest of the day he spent by the pool, wearing a Dodger baseball cap and a pair of droopy blue bathing trunks that extended to just below his knees. Unlike the other men his age, Max paid no attention to the sleek starlets who paraded around the deck in their skimpy bikinis. The girls that captured his eye, the ones who made his head feel light and his heart lurch, were the *little* girls splashing in the shallow end, the nine- and ten-year-olds, their skinny arms and legs made bubble-gum pink by the sun's bright warmth.

At least twice a day Max paged himself, and with a great sigh he would stand at the sound of his name over the intercom, ignoring the phone inside Jack Rose's cabana and walking instead through the clots of sunbathers until he reached the white house phone next to the outside bar.

"Max Rheingold," he would growl into the receiver. Then, with the dial tone buzzing in his ear, he would launch into a seamless but imaginary conversation with a superstar actor or a bankable director. "Yes, yes, Warren, I totally agree with you one hundred percent. The script needs work, of course, but I spoke to John Huston and assured him that Waldo's rewrite would solve all our problems. Of course I understand your concerns, but what *you* must understand is that I would never have the name Max Rheingold associated with any project that was not distinguished."

This pathetic ruse to elevate himself in the Hollywood hierarchy never fooled anyone sitting poolside. But if Max noticed the eyes rolling or heard the embarrassed titters that followed him back to his chaise in front of Jack Rose's cabana, you would never know it by the fresh light in his eyes and the triumphant smile on his face.

★

PART THREE

A VERY

LONG

WEEKEND

★

Twelve

Saturday:

Burk

Meets

Max

Rheingold walked into the coffee shop and took a seat at the counter, groaning loudly when he glanced over and saw Burk cutting into his pancakes.

"Jesus, will you look at that plate. You know how long it's been since I had pancakes?" Burk put down his fork and turned a little on his stool. "Twenty-six months. Over two years. No butter, eggs, coffee, alcohol, or red meat either. I brought my weight down from three-oh-seven to two thirty-two. I'm goin' to heaven," he said, and offered his hand.

After Burk introduced himself, Rheingold slammed his fist on the counter.

"Of course! *Pledging My Love*! Great script. Absolutely wonderful. I want to work with you, Ray. Anything you want to do: cop story, Western, romantic comedy, I don't give a fuck. Let's get in trouble together, let's make a picture."

A confused look came into Burk's eyes that Rheingold noticed. "I think you should talk to my agent," Burk said.

"Your agent?"

"Her name is—"

"Maria Selene! I know who your fucking agent is. What am I, some kind of a dipshit? Listen to me, kid," Rheingold said, lowering his voice as he leaned across the counter. "I own the remake rights to thirty films. *Pecos Outlaws, Peace in the Valley, Massacre at Dawn,* just to name three. You ever see *Careless Love?*" Burk shook his head. "Dick Peterson, Della Short, Kenny Kendall. Takes place at a dog track in Tucson. It's got everything: murder, incest, adultery, dead animals, the works. It'd be a terrific vehicle for Beatty and Dunaway. Just needs someone to dress it up a little, modernize it. I'll have Jack screen it for you."

"Jack?"

"Jack Rose. He's my partner," Rheingold said, straight-faced. He took out a long cigar and slowly slid off the cellophane wrapper. "He had your script layin' around his cabana. I read it and gave him my notes."

A waitress came out of the kitchen and glared at Rheingold. An Ace bandage ran from her calf to her knee. "Oh, that's wonderful," she said. "Now you're gonna stink up the place."

Max smiled. "Calm down, Dotty."

"Don't tell me to calm down, Mr. Rheingold. I don't need your advice, thank you very much. He bothering you?" she asked Burk.

"No. Everything's fine."

"If he bothers you, tell me."

"I will."

An elderly man in an expensive gray silk suit walked into the coffee shop. He glanced in Rheingold's direction before he took a seat at the far end of the counter. "I'd like rye toast and a cup of tea," he said to the waitress in an English accent.

As soon as the waitress moved into the kitchen with the order, Rheingold slid over to the stool next to Burk. "We're gonna work together, kid," he said confidently, his fish eyes bulging out. "I can feel it."

Burk began to eat more avidly than he wanted. "Get back where you belong and let this one finish his breakfast," the waitress told Rheingold when she came out of the kitchen. "Stop bein' a pest. And you slow down," she scolded Burk.

Rheingold heaved his bulk over one stool and snapped open the *LA Times.* Manson's picture on the front page made him sneer. "You see this piece of shit," he said. "This prick and his hippie-slut follow-ers were swimming in my pool a week before they killed Sharon Tate and that bunch. Swimming naked in *my* pool." Down the counter the Englishman chuckled softly over the top of his teacup. "Something funny about that down there?" The Englishman scratched his ear and mumbled an apology. "Fuckin' limey asshole."

"Max!" The waitress was pointing toward a wall phone. "One more remark like that and I call upstairs."

"This music guy rented the house next door to me," Rheingold said to Burk, after he shrugged off the waitress. "He was a drummer in one of those English bands. Chocolate Jockstrap or something. I don't know. But they were sex crazed, I can tell you that. And so were their groupies. I used to look out the window and see them bangin' each other in broad daylight. In front of the fuckin' help, for Christ's sake.

"One morning I saw Manson running around over there, chas-ing this cunt across the patio, whipping her back with a heavy belt until she fell and cracked her head on the bricks. He just left her there. I thought she was dead. Finally, she got up and staggered back into the house. A few minutes later the Jap gardener came into the back-yard and hosed her blood into the pool.

"A week or so later, the guy who rented the place moved out. The owner put it up for sale and drained the pool. That Sunday I was taking a snooze when I heard a bunch of screaming and laughing coming from my backyard. I look outside and I see Charlie and his girls splashing in *my* pool.

"First I called the cops, then I got my loaded forty-five out of my dresser. When I came downstairs, Manson right away wants to apologize, offering me a joint, giving me all this peace and love bullshit. Then I noticed plates of food and empty bottles all over the lawn. How about this? They raided my fucking icebox and my liquor cabinet while I was sleeping. When I told him the cops were on their way over, Manson just grinned, showing not the tiniest bit of fear. He said, 'That's too bad, fat man. I thought we could party.'

"One of his girls—Krenwinkle, I think—came over and started rubbin' up against me like a cat in heat. Manson was watching and grinning this evil smile, giving the girl signals with his eyes. When she started to go down on me, I forgot I was holding the pistol, and Manson snatched it right out of my hand. I thought for sure he was gonna put a bullet in my head, but he didn't; instead, he cocked the hammer and rested the barrel against this girl's cheek while she continued to suck me off.

"God knows how I kept a hard-on, but when I shot my wad she stood up and spit the whole deal in my pool. Then, while the rest of his crew got dressed, Manson found his wallet and took out a fifty-dollar bill. He said, 'Thanks for the booze.' I said, 'Keep it,' and he said, 'No deal. I always pay my way.' Then they all took off in a broken-down van that was parked at the end of my driveway.

"In awhile the cops drove up and I told them it was a false alarm. A few months after Manson was arrested, I looked out my window and saw this woman running across my lawn, waving a pistol. By then, all the papers were talkin' about Manson's death list, all the people he planned to kill, so naturally I thought this broad was sent up to take me out.

"As it turned out it was some dingbat psycho from Detroit, an escapee from a mental institution apparently looking to kill Hank Fonda, who lived across the street."

Burk rose with his check and Rheingold followed him over to the register. "Isn't that an amazing story?" he said, smiling, prodding Burk in the side with his elbow. "And the whole thing is true. Every word." Burk was making an intense effort not to smash his fist into Rheingold's fat face. He received his change and moved into the hallway that led to the elevators and the main lobby. Beside him, Rheingold was saying, "Every nutball in the country ends up here, sooner or later. That's why I love this town. Anything can happen."

Burk stopped in the middle of the lobby and stood in silence for a moment, glaring at Rheingold. Then, in a voice that was quiet but communicated his anger, he said, "Stop following me."

Rheingold looked visibly hurt. Sputtering, he said, "Following you? I'm not following you. We're having a conversation. But look, I'm sorry—"

"Just leave me the fuck alone," Burk said, stopping Rheingold before he could launch into an apology. "You got it?"

Rheingold hesitated, waiting until he could lift one corner of his mouth into a smile. "Sure," he said. "No problem. I don't work with prima donnas, anyway."

The phone rang while Burk was shaving. When he picked up, Maria Selene sounded relieved. "I don't believe it. It's actually you."

"Hi, Maria."

"I've left umpteen messages."

"I'm sorry."

"Forget about me. Paramount's paying you a thousand a week. You can't just disappear for three days. They want to know where you are."

"I'm around."

"Did you get Talbott's memo?"

"Yeah."

"And?"

"I'm not sure I want to change the scene with Eric and Barbara up on Mulholland."

"The rest?"

"I can live with most of it. The scene inside the motel always needed work."

"I'll get you another five grand."

"I don't need to get paid, Maria."

"You write, they pay. That's the deal," Maria said. She sounded determined. "You already gave them a free set of revisions and a producer's read."

"Do what you want. I'll send down the pages."

There was a short silence. "From where?"

"Berkeley."

"You're leaving? When?"

"Tomorrow night."

"They want you here for the reunion. Warren said it was important. They really need you, Ray."

Burk moved to the window. Down below he saw a lazy-looking girl in a tennis outfit walk out of the hotel. She was no older than sixteen. Standing behind her, stroking her arms, was a slim, middle-aged man wearing a clean white T-shirt and pressed bell-bottom jeans that had sunflowers sewn into the back pockets. The couple got inside a blue Mercedes convertible that was waiting by the curb. When they pulled away, Burk said, "Let me think about it. Maybe I'll stay over till Monday."

Maria said, "That's very generous of you."

Burk was still watching the front of the hotel. Max Rheingold came outside and stood underneath the green awning. He was holding a Bloody Mary in a tall glass. A moment later Burt Driscoll, the hotel's general manager, was standing by his shoulder. There was a short but heated conversation that ended when Max spun around and stalked angrily back inside the hotel.

Burk looked up. The sky was milkier than it was an hour ago. Maybe the sun would finally come out, he thought, as he returned his gaze to the front of the hotel. Eventually he said, "I gotta go. I gotta pick up my kid."

On his way out of the hotel, Burk noticed Max Rheingold sitting on the steps in the shallow end of the pool. A short distance away, a girl of six or seven was floating on her stomach, buoyed by a pair of pink water wings.

As he passed by, Burk heard Rheingold say, "You're a very pretty girl. Did anyone ever tell you that?"

"*Everyone* tells me that."

"Do you believe them?"

"Of course I do," the little girl said. "Wouldn't you?"

"I would if I were as pretty as you."

"But you're not," she said matter-of-factly.

"No."

"I'm a tiny angel and you're a fat old man."

The muscles tensed in Rheingold's back as he struggled not to look angry or hurt. After a thoughtful pause, he said, "That wasn't such a nice thing to say."

"I know," the little girl said as she churned the water with her hands.

"Then say you're sorry."

The girl paddled into the center of the pool and flipped herself over on her back, remaining silent as she looked up at the sky with a tiny smile on her lips. Max Rheingold stared at her helplessly for several seconds. Then he got to his feet and started walking across the lawn, taking the most direct route back to Jack Rose's cabana.

Once inside he stood absolutely still for a long time, looking down at his shadow, which lay flat on the floor. "You're nothing, Max," he whispered, his ugly, malicious face stretched into a grimace of pain. "You never were."

Thirteen

Louie

Arrives

In Burk's mind the possibility that he could miss Louie's flight was linked up with a painful childhood memory: a Saturday afternoon in the late summer of 1954. He and Gene were coming home from Trinity Ranch, a boys' camp located deep in the rugged mountains east of Lake Arrowhead. The drop-off point was in the north end of Griffith Park, behind the zoo. But when the yellow school buses filled with singing campers pulled into the parking lot at four o'clock—the designated time of arrival, confirmed by a postcard sent to each parent one week before the end of the camp session—Burk did not see his father's face among the moms and dads waiting expectantly by the open tailgates of their station wagons.

No one answered when Gene phoned their house. "He's probably on his way," he told Burk, "or maybe he got a flat or something. Don't worry, he'll be here."

"Call the newsstand," Burk said, but he wasn't there either.

Thirty minutes passed. Then an hour. Finally, when the lot had emptied, Don Haverford, the camp director, drove them home.

* * *

Their father came in the front door around eight that evening. With him was Ada Furlong, Ricky's mom. They were both drunk.

"What the hell's goin' on here?" Nathan Burk said, staring at the duffel bags and fishing gear dumped in the center of the living room. "You're supposed to be back tomorrow."

Gene shook his head. "Today, Dad."

"That's nuts. I had it marked on the calendar. Sunday the twenty-eighth."

"Sunday," Ada Furlong said, swaying. "That's what he told me."

Don Haverford was sitting on the couch. He stood up. He was military-trim and well muscled, a college wrestling champion, according to his biography in the camp brochure. "Today's the twenty-eighth," he said, faking a friendly smile. "But it was no problem. I was happy to drive them home. They were terrific campers. Two of the best."

Without responding, Nathan Burk turned and went into the bathroom and began to pee. Ada Furlong moved unsteadily toward the front door. She tripped over a fishing pole, ripping a long run in one of her stockings. "I gotta get going," she said loudly, using the back of the sofa to regain her balance. "I'll talk to you tomorrow, Nate. I'll tell Ricky the boys are back. He'll be pleased."

Don Haverford shook hands with Nathan Burk when he came out of the bathroom, and then he followed Ada Furlong outside, into the soft blue late-summer evening.

"She means nothing to me," Nathan Burk told his sons, when they were alone. "Ada's just company. That's all."

"It's okay," Gene said. "You don't have to explain."

Nathan Burk took a seat on the couch. There was a pained look on his face. "I messed up today," he said, aware that Gene and Burk were staring at him. "I forgot. I forgot what day it was. I'm sorry."

Gene said, "It's all right, Dad. We got home safe and sound. That's all that counts."

"Did you miss us?" Burk asked.

Nathan Burk nodded. Then he spread his arms and pulled his boys in close to his chest. "Yeah," he said. "I missed you guys a lot."

★

By the time Burk made it to the airport, Louie's flight was already on the ground and the curb in front of the PSA terminal was clogged with taxis and shuttle vans. Panicked, he double-parked in a red zone behind a limousine, slipped the Sky Cap a twenty to guard his car, and sprinted up the outside escalator. In less than a minute he arrived at the gate check-in counter, sweating and out of breath.

"I'm looking for my son," he said to the woman agent in charge. "He was on Flight 232."

The agent was humming to herself as she meticulously sorted boarding passes, placing the first class and coach in separate piles. Without looking up, she said, "Are you Raymond Burk?"

"Yes."

"He's waiting for you by the administration office. Take the escalator down and follow the signs."

"There was an accident on the freeway," Burk said, needing to explain his tardiness. "I should've left earlier, but I got hung up." He looked around, confused. "The administration office? Where again?"

The agent lifted her face. She was fairly young, in her twenties, with high cheek bones and a prim, delicate mouth that was set in a frown. Pointing over his shoulder, she said, "Down and follow the signs."

Louie was sitting next to the baggage conveyor, straddling his suitcase, when he saw his father step off the escalator. "Yippie! There he is! There's my dad!" he shouted, and a black stewardess who was seated nearby looked up from her newspaper. "Dad! Over here!" Burk stood frozen, his head twisting from side to side. Louie waved his arms over his head. "Here I am, Dad!" Burk finally saw his son and rushed forward, scooping him up with both hands and burying his face in his neck. "I knew you'd be here," Louie said. "I knew you wouldn't forget me."

Burk felt suddenly weak, as if he were on the verge of tears. "You have quite a boy," the stewardess said, moving forward with Louie's suitcase. "He has a wonderful imagination." She extended her right hand. "Madeline Wells," she said. "I was one of the stews on Louie's flight."

"Thank you for staying with him."

"No problem. It's part of the job."

"I got screwed up with the time."

"Those things happen. It's no big deal."

Burk looked away. "Yes it is. He's my kid."

"And he knew you would be here," she said. Her hand was on his arm. "Don't worry. He was fine."

Burk looked into Madeline Wells's face now. She was staring at him levelly, with a slight smile. "Can I give you a lift somewhere?" he asked her.

"I live in Westwood. Is that too far?"

"No." Burk reached for the suitcase. "It's right on the way."

In the car while Louie squirmed in the backseat, Madeline Wells described his behavior on the flight south. Although she made it sound amusing, trying for a comic effect, she could tell that Burk seemed concerned. "Does he act like that a lot?" she asked him.

"No," Burk said, meeting her eyes for a moment, "not really."

"He says he has a movie screen inside his head."

"I do," Louie said.

"Part of the time he seemed like he was in a trance. I thought he was just goofin' like kids do, so I left him alone. But this fat lady sitting next to him was having a fit. I thought she was gonna pass out when he said our flight number—two thirty-two—was an unlucky number."

Burk looked into the rearview, but Louie hid his face below the seat. "He's just a kid. He makes things up." Burk glanced over his shoulder. "Right, Louie?"

Louie shrugged. Madeline Wells said, "He told me his mom was in prison."

Burk nodded, reached across her lap, and flipped the radio over to KGFJ, the rhythm-and-blues station. "What else did he tell you?"

"That you two are goin' out to visit her."

"He tell you she killed a guy?"

"Self-defense," she said. "Is that right?"

"Yeah."

The Wilshire off-ramp was coming up, and Burk veered into the right lane. "What about you?" he said.

"What about me?"

"Are you from LA?"

"Nope. Oakland. I came down here to go to college."

"Where?"

"UCLA."

Burk pulled off the freeway. "That's a good school."

"Turn right at the second signal."

"Did you graduate?"

"Of course I graduated," she said, looking at Burk sideways. "In 'sixty-three. I was a probation officer for two years. I quit after the Watts riots."

"My brother was a cop."

"Yeah?"

"He quit too."

Louie's eyes were open. "Am I gonna see Gene while I'm here?"

"Maybe."

"Take a right on Veteran," Madeline Wells said, pointing. "It's the third building on the left. The Veteran Plaza."

Burk's tires rubbed up against the curb when he parked in front of the apartment. A boy in his teens walked up the street singing to himself, watched by a heavyset woman who was sitting on a low stone wall that bordered the sidewalk. Recognizing Madeline, her worn-out face melted into a smile.

"Don't like to see me dating white men," Madeline Wells said, barely moving her lips.

"This isn't really a date."

"She don't know that."

Madeline Wells was staring at Burk, and there was something in her face he couldn't read. They both turned away at the same time, breaking the tension that was rising in the air. Louie said, "What about Grandpa? When do I get to see *him*?"

"Later, Louie."

"Maybe I can sleep over."

"Maybe."

Louie turned around and shaded his eyes against the hard sunlight that slashed through the back window. "How come we're sitting here, Dad?"

"Because this is where I live," Madeline Wells said. "I'm saying good-bye to your father." She reached down for her purse and a small carry-on bag that sat on the floor by her feet. "Thanks for the lift."

"Maybe we *should* have a date," Burk said. His hand was on top of hers.

"You think so?" Madeline Wells's skirt was bunched up around her thighs and their fingers were interlocked in her lap. "Where are you staying, Mr. Burk?"

"Beverly Hills Hotel."

"Fancy."

"Give me your number."

"No. I'll call you."

"Tonight?"

Madeline Wells glanced at Louie. He was lying on his back, moving his lips silently while he traced words in the air above his head. "I think you should spend some time with your son," she said. Burk leaned across the seat. A moment later he was kissing her mouth. She moaned softly when their tongues touched, then quickly pushed him away with both hands. "No. We can't do this, Mr. Burk. Not here," she said, and pulled her hand out of his grip. Her eyes were glowing and her skin shone like burnished wood. "I'll call you."

"Tonight."

"Sometime."

Madeline Wells stepped out of the car, smoothed out the wrinkles in her skirt, and walked over to the row of mailboxes built into the wall next to the front door. After she fumbled in her purse for her keys and disappeared inside the building with her mail, Burk switched on the engine and lowered the convertible top.

To the east one block, on Sepulveda, he could see his boyhood Little League field and the empty parking lot flanking it. A large green scoreboard rose up beyond the fence in center field. Burk's hand was frozen on the ignition, his memory backing up fast to that Sunday morning when he and Gene and Ricky Furlong all tried out together.

During batting practice drills, Burk swung and missed on twelve straight pitches, never once making contact, not even a foul tip. In the outfield he muffed two pop flies and nearly beaned a coach with a wild throw back to second base. He was cut in the first round.

"I don't care. I'm no good and I know it," he told Gene, and he watched the rest of the tryouts in the grandstand with several rows of nervous parents.

Gene made it through the second and third rounds, but one of the coaches—an older man with watery blue eyes—pulled him aside after he was timed running the bases. "You're a good athlete, but you're not quick enough," he told Gene.

"I can get quick. I'll lose weight," Gene said. "I'll start tonight."

The coach's hand was resting on Gene's shoulder. "Give it a shot next year," he said gently.

Gene's eyes were filling up. "I can't. I'll be too old," he said, turning away to avoid the looks of the boys standing nearby. "This is my last year."

"He's a good fielder," Ricky Furlong said, passing by the coach on his way into the batting cage. "Damn good."

Another coach, a younger man with a slight limp, moved over. "Everyone can't make the roster," he told Gene.

Gene smacked his thigh with his glove. "I'm as good as anyone out there, except maybe Ricky."

"He did okay at third and he put one near the fence," the older man said. "It was between him and Dixon for the last spot."

"I'm better than Dixon," Gene said. He could hardly get the words out through his tears. "I know I am."

The older coach shrugged. "Dixon ran the bases in eighteen point two. You couldn't break twenty."

From the grandstand Burk saw his brother angrily kick his spiked shoe into the third base bag. Then he turned and started walking slowly toward the dugout with his head down. "My brother didn't make the team," Burk said to the woman seated next to him, an overtanned blonde with a grim face.

"Got cut," she said, snapping the gum in her mouth. "That's too bad."

Burk heard the crack of the bat and the crowd rose as one, following the flight of the ball until it bounced off the top of the scoreboard. There was a moment of awed silence before the woman sitting next to Burk said, "Holy Christ! I never saw a ten-year-old hit like that kid Furlong."

"I remember this street," Louie said, when they were back on Wilshire, moving east in the middle lane. "The hospital where Mom stayed was around here someplace. Right? When you hurt her jaw. I wonder what she looks like now."

"We'll find out tomorrow," Burk said.

At Beverly Glen they stopped for a red light. Next to them a city bus idled loudly, belching black smoke from the exhaust. In a window a young woman with a blond ponytail looked up from a magazine. She caught Louie's eye and waved, and he grinned and waved back.

"What if she doesn't recognize me?" Louie said, when the light changed.

Burk abruptly felt his heart pound. He forced a laugh that sounded hollow. "C'mon, Louie, she's your mom. She'll recognize you."

"But what if she doesn't?" he said. "She hasn't seen me in a long time."

"She's got pictures," Burk said. "I sent her pictures."

Louie sat up. "You did? She's seen me? She knows how big I've gotten?"

Burk nodded. "I sent her the ones we took at Tilden Park, with Tim and his girlfriend Juliet."

"The picnic where we flew kites?"

"Right."

Burk made a left on Whittier Drive and drove north through the residential part of Beverly Hills. Near Sunset a black maid in a white uniform stood in front of a driveway leading up to a large estate that was invisible from the road. In her hand was a thick bundle of letters that she had just retrieved from the gray metal mailbox. Two doors away a boy with a serious face sat behind a card table that was set up on the sidewalk. A sign said FRESH LEMONADE, 25 CENTS A GLASS.

Burk pulled over. He gave Louie a dollar to hand to the boy. "Two glasses," Burk said, "and keep the change."

A woman wearing shorts and a green tank top stood on the porch of the house across the street. Down her driveway came a Chevy El Camino with POOL ACE lettered on the front fender. The boy behind the table handed Louie two paper cups filled with lemonade. He said, "Do you live around here?"

Louie shook his head.

"Where do you live?"

"We used to live here," Burk said. "We moved away."

Burk put the car in drive and accelerated slowly up the street. The steering wheel underneath his hands felt warm from the sun. When he turned right on Sunset, he felt something lurking in his chest, something dark and threatening, a nameless terror that made him fearful for himself and for his son. Louie saw the look on his face and said, "What's wrong, Dad?"

"Nothing."

"Something's wrong."

"No, I'm fine," Burk said, trying to reassure him with a smile. Then he took a deep breath and drove back to the hotel.

Fourteen

**Saturday
Night:
Burk Finds
His Past
in the Dark**

Later that afternoon, having dropped off Louie at his father's house, Burk decided to stop for a drink at the Cock and Bull. There were only two customers at the bar, a roly-poly man wearing tight beltless slacks and an attractive but cold-looking woman with her left arm in a red silk sling.

She had broken it a few months earlier, Burk overheard her tell the bartender. "During the Sylmar quake. I was sleeping when it hit. I got thrown out of bed and the ceiling fell on me. The neck brace came off yesterday, but I still have my ribs bandaged."

"My cat disappeared," the bartender said. "Three-year-old calico named Bill. Just dove through the window and that was that. Last I saw of him."

"Animals freak. They can feel it before it happens," the woman said, pulling a Viceroy out of the pack sitting on the bar.

The man she was with lit her cigarette with a silver lighter. "The apartment building next to mine fell down like it was made of tinker toys," he said. "The next day they found two kids dead underneath the rubble."

"Price you pay to live in paradise," said the woman, smiling tightly as she studied her face in the mirror behind the bar.

"I don't buy that," said the man with her. "Buildings should be made to stand up better."

"God doesn't care about building codes," said the bartender. "You can count on that."

Burk swigged down three double screwdrivers before he went back to the pay phone and found Madeline Wells's number in the Western directory. No one answered so he called his brother, who picked up on the second ring.

"Gene."

"What's up, Ray?"

"Not much. Just thought I'd check in."

"I tried you at the hotel. I wanted to talk to Louie."

"He's spending the night at Dad's. I just dropped him off."

"Where are you now?"

"Cock and Bull."

"You sound ripped."

"I'm okay."

"Why don't you stay at the hotel and drink?"

"Don't lecture me. Okay? Monday I'm on a plane. I'm out of your life."

"No, you're not. You're just four hundred miles away."

Burk started to laugh.

"What's so funny?"

"You're gonna think I'm crazy."

"You *are* crazy."

"No, really."

"Really."

"Gene, listen. And don't fuckin' make fun of me. Guess who I've been seein' around town?"

"Who?"

"Ricky Furlong."

"Bullshit."

"I knew you'd say that."

"Where?"

"Around."

"Come on, Ray. Around. In the sky? In a car? Sitting on top of the Hollywood sign? *Where?*"

"In front of the studio collecting autographs. Outside the Rexall on Beverly and La Cienega. Today, at the pool by the hotel."

"By the pool?"

"Yeah."

"Ray, exactly how many drinks have you had?"

"Gene, I'm not shitting you. It's him. He's always with this goofy-looking kid with these huge saucer eyes. And they dress alike too. It's spooky." There was silence on the other end. "Gene?"

"Maybe you just think it's him."

"It's Ricky Furlong, Gene. I know it's him."

When Burk came back to the bar, the squat man was gone, his place taken by a wiry, nervous-looking guy with a face filled with false generosity. Burk ordered another drink and the bartender said, "Let's make it a single this time."

"I'm not drunk," Burk said.

"Just my advice."

"I don't need your advice," Burk said, sounding angrier than he really was.

The nervous guy snickered. "Give the kid what he wants," he said, then he winked at Burk and introduced himself. "Eddie Cortese."

"Ray Burk."

The bartender leaned toward the woman wearing the sling. "He's a writer," he said, trying to sound confidential. "They all got problems with the stuff."

"What does he write?" the woman said, catching Burk's eye as she pushed a wisp of hair away from her beautiful black eyebrows.

"Maybe he should write about you," Eddie Cortese countered quickly. "Huh, Judy? You could tell him some stories. Talk about a crazy life."

The woman turned her head and gave Eddie Cortese a scathing look. "I don't think we need to go into that."

"He wouldn't believe it anyway."

"Eddie," the woman said, "will you please shut the fuck up?"

"I'd like another drink," Burk said. "Make it a single."

The bartender smiled. "Comin' right up. What about you, Miss Exner?"

"No. I'm through for the night. Call me a cab."

After the woman left the bar, Eddie Cortese ordered a martini, drank part of it, then glanced at Burk. "Judy's got a lot of friends in high places. If I told you some of their names you wouldn't believe me."

"She's been in here with Peter Lawford," the bartender said. "Couple of times."

Eddie Cortese shook his head. "Bigger than that."

"Sammy?"

"Bigger."

"Sinatra?"

"Bigger."

"Nobody's bigger than Frank."

From somewhere in the restaurant Burk heard a woman talking much too loudly about Charles Manson.

"I used to go out with Polanski. Jay Sebring introduced us," she said, mentioning one of Manson's victims. "He did my hair for the last three years. Nobody's got it right since."

Burk glanced over his shoulder. The woman speaking was sitting in a booth against the far wall. She was about twenty-two, with cheap-looking makeup and platinum-blond hair that was cut in a shag. Seated across from her was a powerfully built middle-aged man with squashed ears and a sensitive mouth that was too large for the rest of his vacuous face.

The stumpy guy in tight slacks came back inside the Cock and Bull and joined the couple in the booth. "I was telling Art about Jay," the blonde said.

"She said she met him at the Daisy."

"The fat guy's a photographer," Eddie Cortese said to Burk. "The other one is in distribution. Art somebody. The chick works down the street."

"She wants to be a centerfold," the bartender said. "Her name's Callie. She's from someplace in Ohio."

"Fucking Hefner," Eddie Cortese said, shaking his head. "Can you imagine the pussy that man gets?"

Burk excused himself and walked back to the pay phone. This time when he dialed Madeline Wells her line was busy. He hung up and waited. From the bar he heard Eddie Cortese say, "What's the scoop on the kid?"

"He's got a picture at Paramount."

"Yeah? Don't look too happy about it."

"Writers are never happy," the bartender said. "Fitzgerald, Mankiewicz, Faulkner: all a bunch of sad sacks. Chandler was the worst. Mister Doom and Gloom."

Burk heard himself laugh but wasn't sure why. Madeline Wells's line was still busy so he dialed Loretta's number in Encino. No answer there. He slammed the receiver down hard and stood by the phone. Inside, he could hear the blonde talking about her latest visit to the Playboy mansion. She said, "Jack Nicholson was there. He came with Candy Bergen and Ann-Margret. They're doing a picture over at Fox."

The photographer said, "I shot her eight-by-tens."

The blonde sat up erect. "Whose? Ann-Margret's?"

"Candy's. Edgar and I go way back."

"I liked her in *The Group*," the distributor said. "It did nine million here but very little overseas."

"Another round," the blonde called out to the bartender. Then, to both men, she said, "Let's talk about me."

"Miss February is still open," the photographer said. "Hef's gonna look at the proofs on Monday."

"What do you think my chances are?"

"Fifty–fifty. If he says he wants to see you in person, they go to seventy-five–twenty-five."

"What if I fuck him?"

"You have to fuck him regardless."

"Just like I had to fuck you."

"Without pictures you have no calling card."

"This is not an easy town," the distributor said. Underneath the table his hand was resting on her knee. "A lot of girls out there wanna be Miss February."

The blonde said, "What do I get if I fuck you?"

"The clap."

Burk heard everyone in the booth laugh. He was laughing too. Eddie Cortese came by the pay phone on his way to the men's room. He handed Burk a drink. "Pete says it's on him."

Burk dialed Madeline Wells. This time the line was clear but no one answered. After ten rings Burk said, "Fuck it. I'm out of this place."

* * *

At midnight Burk found himself parked across the street from the Veteran Plaza Apartments. Televisions still glowed in several windows, and behind one of the curtains he glimpsed a stocky couple dancing a foxtrot in their living room. On the wall behind them was a painting of a deer.

"Excuse me?"

Burk turned his head and saw an old man standing in the clotted darkness. A white terrier with a bandage over one eye sat by his feet.

"Your lights are on."

Burk hesitated for a moment before he leaned forward and pushed in the switch. "Thanks."

"Last week I did the same thing," the old man said. "Had to call the Auto Club. By the time they got me charged up, I missed my dentist appointment. You live around here?"

Burk shook his head. "No. I'm just visiting someone."

A couple moved up the sidewalk and turned into the entrance of the Veteran Plaza. The woman gave the man a key, and he let her inside. In the lighted foyer Burk saw that the woman was Madeline Wells. Her date was a black man with long storky legs.

"Are you all right?" the old man asked Burk.

"Yeah."

"You don't look too hot."

"I'm okay."

The old man took a step closer, until he was standing in the pink glow of a streetlamp. "Don't take this the wrong way," he said, "but I think you maybe had too much to drink."

"That's probably true." Burk realized with a lunge of surprise that he recognized the old man's face. "I think I know you."

The old man blinked. "You do?"

"You're Frank Dunlop," Burk said. "You taught American History at Westside High. Right?" The old man remained silent. "My name's Ray Burk."

The old man nodded, the confusion that clouded his face slowly giving way to a small smile. "Yes, of course. Now I remember. And you had a brother."

"Gene."

"Gene. That's right. A tough character," the old man said, making a fist. "Very tough."

Burk looked away. "I plagiarized a paper in your honors class," he said reluctantly. "It was on American political cartoonists between the wars. I copied everything straight out of a library book. You gave me an *A*. I didn't deserve it."

"Then do it over."

Burk turned and stared at the old man. There was nothing in his tired-looking face that said he was joking. "Do the paper over?"

"If it's bothering you, do it again. Send it to me and I'll grade it." Now the old man was smiling. "You're not the first, Mr. Burk. You don't have to be ashamed."

"I'm not ashamed."

The old man sighed. "Of course you are," he said. "You cheated. But you were bright, you didn't have to. You could have done well, regardless."

"I thought I needed help," Burk said, feeling both embarrassed and excited at telling the truth. "I didn't think I could do the work by myself. Can you understand that?"

"Yes."

"It's been bothering me. I didn't realize it until right now. I still think I need help," Burk said. He turned in his seat and pointed to the west, where a bank of lights were hidden in the dark trees. "See that field over there? That's where me and my brother tried out for Little League. Neither of us made it, but Gene should've."

"If he'd made it, would it have been easier for you?"

"Yes."

"How?"

"He was my big brother."

"And you needed him on the team."

"Yes." Tears washed into Burk's eyes.

"Did he ever get to help you?"

"He helps me now, because I'm having trouble with my life."

"Life can be very difficult. You will always need help."

Burk wiped the tears out of his eyes with the sleeve of his shirt. "My son needs help too."

"Then you will help him," the old man said, turning away.

"Wait," Burk said. The old man looked over his shoulder. "Do you really remember me?"

"Yes," the old man said. "I do. You were funny. You told funny stories in class. You made us all laugh. And you had a best friend?"

"Timmy Miller."

"And a mother who left."

"Yes."

"And your father owned a newsstand."

"Yes."

"That's all I remember," the old man said. Then, in a completely different tone, as if he were talking to an old friend, he said, "Why are you here tonight, Ray? A woman?"

"Yes."

"She can't help you. Go home." The old man began walking slowly up the street, leading his dog. Before he disappeared into the darkness—over the jingle jangle of the choke chain—Burk heard him say: "Write the paper. Do it soon."

It was 3 A.M. and Burk was in his car, listening to Radio Ray tell his audience that he was leaving the airwaves. "For good. This is my final show," he said, before he opened the phones. "I've been thinking about this for quite awhile, but I'm making it official tonight. Whoops! I guess I took my engineer by surprise," he said, allowing himself a little laugh. "He just spilled his coffee in his lap."

"What're you gonna do?" asked the first caller, a man named Rex.

"I'm not sure. Travel. Garden. Read. Try to find a girl and maybe settle down."

"Have some kids."

"That's in the plan somewhere."

"Put it on the top of the list. Kids are where it's at, as long as you don't expect too much from them when they're grown. Take my word for it. I spawned five, so I know. They all turned out fine except one, the middle son, Lee. Somewhere he got this name inside his head that he can't get out: Edgar Peters. Repeats it over and over and over. All day long. Ask him who this fella is and he just shrugs. Don't know him from Adam's house cat, he says. Can't hold a job or lead a normal life if you got that goin' on upstairs. He's up at Patton State Hospital now, where they're tryin' out a new drug."

"Let's hope it works."

"I ain't holdin' my breath."

Radio Ray's next caller said he was using a pay phone in Culver City.

"Right now I'm gassin' up my car," he told Radio Ray. His voice sounded optimistic. "Actually it's a Ford Ranchero. I'm on my way up to Sacramento to visit an old war buddy."

Radio Ray said, "Jimmy Fain, this boy I grew up with, he had a 'fifty-nine Ranchero. White."

"Mine's black," said the caller.

"Jimmy missed a turn comin' back from Lake Ballard. Three kids riding in back were killed: the Boulton brothers, Pete and Greg, and Mary Sperling. That was in the summer of 'fifty-nine. 'Personality,' by Lloyd Price was all over the radio that summer. That was Jimmy Fain's favorite song. Mine was 'Only Sixteen' by Sam Cooke."

"Gene had those," Burk said out loud, speaking directly to the radio. "He owned every oldie you can think of. But there were no oldies back in 'fifty-nine. Everything was new—all the tunes, the chicks, sex, everything. It was a cool summer," he said, looking out the windows at the star-scattered sky. "A lot of things seemed better back then."

Although there was still one more hour left, Radio Ray accepted only one more call, the last he would ever take. It was from a woman who chose to remain anonymous. She said, "Life? There is no meaning. Love? It never lasts. The truth is you never know the truth. Be grateful. Face reality. Stay out of the future. Treat people decently. There is only integrity. That's it. That's all you'll need to know."

That night Burk dreamt he was inside the Grauman's Chinese Theatre on Hollywood Boulevard, watching Doris Day dance with James Cagney in the musical *West Point Story*. His father was sitting next to him and his cousin Aaron was in the same row, but they were separated by three seats.

In the middle of a production number, Ricky Furlong came down the aisle and sat behind Nathan Burk. He said, "I've got Doris Day's autograph in my book. I was on the set. My dad took me. I got James Cagney's, too, and Virginia Mayo and Gordon MacRae."

Aaron spoke to Ricky while Burk and his father watched the action on the screen. "I knew Cagney in New York," Aaron said. "He was a tough guy, real tough. But not as tough as me. Right, Nate?"

"Right," Nathan Burk said. He leaned toward his son and spoke out of the side of his mouth. "Every Sunday after church, Doris came by the newsstand. I gave her a copy of the *Cincinnati Enquirer*. That's her hometown. She went to high school with Vera-Ellen.

That's a little-known fact. She started out as a dancer. Her mother sewed all her outfits until she was sixteen and went on the road. She once owned a French poodle she called Smudge Pot. She's a great gal."

In the dream that followed, Burk was inside Bonnie Simpson's apartment in the Argyle Manor. On her television, two middleweight fighters from the fifties were slugging it out in Madison Square Garden. The picture was in black-and-white until one fighter was cut over his eye; then the blood turned red as it ran in jagged lines down the side of his face.

Bonnie came into the room and sat on the edge of the bed. Her hair was freshly washed, and she was wearing vanilla corduroy trousers and a dark blue v-neck blouse that exposed the tops of her breasts. In her hand was a drink that looked like whiskey.

Burk said, "My mother wore the same skirt when she visited me once."

Bonnie smiled softly before she finished her drink in one swallow. After she put her empty glass on top of the nightstand, she stood up and casually stripped off her clothes. On the television there was a close-up of the spectators seated at ringside. Aaron was there, sitting next to Ricky's mother. Frank Havana, Max Rheingold, and Jack Rose were in the expensive seats, too. Grace Elliot was seated between them, the front of her white dress spotted with blood.

In the dream, Burk heard Bonnie say, "Tell me what you want me to do. I'll do anything you want."

"I want you to stay."

"You want me here when you wake up?"

"Yes."

"Then you'll have to be good to me."

"I will."

"I know you will," she said, "because you love me. Don't you?"

"Yes," Burk said in his dream. "I do."

★

Fifteen
Sunday

Max Rheingold was bloated and soaked in sweat when he woke up before daylight on Sunday morning. He tried to lift his clammy body out of bed but was thrown backward by a stabbing pain that quickly burrowed deep into the folds of his stomach, searing his insides. "Jesus, not again," he said in a terrified whisper.

He reached for the phone to call Arthur Schlumberger. "He's not on duty this weekend," the operator said. "But I can have his associate, Dr. Marx, get back to you shortly. Is it an emergency?"

Rheingold gasped. 'Schlumberger's my doctor," he said, in an anguished voice. "I don't know Marx."

"I'm sorry, Mr. Rheingold, Dr. Schlumberger is not available."

"Find him."

"Mr. Rheingold—"

"Find him. Have him call me." Max Rheingold dropped the receiver on the floor and lay motionless, fighting a scream as the brutal pain circled slowly through his body, leaving him dizzy and breathless.

How did I get here? Max wondered through clenched teeth. How did I end up like this: a fat, pathetic old man dying of butt cancer in a hotel cabana that smells like wet towels? They took away my home; they didn't have to do that. I was only four months behind in the mortgage. Jack could've fronted me, that sonovabitch!

Max Rheingold suddenly moaned, not from the pain this time but from the memory of the phone call he'd received on Saturday afternoon. Jack Rose had called him from the card room at the Friars' Club, and his voice was filled with disappointment. "I got the hotel bill today, Max. You're spending way too much on food."

"I gotta eat, Jack."

"You eat like a pig," Jack said. Then he passed along what Burt Driscoll had told him earlier that day. "He said you were getting drunk, acting nuts, pushing people around in the lobby, and kicking over their luggage. Burt said a little girl complained to her mother about you. She said you were being overly friendly by the pool. He says it happens again and you're out. Nothin' I can do about it. I can't protect you," Jack said sternly.

"Protect me?"

"That's right, Max. You're a pervert."

"Don't fuckin' say that to me. We've been friends for thirty years. We went to Del Mar together, Jack. Tijuana. I watched you fuck two women in Vegas at the El Rancho Hotel. We were that close."

"We were never close."

"I was in the bed next to you. I could've reached out and slapped your bony ass. That's how close we were."

"I hardly know you."

"I started you out."

"You helped. I helped back."

"This is a business of friends, Jack."

"Friendships end."

"You can't put me out on the street."

"I'm hanging up."

"No."

"We're done here."

Click.

★

Burk drove east on the Pomona Freeway, steering the car with one hand while he fiddled with the radio until he found the signal for KIEV, the soul station in San Bernardino. Directly ahead of him, above the foothills, silver clouds were rushing across the sky like sheep through a blue pasture.

"Lookit this one," Louie said from the backseat, where he was sorting through a packet of snapshots his grandfather had given him that morning. "It's you and Uncle Gene."

"I'm driving, Louie."

"Here." Louie leaned forward, their cheeks almost touching as he displayed the photograph in front of Burk's face. "See, look."

In the picture Gene wore a holster and chaps and boots with silver spurs. His head was bent slightly, his eyes sighting down the barrel of a toy pistol that he pointed at the camera. Burk was dressed normally, in jeans and a long-sleeved shirt that was open at the neck. A leather football was tucked underneath his right arm. In between them stood their mother, her face set, determined. One hand was on Gene's shoulder, the other was shading her eyes against the watery sunlight.

"How old were you, Dad?"

"I'm not sure. Nine, maybe."

"You look angry," Louie said, and it was true: He was scowling, probably to hide the wide space between his teeth.

Louie held up another photograph of Burk's mother. She was wearing the same outfit—white slacks and a white sweater—but standing alone, her smile not quite hiding the sadness in her eyes. Behind her an open gate led into a tennis court where a game was in progress.

"She looks pretty," Louie said.

"I know."

"That's probably how my mom looks."

Burk didn't say anything.

"What's wrong?"

"Nothing. I was just trying to remember when these were taken."

Burk sifted through his memory until he found the year: 1951. It was in December, the week before Christmas, and his mother had arrived on their doorstep unannounced. "I'm only in town for one day," she'd said. "Just a surprise visit. So we can't tell anyone. Agreed?"

"Not even Dad?" Gene asked.

"No."

"Why?"

"Because it will make him sad."

Once they were sworn to secrecy, Burk remembered a taxi ride to Playland, a small amusement park on the outskirts of Beverly Hills. While their mom made a series of calls from a pay phone on the corner, he and Gene spent the rest of the morning riding the ponies and the bumper cars. Around noon, they bought soft ice cream and walked down La Cienega until they reached the municipal tennis courts on Olympic. There they watched a tanned but overweight teaching pro lose a match in straight sets to Buddy Jacobs, an itinerant gambler and tennis hustler from Baton Rouge, Louisiana, and Esther Burk's latest traveling companion. After money was exchanged in the clubhouse, they all piled into Buddy's 1947 Buick Roadster and drove up Fairfax to the Farmers Market. And that's where they bought the cowboy gear and the football, Burk recalled, and the camera, and the new tennis sweater his mother was wearing in the photograph.

"Are we getting close, Dad?"

"A few more miles."

Louie looked off down the road; then he sought out Burk's eyes in the rearview mirror. "Do you remember the day the police came to nursery school because Mom was drinking wine in her car outside the playground? Your mom never did anything like that, did she?"

"No, not like that."

"And I bet she didn't make a bunch of jigsaw puzzles and glue them to the walls of the kitchen. Or go to the supermarket in her pajamas and slippers." Louie giggled into his hands. "Nobody at school believes me when I tell them that stuff. They think I'm making up stories."

"Sometimes you do."

"Not about Mom, I don't," Louie said. He sat back in his seat and crossed his arms against his chest.

They were quiet for a moment and Burk gazed out at the cluster of low-roofed buildings that sat on either side of the highway: factories with their windows broken or boarded up, a coin laundry, a radiator shop, and a cheap motel where a mother and child splashed in the shallow end of a pool that was half hidden from the interstate by a ragged hedge.

The deejay on the radio introduced an oldie by the O'Jays. The song, "One Night Affair," was the same song that was blasting on the radio back in the spring of 1968, when he came home sick one afternoon from his job at the network, surprising Sandra. He found Louie sitting on the front steps, rolling a toy truck across his lap. His next-door neighbor was pretending to water his lawn while his eyes scanned the windows in Burk's living room. "Mommy's dancing with her clothes off," Louie said. "The music was so loud I couldn't hear *Sesame Street,* so I came out here."

Burk remembered walking inside and quickly closing the curtains that faced the street. When he snapped off the radio in the kitchen, Sandra continued to gyrate naked through the house with her eyes blazing.

Burk caught up with her in the narrow hallway leading to their bedroom. He seized her arm and pushed her hard against the wall. "You've got to calm down," he said, but she continued to frug wildly, tossing her head from side to side. When he finally gave up and dropped his hands to his sides, Sandra stumbled backward for a moment, then breathing hard and, smiling contemptuously, she said, "This is my house too. I can do what I want."

"You're right, Sandra. But you can't scare Louie."

"I can drink. I can dance naked. I can play music loud. Anything."

"No."

"Yes, I can," Sandra shouted, and Burk stood there paralyzed by anger and shame, while she turned and disappeared inside their bedroom and locked the door.

Later that night she came into the living room while Burk was sitting in the dark. She had a sheet pulled around her shoulders. The radio was on and Radio Ray Moore was speaking to John Beal, who was describing his wife. "She was tall and stately, and her hair was practically white by the time she was thirty. She had a bachelor of science degree from the University of Nebraska. In hydrology. That's the study of water."

Sandra said, "Is it okay if I sit with you? Do you mind?"

Burk remained silent but indicated that it was by shifting his body to make room. When she sat down, John Beal said, "She overturned her car comin' back from her folks' house outside Lincoln. The coroner said she never had a chance."

Burk heard a door open and the soft tramp of footsteps in the hallway. In a moment Louie was standing in the doorway to the living room. Behind him his shadow was outlined on the wall, twice his size. "Dad?"

"Yeah."

"When are you going to sleep?"

"Soon."

"Are you guys friends again?"

"We sure are."

"Good."

Louie moved back into his bedroom, waiting a moment before he switched off the Snoopy lamp on his nightstand. From the living room he could hear his mother begin to giggle. "Crazy? How can you *say* that?" she said.

"You are."

Louie crawled into bed and pulled the covers up to his chin. "Good night," he called out.

Burk said, "Good night, Louie."

"I love you," Louie said.

Sandra said, "We love you too, sweetheart."

Louie closed his eyes. A light rain begin to fall. It fell for an hour. Louie was asleep before it stopped.

★

Sandra had gained weight. Burk noticed that as soon as she was brought into the private room where he was waiting. At least twenty pounds. And her skin was the same grayish color as her shapeless prison dress.

She took a chair across from him at a small table and smiled. When he forced a grin back, she put her hand over his knuckles.

"Hey."

Burk turned and looked at the female guard, who was standing by the door. She was a short, thick-bodied black woman in her early thirties.

"Holding hands," she said in a warning tone. "That's all."

Burk nodded. Then to Sandra he said, "You look good."

"No, I don't. I look terrible."

"You look fine."

"Please don't lie, Ray. I'm fat and dumpy. It's all the starch I eat. When I was pregnant I was big, but my skin was tight. Not like this," Sandra said, and she pulled at her face with her fingers. "I'm a pig."

"Come on."

"I am."

Perspiration had broken out on Sandra's forehead. She looked frightened. The guard said to Burk, "When do you want me to bring up your son?"

"Soon. In a couple of minutes."

Sandra stared off. "How is he?"

"He's doin' great."

"That's good."

"He really likes Berkeley. Up there, having a mom in prison makes him a hero. You're considered a political prisoner."

Sandra laughed, but when she stopped her face was trembling.

Burk said, "I think about us a lot."

"You and me?"

"And Louie. The three of us."

"It'll never be like it was."

"I know."

"Neither will I."

"You're gonna be fine, Sandra."

Sandra reached into the pocket of her dress and took out a wrinkled envelope. She gazed at Burk blankly for a moment before she handed it across the table. "Open it."

Inside were several articles clipped from the entertainment section of the *LA Times*. In each there was some mention of *Pledging My Love*. When Burk's name was included as the screenwriter, Sandra had underlined it in red ink.

"I'm really proud of you," she said. "You did it."

Burk glanced up at her. He was smiling. "Yeah, I did."

"You know who must be really surprised?"

"Who?"

"Dicky Solomon."

Burk was silent. He waited for her to go on, observing her closely. "Why did you say that, Sandra?"

"Because . . ."

"Because what?"

"Because . . . I met with him, Ray."

"You met with Dicky Solomon?"

"Yes."

"Why?"

Sandra stared at Burk for several seconds, in no rush to provide an answer. Finally: "I wanted to help you."

Burk stole a look at the guard. With her eyes directly on him, he stood up slowly and walked over to the window that looked out on the prison yard. In a small fenced area, children who were mostly black and Hispanic played on the jungle gym and the swing set while their mothers sat at picnic tables in the shade, visiting quietly with their husbands or boyfriends. Louie stood off to the side underneath a large elm tree, smiling quietly, the wind moving his hair as he watched two female inmates shoot a basketball at a netless rim.

"Tell me," Burk said, trying to sound relaxed. "When did this happen?"

"Right before you got fired from the network."

"You called him?"

"I told him who I was. He asked me what I wanted, but I said we had to talk in person. We had lunch the next day."

Burk came back to the table and sat down. Sandra dropped her head and looked guiltily at the floor. "Go on, Sandra. Tell me."

"It was this little French place near the studio, on Cahuenga. I knew what I wanted to say, but I was really scared, like I am now," she said. "Right away I told him how smart you were, how much you hated being a censor. I told him you were really creative and suggested that he give you a job."

"A job?" Burk said with a pained look. "As what?"

"I don't know. Part of his staff. I said you wanted to be a writer. He liked you, Ray. He really did."

"But he didn't think I could write."

"He didn't know. But he thought you were really bright. He told me that several times."

"Over lunch? He told you that over lunch?"

Sandra hesitated while Burk looked at her face, tapping his finger on the table, waiting for her to continue.

The guard said, "You've only got twenty minutes left."

Sandra said, "Maybe it was after lunch. I'm not sure."

"Because you were drunk."

Sandra shrugged. "Maybe. I guess."

Burk sat very still, trying to breathe slowly. "You slept with him," he said, still managing to keep his voice under control. "Didn't you, babe?"

Sandra's eyes were now filled with tears. "He said he was going to help."

"Help me get a job."

"Yes. He was going to call his friends at the network. He said he had pull. He said he would get you out of Standards and Practices."

"All this he told you . . . after lunch?"

"Yes."

"Where?"

Sandra made a breath to speak, then stopped.

"Where did he tell you this?"

Burk's voice startled the guard, and she quickly came to her feet. She said, "I can't have no fightin' in here." Sandra turned slightly away. Tears started falling out of her eyes. "Pull yourself together," the guard said. "I'm bringin' your son up here soon. He don't want to see his momma cryin' like that." Sandra nodded, using the sleeve of her dress to wipe her face. The guard's eyes moved over to Burk. "No more yellin' or I'll terminate the visit."

The room was quiet for a moment. Then Burk leaned back in his chair, acting as if he were going over something in his mind. "So Dicky took you to a motel," he said, softening his voice. "Is that what happened?"

Sandra nodded. She said, "I couldn't feel you anymore, Ray. You were pulling away. You weren't there."

"I was there."

"But I couldn't *feel* you."

Burk felt his anger boiling into rage. He had to grip the end of the table to stop himself from reaching out and punching her face.

"That was the one and only time I was unfaithful," Sandra said.

"You were pregnant."

"I know."

"And drunk."

"I've made so many mistakes, Ray. I'm not perfect. Don't ask me any more questions about Dicky Solomon," she said. "Okay? I barely moved. I just let him fuck me. That's all."

Sandra stopped speaking and nervously bit down on her lower lip. When their eyes accidentally met, she said, "I want to see Louie now. But I want to be alone with him. I don't want you here. Okay?"

Burk nodded.

Sandra glanced at the guard. "Do you have to be in the room too?"

"Yes."

Burk got to his feet. Sandra looked up. "He beat me with his crutch, Ray."

"Who?"

"Shay Carson, the man I killed. He fractured his foot during the calf roping, which meant he was out of the all-around. He got drunk and came back to the motel and tried to manhandle me. Manhandle. Isn't that a perfect word?"

Burk nodded. He wanted to change the subject.

"Sandra, listen—"

"No. *You* listen," she said, in a voice that was surprisingly hard. "I want to tell you this so I don't tell Louie. Do you understand?" Sandra sat forward and challenged him with her eyes. "When I wouldn't let him in, he broke down the door to my room. He didn't know I had his gun, and when he saw it he laughed. I laughed too, making him think everything was okay. But it wasn't, because I was really scared. I told him to leave, but he sat down on the bed and started taking off his clothes. I told him if he didn't leave I was going to call the police. He laughed some more and swung at me with his crutch. He caught me on the forehead. That's when the gun went off. No. Wait. I didn't say that right. That's when I pulled the trigger. *Boom!* I saw a flash come out of the end of the barrel, and he fell back off the bed onto the floor. A few minutes later the police came and took me to jail. That's it. That's how it happened."

Burk was silent. Sandra stood up and walked over to the window. In profile a tear fell off her double chin and left a dark mark on her collar. Down below a thin ponytailed guard came up behind Louie and tapped him on the shoulder. She said a few words and he nodded his head, his gaze giving away none of his feelings as he followed her across the basketball court.

"Here he comes," Sandra said, still staring out the window. "Here comes my boy."

Driving back to Los Angeles, Louie would tell his father how frightened he was inside that room. "She was standing by the window with her back to me. She was hugging herself, like she was cold or scared. I was scared too. Scared that she wouldn't look at me, that I would just stand there forever holding my breath."

"But she turned around, didn't she?"

Louie nodded. "Her face looked different, didn't it, Dad? It looked . . . wider. And her skin didn't look the same. It used to be so smooth. And she chews her nails, too."

"Was it good to see her, Louie?"

"It sure was. But it was over so fast we hardly got a chance to say much."

"I know."

"She says she's getting out pretty soon. Real soon. Right?"

Burk shrugged.

"She is. But she's not going to live with us. Right?"

"Right."

"But it will be okay for me to see her. That's okay."

"Yes, Louie, that's okay."

Burk switched on the radio and punched the buttons until he found an all-news station. Nixon was bombing Cambodia and someone was strangling and torturing young women in Hollywood. A boy drank poison, and an estranged husband was killed by his wife's lover. In each story the word "anguish" was used once. At the end of the newscast, Burk turned around and looked at Louie in the backseat. "Are you glad we came?"

"Uh-huh."

"You sure?"

Louie nodded his head, but Burk could see that he'd already begun to cry.

"She loves you, Louie. You know that, don't you?"

"Yes."

"She does," Burk said, and he slammed his fist on the dash. "She loves you more than anything in the whole goddamn world."

★

It was near midnight on Sunday evening when Bobby Sherwood and Ricky Furlong left the pool at the Beverly Hills Hotel. The light had gone out of the sky, and the hotel's facade now looked more peach than pink.

After they crossed Sunset, they walked south three blocks on Rodeo Drive, then turned left. At the intersection of Elevado and Bedford, a small elderly man was standing on the corner, puffing on a long cigar. He was wearing a maroon bathrobe over baby-blue silk pajamas. Nearby, a toy poodle turned in small circles while its tiny paws scrabbled a patch of grass next to a mailbox.

Bobby was halfway across the street when he abruptly turned and moved quickly back to the curb. His heart was banging but everything else about him remained calm. "You don't know me," he said, blinking a little as he approached the elderly man. "My name's Bobby Sherwood. I'm from Omaha, Nebraska. My uncle is Daniel Schimmel."

"Bobby Sherwood from Omaha."

"Yes."

The elderly man took the long cigar out of his mouth and peered into Bobby's face. "You're right," he said. "I don't know you."

Ricky was at Bobby's side. He tried to gently move him up the street but Bobby pulled away.

"Don't you know who he is?" Bobby said.

"Of course I do."

"Then why don't you get his autograph?"

"Because I already have it, stupid. That's why."

"Daniel Schimmel," the elderly man said, his face taking on a thoughtful look. "Schimmel and Rheingold. Comedians."

Bobby's face lit up. "Yes, Mr. Burns. They were on the same bill with you and Gracie when you played the Ritz in Indianapolis. My uncle has the poster."

"Terrible act. Absolutely dreadful. You said Rheingold was your uncle?"

"No, Daniel Schimmel."

"Him I don't remember. Rheingold was a pig. Used to hang around the kid acts backstage with his fly open."

"My uncle stayed in Omaha."

"Good for him. He's probably much happier there. And funnier."

"He owns the Hotel Sherwood."

"Never heard of it."

"It's on Dodge and Sixteenth. One hundred and seventy-six rooms. I lived on the seventh floor, in the east wing. Room seven-sixteen. The rugs in the hallways are the same color as your robe."

"No kidding."

"And the walls are painted green."

George Burns puffed on his cigar, still staring at Bobby through the whorls of smoke. "This is a very odd conversation," he said, then turned and looked at Ricky. "And you say you have my autograph?"

"My dad got it," Ricky said, taking out the small leather-bound book he always carried in his rear pocket. "Here," he said, opening to a page with three signatures. "He got you on the same day as Bob Hope and Jane Russell."

George Burns took the book and stepped under the streetlamp, holding the page away from his eyes. "*Blue Skies*. No, wait, that was Bing. *Paleface*. 1948. That was it. I remember visiting Hope on the set. Who's your dad?"

"Nobody."

"He was there. He was somebody."

"He was a grip."

"What's wrong with that? So he wasn't a star or a big shot. He was your dad. Be proud of him. Where is he now?"

"Dead."

"May he rest in peace," George Burns said. "What cemetery is he in?"

"Hollywood Memorial."

"Know it well. Nelson Eddy is buried there. I visited his grave not long ago. I was with Jessel. We came by after we had lunch at Perino's."

Ricky said, "My mom picked out a plot by the pond so my dad's feet would be pointing toward Paramount Studios."

"If he sat up he could see the Hollywood sign," George Burns said, grinning.

"Marlon Brando was born in Omaha," Bobby said, after a moment. "When I was fourteen I sat next to him at Chloe's, this diner on Dodge. He had a Reuben sandwich and an order of fries. He said he'd been coming to Chloe's since he was a kid. He knew all the cooks and waitresses by name. Our waitress that day was Edna. One of the cooks was named John."

Bobby stopped speaking when he saw that George Burns was giving his face close consideration. A phone rang inside one of the houses on the street, and Ricky said, "Bobby moved to Los Angeles a couple of weeks ago. I met him the morning he arrived. He was polishing a star on the Walk of Fame."

"We became friends," Bobby said, keeping his eyes lowered but reaching covertly for Ricky's hand. "Really good friends."

"I see," George Burns said. For the first time a hint of fear crawled into his eyes. "Well, I have to go," he said. "It's been a pleasure talking to you boys."

"My grandmother came out to LA in 1942. She came by train," Bobby said to George Burns's back as he crossed the street with his dog. "She died in 1949. She's buried in Hollywood Memorial too. On Paradise Drive, right next to my mom."

Once George Burns was safely back inside his house, he sat in his favorite armchair for several minutes, contemplating the strange encounter he'd just had on the street. He reached for the phone to call the police, then stopped. What would he say? Get a squad car up here right away! There's a couple of fags talkin' about Omaha, Max Rheingold, and the Hollywood Memorial Cemetery.

Schimmel and Rheingold? George Burns shook his head and smiled to himself without separating his lips. They were one of the worst acts he'd ever seen. Second only to Connolly and Webb, a married couple who did an act called Stormy Finish. Jack Connolly played a piano with bananas and pears while Thelma, his wife, did a bad Charleston with a canary sitting on top of her head. At the finish Jack would describe a tornado they drove through in western Kansas. When he was through speaking everything onstage was rigged to fly off.

Just before he went to sleep, George Burns remembered a pretty young girl who played the Capitol Theater in Lynn, Massachusetts. She was sixteen years old and terribly shy. Onstage she would sit behind a large ancient typewriter with a blank expression on her face, taking dictation from the audience while she read the *Police Gazette*. She took three hundred strokes a minute, and she never once made an error.

In between shows, George Burns told her that he and Gracie wanted her on the bill when they played the Palace. She was thrilled.

But when the day came, he was informed by her booking agent that she was dead.

"How?"

"Cut her wrists after a show in Milwaukee."

George Burns did not want to believe this. Instead he told Gracie that the girl had married and left the circuit. "She's not cut out for this life," he said. "She's going to settle down and become a secretary."

Ricky and Bobby crossed Carmelina, and two blocks later, while they were waiting for the light to change on Wilshire Boulevard, Ricky said, "I enjoy walking through Beverly Hills at night. It's quiet and clean and I always feel safe. After my dad died, my mom would bring me here once a week. We'd eat dinner at Nate and Al's and go see a movie at the Warner's Beverly Theater. Afterward we'd have a soda at Blum's or Will Wright's.

"On the night we went to see *The Greatest Show on Earth,* my mom left her seat in the middle of the show. When the picture was over I found her sitting in a corner of the lobby underneath a small red wall lamp, smoking. He eyes were puffy and her cheeks were wet. I asked her why she was crying. She said she missed my dad. She missed sitting next to him, sharing a Hershey bar or some popcorn or a package of M and M's. She said she missed the tart, sweet smell of his breath when he whispered in the dark.

"We left the theater by a side exit and cut across an alley to Beverly Drive, where our car was parked. When we passed the Brown Derby restaurant, Mother spotted actor Steve Taylor leaving with a group of friends.

"She followed him and his date back up to his house in the hills above Sunset. After they went inside she told me to go up and knock on his door. She said, 'See if he remembers your dad. They worked on *Crossfire* together with Robert Ryan.' I said I didn't think it was a good idea, but she kept insisting, saying it was important, that it was some kind of good omen for us if he remembered. I couldn't believe she was making me do this, until I saw the bottle in her purse. That's when I knew she was drunk.

"When I told her no, she said I didn't have any choice. If I refused I would have to walk home in the dark. Then she took my dad's picture out of her wallet, the one where he's standing next to Audie Murphy. And she said, 'Show him this. If he says he knew Ben, ask him for some money. Say he's dead, that we're having problems making ends meet. And look sad.'

"As I walked up to the front door, I saw the lights go on in the backyard, and I remember hearing a hoot owl high up in the pepper tree that stood in the center of the lawn. Before I pressed the door-bell, I looked through the front window and saw Steve Taylor in the living room, lying on the carpet next to a young girl with long feath-ery red hair. Her white linen pants were unbuttoned and her bra was loose and there was a warm smile on her pale, pretty face. I saw her hand go into his slacks and bring out his penis. I remember how it sort of danced in the air in front of her face.

"I looked away when she lowered her head to lick him. On the street I could see my mom slumped behind the wheel with her face turned in my direction. I faked pushing the doorbell and shrugged my shoulders, then I looked back through the window and saw Steve Taylor follow the girl through the sliding glass doors that led out to the pool. By now they were both naked.

"When I got back to the car I told my mom that no one would come to the door. She didn't believe me, I could tell. Her face was tense and fearful and she kept looking over her shoulder, as if she was afraid we were being watched. She squeezed my hand hard and told me my dad was a war hero, braver than any man she knew. She was really drunk by now, mixing up her words, and it was late and I was tired. The next day I was trying out for Little League and I needed my rest. And I was frightened that she would not be able to drive home, that she would crash.

"So I got out of the car and began walking back down Coldwater Canyon by myself. After about half a mile, this snazzy 1952 Chevy convertible pulled up next to me. The man behind the wheel was surprised when he saw I was just a kid. He said I looked lost, and I told him I was, kind of, but I knew that if I kept walking down the hill that I would eventually reach Sunset Boulevard. Once I made it there, I said, I knew I could catch a bus to my neighborhood.

"He said the buses didn't run after ten on Fridays. I started to cry. I couldn't help it. I told him about the Little League tryouts, and then I told him about my mom, how she was parked up the street drunk. He said I could stay at his house, that he only lived a few blocks away. He said he'd make sure I got up in time and had a good healthy breakfast. Then he'd drive me home.

"His name was George. He had long, pretty eyelashes and dark hair that curled in ringlets around his ears. He said he was an actor, but in high school he was an athlete, lettering in baseball and football. He said he lost interest in sports when he discovered girls. Then he discovered boys and became interested in theater. Eventually he became a regular on a TV series, but I'm not gonna tell you which one."

"Did he touch you that night?"

"No."

"Not even a kiss good night?"

"Nothing. At dawn he got up and fixed me French toast, and then he drove me home. I remember how embarrassed I was about my little house with the fading paint and all the funky furniture in the front yard. My mom was home by then, but she was too hung over to say anything, although I know she heard me run inside to grab my mitt and my rabbit's foot and run out.

"George dropped me off at the Little League field on Sepulveda. He said he wasn't gonna stick around, but for some reason when the tryouts began I could tell he was there, watching me. I thought I saw him standing behind the backstop during batting practice, and when I homered on the first pitch, I'm sure I heard his voice say, 'Way to go!'

"When I got to high school, George would sometimes come by and watch me work out. I'd be shagging a fly or running out a grounder and I'd look up and see him in the bleachers, sitting on the top bench, reading a movie magazine or the *Daily Variety*. Other kids' dads dropped by occasionally, so it didn't seem so odd at the time, even though he dressed real Hollywood, in tight silk shirts and tasseled loafers with no socks.

"After practice we'd get a hamburger or a pizza in Westwood, but when he drove me home he never came in to meet my mom. He said, 'She might get annoyed if she thought I was trying to replace your father.'

"One night I told him that I thought Sam Burroughs, my coach, liked boys. He asked me how I could tell. I said it was just a feeling I got when he looked at me, or when he put his arm around my shoulder and squeezed my neck.

"After that night George didn't come around practice that often. There were times during a game that I'd see him up in the bleachers, but his car was always gone when I came out of the gym after my shower. The last time he came by my house was on a Sunday afternoon. He was with a friend, a blond guy named Mike. Me and Gene and Ray Burk were playing football in the street when they drove up.

"I remember Ray and Gene standing by the fender of the Chevy, flipping the football back and forth while George and I made small talk. The radio was on and Mike was humming along to 'Standing on the Corner,' this new song by the Four Lads. Right before he drove off, George said he spoke to Sam Burroughs. 'He's a good man,' he told me. 'He'll take good care of you.'"

And he did.

★

PART FOUR

MONDAY IS
A BRAND
NEW DAY

Sixteen

Leaving

LA

On Monday morning when Burk came downstairs to check out of the hotel, he saw Eddie Bascom and Gus Tolos standing in an alcove off the main lobby. They were conferring with Burt Driscoll and two uniformed policemen. Other members of the hotel's staff, including Doris, the waitress in the downstairs coffee shop, were grouped near the elevators, chatting nervously, waiting to be interrogated.

"What's the story with the cops?" Burk asked the hotel's cashier, a woman with a pulled-down mouth and a no-nonsense manner.

"Accident."

"Where?"

"In the pool."

"What happened?"

"Someone drowned."

"You're kidding."

"Wish I was."

"Who was it?"

The cashier looked away from Burk. Her face was blank. "Don't know. They haven't told us. Sign here," she said, her eyes still avoiding Burk's face as she pushed his bill across the counter. "Any late charges will be forwarded to the studio."

After Burk signed the bill, he looked up and was startled to see Jack Rose standing on the other side of the lobby. He was talking with Van Wood, the lifeguard, and a burly man dressed in a wrinkled white short-sleeved shirt and gray slacks. He was a cop, one of the three Jerome Sanford bribed after Tom Crumpler was arrested.

"Mr. Burk?" Burk felt a hand on his arm and turned his head. It was Colleen, the hotel's pretty assistant manager. "I saw that you were checking out and I wanted to say good-bye. I hope you had a pleasant stay."

"It was fine."

"That doesn't sound very convincing."

"Everything was great. My life just got a little weird, that's all."

"I'm sorry to hear that." Colleen's hand was still on his arm; she was staring up at him with an expression of sympathy. He couldn't tell if her concern was sincere but he didn't really care. "Well, I hope we see you again."

Burk shrugged. "Who knows?"

"Good luck," Colleen said, squeezing his wrist.

"Thanks."

As he walked away, Burk noticed that Eddie Bascom had returned to his station behind the bell desk. He saw Burk pass and greeted him with a vague nod and a forced smile. But just before Burk could step outside, Burt Driscoll moved into his path, cutting him off. "Mr. Burk, I wonder if I could see you in my office for a few minutes."

"Why?"

"It's a private matter," Driscoll said, making his face unreadable. "Five minutes," he said. "No more. I promise."

Burk followed Driscoll up the stairway to the mezzanine. The general manager's office was at the end of a long hallway—between the gift shop and the jewelry store—and when they stepped inside, Burk saw that Jack Rose and Van Wood were already seated at opposite ends of the large leather couch.

Driscoll moved quickly behind his desk and cleared his throat. "We all know each other so there's no need for introductions. Please sit down," he said to Burk, nodding toward the two plush armchairs that faced his desk.

"Max Rheingold drowned last night," Jack Rose said to Burk as he sat. "The police assume it was an accident—he was probably drunk or doped up on pills—but we won't be sure until the lab reports come back tomorrow from the coroner."

"Suicide is a possibility," Driscoll said. "But intentional drowning is extremely rare. They haven't ruled out homicide, either," he said with a flip of his hand, "although there is nothing to point in that direction."

Jack Rose laughed sarcastically. "That's not to say he didn't have enemies. At one time he may have been the single most disliked man in the entertainment industry."

Burk's heart was beating uncomfortably. "I don't get it," he said. "What does this have to do with me?"

"You knew who he was," Jack Rose said. "Right? He read your script. He said you were a helluva writer, like I didn't already know that." Jack Rose shot a look at Burt Driscoll, who stared at him vaguely. "Burt, you ever see the movie *Gun Crazy*?"

Driscoll thought for a moment. "John Dall and Peggy Cummins?"

"That's the one. You see that movie, Van?"

Van Wood shifted his position on the couch. "Not that I recall."

"Came out in 'forty-nine. United Artists. Eighty-seven minutes. Moved like a freight train. Don't know why that film popped into my mind," Jack Rose said. He reached for the cigar in his breast pocket. "Okay! Yes, I do. Writers. We were speaking about writers. You know who wrote that picture?" Jack Rose was looking at Van Wood, but Burk knew the question was directed at him. "Not MacKinlay Kantor or Millard Kaufman, the guys on the credits. Forget those names. Fronts. Trumbo wrote it. Dalton Trumbo. You know how I know that?" he said, turning now to look directly at Burk. "Because I went down to San Diego and picked up the script when Trumbo came in from Ixtapa. I brokered the deal for Joe Lewis, the director, and the studio. I was just a schmuck agent but they trusted me." Burt Driscoll raised his chin, as if he were getting ready to speak. "Burt, don't cut me off. I'm just getting to my point."

"I was—"

"I know what you were gonna say. Mr. Burk here is in a rush. I can read his face. I see the anxiety. He's got a set of revisions in his shoulder bag that he's on his way to deliver to Jon Warren. Am I right?"

"I've got a plane to catch too," Burk said, remembering that he had to pick up Louie at his grandfather's house, which was on the way to the aiport.

Jack Rose stuck out his hand. "Gimme the pages. I'll take them out this afternoon."

"No," Burk said, shaking his head emphatically. "I want to deliver the script in person."

Jack Rose smiled a quick smile. "If the picture's a hit it's because of the script. This kid here's got a gift," he said to Driscoll. "He's not a schticktician like most of these clowns. He's the genuine article." Jack Rose glanced at Van Wood. "You had a gift, Van. Yours was swimming. You were a goddamn dolphin in the water. That's where you belonged."

Jack Rose found a gold lighter in the side pocket of his jacket. He stuck the cigar in his mouth and slowly rotated the tip underneath the flame until it was glowing brightly.

"He took a shot at acting, but it didn't go anywhere," he said to Burk. "The man belongs in the pool. This pool, right here. Max wouldn't have drowned if Van was on duty. There's never even been a close call when Van's in his chair. Am I right, Burt?"

Driscoll nodded. "We have a clean slate."

"Me?" Jack Rose said. "I can't swim for shit. In fact, I'm gonna tell you a secret: I can't swim at all. Not a stroke. Is that hard to believe or what? A goddamn pool in Bel Air behind my house, a pool right here in front of my cabana, and I gotta hang onto the sides like a three-year-old."

"I could teach you," Van Wood said under Jack Rose's voice.

"Teach me?" Van Wood nodded his head. "Too late."

"Why is it too late?"

"I'm seventy-four. I don't need to swim."

"It's good for you," Burt Driscoll said. "It's good exercise."

"I get my exercise on the golf course."

"Van could teach you in a couple of lessons," Burt Driscoll insisted. He leaned forward and put his elbows on his desk. "He taught all three of my kids."

Burk spoke. "Didn't you ever want to learn?" he said.

Jack Rose looked at Burk thoughtfully, turning this question over in his mind. "Only one time. I was down in Coronado. This was back in 'forty-three or 'forty-four. I was staying at the old Coronado Hotel. Big fancy place. Max was previewing a picture in San Diego, and one of my clients had a small role. Mexican broad, you never heard of her. But since I was screwing her, we had adjoining suites.

"After the preview we came back to the hotel and took a walk down by the shoreline. We couldn't see them but we could hear a boy and a girl splashing in the waves. By the sound of their voices I could tell they were young, in their twenties. For some reason the girl kept saying, 'Wait a minute, wait a minute.' She kept saying it over and over and then she said, 'Tell me you love me, Danny.' And the boy said, 'I do.' She said, 'No. Say it right. Use all the words.' And he said, 'I love you, Regina. I love you more than anything in the world.'

"The woman I was with, Lucy, the actress, she said, 'Let's go in. Let's take off our clothes and swim naked.' Jesus, did I want to go in, but I couldn't tell her the truth, so I gave her some dumb excuse. I think I said I was dizzy from too much champagne.

"Of course she was disappointed. She broke away from me and walked out to the end of this long pier. When I caught up to her, I told her I wanted her to come back to the room. I said I wanted to fuck her. She said no, she wanted to swim in the ocean. Then she took off her clothes and piled them up on the dock. That's when I lost control and slapped her across the face. She said I just ruined her weekend. I slapped her again, and a little blood spilled from her nose. Then she turned and dove off the pier.

"I came back to the hotel and sat in the bar and waited for her. When she didn't show up by two A.M., I went back to my room. In the morning one of the towel boys found her curled up in a chaise by the snack bar. He said she ended up hitching a ride back to LA with Max.

"Of course I had to dump her as a client. She was starting to booze too much anyway, and her looks were starting to go. Once or twice she called and left messages on my service, but I never called her back. Eventually she committed suicide."

Van Wood smiled wanly. "Did you love her, Mr. Rose?"

"Did I love her?" Jack Rose glanced at Burk. "What do you think, Burk? Did I love her?"

"Sounds like you did."

"She was a Mexican slut and a lush. But you're right. I loved her," Jack Rose said. "And sometimes I wonder if things would have turned out different for everyone if I'd learned how to swim."

Burt Driscoll shook his head. His hands were clasped on the desk in front of him. "I don't think so, Jack."

"I gotta get goin'," Burk said. "I'm late."

"We're not done," Jack Rose said. His voice was matter-of-fact, but there was something hard behind it.

Burt Driscoll said, "Van, tell Mr. Burk why he's here."

Van Wood hesitated. He seemed uneasy. "Go on," Jack Rose said. "Tell him."

There was no movement in Van's face as he began to speak. His voice was a monotone. "Yesterday I noticed these two guys sitting at a table up on the pool terrace. I'd never seen them before, but I took them as guests. Either that or they were visiting someone. But they looked odd enough to capture my attention," he said. "Both were pale as ghosts. One wore a cap and was kind of loose-jointed; the other had sort of a moon face. They looked like the types you see behind the ropes at premieres. Stargazers. The hotel's policy is to let them sit and watch the action, as long as they don't pester anyone, which they didn't."

Jack Rose leaned forward and tapped Burk on the knee. "They were queer, which is not important here. But what is important is that they left and came back later that night."

"I was cleaning the pool and I saw them standing inside the side gate. They were standing still, almost like statues," Van Wood said, his face becoming animated for the first time that morning. "I told them the pool was closed, which it wasn't really. For swimming it was, but you could still order drinks and sit around under the umbrellas. The one with the cap said they were meeting a friend in the lobby. They were early so they came out by the pool."

"He said they were waiting for you," Jack Rose said to Burk. "Isn't that correct, Van?"

"I think so. I think that's what they said."

"Did they or didn't they?"

"Yes."

Jack Rose turned to Burk. "Well?"

"Your name was mentioned," Burt Driscoll said with a shrug. "We're just trying to clear it up. That's all."

Jack Rose said, "So you weren't waiting for anyone that night?"

"No."

"You're sure?"

"This is total craziness," Burk said. He started to stand.

"Listen to me," Jack Rose said, and his expression turned unfriendly. "A man drowned last night. A man who was living in my cabana. This is bad publicity for me and for the hotel, especially if it was not an accident. Hollywood's a strange town. Scandals come out of nowhere and ruin people's lives. We already got bad press on our picture. I don't need any more grief in my life."

Burt Driscoll said, "There were no bones broken or signs that he was beaten. No choke marks. We're assuming an accident. But these fans—fags, whatever—they mentioned your name and they were the last people to come by the pool before Van locked up. Your name came up. A coincidence?"

"They probably heard him paged over the intercom," Van Wood said.

"That's a possible explanation," Burt Driscoll said. He looked at Jack Rose. "I could see how that could happen. That work for you, Jack?"

"The prick was on his way out anyway," Jack Rose said. "Cancer. Six months, a year; either way he's gone. And we're better off. Right, Van?"

"Everyone by the pool laughed behind his back," Van Wood said.

"Of course you laughed," said Jack Rose, nodding. "The way he ended up, Max was a joke. He never commanded much respect, but there was a time he could get a good table at Ciro's or a ringside seat at the Olympic. Ask your dad," Jack Rose said, pointing his cigar at Burk. "Ask him about Max Rheingold."

Burt Driscoll said, "In 1957, when I was waiter at Chasen's, Max came in all the time. And he was treated very well, as well as anyone."

"Of course he was. In the fifties that teenage-bikini-monster shit was huge in the drive-ins. 'Max Rheingold Presents' meant money in the bank. He was the king of the schlockolas."

"I was a sucker for musicals," Van Wood said, with a girlish laugh. "I still am."

"Burt was a dancer," Jack Rose said, smiling. "He auditioned with Rita Hayworth for *You'll Never Get Rich.*"

Burt Driscoll was gazing nostalgically out the window. "I was too short," he said. "Of course, I couldn't dance like Astaire, either. Who could?"

"No one," Jack Rose said, and stretched his arm across the back of the couch. "Still, I bet you had some moves. Come on, let's see something." Burt Driscoll started to protest but Jack Rose pivoted his head back to Van Wood. "Burt was a real smoothie. A pussy hound par excellence."

The phone rang on Burt Driscoll's desk. He stared at it gratefully before he picked it up. "Hello. . . . Yes . . . that's correct. This morning, sometime before eight. . . . No. . . . Yes. I'll call you then." Driscoll hung up the receiver and nervously pulled at his mustache. "*LA Times.* They want details. I told them I would call them after the police report was released."

Jack Rose turned toward Driscoll and crossed his legs. Several seconds passed. Burk felt he should say something, that it was his turn, but this impulse to speak was overwhelmed by an unwanted memory that forced its way into his mind.

He is ten years old and Gene is twelve. They are playing baseball in the street in front of their house. Gene is pitching and Ricky Furlong is at bat, standing over a shirt cardboard that serves as home plate. When the pitch comes, Ricky hits a line drive, and the tennis ball they are using caroms off a lamppost and bounces into a flower bed beneath the shiny windows that look out over Burk's front lawn. While he searches for the ball, Burk glances up and sees his father standing by the sink in the kitchen. He's slicing a large red onion. Next to his elbow is a platter of hamburgers massaged into thick patties. Ada Furlong is sitting in the kitchen nook, flicking the ashes of her cigarette into the palm of her hand.

From outside this window Burk can see through the kitchen into their small backyard, where bees and dragonflies circle the bowls of potato chips and the open bottles of mustard and relish that are placed in the center of the patio table. He cannot see the barbecue from this angle—it's below the windowsill and too close to the house—but the flames that leap up are reflected in the panes of glass.

Burk hears Ricky's voice. He says, "Let's go, Ray. Hustle it up."

Gene's voice follows quickly. "To your right. It's over to your right."

Inside the house Ada Furlong stands up; she is wobbly but smiling a stupid smile. On a side counter is an open bottle of bourbon. She reaches out but Burk's father slaps her arm away.

"Come on, it's starting to get dark," Ricky shouts, and Burk hears him jog across the lawn. In the kitchen Ada Furlong's hands are striking out blindly, the smile no longer on her rage-twisted face.

"Your mother drinks too much," Burk says, when he feels Ricky standing behind his shoulder. Burk's father has Ada Furlong backed up against the icebox, holding her wrists.

Gene reaches inside a low hedge that runs along the driveway. His fingers come out grasping the tennis ball. He holds it in the air. "Let's go. Play ball."

"Wait!" Burk now has *his* hand up.

"I hate it when they touch," Ricky says.

Burk speaks into Ricky's eyes, which are mirrored in the window. "I hate it too."

Gene bounces the ball twice in the driveway. Ada Furlong squirms away from Nathan Burk and pounds her tiny fists into his chest; then she turns her back and sobs into her hands. "She's always crying," Ricky says. "All the time. I hate it."

"My dad cries sometimes," Burk says, as his older brother joins him by the window. In a moment he feels Gene's fingers close around his upper arm, squeezing him hard.

"Stop spying," Gene says, and Burk allows himself to be pulled away. "Come on, let's finish the game."

Ricky turns and starts across the lawn.

Gene says, "It's gonna be all right, Ricky. Don't worry. They won't stay mad."

Ricky says, "I wish she would go back to our house."

Burk says, "I don't want her around either."

Ricky gives Burk the middle finger. "Pitch the ball," he says to Gene.

"Gene doesn't want her around," Burk says. "Do you, Gene?"

Gene glances over his shoulder at his brother. "Drop it, Ray."

"Do you?"

"I'm quitting," Ricky says. He kicks the shirt cardboard into the gutter and flings the bat against the curb, cracking the handle. "I'm going home. Tell my mom."

Burk walks forward. "You tell her, asshole," he says when he's standing next to Gene. "She's your mom."

"They were just having an argument," Gene says. "That's all."

"I'm going home," Ricky says again. This time Burk can hear the ache in the bottom of his throat. "Tell her."

Burk arrived at the studio just before lunchtime. After he found a vacant parking space outside the administration building, he glanced over and saw Jerome Sanford standing next to a blue chauffeur-driven limousine. He was talking to Bernie Leeds, the head of distribution, a handsome gray-haired man who was wearing dark blue crepe slacks and white Gucci loafers. When he made eye contact with Burk, Sanford gave him a small smile of acknowledgment before he turned back and resumed his conversation.

On his way over to the sound stage, Burk passed by some gaffers and other members of the camera crew he recognized from his earlier visits to the set. They were heading toward the commissary. Before they walked inside, someone (Burk thought it was a hung-over-looking prop man wearing a plaid golf cap) said, "That's the writer. What the fuck's he doing here?"

As soon as he turned the corner at the end of the street, Burk noticed Boyd Talbott steer a striped golf cart up to the stage door. Snake Myers was standing nearby in the shade, chatting with the teamster captain, the same guy who turned Burk away from the location in Griffith Park. When they saw Burk approach, Myers's eyes showed alarm and he mouthed the word "fuck." Simultaneously the stage door opened and Jon Warren walked into the noonday sun with his arm around Loretta Egan's shoulder.

Talbott got out of the golf cart and Warren took his place behind the wheel. Loretta slipped into the seat next to him. Both had their backs turned away from Burk, unaware that he was nearby, until Snake Myers shifted his eyes and said, "We got trouble, Jon."

Warren glanced over his shoulder and saw that Burk was walking toward him with a smile on his face that was not real. "Got the revisions right here," Burk said, pulling a manila envelope out of his shoulder bag. Loretta turned around and Burk waved and continued to smile, and she smiled in return before she dropped her eyes. "Sorry I was late. Something came up at the hotel."

"I think we better have a chat," Talbott said. He started to move forward but stopped when Snake Myers raised his hand.

"This is a big surprise," Burk said. He was speaking to Loretta now, and he was still smiling, but there was a note of anger in his voice. "Couple of lovebirds. When did all this happen?"

"Don't jump to conclusions," Loretta said, leaning away from Warren. "This is just business."

"Business?"

"We're not going to need your revisions," Warren said. He unfolded his legs and stood up to face Burk. "We're going in a different direction. You're off the picture."

"Off the picture." Burk carefully repeated the phrase to himself as his eyes flicked across Loretta's face and back to Warren's. "No kidding. I'm off the picture."

Snake Myers saw the smile leave Burk's mouth. He said, "Take it easy, Ray."

Talbott said, "Jon spoke to Maria Selene this morning. You must have already checked out."

"You did a really good job," Warren said, "but I thought we needed a different touch."

"A woman's touch," Burk said, and Warren nodded.

"It's just a polish," Loretta said. "I'm not changing the structure. You'll still get all the credit."

Warren added, "And just so you know—when I hired Loretta, I didn't realize you had a thing going."

Snake Myers moved alongside Burk and put his hand on his shoulder. "C'mon, let's go across the street and get a drink."

Burk opened his mouth to say something but shut it quickly when the thought got lost in his mind, overwhelmed by an insistent ringing in his ears. The skin on his face was hot and his body was trembling, out of control, unable to absorb the excruciating feelings of embarrassment and betrayal that raged through his chest.

"There's something wrong here," Burk said as he flexed his fingers and shifted his weight from his right leg to his left. Then, without hesitating, he dipped his shoulder slightly and threw a left hook that landed on Warren's chin, knocking him out cold.

Maria Selene was sitting at her desk, chain-smoking, when Burk's call came in from LAX. "Tell him I'll be on in a sec," she told Nora, in a voice that was deceptively casual, disguising what she had just learned from Jerome Sanford: that when Burk came by the set to drop off his revised pages, he and Warren got into an altercation that escalated into a full-scale brawl.

"Burk decked Warren," Sanford told Maria. "Then he went after Talbott and the teamster captain. Fortunately, Snake Myers tackled him before he did any more damage."

"What's going to happen?"

"Warren lost two teeth, so we're going to have to shut down the picture for at least a day. After that—"

"No. I mean to Ray."

"Nothing."

"What do you mean?"

"Jack Rose spoke to Warren. They worked something out. But now Crumpler has decided he won't say a line unless Burk writes it. And he's not kidding." Sanford drew in a long breath. "What a fuckin' mess," he said. Maria suddenly heard his side of the connection click off and the dial tone resume.

"Ray?"

Maria's voice surprised Burk when she came on the line. He was standing inside a phone booth, sweating and nervous, his face glowing from the four straight shots of vodka that he'd gulped down in the airport lounge. In the booth next to him was a short, pretty woman with shapely hips and pale-blue eyes. She was speaking with someone called Leslie, and every few seconds she would repeat the phrase, "What a shame."

"Ray? Are you still there?"

"Yeah. I'm here."

"I heard."

"Yeah?"

"You fucked up, but it's not fatal."

"I did the rewrite, Maria."

"I know."

"I had it with me. It was good stuff. They had no right to bring in another writer."

"They own the script. They can do anything they want."

"They've been fucking with me all week."

"Welcome to Hollywood, Ray."

Burk suddenly felt a sharp pain in the center of his back, the result of the fall he'd taken outside the sound stage. He remembered blacking out for a short period of time, maybe ten seconds; then he heard a flurry of excited voices and felt the weight of Snake Myers's body holding him down. "Take it easy," Snake said, through his panting breaths. "Just take it easy."

When he was finally allowed to stand up, there were two beefy security guards on either side of him, tightly gripping the flesh above his elbows. A knuckle on his left hand was gashed and a thin trickle of blood ran diagonally across his fingers. Off to the side he was aware of Warren lying on the ground, attended by Loretta and a studio nurse. Someone said, "Jack Rose is on the way down," and thirty minutes later Burk was escorted off the lot.

Burk turned his face away from the mouthpiece. A cowboy past his middle years was sitting next to Louie in the airport lobby. He wore a bolo tie and a Stetson hat that was flawlessly white. In his eyes was a compassionate look.

"Ray?"

"Yeah."

"Go home and come up with an idea for something new."

"I already have one."

"I'd love to hear it when you've worked it out."

"I have worked it out."

"Ray—"

"It's about these two kids, Jack and Diane. She's fifteen, he's fourteen. Think Romeo and Juliet in LA," Burk said. His voice, which was faintly slurred in the beginning of the conversation, now had a confident tone. "She lives with her dad, a cop. His mom's an emergency room nurse. The boy's a rockabilly fanatic. The girl's a genius car thief. The whole thing takes place over Labor Day, on the three hottest days in the history of the city."

"Ray, can't we do this—"

"Just give me five minutes, Maria. Just five. Okay?"

Maria was silent for a moment. Then her voice came out sounding tired, without enthusiasm. "Okay," she said, "let's hear it."

Burk began to speak quickly, outlining the plot. At first it seemed to Maria that he was making up the story on the spot, but with the steady advance of his words it became clear that all the elements—the characters, their relationships, the key locations, the setting and mood, and so on—had been worked out in great detail.

"I think it works," Maria said when Burk finished his pitch. But it didn't just work; she thought it was so fresh and relevant that she could walk into Fox or Warner's—or any studio in town, for that matter—and quickly set up a development deal for Burk. Seventy-five thousand for a first draft and a set of revisions was not out of the question. If he wrote it on spec the price could go much higher, maybe even triple. "Have you got a title?"

"*Jack and Diane.*"

"Hmm. I'm not sure that's it. I mean, eventually the parents and the kids end up together, so the piece is really about four people. What about something with 'love' in it?"

Burk said nothing for a moment. The woman in the booth next to him was holding a match up to a cigarette while she spoke into the mouthpiece. "I've got to go. I'll call you when I get in," the woman said. "My plane leaves in ten minutes."

Burk said, "What about—"

"What? I can barely hear you," Maria said.

Burk raised his voice a notch higher. "*Crazy Love.* What about that for a title?"

"That's not bad," Maria said. "I like it."

"I don't," Burk said. "I just wanted to hear how it sounded out loud."

Maria tried to laugh away the rebuke.

The woman next to Burk had hung up the phone. She was standing outside the booth, looking uncertain in which direction she should move.

"The script's about love," Burk said, aware that the woman was listening. "But it's about other things too. It's about finding a safe place. That's what kids and parents are looking for: someplace inside their hearts where they're not scared; a sacred space. And it's about family, because without family there is nothing at all." Burk's eyes wandered back over to his son. Louie and the tall cowboy were now involved in a serious game of gin rummy. "I know what it's called," Burk said, and a weird tenderness crept over him. "It's called *Take Me Home.*"

★

As they boarded their flight to San Francisco, Louie tried to convince his father to sit in the front of the aircraft. "It's safer up front," he said.

"It's safe anywhere."

"Not on the wing, it isn't. If a bird gets sucked through an engine, it can explode."

"I don't think that's going to happen today."

"I hope not. How about here?" Louie said. He was standing by a row of empty seats.

Burk glanced at a seat number. "I can't smoke here."

"You don't have to smoke, Dad."

"Yeah, I do."

"For an hour, you don't."

"Back here," Burk said, guiding Louie toward two rows of seats that faced each other in the rear of the cabin. "You take the window. I need room to stretch out my legs."

A stewardess with a phony smile moved forward to help Burk stow his carry-on gear in an overhead rack. "What row are we in?" Louie asked her.

"Thirty-two."

"Oh."

"Is that good or bad?"

"It's neither," Burk said as he dropped heavily into his seat on the aisle. "Right, Louie?"

Louie shrugged, avoiding the questioning looks from both his father and the stewardess. Over the white noise of the engine, Burk heard a familiar-sounding voice. "I work for I. Magnin," said the woman seated across the aisle, the same woman who was on the phone next to him in the lobby. She was talking to the man in her row: a younger man, dark and slender, dressed in a gray suit. "I'm a buyer in men's sportswear. What about you?"

"I'm in municipal bonds."

"*In* meaning what?"

"I trade them. Buy and sell. I'm a broker with Paine-Webber."

"I see," the woman said. "Yes."

The plane began to taxi toward the runway. Louie said, "I've got butterflies in my stomach. I'm scared."

"Don't worry," Burk said. "We're gonna be fine."

The woman across the aisle turned her head, her eyes bypassing Burk's face. "Why are you scared?" she asked Louie.

Louie remained silent, his eyes shut tight and his elbows digging into the armrest. The woman looked at Burk, staring at him as if she were trying to pull him into focus. He pointed to the seat number. "Certain numbers frighten him," he said.

"Like what?"

"Two and three in certain combinations. And some numbers that add up to ten. Like one and nine."

The aircraft had reached the beginning of the runway. The pilot said, "Flight attendants prepare for takeoff."

The man in the gray suit checked the number above his seat. "I'm sitting in thirty-two E," he said in a worried undertone.

"Maybe he should see someone," the woman said to Burk. Her voice sounded worried too.

"He's fine. It's something he'll grow out of."

"My birthday's February nineteenth," said the man in the gray suit. "What does that mean?"

"That means you're a Pisces," said the small well-dressed black man sitting across from him. He wore rimless glasses and spoke with a slight British accent.

The aircraft started down the runway, gathering speed. As they lifted into the air, Burk put his hand on Louie's shoulder. "We're up, pal. We're on our way."

Louie opened his eyes. He was looking out the window. Underneath the scattered clouds the city glittered in the bright sunlight.

"Do you live in San Francisco?" the woman asked Burk.

"Berkeley."

"I live across the bay, in Sausalito."

"I really dig Sausalito," said the man in the gray suit.

"I teach in Berkeley," the black man said. "I'm a cultural anthropologist."

The man in the gray suit looked annoyed. "Anthropologist? I thought maybe you taught astrology."

The black man made a froggy-sounding laugh. "Astrology. That's very good. But no," he said, still laughing, "astrology is just a hobby."

Louie opened and closed his fists three times. He said, "Thirty is three times ten. But thirty is a good number. That's how old my dad will be next year."

"My best friend, Leslie, is a child psychologist. She lives in Berkeley," the woman said to Burk. "If you want her number I would be glad to give it to you."

The black man and the man in the gray suit were watching Burk, waiting for him to reply. The seat-belt light blinked off and the stewardess who was sitting near the galley stood up. Burk caught her eye. He said, "I'd like a Bloody Mary."

"We'll be serving beverages in a few moments," the stewardess said, keeping a happy smile on her face but showing just a sliver of irritation in her voice.

Louie said, "Don't drink too much, Dad."

Burk put a finger to his lips and Louie hunched his shoulders, apologizing with his eyes.

"What sign are you?" the black man asked the woman sitting across from him. "I'd guess either a Capricorn or a Leo."

Louie said, "I'm a double Gemini."

"I'm a Virgo," the woman said.

"Cultural asshole," said the man in the gray suit.

"I think that's enough," the woman said, disgusted. She unfastened her seat belt and stood up. "Would you mind?" she said to Burk, pointing at the empty seat next to him.

Burk stood up to let her in. "Be my guest."

The man in the gray suit crossed his legs and smoothed the crease on his knee. His lips were smiling, but there was a hard gleam in his eye. The stewardess came down the aisle and handed Burk a Bloody Mary. "What can I get you?" she asked Louie.

"A ginger ale and a bag of peanuts."

"I'd like a double scotch on the rocks," said the man in the gray suit.

"This is a tough time for Pisces," the black man said. "The Jupiter–Neptune conjunction puts you in the astrological strike-out zone. It can last for months," he said, trying to look apologetic. "I'd suggest moderation in all affairs. Take no risks."

Burk glanced at the woman seated next to him. "You were on the phone next to me in the airport."

"Yes, I know. By the way," she said, "my name is Barbara Nichols."

Burk gently squeezed her outstretched fingers. "Ray Burk. And this is my son, Louie."

Louie turned and gazed up at Barbara with an unchildlike expression on his face. "My mom's in prison," he said. "I saw her yesterday. That's why I came down to Los Angeles."

The black man grew suddenly tense. "What an odd coincidence," he said, his eyes blinking rapidly. "On Monday I'm flying to Mexico to interview women who are incarcerated in a jail in Sonora. It's part of a cross-cultural study of prostitutes, for which I've received a rather large grant."

Barbara glanced quickly at the black man before she refocused her attention on Burk. "Out of curiosity," she said, "what kind of a crime did—?"

"She shot a guy," Burk said. He drained the Bloody Mary in one gulp and held the plastic cup in the air, rattling the ice.

Louie tapped Barbara on the wrist. In a whisper he said, "It was self-defense. He was trying to kill her. She gets out in a few months. We're all going to live together."

Burk looked down at Louie hard. "I never said that."

"Not right away . . . but someday."

Barbara opened the purse in her lap. Her eyes stayed on Burk's face as she pulled a cigarette out of a fresh pack. The black man leaned across the aisle with a match. "Thank you," she said, coughing slightly after she exhaled the first puff.

On her way back to the galley, the stewardess took Burk's cup out of his upraised hand. "One more for me too," said the man in the gray suit.

Louie said to his father, "Don't get drunk. Okay?"

"Okay."

"My mom drinks too much," Louie said to Barbara. "That's one thing I remember a lot."

The stewardess came back with a Bloody Mary for Burk and a double scotch for the man in the gray suit. She looked mildly surprised when the airplane suddenly lost altitude, nearly throwing her into Burk's lap. A moment later, the pilot's voice came over the intercom. "We will be experiencing turbulence for the next five or ten minutes," he explained, "until we get to our cruising altitude at thirty-two thousand feet."

Louie was staring out the window, scratching the glass with his fingernails. Under his breath he repeated the number: "Thirty-two thousand."

Burk glanced at Barbara. She held his look. "He's been to a psychologist," he said, after several seconds. "Maybe I should send him to see someone else."

"I think that would be wise," Barbara said. "I'll give you Leslie's number before we land."

"I'd like yours too," Burk said.

Blood rushed into Barbara's face. "Oh? You would? Well, I'll have to think about that," she said, smiling coyly. "But that's not to say I don't find you attractive—despite the bruises on your face, and the fact that you were obviously drunk when you got on the plane."

"I've had a rough day," Burk said.

"I can imagine."

"I'm not sure you could."

At that point, Burk described the events leading up to his fight with Jon Warren. Halfway through this story Barbara yawned and arched her back. "Am I boring you?" Burk said, trying not to stare at her plump, pointed breasts.

"I heard all this before, while you were speaking on the phone."

"You were eavesdropping."

"Like you."

"I was checking out your body," Burk said, the words coming out of his mouth unexpectedly.

Barbara didn't seem surprised. "Like you were a moment ago," she said, her eyes gliding across his lap. "You guys are so obvious."

"So where does that leave us?" Burk said.

Barbara slid off her shoes and crossed her legs in a way that drew her skirt above her knees. "I don't know," she said. "You tell me."

"Are you seeing someone?"

"Yes."

Burk stared at Barbara's face, wondering why he was so attracted to her. It was her smile, he decided. The way it crinkled her eyes reminded him of his mother. "Everyone's seeing someone," he said, glancing away. "Until they meet someone else."

"That's not always the case. Sometimes people stay together and get married and have kids."

"I tried that. It didn't work."

"Part of it did."

Burk turned and looked at Barbara looking into his face.

"You've got a great kid."

Burk flinched but didn't look down when he felt Barbara's fingers moving lightly over his wrist. "I know," he said. "He's the best."

Burk heard the stewardess laughing noisily in the front of the cabin. When he looked down the aisle, he saw her standing over a Marine corporal with Native American features. "We're passing over Big Sur and Monterey on our right," the pilot said. "And for you golf-ers on the starboard side, you'll be able to get a glimpse of Pebble Beach. In just a few minutes we'll be starting our descent into the Bay Area. Have a great day and thanks for flying PSA."

"My brother went to Monterey Pop," Burk said. "He was never the same after that weekend. He was a cop. When he came home he quit the force. I think drugs—acid, especially—had something to do with it. I don't know, I'm not sure. But I know he changed."

"I spent my honeymoon in Big Sur," Barbara said casually, let-ting her fingers fall away from Burk's wrist.

"You were married? When?"

"Awhile ago. You look surprised."

"I'm not." Burk looked down at Barbara's fingers, moving ner-vously on the armrest. She was wearing a thin gold wedding band. "I saw your ring when you got on."

"Sure."

"I did. Really."

There was a small, almost trancelike smile on Barbara's face. Keeping her eyes away from Burk, she said, "My husband went to language school in Monterey. He was stationed at Fort Ord. We got married in July, a few months before he was sent to Vietnam. I had just graduated from Cal that spring, in 1963, right before the Free Speech movement."

Timmy Miller had graduated from Berkeley in the same year. Burk wondered if by chance they'd ever met. He decided that the chances were so slim that to bring it up would make him sound stupid. Instead, he asked her where her husband was stationed now.

"In North Vietnam," she said, in a voice that was empty but not hard. "He's a POW."

The woman sitting in front of them turned around and peeked at Barbara through the crack in the seats. The one eye that Burk could see was moist with sympathy.

Louie unfastened his seat belt. "I have to make," he said, stand-ing up.

The small black man was awake, cleaning his glasses with the bottom of his tie. A magazine with Eldridge Cleaver on the cover was open in his lap. The man in the gray suit shifted in his seat, his face grim and his eyes heavy with scotch.

"He was captured in 1968, during Tet," Barbara said. "At first I was told he was missing in action. That could mean anything, right?" Burk nodded, but his face expressed doubt. "I know he's alive."

"How do you know that?"

Barbara tugged the hem of her skirt over her knees. "I just do," she said, and they were silent for several seconds.

Louie had a serious look on his face when he came out of the rest room and squeezed back into his seat by the window. The NO SMOKING light came on, and Barbara put out the cigarette she'd just lit. Burk turned his head. "I'm sorry," he said.

"For what?"

"I don't know."

"There's nothing to be sorry about," she said. A tear dropped out of her left eye and rolled down the side of her face. "Would you like to see his picture?"

"Sure."

Barbara took a photo out of her wallet and passed it to Burk. "I took that at the Carmel Valley Inn," she said. "That's where we stayed on the night we were married."

The young man in the picture was tall, with wide shoulders and very straight blond hair that was parted in the center of his forehead. He was standing by the entrance to the hotel.

Burk said, "He's a good-looking guy."

"Yes, he is," Barbara said, smiling proudly. "Do you have a picture of your wife?" Burk nodded his head tentatively. "Can I see it?"

Burk found a small snapshot of Sandra tucked behind his driver's license and his triple-A card. It was taken by his brother during Sandra's first summer in Los Angeles, when she was already pregnant with Louie. She was sitting on Gene's redwood deck, wearing white shorts and a blue T-shirt with UNIVERSITY OF WISCONSIN lettered across the front. Behind her in the gathering twilight were the outlines of housetops and a sky that was singed with red.

Barbara looked at the picture silently for several seconds. Burk felt he detected something cold—even hostile—in her appraisal. "She's much prettier than I am," she said, and an uncomfortable silence dropped between them.

The landing gear came down, giving the aircraft a slight jolt.

Louie pointed out the window. "Look, Dad, we're comin' in over the water."

"I can see."

"We're almost home."

"I don't want you to call," Barbara said to Burk. Her face at that moment looked tired and a little bit frightened.

"Are you sure?"

Barbara nodded her head. But when the wheels of the plane touched the earth, she said, "No."

★

PART FIVE

FINAL

THINGS

★

Seventeen

What Bonnie
Told Bobby
and
Putting
Max to
Rest

On December 3, 1969, three days before her death, Bonnie's Greyhound bus stopped for repairs in Council Bluffs, Iowa. When she found out there would be a one-day layover—the brake linings needed to be replaced, along with an engine mount—she quickly left the station and took a taxi across the Missouri River into Omaha.

"Marlon Brando was born in Omaha," Bonnie told the driver while they were stopped at the intersection of Ames and Leavenworth. "Did you know that?"

The cabdriver nodded his head. "Yes, I do. And so was Dorothy McGuire."

"Henry Fonda was born in Grand Island but he grew up near Thirty-second and Davenport. You can see the top of his house from the seventh floor of the Hotel Sherwood. Now, of course, he lives in Los Angeles. I plan to go by and see his house when I get there."

"Sounds like you're a fan of Mr. Fonda."

"Yes," Bonnie said, "I am."

Up the street, across from radio station KKOW and the redbrick YMCA, was the marquee of the Orpheum Theatre. When the light changed to green, a young man with a round pink face walked out of Chloe's Diner and started pacing back and forth in front of the box office.

Bonnie sat up in shocked surprise. Although she had not seen Bobby since 1954—on that mild spring afternoon when he stepped out of the Hotel Sherwood wearing khaki shorts and a loose-fitting white polo shirt—she knew without a doubt that this young man, blond and ruddy and radiating fitness, was her son.

And she knew she would find him later, when all the streetlights were on and the sky was thick and dark.

★

"I was sitting in the balcony," Bobby told Ricky on the morning of Max Rheingold's funeral. They were standing next to a transplanted palm tree on the corner of Western Avenue and Sunset Boulevard, eating sugar doughnuts out of a paper sack while they waited for a city bus. "She sat down in the seat right next to me in the front row."

"Right next to you? That's pretty weird."

"I know. Since the theater was almost empty."

"What did you do?"

There was a thoughtful pause as Bobby summoned his mother's haunted face out of the crowd of people floating inside his head. "Nothing," he said.

He turned and looked at Ricky, who still questioned him with his eyes.

"When the movie was over I heard her say my name so softly that I wasn't sure if I'd imagined the sound. The lights came up and she said, 'You don't know me, Bobby, but I'm your mother.' I remember almost losing my breath and wanting to scream out loud. I said I didn't believe her, but she said my name again, and when and I met her eyes, I felt all the broken chunks inside me come together for the very first time."

It was already dark when Bonnie and Bobby left the theater and began walking south on Jackson Street. At Dodge they cut a path through the parking lot behind the main library and came out on Hayes, a small dark street that led down to the Missouri River. And it was there, sitting on a bench by the riverside with the lights of the city behind them, that Bonnie told her son about her life.

She told him first about her mother, Grace Elliot Simpson, about the day she took the train to Los Angeles, leaving Bonnie to live with her grandparents in a broken-down house by the railroad tracks. It was wartime and Bonnie's father was a soldier fighting overseas against the Japanese.

In the spring of that year a man in uniform came to the house with a letter from her father's commanding officer. Bonnie remembered the soldier's long legs, his droopy face, his nervous voice; the presence of her grandmother behind her, the odor of stew in the kitchen cooking in an iron skillet; her grandfather, who was almost deaf, saying, "What, what, what?" and her grandmother answering, shouting, "He's dead! Tommy's dead!"

Grace Elliot Simpson came back for her husband's funeral but left again the following day. Bonnie remembered sitting in the rocker on the side porch watching her go, the dark clouds overhead, her toes and fingers numbed from the cold. When the taxi pulled away, her grandmother came through the screen door and knelt beside her. She smelled of nicotine and medicated ointment. She whispered to Bonnie, "Come on back inside and help me cook."

Bonnie went out to Hollywood on the Union Pacific, the same train that took her mother. It was the summer of 1949 and she was thirteen and pretty, with light-colored eyes and perky breasts.

She remembered the orange trees, the fast clouds and salty air near the ocean, the red and gold twilights and the dark clear nights that followed. She remembered riding in convertibles and limousines, and parties where lovely women whispered and giggled in small groups, their gold rings sparkling on their long slender fingers.

She mentioned to Bobby a girl named Maria Schlumberger, riding horses with her in borrowed clothing. She remembered getting caught in a thunderstorm, then bathing later at Max Rheingold's house. She said the scariest thing was not the rape itself, which happened a few days later in his office at the studio, but the way Rheingold's rough fingertips felt on her skin, and the way his eyes were blood-streaked and shiny, like some wolf or frantic night beast.

She remembered kicking and screaming, feeling like she was in a car skidding sideways, out of control, with a passenger on top of her, crawling across her body, her heart exploding with fear; then, standing up, dripping blood on the Oriental rug, seeing his fat belly and chest hair sticky with semen and sweat, a hideous smile separating his bloodless lips. She told Bobby she felt like a flower that was ready to bloom and was suddenly trampled to death.

Bonnie said the memory of her mother's death in the fire was too painful to speak about. She attended the funeral but remembered only that the casket was closed. On the train back to Omaha she was given a private berth, which she later learned was paid for by Max Rheingold. She ate Belgian waffles every morning and played a loose game of casino with a Cajun lady and a man named Bill Oliphant. Oliphant worked for an outfit that sold land in Florida and Texas. He claimed he went to high school with Alan Ladd.

Daniel Schimmel and his wife, Madge, met Bonnie at the train station. To help out at the hotel, she worked as part of the housekeeping staff, changing the flowers in the dining room and waxing the woodwork in the lobby. She had keys to the empty rooms on the upper floors and sometimes made long-distance phone calls to her grandmother in Michigan, telling her not to worry but not letting her know where she was.

Once she called Maria Schlumberger in Los Angeles. They talked for over an hour. Bonnie spent the whole time lying about her record collection, her boyfriends, her clothes and jewelry, and whatever else she could think of.

Bonnie spoke briefly about leaving Omaha after Bobby was born, never mentioning the tough times but only how free she felt bumming around the country for those three years, riding the freights and road-gossiping with men with names like Louisiana Slim and One-Armed Kelly. Then she skipped ahead to 1963, when she was living in Chicago with a man named Gil Frost.

Gil was a small man, smaller than her, but she considered him handsome despite the fact that his neck was too fat and his curly black hair was thinning fast. He'd recently graduated from Northwestern University and worked as a copywriter for Leo Burnette, the advertising agency for Procter and Gamble.

He took her to twenty Chicago Cub games that summer. Because they were the same size, she wore his Levi's and his cotton knit pullovers with the alligator scooting across the front. He told her he loved the way she kissed. Nobody had ever told her that before.

When Kennedy was shot he cried for four straight days. After that he started losing interest in his job. He said working on an ad campaign for Kraft cheese made him feel corrupt. He said he wanted to write a novel or direct a film. After lunches with clients he liked to sneak away to play chess in coffeehouses near the University of Chicago. Nuclear war frightened him. He could talk about racial discrimination for hours. Eventually he got fired.

He began to sleep during the day. At night he smoked marijuana and listened to records by Leadbelly and Muddy Waters and other black blues singers. Women who were paranoid and obese started to drop by at odd hours. They wore dark shapeless clothes, and read aloud from Jack Kerouac's *On The Road*.

Bonnie began sleeping on the couch. On the day she left, Gil was nearly bald.

He gave her five hundred dollars.

She took the Greyhound to Detroit. She lived in a motel near the airport. At the Pontiac Lounge, a bar located directly across the highway, she became friendly with a group of rowdy engineers who worked for General Motors. She started going with a guy named Herb Freeman. Everyone called him "Herb the Heeb." She said he looked a little like Tony Curtis. His father, Leon, was a bookie.

In Las Vegas, where they were married, Leon arranged for Bonnie and Herb to stay free at the Sands Hotel, and they received complimentary front row seats for Dean Martin's show in the Copa Room.

Several months later, back in Detroit, Bonnie saw Herb kissing a well-dressed woman on Michigan Avenue. "Giving her his lips," was the way she described the scene to Bobby. She was inside a department store, looking out. She became dizzy and stumbled, nearly knocking over the cosmetics on the counter in front of her.

The next day she moved into a rooming house and found a job at a soft drink bottling plant in a run-down section of the city. At work one day a janitor came into the washroom while she was sitting on the toilet. He looked over the top of the stall and laughed at her; then he turned off the lights on his way out. She left the building immediately, without picking up her paycheck.

That same afternoon she gave blood and volunteered to work for Tom Carter, a light-skinned liberal black who was running for mayor. His father was a distinguished judge and his daughter, Kimba, sang in a Baptist church choir led by the Reverend James Franklin, Aretha's father.

Bonnie and Tom Carter had a brief affair. He was a trained hypnotist, and several times they made love while she was in a trance. She remembered absolutely nothing of these experiences, except that she was dissatisfied afterward. When they broke up, Carter told Bonnie she could never love another man because he'd hypnotized her soul.

She quit the campaign, spending her afternoons going to movies that only starred black actors. One Saturday she met her second husband, Freddie Bousquet, while she was watching Jim Brown in *The Split*. She picked him up. It was her choice, she said.

He lived in a redbrick ranch-style house in a new development on the west side. On the walls were illustrations of animals that were extinct or ecologically endangered. He said he had a brother who fought in the Bay of Pigs. He brushed his teeth for an unusually long time each morning and night. When he smiled, his eyes looked desperate, reflecting the light like chips of blue glass.

Behind the house was a thickly wooded area where Bonnie said she went for long walks in the afternoon. She fed the birds and squirrels and picked marsh marigolds and wild roses beside a murky creek. One day a man wearing cracked black boots passed her on a path and squeezed her arm. His eyes were hidden by a strip of white gauze.

After that she couldn't sleep through the night. She cried uncontrollably for hours at a stretch. Thoughts bounced around inside her brain, then suddenly disappeared as if they were sucked out her ears. She knew she was going mad and finally called the psychiatric unit at Wayne State Hospital. The woman who answered made an appointment for the following day.

★

"That's it. You know the rest," Bobby told Ricky as the bus they were riding slowed and then stopped at a traffic light on Beverly Glen and Sunset. A dark blue Mercedes convertible passed through the intersection and Ricky sat up straight in his seat. He said the man driving looked like actor David Janssen.

"It was," said the woman sitting across the aisle, in the long seat behind the bus driver. She was black, in her fifties, dressed in a starched white nurse's uniform. "Mr. Fugitive. Same time every day. Right, Russell?"

The bus driver glanced over his shoulder. He too was black, with wide, flaring nostrils and a heavy stomach. "Seven A.M. sharp. Ain't no fugitive from us," he said, turning away when the light changed.

"Can't run away from his problems with the bottle, either," the black woman said with an expression of authority. "Nossir."

"Miss Brenda's got the dirt on everyone."

The black woman nodded her head. "I know what I know."

Ricky took out his autograph book and quickly turned the pages. When he came to Janssen's signature he nudged Bobby in the ribs. "I got him while he was doing *The Green Berets*," he said in a low voice. "I could have gotten John Wayne that day, but my dad already got him in *Wake of the Red Witch*."

Bobby looked at the page. David Janssen was from Nebraska, not Omaha but Naponese, a small town in the southeast quadrant of the state. Janssen's cousin, Jack Crockett, was one of the state troopers involved in the capture of Charles Starkweather and his girlfriend after their three-state killing spree in the summer of 1957.

The black woman said, "I work for Mr. William Holden now. Last year I worked for Mr. Gig Young. When they're not working, they both sit around all day drinking in their bathrobes, watching the TV, waiting for their agents to call. You can have the glamorous life if that's where it gets you."

"They're both fine actors," Ricky said, unaware that *Wake of the Red Witch* was one of Gig Young's first movies.

"That's what I heard. I wouldn't know. I don't go to movies," the black woman said. "I go to church."

Ricky said, *"Buck and the Preacher."*

The black woman stared across the aisle. "Say what?"

"It's a movie that's coming out next year. Sidney Poitier plays a preacher."

"Lotta preachers sound like actors to me," the bus driver said. "Instead of readin' from a script, they're readin' from the Scriptures."

"Big ol' difference between the word of God and the word of man," said the black woman.

"Amen, sister," called out a dignified but fierce-looking black man seated in the rear of the bus. His round head was cleanly shaven and he had on a black tight-fitting suit. Beside him was a plumpish, coffee-colored little girl with her hair tied in pink pigtails. "You sound like someone who knows the truth when he hears it."

"I do that," the black woman said.

The black man was sitting erect in his seat. He held up a copy of *Muhammad Speaks,* the Black Muslim newspaper. "Elijah Muhammad speaks the truth."

The black woman clamped her gums together and shook her head. "Not to me he don't."

"Elijah Muhammad speaks the truth to everyone," the black man said.

At the next light the bus driver made a left and started down Hilgard, a wide tree-lined street that bordered the eastern edge of the UCLA campus. Small groups of athletic but unreflective-looking coeds stood chatting in front of sorority houses, all of them dressed alike in polished khaki skirts, knee socks, and brown loafers.

The black man snorted with contempt. "Look at those white devil bitches. Ain't you glad you don't look like that?" he asked the little girl next to him.

"Yes, I am."

"What are you?"

"I'm black and I'm proud."

The bus driver called out the next stop. "UCLA, Royce Hall, Manning Avenue."

Bobby turned his head. "What're you lookin' at, sissy boy?" the black man said coldly.

"I'm from Omaha, where Malcolm X was born," Bobby said. "My uncle knew him."

The black man stared at Bobby for a long time before he spoke. "He *knew* Brother Malcolm. What does that mean?"

"His auntie worked at the hotel where I grew up. The Hotel Sherwood. Sabrina Little. She was a maid. She used to walk me to school."

"Now that don't surprise me none," the black woman said. "Nossir. A maid. We all maids, us black women."

"Malcolm Little," Bobby said. "That was his name back then. My uncle's name was Daniel Schimmel. He wasn't really my uncle. He said he was my father, but he wasn't that either."

"They killed Malcolm's daddy," the black man said. He was on his feet, pulling the black girl toward the front of the bus. "Burned down his house, then ran over him in the street. Lynching him would've been kinder."

Bobby said, "I didn't find out who my father was until two years ago."

Ricky said, "My dad died in a car wreck when I was eight."

"My daddy's never gonna die," said the little girl, her fingers closed tightly on her father's wrist.

"Wilshire Boulevard comin' up," the bus driver said. "Thrifty Drugs, the Crest Theatre, and Westwood Park and Memorial Cemetery."

Ricky tapped Bobby on the shoulder and they stood up together. "Westwood Memorial Cemetery. This is our stop," Ricky said. "This is where we get off."

The bus driver tilted his head in Ricky's direction but kept his eyes on the road. "You boys goin' to a funeral?" Ricky nodded. "Family?"

"Someone."

"Someone?"

"Someone who was bad," Bobby said.

The black man pushed his daughter forward until they were standing by the change box. "We be gettin' off first," the black man said to the bus driver.

"Whatever you say."

"I said it."

The bus driver turned his head and gave the black man a long, penetrating look. "You need to relax, brother."

"Don't call me that name," the black man growled. "I ain't your brother. A brother of mine don't drive no bus."

"What's wrong with drivin' a bus?" said the black woman.

The black man pulled one of his daughter's pigtails. "Tell her what's wrong, Clothilde."

As if on cue, the little girl said, "Either you're part of the solution or you're part of the problem."

The black woman laughed scornfully. "What rubbish. That child should be in school."

The black man stared at the black woman, his mouth partly open, surprised by her boldness. Then he smiled. "You're a maid. What do you know?" he said, then he dramatically curled his thumb and forefinger into a circle. "Nothing. Zero. *That's* what you know. You just a slave to the white blue-eyed capitalist pigs."

The bus driver slowed to a stop on Wilshire Boulevard. "You ain't welcome on my bus," he said, looking hard at the black man. "Now get off." He jerked open the door, but the black man remained standing on the first step. *"Now."*

The bus driver stood up. There was something tight and threatening in his face. The little girl moved behind her father's legs, holding her straw purse up to cover her eyes. "Nigger. A year ago you'd be dead," the black man said almost tenderly.

"Is that right?"

"Tell him, Clothilde. Tell him what I would've done."

The little girl snickered behind her purse. "My daddy would've cut you up," she said.

The black man smiled at the bus driver with satisfaction. "If you were a man," he said, "you would walk off the bus with me right now and join us in the revolution. The nation of Islam needs you."

"I got other obligations," the bus driver said stonily.

"A righteous man has no other obligations. A righteous man needs only Allah."

"You can tell Allah to kiss my black ass. And you got five seconds to get off my bus: five . . . four . . . three . . . two . . ."

The black man suddenly clapped his hands in front of the bus driver's face. "I'm goin'. I'm on my way. But I want you to understand one thing," he said, as he backed down the steps. "If you didn't eat meat, you'd see it. Right, Clothilde?"

"Right, Daddy."

"Tell him."

"If you didn't eat meat, you'd see it."

"Tell him again."

"If you didn't eat meat, you'd see it," the little girl shouted, then she followed her father through the open door. "Praise Allah! Praise the true prophet!"

The bus driver took his seat behind the wheel. "Someone should throw a net over that one," the black woman said.

The bus driver closed the door and laughed in a pleasant way as he watched Ricky and Bobby cross in front of the windshield. The light changed and the black woman said, "Ought to throw a net over those gray boys, too."

   The bus driver nodded and sat back and worked his muscular shoulders into his seat. "I hear you, Miss Brenda. Uh-huh. I sure do."

★

Because Max Rheingold had no living relatives and his only friend, actor Kenny Kendall, was serving a one-year jail sentence for selling cocaine, Jack Rose reluctantly put himself in charge of the funeral. Once he chose the cemetery, he decided that Max's final resting place should be under a shady camphor tree, just a few yards away from Marilyn Monroe's sealed crypt.

   "He discovered her. All the other schmucks take the credit," Jack Rose told the cemetery manager, a short, intensely focused woman with kinky hair and a small bruise on her chin. "But it was Max. He spotted her walking down Las Palmas near Nate's News. He put her in *Rustler's Roundup,* this oater he was making at Monogram. Gave her one line but she blew it. Ended up on the cutting room floor. But Max was the first."

   "And I never fucked her," Max told Jack after she became a star. "Can you believe it? I just thought she was a nice kid who needed a break. Not too bright but she had a look."

   Jack said, "That's called star quality."

   "Who knew?"

   "Obviously you didn't."

   In 1962, on the morning she committed suicide, Max called Jack. "She had a lousy life," he said. "I hope she's happier where she is."

   "Ask her when you get there," Jack told him.

   "I plan to. I plan to fuck her, too."

Only three mourners had arrived by eight-thirty: Bobby Sherwood and Ricky Furlong, who stood together, whispering, and a gray-bearded cowboy wearing a bolo tie over a Western-stlye shirt with blue piping and pearl snaps for buttons. He held a white Stetson hat by the side of one leg.

   Across the newly mowed grass, Jack Rose's limousine could be seen idling on the narrow road that separated the gravesite from the memorial chapel and the outside mausoleum.

"Bela Lugosi was buried in his cape," Ricky said, as he watched the Mexican gravediggers lower the casket into the grave.

Bobby said, "Who told you that?"

"I read it somewhere."

"His cape. That's funny," Bobby said, without smiling.

A bell began to toll loudly from the Mormon Church down on Santa Monica Boulevard. As soon as the ringing stopped, the cowboy bent down painfully and used his hat to sprinkle some dirt over the casket. "You boys know Max?" he said, standing up. He was looking at Ricky.

Ricky said, "Sort of."

"Yeah?" The cowboy looked over at the limousine. "You come with him?"

"Who?"

"Mr. Moneybags in the stretch. Jack Rose."

Ricky shook his head. "We came on the bus," Bobby said.

"I flew down from Fresno," said the old cowboy, looking up at a sky that was just a shade darker than the piping on his shirt. "Wind's blowin' from the north. That's why the air seems so clear. Used to be like that every day of the week back in the forties." The gravediggers laughed, interrupting the cowboy, and he looked in their direction without any expression on his face. "I speak Spanish," he said. "Picked it up in Durango when I did *Hangtown Mesa.* Max produced that one. Made about two cents."

"Are those guys laughing at us?" Bobby asked the cowboy.

"They called you queers," he said, and smiled over at the brown faces watching them. "If you ask me, it's no business what a man does with his dick."

"As long as he doesn't hurt anyone," Ricky said.

The cowboy said, "That's assumed."

"He hurt my mom," Bobby said, looking down at the casket. He swallowed hard to hold back the tears.

"Max had a cruel streak. He hurt a lot of people."

"He hurt her bad. I hurt him back," Bobby said, and spit into the grave.

The cowboy glanced at Bobby, looking at him silently for several seconds. "How'd you do that?"

"It doesn't matter," Ricky said.

"It don't?"

"No."

The cowboy waited a moment, and, strangely, a small laugh came out of the side of his mouth. "I guess you're right," he said, grinning, "since he's already dead."

Ricky reached down and lightly squeezed Bobby's hand. "Let's get some breakfast," he said. He turned and pointed across the street to Ship's, the coffee shop on the corner of Wilshire and Glendon. "They make a fabulous Western omelet."

"Speaking of chow, I played the chuck wagon boss in *Desperate Trails*," the cowboy said, beginning to ramble on as Ricky and Bobby moved toward the street. "They shot it over there at Republic. That's where I met Max. He had an office on the lot next to Abbott and Costello. Now Bud Abbott—"

"Take it easy, Tibbles."

The sound of his own name startled the cowboy. He turned and saw Jack Rose standing at the edge of the open grave, dressed in a dark blue suit. In his right hand was a small brown paper sack. "I didn't see you walk up, Mr. Rose," the cowboy said, wincing at how nervous his voice sounded. "You kinda scared me."

"It's been awhile, hasn't it? What, twenty years?"

"Around that."

Jack Rose nodded his head. He was gazing at the cowboy, evaluating him but not in an unfriendly way. "How's your ranch?"

"I'm makin' out all right. Switched over to almonds last year. Almonds are a good crop."

"I like almonds," Jack Rose said.

"I'll send you some."

"You don't have to."

"I'd like to," the cowboy said.

Jack Rose gave the cowboy a hard stare and held it, working his jaw silently for several seconds. Then he took his hand away from his body, muttered a few phrases in Hebrew, and dropped the brown paper bag into the grave. "Pastrami on rye from Nate and Al's," he said. "Max's favorite sandwich."

"He liked chili dogs, too," the cowboy said. "One time at the Tail of the Pup I saw him put away six, one right after another, piled high with all the trimmings."

Jack Rose said, "Max had an appetite."

"He sure did."

Jack Rose looked off in the distance, allowing a long significant silence before he spoke again. "'Forty-seven. Is that the year we met?" he asked the cowboy.

"In the summer. Up in Crestline. I was doin' a Johnny Mack Brown picture. You represented the girl."

"Which one?"

"The second lead. A blonde. I don't remember her name."

"Max liked blondes. The younger the better," Jack Rose said, and the cowboy squirmed underneath his gaze. "Right, Tibbles?"

"Max had problems, like all of us."

"Problems with little girls."

The cowboy shrugged this off. "He always treated me okay."

"You remember Grace Elliot?" Jack Rose said, his smile turning gentle.

"The name sounds familiar."

"She was an extra, mostly in Westerns. Tall, auburn hair, strong jaw. Eyes were an extraordinary shade of blue."

The cowboy looked down at his feet. "I think I know who you mean."

"In 'forty-nine Max did a picture up in Big Bear. It was called *The Crooked Man*," Jack Rose said, his smile slowly drifting off his face. "Grace Elliot was in it. There was an accident. The picture never got finished." The cowboy stood quiet, remembering. "She brought her daughter out that summer. I guess she was around thirteen. Bonnie, I think her name was."

"I was up there," the cowboy said. "I did some stunt work."

"And some special effects. Everyone doubled on Max's films. Right?"

"Yeah. That's right. I did effects," the cowboy said. The way he said it sounded like a confession. "I cared about Grace," he said.

"Of course you did, Tibbles."

"Max knew I did, too."

"And he knew the accident wasn't your fault. It was just that— an accident."

The cowboy made a move to turn away, but Jack Rose said, "No. Not yet."

Tears came out of the cowboy's eyes. "I came down here to pay my respects," he said. "That's all."

"I'm here for the same reason," Jack Rose said evenly. Then, in a quick but agile move, he stepped across the grave. The two of them were now standing very close together their gray hair shining in the sunlight. "Still, it's important to know the truth."

"I know the truth," the cowboy said.

"No. I don't think so. Not all of it. Part of it you know. Part I know. And part no one will ever know, because it's buried with Max." Jack Rose gripped the cowboy's bicep and moved him toward the limousine. "Come on, I'll give you a ride."

On the way to the airport, Jack Rose sat so close to the cowboy that their knees touched lightly whenever they turned a corner. Neither spoke until the limousine pulled onto the freeway, then Jack mentioned, casually, that he drove Grace Elliot's daughter to the train station back in the summer of 1949.

"I sent her off to Omaha," he said. "Never heard from her again."

"Maybe she grew up and had a normal life."

"I hope so," Jack Rose said, remembering the little girl's sad, defeated face.

"So do I," the cowboy said, and once more he saw the cabin explode in his mind, a wall of flames, and a woman staggering into the apocalyptic sunlight, crying out for release. "It would only seem right."

★

Eighteen

Going

Home

May 29, 1971

Four days after Max Rheingold's funeral, Ricky found Bobby on his knees on the south side of Hollywood Boulevard, between Hudson and Cherokee, bent over a star he was polishing on the Walk of Fame. The blue sky above him was immense, infinite, and the shadows from the power lines fell across his yellow polo shirt, tiger-striping his back.

A few paces away, a man dressed in cook's whites stood in the open doorway of a luncheonette. A waitress with a bossy face came outside and stood next to him. Pointing a finger at Bobby, she said to Ricky, "You know this guy?"

"Yes."

"That star ain't got no name on it. How come he's polishing it?"

"I guess he's getting it ready."

The fry cook laughed a smoker's laugh. "Ready? For who?"

"For whatever name they decide to put there."

The waitress gave Ricky a withering look. "He's fucking crazy. You both are," she said. Then she turned around and stepped back inside the luncheonette.

The fry cook spit on the sidewalk by Bobby's knee. "Get him out of here," he said to Ricky in a threatening voice. "He's blocking traffic. Get him away from my door."

Ricky tapped Bobby lightly on the shoulder. "Come on," he said, urging him to stand with his voice. "I think we better go."

Bobby glanced at the fry cook's hostile face, sizing him up; then he slipped his handkerchief and his bottle of Brasso into the front pocket of his khaki trousers. When he stood up, Ricky threw his arm around his shoulder in a masculine fashion. "Guess who I saw when I was walking past the Columbia lot?"

"Who?"

"Carol Lynley."

"Did you get her autograph?"

"I already have it, dummy. Remember? *Bunny Lake Is Missing.*"

"That's right. I forgot," Bobby said, nodding slowly as they started up the street. "Did she say anything?"

"No. But she looked over."

"That's all?"

"I think she recognized my face."

Near Frederick's of Hollywood, Ricky and Bobby stepped around a circle of French tourists who were snapping pictures of Jerry Lewis's star on the Walk of Fame. Ahead of them, just west of Highland, was the El Capitan theater. *Diamonds Are Forever* was triple-billed with *Wild Rovers* and *The Ballad of Cable Hogue.*

Outside the theater a construction crew was repairing potholes in the right lane, slowing the midafternoon traffic along the Boulevard. A girl in a tight sweater stood by the curb with her chest pushed out, ogling a long-haired man operating a jackhammer. The scrawny dog she was holding was turning in circles, his leash becoming tangled around a parking meter, his frantic barks swallowed up by the noise of the street.

Bobby and Ricky crossed with the light. Away from the hectic sounds, Bobby said, hesitantly, "When I came back from the Laundromat this morning, there was a letter from my uncle at the desk. He wants me to come home. He wants me to come back to Omaha. He says they're opening a florist shop and a travel agency in the hotel. He said I could work in either one—or maybe I could be in charge."

Ricky and Bobby glanced at each other quickly as they walked east on the boulevard; then Ricky put his hand on Bobby's arm, stopping him on the sidewalk so a car could pull into the busy lot next to Musso & Frank. "What do you know about flowers?" Ricky said, as they resumed walking.

"I know a little."

"You have to know more than a little."

"Dandelions and goldenrod are everywhere in Omaha," Bobby said. "And roses, of course. In the hotel dining room in the spring there were always yellow and pink roses standing in vases on every table." Bobby paused in front of a store with windows blocked out with wood. "You could come with me."

"To Omaha?"

"I called my uncle collect after I got the letter. I told him I had a friend. He said, 'Bring him out if you want.'"

"Does he—?"

"He knows," Bobby said, starting up the sidewalk once more. "It doesn't matter to him."

For the next two blocks Ricky remained quiet, struggling with the possibilities of this offer, turning it over in his mind. Crossing Ivar he said, "I get money every month from the state. That's how we live, Bobby. That's how I pay the rent and buy the food."

"We don't need that money anymore," Bobby said. "We could stay at the Sherwood. Free. Including our meals. You could work there too. We would both have salaries. Then, maybe, eventually we could rent a house with a yard big enough for a dog. A golden retriever. Sam. That would be his name."

At Vine, Ricky slowed by the open doorway of the Taft building and pulled Bobby out of the sunlit air. He said quietly, looking at him, "I grew up in a house in a nice neighborhood. We had pets and played ball in the street. We did all that, Bobby. But it didn't work out for me."

"We'll be in another city, where the seasons change," Bobby said. "It could work out differently this time."

"I don't know that."

"Don't you think I was scared to leave Omaha? It took me two years before I could get on the Greyhound bus with my bags packed. But I made it here. I had to do something important and I did it. Now I get to go home."

Ricky put his hand on Bobby's shoulder and gently pushed him back on the sidewalk. There was another long silence that continued to stretch as they walked east with the sun warming their necks.

Finally, in a voice that Bobby had never heard before—a voice that seemed to throb in his throat—Ricky said, "When I hear the Dodger games on the car radios in the traffic, it takes me back to high school. I was a wonderful ballplayer, Bobby. That's the word Coach Burroughs used: wonderful. 'You've got a wonderful swing, Ricky,' he would say, or a 'wonderful arm.' And when he touched me underneath my shirt, he would tell me I had 'wonderful skin.' I remember one time at the end of the dugout he held my head between his hands and let his thumbs slide slowly down my cheeks. 'Just peach fuzz now,' he said. 'But later when you're older you'll have a wonderful beard.'

"And once, before a geography test, he unlocked the gym and made me shower, so he could watch me and tell me where to soap myself and for how long. When I was done he had me lie down on the trainer's table on my stomach. Right away he made the moisture flow inside me with his finger; then he climbed up on the table and pushed himself into my wet place. For the next half hour, while he traced the map of the world on my back with his tongue, he tested me over and over on the names of the countries on each continent.

"When we were finished, after I got every question right, he took a shower with me in the dark. Through the transom I remember hearing someone practicing drums in the music room next door, the sound of the bass bouncing off the tiled walls surrounding us, echoing the heartbeat sounding in my ears.

"And then that spring all the scouts started showing up after school. Instead of being called wonderful, instead of that word, they used the word 'great.' Like he has 'great power' or 'great balance' or 'great instincts.' And my coach would say, 'Yes, he's a wonderful boy.'

"They didn't get it, Bobby. Wonderful was a safe place. Great was something else, something I had to live up to. At least that's what I felt. I was terrified of 'great.' Say *great,* Bobby."

"Great."

"See how it sounds: all hard edges, like a piece of furniture you trip over in the dark. Wonderful is soft, like . . . like . . ."

"Like a bucket of bunnies."

Ricky laughed loudly, uncontrollably, a sound that drew stares from the passersby.

"You don't belong here anymore," Bobby said. "Neither of us do."

They were standing in front of the St. Francis Arms. Ricky's eyes were still gleaming with joy, but inside he was frightened. "What about autographs?" he said, the panic now showing on his face. "What will I do? There's nobody there."

"We'll be working, Ricky. We'll be busy," Bobby said. "We won't have time for all that."

Ricky nodded, thinking, his eyes moving away from Bobby's face. "Marlon Brando. You said he was from Omaha. Right?"

"Right."

"He probably comes home sometimes to visit. Right?"

"I guess."

"And maybe he goes to church or stops by the hotel for a meal. If I was around I could get his autograph. True?"

"That could happen," Bobby said.

"And Henry Fonda and Jane and Peter, and Fred Astaire and Dorothy McGuire. They could show up too."

"You already have Henry Fonda."

"I could get him again," Ricky said, with a grin of delight. "Doubles are okay, when they're far enough apart in years. I'd like to get Henry and Peter and Jane to sign on the same page, like my dad did with Walter Huston and his son John." Ricky reached for his autograph book. "You want to see?"

Bobby put his hand on Ricky's arm and smiled patiently. "Let's go inside," he said. "Let's go up to the room and pack."

Ricky made a sound of resignation as he stared into Bobby's face with an expression of blind trust. Then, ever so slowly, a moment from their recent past, started to fill the space in the air between them.

It's late at night and Bobby takes off all his clothes before he steps into the shallow end of the large swimming pool behind the Beverly Hills Hotel. He pushes off the wall and begins to sidestroke silently through the water, his breath unaccountably soft as he pulls alongside a man floating in the lane next to him. There is light on the water from the moon, reflecting Bobby's face. The man raises his head and says, "Who are you?"

"My name's Bobby."

"Get the hell away from me. You're not supposed to be in the pool."

"Why not? You're in the pool . . . Max."

"You know my name."

"Uh-huh. I know everything about you."

"What're you, an actor or something?"

"No, Max. I'm your son."

Max is now treading water with his hands, trying to ease himself toward the side of the pool.

"I don't have a son."

"Yes, you do."

Bobby grins like a dolphin. There is something in his eyes like joy. Overhead a star blinks twice—a celestial signal—and he places his palm on top of Max's head, pushing down hard.

"You cocksucker! Get your hands off me!" Max shouts, his eyes bulging in fear as he frantically tries to break away and swim to safety. "You're trying to kill me!"

A few yards away Ricky is relaxing on one of the lounge chairs scattered around the deck. He's laughing softly, his chest rising and falling, watching Max's head disappear underneath the water—once, twice, three times!

Max is taking in water, unable to breathe, a white-hot pain screaming through his chest; then finally, in the sweetness of surrender, his life quickly unravels behind his eyes and all that he knows of hope is gone.

"Oh, sweetheart, oh, Holy Mother. . . ."

Those are Max Rheingold's final words: tiny green bubbles rising to the water's surface, words no one will ever hear.

Three Memories

I

A warm starless night, the sky a syrupy deep black.
Burk and Sandra are driving from Topanga Canyon to Hollywood, using Mulholland Drive. In the half-light of the moving
car, there is something unknowable in her face. He wonders
what she's thinking but doesn't ask.

Near Coldwater Canyon she says, "It would be nice to
live up in the hills, away from everything. Is that just a silly
dream?"

He shakes his head. He feels her fingers prowling
through the hair on the back of his neck.

"It isn't?"

"I'd like a house with big decks and lots of wood," he
says. "Decks that go all the way around the house."

"So when it's clear we can see the ocean," Sandra says,
and lets her head fall on his shoulder. "What about a swimming pool?"

"Sure."

"We'd have to get rich to have a house like that."

"It's possible."

"How?"

"I don't know. If we work hard."

"You mean you. I'm having a baby."

He looks away from her glance. His armpits are wet. She can't see his face when he says, "I'm not talking about jobs. I mean working together as partners. If you believe in each other—"

"I believe in you, Ray," Sandra says, pushing her breasts into his side, "or I wouldn't be here."

Ten minutes later they are parked in their driveway. Behind them Burk can hear the freeway they just left. There is something he wants to say. Sandra knows this, she can tell by his breathing; she waits, her hands folded neatly in her lap.

She thinks, Up on Mulholland we were two different people: a boy and girl in love. We're still in love, but it's different. Down here we're scared. I know I am, she thinks. I'm scared of the thoughts that move in and out of my mind. And sometimes when I laugh it sounds canned, like the laughs on the television shows Ray censors. Lots of times I just say "Ha-ha" out loud, instead of laughing. When Ray asks me why, I tell him I don't know. He knows something's wrong with me.

Minutes pass in silence.

Finally, as if he's compelled to tell the truth, Burk says, "I bought a book last week. It's called *Introduction to Teleplay Writing*. It tells you how to write a TV script. I didn't show it to you. I thought you might laugh."

Sandra takes his hand. It feels hot. "Why would I laugh?"

"I don't know. All of a sudden I'm trying to be a writer. Maybe that would sound goofy to you."

"Is that what you want to be?" Sandra asks.

"I don't know." Burk hears his voice go up. "Maybe."

"Television's pretty dumb. Maybe you could write a movie."

Burk's heart is pounding against the wall of his chest. He wishes he were stronger, that he'd held onto his secret. He says, "Maybe. I could try."

Sandra turns her head to Burk. Their hands are sweating. "I think you're brave," she says.

"What if I can't? Will you still love me?"

Sandra laughs, "Ha-ha," but Burk sees a tear fall past her lip when she says with conviction, "Of course I will."

★

2

"She loved you, Ray." This is Gene speaking on the day Sandra is to be released from prison. "She believed in you, big time."

"She left us, Gene. Just got in her car and left."

"She had to do what she had to do."

"Like Mom."

"It's not the same."

"It feels the same."

"Sandra danced naked to pay the bills. She did that so you could write. That's how much she loved you."

"What about Louie?"

"What about him?"

"It's not fair."

Before he hangs up, Burk tells Gene that he almost stole "Daddy's Big Dick" back in December of 1969.

"You're kidding."

"No. Really."

"I can't believe you would do something like that. We're brothers, Ray. We're blood. We don't steal from each other."

"I know. I'm sorry. I was fucked up, then. You pissed?"

"Maybe, I don't know."

"I put it back, Gene. Go look. It's still there. I promise."

★

3

It's May 14, 1971, three days before *Pledging My Love* goes into production. He and Loretta Egan are eating dinner at Musso & Frank. They are seated in the front room, in a booth by the wall. Across the room Clint Eastwood is dining with a trim, tough-looking man in his mid-sixties.

Loretta says, "I don't think I can enjoy my meal with him in the room."

Burk remains silent, raising a lit match to the cigarette stuck between his lips.

"When you don't answer I think you're judging me."

Burk looks at her briefly. "I'm not judging you. It just feels that way," he says. A few seconds later he says, "Let's see if we can have a good time."

"You can't feel the vibes? I can."

At that moment the man in the booth behind them says, "That's Don Siegel. He directed *Coogan's Bluff*. They're doing this thing called *Dirty Harry* at Warner's."

Loretta says, "See?"

The waiter arrives to take their order. They decide to split a Caesar salad, and Burk orders a steak, rare. "And I want another martini," Loretta says. "Make it a double."

Suddenly heads turn in the restaurant and Loretta's eyes fly past Burk's face: Walter Matthau is standing next to the maître d'; with him is an intense-looking woman dressed in tight black jeans and a black turtleneck sweater.

"That's not his wife," says the woman sitting behind Burk. "His wife's a blonde. She used to be married to William Saroyan."

"That's Elaine May. She's directing her first movie," someone else says. "She wrote the script, too. I saw her and Mike Nichols live on Broadway."

Burk and Loretta are listening to all this, listening in silence. The envy on Loretta's face turns into pain. "Elaine's a talented woman," she says. Burk nods, keeping his face neutral. "Fuck it. So am I."

The waiter returns with Loretta's martini. She gulps down half in one swallow. The man behind her says, "I think the most gifted of the bunch was Nathanael West. Have you read *Miss Lonelyhearts*? Ninety pages and it took him four years. The sonovabitch was a stonecutter."

"What about Chandler?" the woman asks.

"Chandler's good but he's not West. West hemorrhaged pain on every page."

Once Matthau and Elaine May are seated, they are joined by Jack Rose and a tall brunette with an aloof, almost-pretty face. From another part of the restaurant, Burk hears someone mention the name of his script. Loretta hears it too. She closes her eyes. "I can't stand this," she says.

"I'm sorry," Burk says, conscious that he looks somewhat pleased.

Loretta opens her eyes and lifts her chin. "Don't look at me like that. Don't patronize me."

Burk feels anxiety burning into his stomach. The coke he snorted earlier is wearing off. He excuses himself. On his way to the men's room he hears a woman say his name. He turns around, trying to put the face with the voice; she's in her forties, willowy but brittle looking. Flanking her at the bar are two men wearing leather jackets and cowboy boots. All three are smoking cigarettes.

Burk thinks, They don't know who I am, but they know I'm here.

Loretta has already started eating her salad when Burk returns to the table. In between bites she looks at the side of his face and sees that his eye is blinking. "Are you okay?" she asks him.

Burk nods, looking into space.

Loretta shakes her head. "Go easy."

The waiter returns with a round of drinks. "Compliments of Mr. Rose," he says.

Burk and Loretta don't speak again until Burk pushes aside his plate. "I'm not hungry," he says.

"Because you're wired."

"Maybe."

"You should pace yourself, Ray."

Burk points at Loretta's empty glass. "Like you."

Loretta smiles, unable to hide the anger in her eyes. "Fuck off."

Burk's knee is jumping. He lights a cigarette and blows a cloud of smoke above his head. "We lost our sense of humor, Loretta."

"Tell me about it."

A handsome couple move by their table on the way out the door. They are holding hands. Staring after them, Loretta says, "When was the last time we held hands, Ray?"

Burk can't remember.

"What about the first time?"

Burk looks away. He's reaching back, past his relationship with Loretta. He's with Sandra now in Madison, walking across the grass in front of the university library. They're laughing at each other's jokes. He takes her hand, and a moment later her leg comes up and she toe-kicks him in the butt.

"We were in line to see *Catch 22,*" Loretta says. "In Westwood."

"That's right."

"You don't remember."

"Yes I do."

Loretta kills her drink. "You're lying to me, Ray," she says calmly. "Let's get the check."

On the way back to the Beverly Hills Hotel, Loretta quietly begins to weep. Because he's too stoned, Burk is unable to summon the words to console her; the best he can do is to reach out and touch her arm.

At North Foothill Road he turns left and parks under a streetlight in the middle of the second block. Loretta rolls down her window and angles her head to the side so the night air can dry the tears on her face.

"That's where Groucho Marx lives," Burk says. He's pointing at a redbrick two-story house on the opposite side of the street. "I was inside there once. Back in high school, me and Timmy Miller crashed one of his parties. We used to do that a lot during the summertime: cruise up and down the streets until we found a big bash, then sneak in.

"There must have been three hundred people at Groucho's that night, most of them outside, all around the patio and the pool. Anthony Perkins was grilling steaks on a

huge barbecue. I remember that because Timmy and I had
just seen *Psycho* the week before. Betty Grable was there too.
She did a tap dance around the deck with a champagne glass
balanced on her head. A lot of old-time stars were there. But
there was a young crowd, too.

"I remember Dennis Hopper consuming endless gin and
tonics. Elizabeth Taylor was there. Timmy told her he was a
premed student at UCLA. She acted like she believed him,
telling him all about some back problem she had, but I was
sure she was putting him on."

"What did she look like? Was she beautiful?"

Burk closes his eyes, nodding and grimacing a little
as he retrieves another memory. "Lana Turner came to
the party. She was with the guy who played Tarzan in the
movies."

"Johnny Weissmuller?"

"No. The one after him. Big stone-faced guy. Lex Barker!
That was him. They were married once, but I think they were
divorced. He was drunk, I remember that," Burk says, and
when he opens his eyes they are bright, maybe too bright. "He
got up on the diving board and did this yell, not a yell like
Tarzan but something different, howling like he was in
terrible pain. I remember people applauding like he was
doing some kind of act. But he wasn't. Eventually he sat
down on the end of the board and started to cry. Tarzan,
crying. It was so weird. I mean it seems weird now, but I don't
think Timmy and I ever talked about it."

Burk rubs the palm of his hand across his forehead, as if
he is trying to erase some painful thought or image that is
forcing itself into his consciousness.

"I saw my mother the next day," he says suddenly,
startling Loretta. She looks down: His right hand is on the
seat between them, his fingers curled in a way that seems to
be drawing her to him. "I was working at the Ambassador
Hotel. My dad knew the manager. I was a lifeguard that
summer. That Sunday, the Sunday after Groucho's party, I
gave a swimming lesson to a twelve-year-old girl who was
blind. She and her mother had come out from Ohio to go to
Disneyland. The girl's name was Eden and I remember

supporting her in the water, teaching her first to float. One hand was under her legs and the other was flat against her stomach. As I turned her in a circle, her hair fanned out in the water and I could feel her heart racing underneath my palm.

"When I asked her if she was okay, she said, 'I'm fine. I'm just excited.' Then she turned her face toward my voice and asked me whether I thought she was pretty. I said she was and she said, 'Is my body pretty, too?'

"For a while I didn't answer. It felt strange to be holding a girl that age and talking about her body. Finally, she started to giggle. 'That's okay. I know my body's pretty,' she said. 'You know why? Because my daddy tells me it is. Every night at home he comes into my room and rubs lotion all over me and tells me how soft my skin is. But his skin is not as soft as mine, and sometimes he tickles me too hard. I don't like his whiskers either, especially on my bottom, and sometimes he whispers things that scare me.

"'One time my mom came in while he was rubbing me and she told him to stop. She said it in a really mean voice. He said I was as much his as hers, and they started shouting at each other. After school the next day she asked me if I wanted to meet Mickey Mouse. I said yes and we drove to the airport.'"

Burk closes his eyes and lets his forehead rest on the edge of the steering wheel. He feels Loretta take his hand and squeeze it in a familiar way as she slides across the seat. In silence he thinks about that Sunday, the shock of the little girl's story and his clenched teeth at the end. Just before he speaks again, Loretta slips her arm around his shoulder and kisses him tenderly on the cheek.

He says, "The Philadelphia Phillies checked in later that morning. Usually the baseball and football teams stayed downtown, at the Biltmore, to be closer to the Coliseum where the games were played. But a convention of dentists had reserved all the rooms that weekend. We were filled too, mostly with foreign tourists and families. The Hollywood types stopped coming in the early fifties, except for Walter Winchell. He always stayed at the hotel for three weeks every summer. He was there that Sunday, sitting in front of his cabana in his street clothes. I remember he was interviewing Coleen Gray."

Loretta says, "Coleen Gray. I remember her. She was the girl John Wayne lets get away in the beginning of *Red River*."

"She was a has-been in 1960. Either Winchell was screwing her or pumping her for gossip, or both. There was another actor in the pool that day," Burk says. "The blond guy you liked in *Sometimes a Great Notion*."

"Richard Jaeckel."

"He was doing some bullshit teenage picture. *Platinum High School* or something. When I noticed him, that's when I saw my mom. She was directly behind him, sitting with a couple of the Phillies. I recognized her voice first, then her smile. Her hair was different, though. It was cut short and dyed a dark red."

"Did she recognize you?"

"No. Her eyes passed right over my face."

"Are you sure?"

"Yes."

"What did you do?"

"Just watched her. She seemed to know all the players, but she was especially friendly to this older guy. I think he was the pitching coach. She was wearing his cap tilted back with the bill snapped up. Boy, it was really weird, Loretta, seeing your mom like that with a bunch of men. Seeing her, but her not seeing you."

"How long had it been?"

"Four years."

"You probably looked a lot different. Why didn't you just go over and say something?"

Burk shakes his head. He is frowning. Telling the story makes him feel helpless. "She was with these guys," he says. "Don't you get it? A bunch of ballplayers. I saw what was going on. She wasn't there to see me. That night I told Gene. He didn't believe me. He said I was fucking crazy. Then I showed him the last postcard she sent us. It was from Bradenton, Florida, where the Phillies go to spring training.

It was postmarked the second of March. He still didn't believe me."

"I believe you, Ray."

"I was off on Mondays," Burk says. "On Tuesday and Wednesday the Phillies played the Dodgers in day games, and they checked out before their game on Thursday night. My mother never showed up by the pool again, and she wasn't registered at the hotel because I checked. Under her real name, anyway. Just that one Sunday she was there, on the deck, drinking rum drinks and playing kneesies with that old man. I don't get it. I just don't get it," Burk says, staring meditatively through the windshield. Then he starts the engine. "That was the last time I saw my mom, Loretta. Okay? End of story."

Loretta says, "What about the blind girl? What happened to her?"

"I gave her two more lessons. By Friday she could do a width of the pool without my help. Before she left the following Sunday, her mother came down to the pool and gave me a fifty-dollar tip. She was wearing a Disneyland T-shirt. I asked her if Eden got to see Mickey Mouse. She said, 'No, Eden can't see. But she gave him a hug and he let her feel his ears. She said they were as soft as silk.'"

★

PART SIX

THE DARKNESS
AROUND US
IS DEEP

★

Nineteen

And the Stars
Will Make
You Blind

April 14, 1983

Sandra Burk died in Los Angeles with puke and blood crusted around her lips in April 1983 in the middle of a cold rainy spring. For the last four years of her troubled life—a life that confounded Burk and was the source of endless guilt—she lived alone in a tiny apartment above a garage in West Hollywood. This property and several others in the predominantly gay neighborhood were owned by Eddie Cornell, Gene's partner for one year back in the mid-sixties, when they worked undercover vice out of the Hollywood division.

"She drank herself to death," Gene told Burk on the morning that her body was discovered. "At least that's what Eddie thinks. He said there was no sign of any violence, just her cats and an empty half-gallon of cheap vodka. The coroner said she probably had been dead for three days."

Burk was silent. He had the sensation of feeling both furious and relieved at the same time. When he was able to trust his voice he said, "This is hard to take in, all of a sudden."

"I know. You're in shock," Gene said. He waited a moment. Then he brought up the question of funeral arrangements.

"I want her cremated," Burk said. "I think she'd prefer that. I don't know why, exactly. But I just do." There was another silence, in which Burk could feel his tears start to come. "I gotta call Louie."

"Ray?"

"Yeah."

"You're gonna be okay."

"I know."

"I'm here if you want to talk."

After he hung up the phone, Burk thought back to the last time he and Louie had seen Sandra. It was in San Francisco, in the summer of 1975. Warner Brothers was sneaking *Take Me Home* at the Coronet Theatre on Geary, and she arrived unexpectedly with Eli Cook, a skinny guitar player she'd met at Serenity Knolls, an alcoholic rehabilitation center in Petaluma.

"I saw your name in the ad and screamed. I had to be here," she told Burk, when she found him in the corner of the lobby, smoking nervously, surrounded by friends and a steady stream of well-wishers. Cook was standing behind her, looking slightly dazed and uncomfortable. "Where's Louie?"

"Inside. He and Timmy are sitting together."

"Timmy is Ray's best friend. They went to high school together," Sandra told Cook, who tossed his rock-star hair behind his shoulders before he stuck out his hand and introduced himself.

Sandra said quickly, "Eli loved *Pledging My Love*."

"Yeah. Cool flick." Cook nodded and smiled dumbly, retreating a step with his eyes half closed.

It was obvious to Burk that Cook was stoned out of his mind, probably on downs or some extra-strong grass. But Sandra was standing straight and clear-eyed, dressed in a man's white shirt that was tucked into tight bell-bottom jeans. "Why don't you grab a seat?" Burk suggested. "We'll talk after the show."

Sandra started to walk away. After a few steps she stopped and looked over her shoulder, weighing the question she was about to ask. "Is she here?"

"Who?"

"Your girlfriend. The one you met on the airplane."

"We're getting married in November."

Sandra made no reply to this as she stared at Burk, allowing a silence to develop that lasted for several seconds. Finally she took Cook by the elbow and walked him inside the theater.

Just before the lights went down, Burk found his seat next to Barbara Nichols in a small roped-off section on the side aisle. Two rows ahead he could see Louie's head bobbing up and down as he bounced nervously in his seat between Timmy and his girlfriend, Juliet.

Barbara reached down and squeezed Burk's hand. "Good luck."

"Thanks."

This would be the second time Burk had seen *Take Me Home,* the first with a paying audience. Earlier that month, at the screening for the cast and crew in Los Angeles, the response was enthusiastic, but he was still bothered by a long talky section in the second act where everything seemed to sag. "It'll get decent reviews," Burk told Barbara when he phoned her that night. "I don't know about the box office."

"Was Gene there?"

"Yeah."

"What did he think?"

"He liked it."

"Well?"

"Barbara, he's my brother."

For the sneak in San Francisco, there was a new song by the Beach Boys and several scenes were either shortened or edited out, clarifying the story and vastly improving the film's overall pace. Also, the audience seemed looser and less judgmental, laughing in all the right places. And as far as Burk could tell, the people who did walk out came back after buying popcorn or using the rest room.

When the movie ended and the people around them were applauding loudly over the closing credits, Burk whispered to Barbara that Sandra was in the audience. Barbara's face, which a split-second earlier was glowing with excitement, now took on a look of blank disbelief.

Burk said, "You wouldn't have enjoyed the movie if I told you before it started."

Barbara shook her head. She was smiling, but her face expressed disgust. "I cannot believe this."

"What was I supposed to do, tell her to leave?"

"Yes."

"I couldn't do that. Besides, I had no idea she would show up."

"So now what happens?"

"Nothing. She wants to say hello to Louie. That's all. It'll take five minutes."

"I don't want any part of this."

"Why don't you just say hello."

"Oh, please." Barbara stood up. "Get a ride home from Timmy." Burk reached for her arm as she tried to work her way toward the aisle. "Don't," she said, twisting away but not looking at his face. "Don't touch me."

Barbara's car was not parked in the driveway when Burk arrived home that evening. On the table in the dining room was an envelope with his name printed on the front. The short note inside said:

> *Ray,*
> *The movie was sweet and funny and moving. You're*
> *a wonderful writer. I'm sorry I bailed out, but I couldn't*
> *stand the thought of seeing Sandra. I don't know why I*
> *despise her so much, but I do. Maybe it's because of*
> *Louie, because I've grown so very attached to him and*
> *don't want to see him hurt. I'm going down to Big Sur for*
> *the rest of the weekend. I need some time to myself. I*
> *still . . .*
> *Love you,*
> *Barbara*

Once Louie was asleep, Burk called Gene, and with the sound of panic still in his voice he told his brother what had happened after the screening.

"The movie played great, much better than when you saw it. Big laughs, big applause at the end. Louie was sitting with Tim and Juliet. He was really proud and excited. Before I could get to him, this publicist from Warner's grabbed me. She needed some information for my bio. She said it would just take a minute.

"Out of the corner of my eye I saw Sandra pushing her way through the crowd, bumping people aside. There was this strange, almost desperate look on her face. I knew something was wrong, but I thought Timmy could handle it."

Gene said, "That was your mistake. Right there."

"I know. I fucked up. Timmy went to get the car, leaving Juliet alone with Louie. That's when Sandra came up from behind and put her hands over his eyes. Juliet assumed she was the mother of a classmate or one of Barbara's friends. She didn't realize who she was until Louie spun around and she saw the startled expression on his face.

"Sandra said she had a lot of things to tell him. She grabbed him by the wrist and started to lead him up the street. Juliet could sense something was off. She grabbed Louie's other wrist. Now there was a tug of war in the middle of the sidewalk. Sandra was screaming and cursing, losing it, punching Juliet in the face with her fist."

Gene said, "This is unbelievable."

"I know."

"And all the time you were talking to this publicist."

"Hey, I didn't know what was going on. I thought Timmy had it covered. I told you, I fucked up."

"What happened? Go on."

"The theater manager called the police. By the time I made it outside, Sandra was already in the backseat of a black-and-white with her feet up, raging like a lunatic, trying to kick out the rear window. She kept screaming, 'Let me talk to my son! Let me talk to my son!' I swear to God she was actually foaming at the mouth. Finally, when I said I'd bail her out, she started to calm down."

"Forget about bail. They're gonna put her on a seventy-two-hour psych hold. The whole thing is really sad, Ray."

"I know."

"Did Louie talk to her at all?"

"No."

"What a drag," Gene said. "I'm sorry."

"For what?"

"I don't know. For you, I guess. For the way things turned out."

"Things turned out okay. Hey, I think I got a hit movie," Burk said, laughing, trying to sound lighthearted and confident. But when Gene remained silent, Burk felt suddenly ridiculous, because he realized then that his brother had been speaking about his marriage to Sandra, really about *her* life, a life filled with furious suffering, a life that went all wrong.

After they hung up Burk stayed awake, smoking, not really thinking about anything as he stared at the shadows on the ceiling. In the hallway he heard Louie's familiar footsteps before he saw him standing in the doorway, pulling at the waistband of his pajama bottoms.

"I couldn't sleep."

"Yeah. Same here," Burk said, and found a cigarette and lit it.

"You should quit smoking, Dad."

"I know."

Louie came forward and Burk pulled him down on the bed next to him. As he caressed his son's back and shoulders, he thought of the many times he'd woken from a terrifying dream, his heart racing, wanting to be held, to be comforted. And once more he relived a memory from his childhood.

It's the middle of the night. He's twelve, Louie's age, and he's standing outside his father's room, dizzy and disoriented in the deep silence. The door is open slightly and there are two bodies sleeping underneath the blanket. He knows the woman is not his mother, because he can see the silver Speidel watchband and red polish on her nails. His mother's nails were colorless and she never wore a watch.

He does not move, not even when he feels his brother standing behind him in the darkness. At some point the woman sits up and takes a sip from a glass by the bed. She never sees him, or, if she does, she shows no interest in his hate-filled face.

Louie's voice, worried but soft, nudged Burk out of the past. "Do you think Mom will be okay? Will they hurt her?"

"No."

"People in jail get beat up all the time."

"She'll be okay, Louie."

"Will you get her out?"

"I'm gonna try," Burk said, and he ground out his cigarette in the overflowing ashtray in his lap.

"Try your best."

★

Louie's flight left New York's Kennedy Airport at 8 A.M., which put him into Los Angeles a little before noon, Pacific Daylight Time. That gave him an hour to kill before his father's plane from Oakland touched down at one.

The plan was to meet downstairs at the baggage claim, rent a car, and drive directly to the Hillside Cemetery, where Gene would be waiting with the rabbi. The funeral for his mother was scheduled to begin at 2 P.M. and, as far as Louie knew, they would be the only mourners at the gravesite.

The choice was his to keep things small. "I don't want people there who didn't really know her," Louie told Burk when they spoke over the weekend. "Does that make sense?"

"Sure."

"But if you want to bring Barbara you can."

"She doesn't want to come."

"What about Timmy?"

"It's up to you."

"Let's make it just family."

"Fine."

"Did you talk to Grandpa?"

"He's not feeling so hot. I think it would be too much of a strain."

"I feel really sad."

"So do I."

"But I can't cry."

"You will."

"I want to. I just can't yet."

Louie bought a hot dog at the snack bar and ate it standing up while he paged through a leftover copy of that morning's *LA Times*. Because he wasn't looking for it, he was taken by surprise when he saw his mother's name listed among the obituaries in the Metro section.

Sandra Burk
  Funeral services for Sandra Burk will be held at the Hillside Cemetery in Culver City at 2 p.m. today.

Preliminary autopsy findings indicate that Ms. Burk died of acute alcohol poisoning in her apartment at 1102 Huntley Drive in West Hollywood. She was 39.

Since she moved to Los Angeles from Santa Rosa in 1981, she had worked as a cake decorator, a veterinary assistant, and a part-time receptionist for Apex Pest Control. She was also a volunteer for the American Red Cross and coordinated the Bloodmobile Drive for her neighborhood.

Burk, a graduate of West Central High, in Harrisburg, Pennsylvania, spent two years at the University of Wisconsin, where she planned to major in philosophy before she dropped out to marry her former husband, Raymond Burk, the screenwriter and playwright. They were divorced in 1971.

Her son Louis, a student at New York University, is her only survivor.

Louie stood uneasily at the counter, his face looking slightly troubled as he read over the obituary for the second time. When he was done he pushed the newspaper aside and rolled his neck a little before he looked up. Standing across from him, sipping coffee from a paper cup, was a thoughtful-looking black man with horn-rimmed glasses and a small goatee. A large black case that was shaped to contain either a stand-up bass or a cello was propped up against the counter next to him.

"My mom died on Friday," Louie said, his voice cracking. "It's in the paper."

The black man put down his coffee and his blank face underwent a change that softened his features. "You mind if I have a look?"

"Go ahead," Louie said, pointing. "She's the fourth one down. Sandra Burk."

The black man ran his finger slowly down the page. "Tarzan died yesterday," he said. "How about that?"

Louie looked confused. "Tarzan?"

"Buster Crabbe. He was in all these serials when I was a kid. Flash Gordon. Buck Rogers. My mom used to take me," the black man said. He took out a pack of Kools and fired one up. When he finished reading Sandra's obituary, he frowned and shook his head. "Thirty-nine. She was a young woman."

"It's just a bunch of words. That's not who she really was."

The black man made a sound of agreement as he adjusted his glasses. "That's right. Just words. Too bad there wasn't a picture. I bet she was good-looking."

"She was . . . when she took care of herself."

"Tall?"

"Five-eight, I think."

"Good-sized. Dark hair?"

"Except during the summer, when the sun bleached it out. I didn't see her all that much. She left when I was little."

"How little?"

"I was five."

"Yeah? That's how old I was when my daddy took off. His name was Louis, too. Just like you."

"That's not my name," Louie said. "They spelled it wrong. It's Louie without the *s*. I was named after the song, 'Louie, Louie.'"

"No kidding?"

"Really."

"Whose idea was that?"

"My mom's."

The black man smiled as he inhaled on his cigarette. "The more I hear about your mom," he said, "the more I like her."

"Everyone liked her. Everywhere she went she made friends," Louie said. "That newspaper doesn't tell you anything about her."

"Tell me about her, Louie."

Louie stared at the black man, holding his gaze for a second before he turned around to check the clock. "I have to meet my dad's plane at one."

"We got fifteen minutes. Tell me some things, anything you want. Right off I know she liked music, because she named you after a song. Right?"

Louie nodded, smiling. "Yeah. And she liked to dance, too. One time she danced for money," he said.

"For money? You mean like—"

"She danced naked in this bar," Louie said, surprising the black man, who raised his eyebrows while he maintained an amused grin. "My dad got fired from his job and we needed the money. She did it to give him time to finish this script he was writing."

"Takes a fine woman to do something like that," the black man said, nodding. "I'm a jazzman. Took me ten years and three wives before I could make a living with my ax. Not many women want to suffer through the hard times with a man. Sounds like she was willing to give it a shot."

"But she still left. She just took off one night while it was raining. I didn't see her again for almost two years. By then she was in prison. She shot a guy," Louie said, looking closely at the black man's face to see if he believed him. "She killed him."

The black man returned Louie's stare as he stirred the end of his cigarette into the coffee pooled in the bottom of the cup. "My father killed a man," he said, his voice dropping to a whisper. "Killed him with a knife after he caught him cheating at cards."

"Did he go to jail?"

"Not for that."

"For what?"

"Other things. Burglary. Armed robbery. He held up a bank," the black man said. Then he lit up a fresh Kool and smiled. "How'd you get me talkin' about my pop?"

"Do you ever see him?"

The black man waited for a second, recoiling slightly before he said, "No. He's dead. He died in the joint."

"Did he ever see you play?"

"Nope. But he heard me on record."

"I'm an actor," Louie said, and cringed when he heard the boasting in his voice. "I mean I'm studying to be an actor."

"That's cool."

They were quiet a moment. Then, in a matter-of-fact voice, as if he were talking to himself, Louie said, "I'm scared."

The black man looked at him, unblinking. "Go on. Tell me about it."

"My mom. She's dead, okay. But I never really knew her. I maybe have seen her four times since I was a little kid. I know I'm supposed to be sad, but I don't feel anything."

"Yes, you do. You're angry."

Without hesitating, Louie said, "I want to smash someone in the face."

"That's good. Feeling angry is good. You can feel angry and not act angry. I learned that. It took me a long time."

Louie nodded. Then he said, "I want to cry, too."

"After my pop died, I couldn't cry for a year," the black man said. "Then one night I was gigging at this place down in the Village. Right in the middle of this tune, out of nowhere, tears started leaking out of my eyes, big-ass crocodile tears I couldn't stop. I cried through the whole set and an encore. Cats in the band knew some shit was comin' up but they didn't say a word. God knows what the audience was thinkin'."

"I wish I could have told her I loved her before she died."

"She knows you loved her."

"I don't know that for sure."

"I do."

"How?"

"I just do. Black jazz guys know things like that. Your dad'll say the same thing."

"My dad's white."

"He's a writer. They got a sense of things."

Louie glanced at the black man, who nodded toward the clock. "You got five minutes. You better get movin'."

"Yeah, I know."

"Nice rappin' with you."

"Same here," Louie said, and started walking out of the snack bar. Before he pushed open the door he turned around. "You know my name but you never told me yours."

"Louis. Louis Jackson, Jr. But my friends call me Louie."

"Really?"

"Really."

"Swear to God?"

The black man raised his left hand and put his right hand over his heart. "Swear to God."

A smile slowly spread across Louie's face. "That's weird. No, that's really weird," he said, still smiling as he stepped through the door.

Sandra's simple burial plot was located in a small patch of grass directly in front of the Al Jolson memorial, a huge monument on a hill just across from the main mausoleum. Gene and an attractive woman dressed in black were already at the gravesite when Burk and Louie parked in the lot next to the chapel. Burk assumed she was Naomi Levin, the rabbi who had called him earlier in the week.

"Tell me about Sandra," she'd said, in a voice that was both cautious and caring. "The more I know, the easier it will be to speak about her at the service."

"She was kind," Burk said. "That's where I would start."

"With her kindness."

"Yes."

"In what way was she kind?"

"If she liked you, if you were her pal, she would do anything for you."

"And you were her pal, Ray?"

"Yes."

"And these things she did, describe them."

"She helped me believe in myself."

"In what way?"

"As a writer, as a father, as a . . . lover."

"And yet—"

"What?"

"She left you and your son."

"Yeah, she did. She left us."

"But you always knew she cared."

"Always."

"Always," the rabbi said, repeating the word in a way that reassured Burk, making him feel absolutely certain he was right. Then she changed the subject. "I spoke to your son."

"When?"

"Just before I dialed your number. He was very sweet, very helpful. At the end of our conversation he said he didn't want me to read the Twenty-third Psalm at the funeral. He wouldn't tell me why."

"He has a thing about numbers. Twos and threes together. It goes way back to when he was a kid."

"I see."

"A good-luck bad-luck thing."

"That he never grew out of."

"Apparently not," Burk said, and the conversation stopped for several seconds. Then, pushing gently, the rabbi asked Burk if Sandra was a good mother. "Yes," he said. "She was a wonderful mother."

"Louie said she loved horses."

"She liked to go to the track. She was an expert handicapper. But she loved all animals."

"You guys had a dog for a while, didn't you?"

"A beagle. He got lost. Did Louie tell you the story?"

"I wasn't sure whether to believe him."

"It's true. It happened. The dog jumped out of the car in traffic. It was hot and all the windows were down. Louie screamed. Sandra didn't hear him. She had the radio turned way up."

"What a terrible way to lose a pet. Maybe that's why she volunteered at the animal hospital, to make amends. I talked to the owner. He said she was witty and smart. All the customers were charmed by her, especially the gay men. He said she loved to bathe the animals and tie bright ribbons in their hair. But he had to let her go when he found out she was stealing pills and making long-distance calls at night."

For a moment there was silence. Gradually, Burk felt a vast loneliness spread through his body and surround his unhealed heart. "I miss her," he said. His voice was smaller now, harder to hear. "I miss her a lot."

"I know. I can tell."

"What am I going to do?"

"Grieve, Ray. Start now. You have time," the rabbi said. "You have all the time in the world."

Sandra's funeral was over at two-thirty. By then the sun had clouded over and three new mourners had joined the small group standing on the gently sloping hillside. Two were women in their seventies, both small and pale, wearing brightly colored paisley scarves tied around their short white hair. Standing between them was a boy around Louie's age. His features were slightly mismatched and he wore a dirty T-shirt with a cartoon character on the front.

"Could we say a word or two?" one of the women asked the rabbi, who glanced at Burk.

"We were her friends," the boy said, making a proud face.

"Wayne worked with Sandra over at the vet's," said the woman who spoke first.

"She looked in on us every day. She brought us groceries when we were sick," her friend said, then looked over at Louie. "She talked about you all the time. She carried your picture in her wallet. She carried yours, too," she said to Burk. "The one at the beach, when you were in college. You had white goop on your nose, and your shoulders were splotched from your peeling sunburn."

"When one of your movies went on television she made us tune in," the first woman said. "We popped popcorn and had a grand old time."

"Iris was in the movies," Wayne said, nodding at the woman who had just spoken. "She was in *Son of Fury* with Frances Farmer and *Our Hearts Were Young and Gay* with Gail Russell and Dorothy Gish."

"Wayne's Lu Ann's grandson," Iris said to the rabbi. "We brought him up by ourselves after his mother joined that commune up in Oregon."

"They don't want to hear about that," Lu Ann said. "This is Sandra's funeral. Let's talk about her."

"I'd like to mention her smile," Iris said. "Among other things she had a lovely smile."

"But she could get angry, too," Wayne said.

"Her emotions ran to extremes," Lu Ann said, "not unlike Frances Farmer, as long as her name was brought up. The Hollywood big shots ruined Frances," she said. "The Hollywood big shots and the press."

Wayne came around the grave and stood next to Louie. Quietly, without looking at anyone, he said, "I know what it's like to grow up without a mother in the house. I hardly ever got a letter."

"My mom wrote me," Louie said.

"I know. And you got a dad. That's good," Wayne said, tipping his head toward Burk. "Sandra was really proud of him. She kept all his clippings and reviews. When you clean out her apartment, you'll see."

"Wayne's father was a surf bum," Lu Ann said.

"He lives in Hawaii," Iris said. "Took off when he found out Dana was pregnant."

Lu Ann said, "Dana's my daughter. Ever since I can remember she ran with the wrong crowd."

The rabbi said to Burk, "We can end the service now if you like."

Burk glanced at his son. "What do you think, Louie? You have anything more to say?"

Louie's eyes were hooded in thought. He was staring down the hill, where another, larger funeral was getting ready to begin.

"I bet that's Buster's funeral," Iris said.

"I bet you're right," Lu Ann said. She glanced over at Burk. "Buster Crabbe died on Friday. That's what's goin' on down there.

He was Kaspa the Lion Man in *King of the Jungle.* Iris worked with him in *Swamp Fire* in 1946. That's where we met. I was doubling for Virginia Grey."

"He was Flash Gordon too," Louie said to Lu Ann, and she widened her eyes.

"Yes, that's right," Iris said.

"Growing up we saw him in a lot of stuff," Burk said to Gene. "Remember? In the serials he was Billy the Kid. Then he became Bill Carson. He had a sidekick named Fuzzy and rode a horse called Falcon."

"He was always dressed in black," Gene said.

"And he was a world-class swimmer," Iris said, tapping Burk on the shoulder with a bony finger.

"And your mother was a fine swimmer, too," Lu Ann said to Louie. "There was a pool in our building that she used—but at odd hours, either very late at night or early in the morning. One time before the sun came up I looked outside and saw her swimming back and forth across the shallow end. Paddling next to her was a golden retriever with a bandaged paw. She was giving him physical therapy, she said."

"That's one of the reasons she got fired," Wayne said. "You weren't allowed to take the pets out of the building without permission."

"But she didn't give a damn," said Lu Ann. "She knew that pup would feel better taking a swim. That's all. And she did it. That's the way she was."

Louie was smiling, looking at his father as if he were remembering something from their shared past. "She liked to play music loud," he said. "She liked the Beatles and the Stones, but her favorite song was 'I Can Never Go Home Anymore' by the Shangri-Las."

Burk said, "She liked 'Dream Lover' by Bobby Darin, too."

Gene caught Burk's eye before he corrected him. "I think that was one of your favorites, Ray."

"But she liked it."

"I think we're done here," said the rabbi, as Iris and Lu Ann joined arms, clinging to each other now as they stepped slowly down the hill toward Buster Crabbe's grave.

Wayne touched Louie lightly on the arm. "At breakfast all they talked about was the muscles in his back, the way they shined when they got all sweaty."

Louie took a small step to his right, away from Wayne's hand. "I don't know what you're talking about."

"I'm talking about him," Wayne said, staring across the grass. "The guy who died. Tarzan."

"The family would like a few moments of privacy," the rabbi said to Wayne, looking at him carefully. "Would that be all right?"

Wayne clenched his jaw but didn't move away. "Your mom liked sports," he said, staring down at Sandra's grave, "especially basketball. The Lakers were her favorite team, and her favorite player was Jerry West, even though he was retired. Zeke from Cabin Creek. That was his nickname. She used to say that over and over when she was drinking. I liked her. She was nice to me," he said, with a sad shrug. Then, cautiously, he glanced up at Louie. Meeting his eyes, he said, "Maybe I'll see you again."

Louie stood silent, watching Wayne walk over to a dark green Toyota sedan that was parked nearby. After he got into the backseat and slammed the door shut, Gene said, "I've got every song that the Shangri-Las recorded. Anytime you want, you can come out and listen to them all."

"She liked The Shirelles, too," Burk said. "And Del Shannon."

"'Runaway,'" the rabbi said and smiled just slightly.

"I've got everything," Gene said.

Louie raised his head and tears slid down his cheeks as he looked up at the sky. "It was raining the night she left. Remember, Dad?"

Burk nodded yes, he remembered, but did not look at his son.

"I was worried about her," Louie said. "I always worried about her."

The rabbi was standing next to Burk. She took his hand. At the same time, Louie felt Gene's arm around his shoulder. Burk finally looked in Louie's direction, and for a moment he saw a flicker of blame in his son's eyes. "It wasn't my fault, Louie. She was going to leave. I couldn't stop her."

"I know," Louie said. "She ran away—just like the song."

"There was something magical about Sandra," the rabbi said. "I can hear it in all your voices. I can't explain it exactly, but I can hear it."

Louie turned away from the grave, unable to check the tears that came out of his eyes. "It's okay," Burk said, staring at his son's back. "It's okay to cry."

"I don't have that many nice memories," Louie said, biting his lip. "And the things I do remember make me angry. I hated her sometimes. I can't help it. I hated her for always picking me up late at nursery school, and all the times she was drunk. And for dancing naked in the house with the shades up so the guy next door could see her. I hated her for that. I hated her for leaving, for going to jail, and for all the times she said she'd visit me and never did." Louie turned around and faced his father. "I hated her."

"I know," Burk said. "I hated her sometimes, too."

"Sometimes I hated you both," Louie said. "It wasn't all her fault."

"Of course it wasn't."

Turning away again, Louie said, "You hit her. You hit her in the face."

Burk nodded, finding it difficult to speak for a few moments. Then he said, "It was a terrible thing to do. I did a lot of terrible things. But my life is different now. It's been different for a long time."

"She was ready to die," Louie said. "That's all. She knew it was time and was just ready to die." Burk came around the grave and embraced his son. "I'm scared," Louie said. "I really am."

"I know."

"Even if I never saw her much."

"She was still your mom and deep down you loved her."

Louie's arms dropped away from his father's back and he took a step backward. Still crying, he said, "Maybe that's what we'll put on her marker."

"What's that?"

"She knew it was time."

Sandra's windowless studio apartment reeked with a rich warm odor of urine and spilled beer. An empty gallon of cheap vodka and a plate of rotten unidentifiable food were left on top of her filthy bedding, surrounded by a ring of tiny ants. Taped on the wall behind her headboard were pictures of pro basketball players scissored neatly from the pages of *Sports Illustrated.*

A troop of roaches marched down another wall, crawling slowly across phone numbers that were scrawled in black ink. Books, mostly warped or with broken spines, were piled against the wall or under the bed; old racing forms were stacked on her nightstand, weighted down by three browned apple cores and a cracked plaster statue of a horse.

"Jesus, this is terrible," Burk said. He was standing in the smelly bathroom with a sick look on his face, staring at the yellowed toilet bowl and the torn linoleum. Gray water dripped from the showerhead and shaving soap streaked with blood was smeared on the mirror above the sink. "She was always so clean. I can't believe she lived like this."

Burk accidentally crushed a roach as he walked back into the bedroom. When he sat on the edge of the bed to pull the flattened insect off the bottom of his shoe, he saw Louie standing in the closet with his eyes closed, turning slowly, Sandra's coats and dresses falling around his head and shoulders.

"I can smell her. I can smell her all over," he said, moving deeper into the closet. Burk felt tearing pain that ripped through his chest, almost taking away his breath. "C'mon inside, Dad."

"I'm okay, Louie."

"No. C'mon. Try to smell her."

Burk rose up slowly and walked into the closet. In the sparse light he could see Louie crouched in a corner, smiling up at him, his face half hidden by a pale pink negligee.

"Do you remember any of these clothes?" Louie said.

Burk ran his hands lightly over a few garments and shook his head. "No. I don't think so."

"There's an old peacoat in back here and some ratty sandals. Are those from college?"

"Not that I remember."

Louie held up a black brassiere. "How about this?"

"That doesn't look familiar either."

"She's got a portable hair dryer on the floor and a paper bag filled with curlers."

"She didn't use curlers," Burk said, breathing in deeply, trying to find Sandra's fragrance in the musty air. "She just washed her hair and brushed it out."

"She had pretty hair," Louie said. "I remember that. And I remember her shampoo. It had an apricot smell."

"That's right," Burk said. He moved in a step and felt the sleeve of a white wool sweater brush against his beard. "I remember this crewneck," he said, pulling the sweater off the hanger. "She used to wear it with blue jeans and white tennies. She always dressed really simply."

"There's a couple of low-cut spangly things back there."

"That wasn't Sandra."

"Maybe."

"Simple and loose. That was your mom's style."

"She's got a kimono. Red with a big black dragon on the back."

"I can't see her wearing a kimono. As a joke, maybe. But that's all."

"She probably had a bunch of secrets," Louie said. When he stood up, there was a pair of black net stockings wrapped around his neck. "A lot of things we don't know about. Things we'll never know."

"You're probably right, Louie."

"You know I am, Dad."

After they checked into the hotel, Burk decided to take a nap while Louie put on his swimsuit and went down to the pool. He came back upstairs twice, the second time Burk was lying on the sofa by the window, rereading the term paper that he planned to hand-deliver to Frank Dunlop, his former high school history teacher, later that evening.

"What's that?" Louie said as he switched on the TV. "New script?"

Burk shook his head. "Just something I wrote."

"What?"

Burk glanced at Louie, then his eyes made an anxious circuit of the room, landing finally on the Devo video that was playing on MTV.

Before he could answer, Louie spoke first, taking him by surprise. "I already read it, Dad."

Burk felt himself blushing, like a teenager who'd just been caught masturbating in his bedroom. "You did? When?"

"Earlier, while you were sleeping," he said, and he couldn't help smiling a little. "I was bored. Why did you write something like that?"

Burk looked into his son's face, trying to rehearse in his head a satisfactory explanation, an explanation that was both amusing and original. But finally he just shrugged and told him the truth. When he was done speaking, Louie was quiet for a moment, his eyes looking somewhat confused.

"Are you disappointed in me?" Burk asked his son.

"Why?"

"For cheating. For copying something out of a book."

"Everyone cheats."

"Not everyone."

"I cheated," Louie said, casting a glance toward his father but not straight at him. "In high school some guys swiped the chemistry exam and sold the answers for two hundred dollars. Ten of us put up twenty apiece. And Steve Jacoby, this guy in my dorm, he told me that he took the SAT for one of his buddies. The guy's dad paid him a thousand dollars. Now that's *really* cheating."

Burk said, "I never felt right about what I did. I wanted to straighten it out."

"Did you ever cheat on a girl?" Louie said. He was looking directly at his father now.

"Maybe . . . yeah, I probably did."

"How many times?"

Burk did not answer. He stood up and walked over to the closet. Remaining silent, he slipped a clean shirt off the hanger and found that his hands were shaking as he fastened the buttons. "I don't know," he said. "I'm not sure."

"Did you cheat on Mom?"

Burk faced his son and nodded his head. "Yeah, I did."

Louie stretched out on his bed while Burk went into the bathroom and brushed his teeth. When he came back out, he stood for awhile, gazing abstractedly around the room. After a long silence he took a seat in the overstuffed armchair next to the fireplace.

Louie started to speak, checked himself, but the words came out anyway. "Did Mom know you cheated on her?"

"No."

"Are you sure?"

"Yes, I'm sure."

"That's good."

The muscles in Louie's face softened, and they looked at each other for a brief moment while Burk patted his pockets to make sure he had his wallet and his car keys. "I gotta get going," he said. "I'll be back in awhile. Okay?"

"Okay."

Burk got to his feet. After he took the manila envelope out of the suitcase, he crossed to the door and stood for a few moments, watching his son and waiting for him to turn his eyes in his direction. When he opened the door, Louie said, "I love you, Dad."

"I love you too, Louie."

★

"Good evening, young man," Frank Dunlop said, smiling, and his sober gray eyes showed a twinkle of excitement as he led Burk inside his apartment. "You're right on time."

Dunlop's living room was small and cramped, decorated with dark red wallpaper and antique wooden furniture that was furred with a thin layer of dust. Jazzy music from an invisible stereo oozed softly out of speakers concealed by tall plants. Next to the fireplace was a small red velvet pillow with gold trim; a dog's silver choke chain was coiled on top.

"That was Woodrow's," Dunlop said, when he saw Burk's eyes settle on the pillow. "He passed away last year. You remember him, don't you?"

Burk said, "You were walking him on the night we met."

"Of course," Dunlop said, and for a moment he looked dreamily sad. "Woodrow was named after Woodrow Wilson, in my estimation one of our finest presidents. He never really got as much credit as he was due." Dunlop turned toward Burk. "Would you agree?"

"I don't remember too much about him."

"Perhaps he should've brought us into the war sooner, but diplomacy in hindsight is always easy to second-guess. I take it that's your paper," Dunlop said, nodding toward the envelope that Burk was holding by the side of his leg. "It must feel good to finally get this off your chest."

"It does."

Dunlop glanced at Burk with a little grin on his face before he started toward the kitchen. "Why don't I make us some tea," he said. "Then we can chat."

When Dunlop came back into the living room, he found Burk standing in front of a small rolltop desk, staring at a framed black-and-white photograph. It was a picture of a young man dressed in an Air Force uniform, leaning against the fender of a 1957 T-Bird. Bright wintry sunlight glanced off the lieutenant's bars pinned on his shoulders.

"That was Mike," Dunlop said, the teacups rattling on the tray as he placed it on the side table. Then he turned back to the picture with a professional expression. "Quite a handsome lad, wasn't he?"

"Is he a relative?"

"Oh, no. Nothing like that. He was . . . well . . . more like a friend."

Dunlop turned away from the picture and took a seat on the couch, and Burk sat across from him in an armchair made out of dark maple wood. "He looks familiar," Burk said, his eyes straying back to the photograph. "Did I know him?"

"I wouldn't think so."

"Did he go to Westside High?"

"No. He was from Colorado. And he was much older than you. He was twenty-four when that picture was taken."

"I guess he was someone you cared about."

"Yes. He was."

For a moment Dunlop looked as though he might cry. Then he took off his glasses, turning his head to shield his eyes while he cleaned the lens with a napkin. After some time had passed—the music on the stereo had changed from jazz to the Broadway soundtrack from the musical *Carousel*—Dunlop said, undramatically, "I'm a homosexual, Ray. In case you didn't already know. It's not something I'm ashamed of, but years ago it was quite different. If anyone had discovered I was gay, I would have been immediately ostracized from the faculty and probably dismissed from my teaching post. I could have ended up like Sam Burroughs."

"Sam Burroughs? You mean the baseball coach?"

"He was just an awful fag." Dunlop said, smiling sadly. "He couldn't keep his hands off those boys. Lucky for him he wasn't sent to prison."

Dunlop poured tea into two cups, laughing lightly when he spilled a few drops on the table. Still smiling, he sat back and began to talk about life in the fifties, and how difficult it was to be a homosexual man, how careful he had to be. As he went on and on, endlessly, Burk maintained a look of interest on his face while a scene from his past drifted slowly out of the wings of his mind.

He and Gene are throwing a football back and forth on the sidewalk in front of their house. In awhile, Ricky Furlong comes down the block and joins them, laughing and talking away while they take turns running pass patterns in the street. Three birds dive off a power line and land in the patchy summer-brown grass that runs down the side of the driveway. For some reason Burk remembers that, and he remembers he is trying to solve an algebra problem inside his head when a baby-blue '57 T-Bird pulls into their street, breaking his concentration. The top is down and the man behind the wheel has long dark hair that falls over the back of his collar. His passenger is younger by a few years, with a sunburned forehead and freckles on his muscular arms.

In Burk's memory it is almost suppertime and he can smell meat cooking in someone's backyard. Ricky drops the football he is holding and walks slowly over to the T-Bird, which is now parked in his driveway with the engine still running. Burk follows Gene up the sidewalk, but they both stop at the same time when they recognize the driver's deep masculine voice. He says, "I just came over to say good-bye. Me and my buddy Mike are taking a trip. We'll be gone for awhile."

Ricky kicks at the ground with his sneakered foot. "You gonna write me?" he asks.

The driver shrugs, waiting until Ricky looks up before he says, "I'm not sure. We're gonna be pretty busy. If I get a chance, I will."

"I just got out of the service," Mike says, leaning forward in the bucket seat. "George is taking me on a vacation. He's a cool guy. He says you're cool too."

Ricky and the man driving shake hands, and then the man reaches up and touches Ricky's face in a way that makes Burk feel excited and guilty at the same time. When the T-Bird pulls away, the neighborhood doesn't seem the same to Burk as it did moments before. It isn't quite as friendly.

Ricky's mother, Ada, appears in a side window, her body turned at an odd angle as she gazes out at the street.

Gene says to Ricky, "That guy George is on TV, isn't he?"

"Sometimes," Ricky says.

"How come you know him?"

Ricky doesn't respond. He is watching the T-Bird turn the corner at the end of the block. When the street is empty, Ricky's mother walks outside. The cardigan she was wearing in the window is now tied around her waist and hips. In a harsh voice she tells Ricky to come inside for dinner.

"Now," she says from the doorway. "And I don't want to ask you twice."

Ricky turns and follows his mother back inside their house. By now the sun is gone, and the only sound Burk remembers hearing is the wind whispering in the trees.

In a moment Gene is standing by his brother's side. They both look troubled, afraid to say what they are really thinking. After awhile Gene throws his arm around Burk's shoulder and turns him away from the house.

"Screw Ricky," Gene said. "He's a jerk."

Dunlop slowly got to his feet and followed Burk over to the front door. After they shook hands he said, "I'm sorry if I took you by surprise. I don't believe I was ever this open with any of my former students.

"Doing your paper over was the right thing. You paid off an inner debt that has been piling up for years. Now you're free."

"I don't feel that way yet."

"You will."

Burk was a mile from the Beverly Hills Hotel when he heard his father's voice come over the radio. Shocked, he made a quick right and parked on a side street south of Sunset.

"I've got a lot of things on my mind, things I kept bottled up for years. I need to talk," Nathan Burk was telling Bill Gleason, the host of *Sportstalk,* the show that replaced *Radio Ray Moore* on KMPC. "That's why I'm calling you."

"I'm here to listen, Nate," Bill Gleason said. "As long as it's about sports."

"That I can't guarantee," Nathan Burk said.

"Those are the rules, my friend."

"Bend them."

"I don't make 'em to bend. I'm a hired hand. I do my shift. I talk sports."

"It's late at night. There's more to talk about when it gets dark. That's when life seems empty and hopeless. Right now, as we speak, I'm sitting in my living room. Through the window I can see a light burning in the house across the street. A woman wearing a bathrobe just opened a cold fresh can of beer that she pulled out of the fridge. Now she's slicing cheese on a wooden platter. She's making a snack to eat in bed. I know this woman. She had a boy who played sports."

"I think we should talk about the boy."

"No."

"I'm intrigued."

"It's a family. You can't separate them."

"I want to put the boy on the field," Bill Gleason said. "I want to give him a glove. I want to see him swing a bat. Paint a picture for me."

"That's not why I called."

"Then hang up."

"That's a cruel thing to say."

Burk whispered, "Dad, go to sleep. Please. Hang up and go to sleep."

"Now I'm on my feet," Nathan Burk said. "I'm standing by the window, looking at the stars blinking in the sky. What I wouldn't give for a woman to come up behind me and put her arms reassuringly around my shoulders. What a surprise that would be! A man deserves to feel a woman's arms around him."

"Sports." Bill Gleason said the word like a threat.

"Yes, I know."

"Talk about sports or I'll cut you off."

"I'll talk about life," Nathan Burk said. "Life is like sports, filled with winners and losers."

"That won't work, Nate. Not tonight."

For a moment there was silence, and Burk tried to imagine the expression on his father's face: humiliated, perhaps, but not discouraged. "My wife was a sports fan," Nathan Burk said.

"That's a start."

"She loved all sports. Tennis, swimming, baseball, volleyball, Ping-Pong. But especially tennis. I have a picture of her on a tennis court, dressed in white tennis shorts and a white polo shirt. It's one of many pictures spread out on my coffee table. If I looked over my shoulder right now, I could see this picture. She's playing a mixed doubles match at La Cienega Park. Her partner is a small balding man named Marvin, a minor comedian from New York who earned a living selling gossip to the tabloids. Ask me how old my wife is in this picture."

"Tell me."

"Thirty, maybe."

"You're not sure?"

"She could be twenty-nine. If it's November then she's thirty. But she looks no older than eighteen."

"What year is this?"

"The year before she left."

"Your wife left you?"

"Yes."

"Where did she go?"

"See. You're hooked. I've got you hooked," Nathan Burk said, and laughed loudly; then something happened and his voice became frantic. "Forget everything I said! It's all a lie! She hated tennis! Hated the game with a passion!"

"Wait a second—"

"No! Listen to me! Pay attention! I'm turning around with the phone to my ear. I'm bending to take a picture off the coffee table. Here it is! A *real* picture. The other I made up.

"We're in Manhattan, my wife and I. We're in front of the Essex House, this big fancy hotel near Central Park. We're standing on the sidewalk with the lunchtime crowd jostling around us. The taxi that dropped us off is just pulling out of the picture. I've got this silly smile on my face. My wife is standing by my side, her shoulder underneath my arm. Maybe she's smiling too. It's hard to tell, because she's staring down at her feet.

"We just got married that morning. I rented a suite at the hotel for our honeymoon, the newlywed suite on the top floor. Later that night we went to dinner at Toots Shor's. The Phillies were playing the Dodgers that weekend and several players from both teams were at the bar. In back a bunch of gangsters were sitting around a big table. When they found out it was my wedding night, they sent over a bottle of the best champagne in the house. Around midnight Aaron came by to help me celebrate."

"Aaron?"

"Aaron Levine, my cousin. He was a boxer, a two-time New York State Golden Gloves Champion in the welterweight division. That night he drank too much and picked a fight with one of the Phillies at the bar. The man was flirting with my wife. A pitcher, Phil something. I forget his last name. Aaron knocked him out with one punch. A brawl started and the police were called. Aaron was thrown in jail and Esther, my wife, took a taxi back to the hotel."

"Was Aaron a drunk?"

"Yes. But he was a fine man when he was sober."

"I don't doubt that one bit."

"He taught my son Gene how to box. I think he saved his life."

It was close to 4 A.M. when Burk arrived back at the Beverly Hills Hotel. Crossing the lobby he saw the night manager, Carl Jorgenson, dozing in an armchair with his long legs stretched out in front of him. On the carpet nearby was a copy of *True Confessions,* John Gregory Dunne's fictional retelling of the Black Dahlia murder and a current best-seller.

The elevator dinged, signaling its arrival in the lobby, and the sound caused Jorgenson to blink open his eyes. When he saw Burk looking at him, he pretended to check his watch before he reached for his book and stood up.

"Did I get any messages?" Burk said, as he stepped inside the elevator, holding the door open with his hand.

Jorgenson brushed an imaginary fleck of dirt off his tie and glanced toward the front desk. "Only one," he said. "Your line was busy for quite awhile, so I had it taken up to your room."

Burk pointed at the book Jorgenson was holding. "Good read?"

Jorgenson nodded. "Oh, yes. A real page turner," he said. He displayed Dunne's signature on the flyleaf. "He was in for breakfast yesterday morning. I had him sign it before he left."

Still keeping the door open, Burk mused, "I'd like to write a book someday."

Jorgenson nodded with approval. "Yes," he said, "you should do that."

"Would you buy a copy, Jorgie?"

"Absolutely, Mr. Burk. And I would make you sign it, too."

Burk's smile was genuine as he stepped back and let the elevator doors close.

"Good night, Mr. Burk."

"Good night."

Louie was lying on his side, breathing noisily into his pillow, when Burk walked into the room and picked up the phone message from Barbara that was delivered earlier that evening.

"Hey, Louie?"

Louie rolled over and pulled the covers away from his face. "Yeah?"

"Who were you talking to?"

"When?"

"A couple of hours ago."

"No one."

"Yes, you were. The line was busy."

Louie sat up and the shadows shifted on the wall behind the bed. "I called Gene."

"How come?"

"I don't know. I was sad, I guess. I wanted to talk about my mom."

"I'm your dad, Louie. You can talk to me. I'll tell you anything you want to know."

"I waited up. I wanted to talk tonight. You weren't here."

Burk heard a note of anger in Louie's voice. "I'm sorry. We can talk now."

Louie was silent for several seconds. Then, tentatively, as he lay back down, he said, "Tell me what you remember most about her. If there was one moment, just one that you could freeze forever, what would it be?"

"That's easy," Burk said. He looked over at his son and their eyes met in the dark. "It was the moment she found out she was pregnant, the moment she found out she was going to have you."

"Tell me what she looked like."

"There was a softness in her face that I'd never seen before, in her eyes especially. She looked like—" and here Burk hesitated, searching for the proper description—"like the joy she was feeling was melting her insides. And then she started to giggle into her hands like a little girl. She said, 'I feel like doing cartwheels.' And that's what she did—all the way home."

Louie was smiling. "That's a cool memory," he said. "That's really cool."

Louie rolled over on his stomach. Inside his head he found a picture of his mother cartwheeling down the street with her wild eyes shining, smiling ecstatically. And he kept that image in his mind—her body whirling hand-over-hand in the September sunlight while all around her people stopped to watch, some disapproving, but many more astonished or amused, their smiles as big as hers—until he, too, was dizzy and breathless and there was nothing left to do but sleep.

He came awake in an hour, feeling anxious, his fading dreams suddenly usurped by the voices in the radio. "Forty-six points against Westchester," a man said. "I set the tournament record."

Louie opened his eyes. Golden sunlight struggled through the curtains, and his father was sitting up in bed, fully clothed. "I know this guy," he said. "He used to work downstairs at the Polo Lounge. Now he's over at the Palm. His name is Gus."

Louie's hand came out from underneath the blanket. He found his watch on the nightstand and brought it up to his face, blinking a few times to clear the cobwebs away from his eyes.

"I ran track too," Gus said. "I tied the city record for the low hurdles in 1957."

Bill Gleason said, "You play ball in college?"

"Arizona State. I got a full ride. Things didn't work out in the desert, but that's another story."

"Sad one?"

"In a way. I had a little problem with the beverage. But no more," Gus said, lowering his voice. "Anyway, I just called to check in."

"Glad you did," Bill Gleason said. "Got anything else?"

"Yeah. The old fellow you were yakking with, Nathan Burk."

"Nate's News."

"Used to be the best newsstand in town. Now I get my magazines over on Pico," Gus said. "Last week I found this new baseball monthly called *The Diamond.* It's a nostalgia rag. Stories about old-timers, lots of pictures, interviews with the greats and near-greats, that kind of thing. I'm surprised no one's mentioned it on the air."

"That's why we're talking sports: to pass it on."

"Had a story in it about one of your listeners, Ed Shaw."

"Name rings a bell."

"He was a scout. Called in once in awhile. He scouted me, in fact. But he could see I had a problem."

"Ed Shaw?" Bill Gleason said the name to himself.

"He signed some good ones. Cal Ripkin, I think. And a bunch of others. He died last week down in Florida."

"Sorry to hear that."

"Get a copy of *The Diamond,* Bill, you'll read it cover to cover. In back they got a bunch of ads for collectibles. Cards are big-time these days."

"And getting bigger."

There was a slight pause. Then Gus said softly, his voice slightly off-key, "They had me pegged for greatness at one time, Bill."

"Potential," said Bill Gleason. "All of us had it in spades."

Burk said to Louie, "Take a shower. It's almost six. We're gonna be late for your plane."

"In a sec. I want to hear this."

"You never know what life's gonna deal you," Gus said. "Years ago I worked at this fancy hotel. Turns out the lifeguard was in the Olympics. Finished fifth in the butterfly at Helsinki in 'fifty-six."

"A near-great."

"Signed a studio contract. Thought he was gonna be another Johnny Weissmuller or Buster Crabbe."

"Buster died the other day."

"Yeah. I know. Nice guy. Used to see him around the hotel."

"I preferred Weissmuller as Tarzan."

"We go up and down," Gus said. "For years I was up, then I took a tumble. Now I just want to stay even. You know what I mean."

"Balance."

"Exactly."

Burk picked up the phone and dialed room service. He ordered hot cereal, coffee, and a bagel that was heated but not toasted.

Louie moved toward the bathroom. "I want pancakes," he said, "with a side order of sausage."

"I miss working at the hotel," Gus said. "I like where I work now, but it's not the same. Nothing's the same."

"Which doesn't make it all bad."

"Most of it sucks."

"That kind of negativity surprises me," Bill Gleason said, "coming from a sober man."

"You haven't seen what I've seen."

"I've seen my share."

"Take me back to 'fifty-seven. Leave me there. Nothing could make me happier."

Bill Gleason laughed, a laugh that came out sounding slightly insincere. "Gotta wind things up, Gus. Any last thoughts?"

"I used to love cool spring mornings like this," Gus said, in a voice that couldn't hide his sadness. "It was the best time to shoot baskets in the park. I could be by myself then, working on my shots, practicing my moves at both ends, turning and shooting, turning and shooting. Just me alone, dazzling the birds. That's over. That kid's gone now."

"He's still inside you."

"No. *I'm* inside me, and I'm shaking. My hands are shaking. What happened to that calm feeling I used to call peace of mind? Where is it? It's gone like my wedding band. Okay, so I'm sober. But is this what my life's about: all-night radio and hoping my radiator don't boil over when I drive to work? I feel trapped, Bill G. Trapped behind a door where no one knocks."

"I'm sorry, Gus."

"You wanted my last thoughts. I'm giving them to you."

"I know, but—"

"I fell off the joy path. Can't you hear the pain in my voice?"

"Yes, I hear you. I hear your pain."

"The music's over and the hair in my comb is gray. I can't see the wild daisies in the woods. Tell me what to do."

"Get on your knees. Now."

"I'm on my knees."

"Close your eyes."

"My eyes are closed."

"Pray."

Burk parked the rental car in the lot across from the United Airlines terminal, where Louie's flight back to New York was scheduled to depart in thirty minutes.

"I'll see you this summer," Burk said, when they reached the security checkpoint. His mouth was smiling, but he looked a little worried, too. "Okay?"

Louie nodded. "Ask Timmy about a job."

"The bookstore or the theater?"

"Anywhere he has an opening."

They were silent a moment. Their eyes did not meet until Burk said, "Your mom did the best she could."

"I know she did."

"She loved you."

"I know. And she loved you too."

When they hugged, when his son's body was pressed against his, Burk could sense the terrible anger and sadness that vibrated his chest. But he knew, also, that there was nothing he could say or do that would make him feel better. He could only tell him that he understood.

Each was holding back tears when they stepped apart. The last call for Louie's flight came over the public address system. Burk said, "That's you. Get going. Call me when you get to your dorm."

Louie walked through the metal detector and followed the other passengers moving toward the gate. After a few steps he stopped and looked over his shoulder. He smiled as if to say everything would be okay, and then he waved and said, "Take care of yourself, Dad."

Burk waved back. "You too. You take care of yourself, too."

★

Western. Wilton. Bronson. Gower. Berendo. Unable to let the past rest, Burk was cruising slowly through East Hollywood in the right lane, making one final farewell loop before he drove back to the airport for his seven o'clock flight. Two hours had passed since he'd stopped for a drink at Ernie's Stardust Lounge—or what used to be Ernie's before it changed ownership in 1980. These days it was a gay bar called the Brig.

But the interior had not changed much—maybe the lighting was a little dimmer—and the same tunes were on the jukebox, only now the customers were all slender, good-looking men under the age of thirty, and *all* of them were dressed in uniforms: firemen, police, postal workers, Boy Scouts, every conceivable group was represented, even the clergy.

To Burk's surprise Miles was still behind the bar, working side by side with another, younger guy, both of them tricked out like Marine drill instructors. Burk tried to say hello when he ordered a Budweiser, but Miles had his Smokey-the-Bear hat tilted down so low they barely made eye contact. If Miles did recognize Burk, he didn't let on.

Burk drank his beer down fast; then he shot a game of quarter pool with a darkly handsome young man who was wearing a New York Yankee uniform with the seat cut out, exposing his hairy pink buttocks. He said his name was Lonnie, but his friends called him Joe D.

When Burk said he was straight, Lonnie just laughed. "Like I didn't know that when you walked in. A lot of straight guys come in here," he said, nodding toward a young black priest who was seated at a table in back. "Nothing wrong with kneeling before God, especially if he's got a nine-inch dick."

"Whatever your pleasure." Burk shrugged, turning his palms up. "I just dropped in for old times' sake. I used to drink here when it was Ernie's. It was a cool place."

"It's still pretty cool," Lonnie said, wiggling his bare ass as he bent over the table to take a shot. "But it can get a little desperate around closing time, when the old queens show up."

Burk left the Brig after three beers, but not before he played "Dream Lover" by Bobby Darin. After the first verse, his past descended on him like a light blanket, taking his reluctant mind back to the year 1969, the year that man landed on the moon. It was also the year of the Manson family's stabbing rage, and the year that Burk spent driving aimlessly through the streets of East Hollywood, contemplating the failure of his life.

"You just drove around? That's all you ever did?" Lonnie asked him. "Come on, you had to stop occasionally."

"Just for gas and smokes. And once in awhile if I had a problem with my car. But that's it," Burk said, his face clouding over. He couldn't speak for several seconds as a memory welled from within.

He remembered that later in that unsettling year was the afternoon in December when Bonnie Simpson entered his life, holding a map to the movie stars' homes and a purse filled with apples.

Burk was parked in front of Argyle Manor with the engine running. A tricycle lay deserted in the driveway, and there was a no-vacancy sign stuck in the well-tended ivy by the sidewalk. Overhead two huge clouds came together in the windy sky, and a blackbird landed on a telephone wire, chirping once before it took off, rising over the sad rooftops, a winged signature scribbled across the corner of a blank white page.

Burk felt a renewed sadness as he glanced up at Bonnie's old apartment on the second floor. He closed his eyes. And suddenly he could see her in that barren room: her honey-blond hair, her haunted eyes, her graceful shoulders, the paleness of her breasts, and the soft curve of her hips as she moved through the changing light. Burk's memory was so strong that when he opened his eyes she was now standing by the uncurtained window, her face filled with a deep tenderness as she stared down at the street.

In time this mirage of desire dissolved slowly into the shadows of Burk's mind. But he was still burdened by an unnameable yearning (and a sudden sense of emptiness and loss) as he made a U-turn and started back down Argyle. At Hollywood Boulevard he turned right. When he passed by Las Palmas and the corner where Nate's News used to operate, he permitted himself another moment of sadness. His father, recovering from a mild heart attack, had sold the newsstand to Larry Havana back in 1972, and now it was called the House of Love, an X-rated porno arcade blaring disco hits: a neon lighthouse that welcomed the simmering lust of the lonely hearted and the self-loathing.

The following year, when his health returned, Nathan Burk opened another newsstand on Sepulveda that Gene managed until 1978, the year he decided to become a private detective, specializing in divorce and white-collar crime. The business flourished, doing so well that after only six months he was forced to expand his office and hire several new employees. But lately he seemed to spend most of his time on the phone to Berkeley, trying to persuade Burk to write a movie about the life and death of rock-and-roll singer Bobby "I Fought the Law" Fuller.

In 1966, the year before Gene resigned from the force, Fuller was found dead outside the apartment in Hollywood he shared with his mother. He was believed to have killed himself by swallowing gasoline, a police verdict that Gene never supported. And for years after he left the force he continued to investigate the case on his own, following rumors of a mob hit that he could never substantiate.

But now he claimed that he'd developed new leads that linked Fuller's manager with Jack Dragna, a notorious gangster who ran the gambling and prostitution rackets in Los Angeles during the fifties and sixties. According to Gene, Fuller's manager was a high-stakes gambler who was into the mob for $50,000.

"They gave him sixty days to pay off," Gene told Burk. "When he couldn't come up with the cash, he sold half of Bobby's contract. Bobby found out and threatened to go to the cops. Two weeks later he was dead."

As Gene laid it out, the story was intriguing—a rock-and-roll mystery set in Southern California in the 1960s: Raymond Chandler meets the Beach Boys—and Burk loved his older brother, but he had a couple of his own ideas he wanted to develop.

"Then fuck you," Gene said, his voice taking on a surprising edge when Burk turned him down. "Remember this conversation when I sell the rights for a million bucks."

Near the intersection of Crescent Heights and Sunset, the road widened and Burk passed a large traffic island that used to be the site of Pandora's Box, one of Hollywood's first beatnik coffeehouses. Mort Sahl was a regular in the fifties, and so were poets Jack Hirschman and Charles Bukowski. And one night coming back from a Drifters concert in El Monte, Burk and Timmy Miller saw Marlon Brando sitting at a table in the cool darkness, playing chess with jazz bassist Charlie Haden.

A block west of Crescent Heights was The Way, a zen macrobiotic restaurant and the former location of The Xanadu, another Bohemian night spot where Burk and Timmy used to hang out in high school—until it became, mysteriously, the meeting place for the Grave Diggers, an outlaw motorcycle gang from Antelope Valley.

It was there in 1964 that actor Lee Marvin came in drunk and sucker-punched Billy Valentino, the lead singer of the Droogs, LA's premier garage-punk band. Later that night Marvin was attacked in the parking lot as he climbed inside his brand-new Corvette. The windshield was shattered and he was beaten so badly that filming on *Cat Ballou* had to be delayed for eight weeks.

Burk stopped at a red light at the end of the Sunset Strip. The last building, a high-rise at 9255 Sunset Boulevard, contained the offices of his former agents, Rheinis and Robins. Burk fired Maria Selene back in 1972, when he discovered that she had sought out Loretta Egan as a client behind his back. She even secretly negotiated Loretta's deal to polish *Pledging My Love* and later took Loretta's side when she petitioned the Writers Guild for shared credit.

The day Burk won the arbitration he had a dozen roses delivered to Jon Warren's house on Alta Way, where Loretta was living. On the card he wrote a two-word message: *Nice try.*

South of Sunset three blocks were the Shoreham Apartments. Actor Kenny Kendall lived at the Shoreham until 1974, when he was found shot to death outside the elevator on the ninth floor. The *LA Times* reported that Kendall had been arrested twice in his last year, both times for possession of cocaine. An obituary ran the following day in the *Hollywood Reporter,* listing several films in which he had appeared. Included was *Careless Love,* a gangster flick Max Rheingold produced in 1948. The obituary also mentioned a daughter, Patty, who was living in New Orleans.

Burk felt a tingling in his neck, then a hot burning sensation, as his mind was teased back to that sweet afternoon in the summer of 1959—an afternoon that was later converted into myth—when he and Timmy and Patty Kendall saw Gene fight Clay Tomlinson in the parking lot at Will Rogers State Beach. All it took was the fury of his quick fists—machinelike fury, executed with a bloody vengeance—and for months Gene's name was on everyone's lips. Everywhere he went people smiled at him or shook his hand.

Siblings. Burk and Gene. That summer of 1959 ended their childhood together. From then on they moved in different directions.

A photograph comes into Burk's mind like a sudden flash: He and his brother are standing side by side. Burk is taller by two inches, though he is two years younger. They are in their backyard with the midafternoon sunlight slanting through the treetops. A flawless day. But there is nothing peaceful in their faces, just stillness, the absent mother feasting silently on their insides with her malignant lips.

A woman walks away from her family, from the two boys who were formed in the cavern of her body. Why did she do that? Burk wonders, her face just a blur in his memory, a faint smudge rubbed into the mirror of his soul. Goddamn you, Mother.

Burk was on the freeway, just minutes from the airport. Off to his left was the Hillside Memorial Cemetery. Behind a cluster of trees, Sandra was lying underneath the soft earth, her very cells broken down into four or five pounds of bone and ash, the drama of her shattered life finally over.

"So long," Burk whispered, and, as soon as he released Sandra's face from his mind, he felt a panic come over him. On the screen in front of his eyes raced the events of his life. The fifties, sixties, seventies—gone in a flash. Years. Days. Months. Decades. All the ordinary and extraordinary moments. Gone.

"No!" Burk screamed, his body lurching toward the windshield in a spasm of terror, the thought of his own death locked around his throat like a necklace of iron spikes. "Not yet!"

And in that terrifying moment Burk dared to ask himself this question: What happens when the last person who has loved someone is gone? Who will remember them?

Who will remember Sandra?
Who will remember Bonnie?
Who will remember . . . ?

★

"It doesn't matter," Burk said to himself almost defiantly, answering the voices that were still chanting inside his head. Outside the window of his airplane he saw a searchlight move slowly across the fathomless sky, a slender silver finger pointed toward the stars. "Because right now I am still alive, and I'm going home. I can remember them. I can remember them all."

ACKNOWLEDGMENTS

Writing this novel was a long, slow journey, most of it trudged through canyons of deep darkness, where the cold wind of fear tanned my face and every other step was backward. Without the love and support of the following people—and God's good grace—I would not have made it home.

These are my friends, and I want to thank them all: Jeremy Larner, Anne Lamott, Katherin Seitz, Michael St. John Smith, Sean Blackman, Michael Blodgett, George Stelzner, Rosie Shuster, Ned Wynn, Steven Isenberg, Margot Kidder, Judy Coppage, Michael Wolf, Lydia Cornell, Thom Mount, Josh and Cathy Kramer, Priscilla Newton, Teresa Tudury, Penny Peyrot, and Irish Black.

This book could never have been started (or completed) without the encouragement and optimism of my good friend, Terry McDonell. Thanks, Terry.

I am also deeply grateful to my editor and publisher, Morgan Entrekin, whose patience and sage advice helped me to write the best book I could.

To my agent, Amanda Urban, I thank you for your honesty and invaluable insights, especially at the end when they counted the most.

Special thanks to Carla Lalli, Judy Hottensen, Elisabeth Schmitz, and everyone at Grove/Atlantic who made me feel so welcome.

Finally, I would like to thank my brother, Mike, who was there from the beginning. He knows the real story.